CRYSTAL
REBEL

Other Novels by Joshua Palmatier:

The "Ley" Series:

Shattering the Ley
Threading the Needle
Reaping the Aurora

The "Well" Series:

Well of Sorrows
Leaves of Flame
Breath of Heaven

The "Throne of Amenkor" Series:

The Skewed Throne
The Cracked Throne
The Vacant Throne

The "Crystal Cities" Series:

Crystal Lattice
Crystal Rebel
Crystal War

Anthologies from Zombies Need Brains:

After Hours: Tales from the Ur-bar
The Modern Fae's Guide to Surviving Humanity
Temporally Out of Order * Alien Artifacts * Were-
All Hail Our Robot Conquerors!
Second Round: A Return to the Ur-bar
The Modern Deity's Guide to Surviving Humanity
Solar Flare * Submerged * Guilds & Glaives * Apocalyptic
When Worlds Collide * Brave New Worlds * Dragonesque
The Death of All Things * The Razor's Edge * Portals
Temporally Deactivated * Galactic Stew
Derelict * Alternate Peace * Noir
My Battery Is Low and It Is Getting Dark
Shattering the Glass Slipper * Artifice & Craft * Game On!

CRYSTAL

REBEL

A Novel of the Crystal Cities by

Joshua Palmatier

Zombies Need Brains LLC
www.zombiesneedbrains.com

PART I

THE
FLATLANDS

Chapter One

The elevator screeched to a juddering halt, all five of the occupants—Raven, Lane, with Devon and Nic supporting the wounded Dalton between them—stumbling. Devon steadied himself with one hand against the mold-slick wall.

"That wasn't terrifying at all," Nic said into the strained silence.

None of the others responded. Devon shifted his pack and adjusted his grip on Dalton. "Where are we?"

Raven faced him, her features shadowed by the pale blue glow of the elevator's controls, their only light source. "The sublevels of the city, beneath Level One."

Dalton coughed, the sound pained. "I didn't know there were any sublevels."

"Most people don't." She pulled her satchel open and withdrew a lantern and flask of oil. Kneeling, she began to fill it, the oil pungent. "There's no lucent down here—all of it was removed and taken to the city above at the Founding. If you've got any kind of light source, we'll need it. Most of what lives down here won't approach the light."

"Most?" Nic asked.

Devon elbowed Lane. "Get my lucent lantern from my pack."

Lane shifted behind him, Nic and Devon jostling Dalton around between them so she'd have room. The elevator that had brought them from Level

Fifteen down to the sublevels was deep but narrow. It had obviously once transported cargo, perhaps machinery or mining equipment.

Devon felt Lane tug on his pack, then root around inside. A moment later, a soft green light joined the blue as she flicked Devon's lantern on. Raven capped the oil and with a snick of a match lit her own lantern, the flame threatening to go out before stabilizing.

She glanced at them all. "Stay close to me."

She punched the lucent node next to the glowing location bar and the doors ground open onto a cavernous room. Their lights only revealed a worn stone floor about twenty feet beyond the elevator cage, but Devon could sense the openness above and to either side.

Raven stepped into the door, looking up first, lantern raised. At some point, she'd drawn her blade, held it defensively before her.

"If you need to," Dalton murmured, "drop me and fight. I can defend myself if necessary."

Raven moved into the darkness, Nic, Devon, and Dalton shuffling behind her, Dalton mostly supporting his own weight, Lane coming up behind. The elevators—three of them—were attached to a flat wall rising up into the darkness, but within thirty paces they fell behind and were lost. The only sounds were their feet scuffing against the stone and, from somewhere distant, the distinct dripping of water into a pool. Raven kept glancing at the floor and Devon realized she was following faint markings that appeared every ten to fifteen feet. Every now and then, she had to brush the layer of dust and fallen stone aside with her foot to see them.

Devon's heart stuttered when a heavy mining cart appeared, canted to one side due to a broken wheel, covered in rust, empty. Raven's pace quickened and shortly after that a wall with a passage carved into it appeared, the stone around the entrance heavily scratched. She ushered them inside, but just as Devon reached it, he heard a skittering from behind, as if something many-legged were crawling across stone.

Raven swore beneath her breath and shoved Devon into the corridor beyond. "Let's hope it remains wary of the light."

"What is it?" Lane asked.

"It's called a skrill. Like a giant millipede, except with serrated pincers at the front that can lop your arm off in a single bite. They're the main reason no one comes down here anymore."

"Lovely," Nic said. "And how big is it?"

"Let's not find out. Move."

Devon, Dalton, and Nic took the lead, Raven and Lane behind, Raven calling out directions when necessary. Within a hundred feet, the corridor began branching out into cross-corridors, smaller rooms, and caverns as immense as the one they'd left behind. At each new intersection, they'd pause and Devon or Nic would verify the branches were empty before continuing. The corridors were braced with metal, some of the rooms containing long-abandoned machinery and equipment.

There were long stretches where they heard nothing behind them and Devon began to think the skrill had been left behind. But then they'd hear that skittering again, sometimes closer, sometimes farther back. The strain of listening for the sound began to give him a headache. His body was already slick with sweat—from the tension and from the exertion of keeping Dalton upright.

Then they hit another cross corridor and before Devon could scout ahead, Dalton shouted, "Raven!"

The Regular shoved forward and by then even Devon could hear it: skittering sounds from both left and right.

"They're trying to cut us off," she said grimly. "No time for sightseeing now. Run!"

She sprinted into the room straight ahead.

"Let go," Dalton ordered and Nic ducked out from under his arm, falling back with Lane. Devon didn't move. "Let go, Devon. I can do it on my own."

Reluctantly, Devon slipped out of his grip. He staggered, but caught himself against the wall and then began jogging after Raven, his other hand clutched at the bandages wrapped around his chest.

"He said he could do it," Lane said. "Trust him."

"What about you? Is your ankle still injured?"

"They had a healer look at it while I was being held in the War dormitory."

Then, at the sound of the skittering behind them, close now, she grabbed his arm, eyes wide.

Without a word, the three of them raced after Dalton and Raven.

Halfway across the room, the skittering behind converged and erupted in a series of clicking. By the time Devon had reached the corridor on the far side, the skittering had surged after them. He shoved Nic and Lane before him, shouted a warning to Raven, whose light could be seen far beyond Dalton's loping form. She shouted something back, but he couldn't understand it.

They came up behind Dalton, gasping and moving as fast as he could. Devon urged Lane and Nic to go around him. The skittering and clicking intensified as the creatures entered their corridor, no longer holding back. Ahead, Raven's light had halted. Devon yelled, "They're coming!"

All four of them emerged into another immense cavern like the first, except a hundred paces out stood a man with his own lantern held high. Dressed in leather breeches and a shirt full of pockets, he held a spear with a hook beneath the head in his other hand, butt planted against one foot, length cocked to one side. Raven had halted twenty paces before him, stance poised.

"Maupin," Raven said, her tone neutral.

"Oh, it's you," he answered. Then he glanced up. "And I see you've brought friends."

It took Devon a moment to realize he didn't mean Lane, Nic, Dalton, and himself.

He spun as two of the skrill emerged from the tunnel entrance directly behind them, both angling vertically up the wall in different directions, their hundreds of pointed legs scrabbling across the stone with that skittering sound. Their heads ended in two serrated, curved mandibles that snapped together, creating the clicking sound. They were just as Raven had described—millipedes with a pincer mouth—except they were as thick as Devon's arm and over twice its length.

"Back up!" Maupin shouted, then gave a harsh, piercing whistle as he dropped the lantern and charged forward.

At the same time, another of the creatures twisted from the opening, only this one was ten times larger. Its mandibles snapped at their small group, the crack as they met and scissored together like a thick branch snapping. Then it reared up before them.

Nic cried out and all four of them stumbled backwards, Dalton tripping and falling to the ground on his back. Devon grabbed for him and hauled him upright, pushing him hard toward the far side of the cavern where seven other men and women, dressed similarly to Maupin, suddenly appeared with their own lanterns, spears, and assorted weapons. They bellowed and shrieked as they charged forward. Raven yelled, "Get to the next corridor!" then joined them.

Lane hoisted Dalton up on his other side and together, Nic following, they loped across the cavern. Behind them, orders echoed back and forth and weapons clashed against stone. Someone cursed, another screamed, the sound devolving into a moan.

As soon as they reached the corridor's entrance, Devon dropped Dalton to the ground and turned, Lane right beside him. They fanned out to cover the opening, Dalton gasping as he righted himself. On the far side of the cavern, one of the smaller creatures lay dead, its head chopped off, thick blood oozing onto the stone. Its mandibles were still clicking together in spasms. Maupin, Raven, and the rest had encircled the larger skrill, most of its length still hidden inside the tunnel behind it. It lunged and snapped at Maupin, catching his spear and splintering it near its head. At the same time, two of the others plunged their spears or swords into the creature's sides, seeking out the flesh beneath the segmented plates along its back or the skin near the base of the its legs. It screeched and reared, the men and women shouting as they dodged beneath it and stabbed up into its underside. Maupin had fallen back to where one of his men lay moaning on the floor, clutching a gash down the length of his arm. He snatched up the wounded man's hooked spear and turned.

The skrill flailed and began to drop, sweeping down and across the group. Everyone shouted warnings and scrambled.

All except Maupin and Raven. He stepped forward and thrust the spear up under the skrill's jaw, into its throat. It flinched and tried to jerk away, but the hook caught and held. Both hands on the spear, the shaft braced against his body, Maupin used brute strength to wrench the skrill onto its side, its body crashing into the floor. At his side, Raven shoved her sword its full length up beside the spear into what Devon assumed was its brain or spine. Whatever she hit, the entire length of the creature went limp. It gave a final pitiable screech as she withdrew her blade, Maupin still holding the spear rigid.

Devon exhaled harshly, hadn't even realized he'd been holding his breath.

At his side, fingers crooked and ready to start a sigil, Lane said, "What happened to the other smaller one?"

Devon heard the skittering a second before Nic shouted, "Look out!"

He twisted in time to see the skrill dropping from the wall above. He raised an arm as it slammed into his body, driving him to the floor. It was heavier than it appeared, its mandibles slicing the air inches in front of his face, held away only by Devon's arm. He heard Lane shout, "It isn't working! Nic, do something!" and then Nic appeared above him. The former gang member drew his knife across the skrill's throat, the blade cutting deep, nearly severing its head clean off. Thick blood spilled onto Devon's face and chest as he flung the limp body aside. He rolled and spat onto the stone repeatedly, but the bitter, tingling taste of the creature's blood remained.

Hands gripped his shoulder and then Dalton knelt beside him. "Devon, are you alright?"

"I'm fine." He coughed and spat again, then glanced at his arm, his shirt riddled with tiny tears. He pulled the sleeve back. "Just some bloody scratches."

On the far side of the cavern, the men and women were whooping and hollering, one or two dancing around the larger skrill's corpse. Maupin and Raven were headed toward them.

Nic kicked the smaller skrill's body. "It's like I didn't kill one myself."

"Nothing happened."

All three turned toward Lane, who was staring at Devon in shock. She raised her crooked hand and motioned, what Devon recognized as the beginning of the base mage sigil.

"Nothing happened when I tried to use magic on the skrill. No rush of power, no pinprick of lights...nothing."

"Did you do the sigil correctly?"

She gave him a flat, angry glare. "I know how to do the sigil. The double pyramid never formed."

"Ah," Maupin said as he and Raven halted before them, "you'll have to ask our resident Historian, Gillian, about that. Magic doesn't work here in the Flatlands."

"What? Why?"

"As I said, you'll have to ask Gillian."

Lane appeared stricken.

Maupin reached down to pick up the body of the smaller skrill, holding it up so the blood would drain from its severed neck.

"What are you doing?" Nic asked.

"Skrill meat is delicious."

"You're joking, right?"

"Unfortunately," Raven said, "he's not. Devon, Dalton, Lane, and Nic, meet Maupin, the leader of the tullers."

"The tullers?" Dalton asked.

"That's what we call ourselves. You'll see why shortly." He scanned them all, returning to Devon at the end, even though he spoke to Raven. "I assume you brought them here for a reason?"

"They need protection. The Council will be searching for them, along with everyone from the Lyceum, as well as Carbolen and the gangs."

Maupin's eyebrows rose. "That's...impressive. Is there anyone *not* looking for them?"

"Not really."

"And how do you intend to keep where you've taken them from Carbolen? What are you going to tell him?"

"I'm not going to tell him anything. I'm not going back."

Maupin finally looked at her, his gaze searching. "Well then. This is a story I'd like to hear."

* * *

"—and then Favian had Proctor Gallean arrest us," Devon said, his throat raw from speaking. "We were taken to the War dormitory, placed in separate rooms, and were waiting to be questioned." He brought the tin to his mouth and gulped down a mouthful, the cold water soothing.

They all sat around a fire in the center of one of the smaller rooms, two of Maupin's group guarding the door, the rest scattered about the chamber on various cots and pallets thrown on the floor. Dalton was snoring, on his side, curled around his wound, back to the fire, but those in Maupin's group had been listening intently as Devon, Lane, Raven, and Nic told various parts of what had happened in the city over the past few days. One of the smaller skrill was roasting on a spit above the flames, the scent somehow spicy.

"That's where we found them," Raven said. "We broke them out and took them to Carbolen. But I knew Carbolen wasn't going to let them go. He was going to use them. It's what he does."

Maupin stood off to one side, back to them, staring up toward the ceiling, as if he could see the city through the stone. "They almost took the city? Seized control?"

"Yes, but they slaughtered thousands to do it."

Maupin was silent. Then, under his breath, almost to himself, "And they had mages."

"Weren't you listening?" Raven asked. "They activated a Warding. On purpose!"

Maupin faced her. "I was listening." He glanced toward two of his own—a man and woman—who nodded and vanished out into the corridors. Then he moved closer to the fire and squatted, twisting the spit. "We haven't been to the city in a month. Obviously, a lot has changed since then."

"No shit," Nic muttered.

Maupin ignored him. "What do you expect us to do with you?"

"Harbor us, for a short time."

"How long?"

"Until we figure out what we need to do."

"And what if the Iandolo Army comes looking for you down here? Or Carbolen?"

"For shards sake," Raven snapped. "If you don't want to be associated with us just say so!" She stood, gesturing to the others. "Come on. We've worn out our welcome."

She strode toward the door, but Maupin snagged her arm.

"I didn't say that," he said. They glared at each other, both tense. "You can be so damned…" Then Maupin's shoulders sagged and he relaxed his grip. "We'll harbor you, but you have to acknowledge that there's significant risk. We haven't remained hidden by taking such risks."

"You haven't remained hidden at all."

Devon started at Dalton's voice. He immediately slid to where Dalton eyed Maupin and Raven from a half-seated position, his sword drawn.

"What do you mean?" one of Maupin's men asked.

Dalton sat up fully and laid his sword flat across his knees. "Your group. The Iandolan Army knows about you. You simply haven't done anything significant enough yet to warrant their attention."

"And we'd like it to remain that way," Maupin said. "If they find out we're hiding you from them, they may change their mind."

Raven stepped away from him. "We won't be with you long enough for that. I promise."

"Good," one of the others said. "Now that that's settled, let's eat."

He moved to the fire and removed the spit. With practiced ease, he slid the skrill from the spike, laying its back on the floor, then used a knife to slit it lengthwise down the center. The rest of Maupin's group shoved forward, each taking a spiked leg and tearing it free, a chunk of meat separating from the shell of the body. One offered a chunk to Devon, who took it hesitantly, then Dalton.

The former soldier sheathed his sword and took a bite, chewing thoughtfully.

"You can eat this?" Devon asked.

"It isn't any worse than some of what the army feeds you. Better, even."

Devon took a tentative bite, surprised at the sweet, juicy flavor. He noticed Lane and Nic doing the same a few paces distant, watched their reactions as he said in a low voice, "So what do you know of these people?"

"Not much. The army labels them bandits. They live outside the city and as I said, they haven't done anything to warrant the army's full attention."

"They don't seem much like bandits to me. Look at the way they dress, their weapons."

"I noticed."

Raven drifted close and Devon asked, "Did we really need to tell them everything?"

"We didn't tell them everything," the Regular said. "We left a ton of it out—how you and Lane work together, how much you pissed off Carbolen, Varenov and Arrend's involvement in your escape. We only gave them broad strokes. Enough to convince Maupin that you were worth hiding. He'll try to use you, just like Carbolen, but I trust him more."

"Did you know he and his men would be here?"

"Of course not. But once we heard the skrill following us, I figured it was our only chance. He sometimes keeps a group here to keep an eye on Iandolo, sort of an outpost. I had no idea he'd be here himself."

"What's with you and Maupin, anyway?"

Raven shot a glance toward the tullers' leader. "It's…complicated." When she turned back and saw their expectant looks, she sighed. "We've worked together off and on, through Carbolen and the gangs."

Devon thought it more than simply "working" together, but Dalton said, "So Carbolen may come here looking for us?"

"Here in the sublevels, yes. Maybe. But the skrill should keep him from finding us. He definitely won't look outside the city. He'd never convince the gangs to go into the Flatlands."

"Not even the Regulars?"

Raven didn't answer.

Dalton switched topics. "What about the two Maupin sent away?"

"Scouts sent into the city to verify what we told him and to find out what's happened since. He likes to keep informed." She motioned to Devon's half-chewed skrill. "Eat. Save what we brought with us that will keep. We've got a few days-worth of travel before we get to the tull."

"What's a tull?" Devon asked.

Raven headed toward Lane and Nic without answering.

* * *

Two days later, Devon and the rest of his group, along with Maupin and their escort of tullers, emerged from one of the corridors into a pocket cut into the side of the cliffs that surrounded Iandolo. An arid, gusty wind blasted grit into Devon's face and he raised a hand to shield his eyes from the overly bright sun. The pocket lay a hundred feet above the Flatlands, a barely distinguishable ragged path leading off from the edge to the ground below. Overhead, the sky was a brilliant blue with patches of clouds scudding by. The ground was a harsh mix of brown and tan sand and broken rock, with striations of more vibrant yellow and red thrown in. Patches of straggly trees and brush were interspersed throughout.

Jutting up from the cracked and barren land were plinths of rock, ranging in height from ten feet to over two hundred. Most were single spires, but a few were grouped together to form jagged walls or clumps that reminded Devon of natural crystals, except made of stone. Far out, hazed by distance, sat the cliffs of a plateau, perhaps two hundred and fifty feet high, a quarter the size of the one Iandolo had been built on.

"That," Raven said, coming up to his side as Maupin and two of his group began to descend along the path, "is a tull."

Lane, Nic, and Dalton clustered around him, staring out at the Flatlands and the tull in stunned silence.

"That's where we're headed?" Devon asked.

"That's where they live." She let them take it in for a moment. "Let's get moving. It will take a couple of days to get there. Don't touch anything on our way. Don't eat anything. And for shards sake don't drink anything unless one of us tells you it's all right. Practically everything out here is designed to kill you."

She headed after Maupin.

Behind them, one of the two from Maupin's group left as a rear guard coughed as a subtle hint.

"I never thought I'd see the Flatlands, let alone go traipsing through them," Lane said.

"I've never even thought about the Flatlands," Nic answered.

Both of them looked awed, but terrified.

Dalton shifted, Devon automatically reaching to steady him. "You can always go back."

Lane stiffened, her face hardening. "No, I'm good."

Nic merely sighed.

They headed toward the sandy trail down through the stone cliffs of Iandolo, Maupin's two guards falling in behind.

Chapter Two

Varenov Illea, arms crossed on her chest, stared at the blackened char on the wall in her quarters, where the ball of fire her daughter had shot at those she'd thought were Brovettan soldiers breaking in had landed before she'd realized it was her friend Devon.

The mathematician. The one who'd caused so much trouble, no matter how inadvertent.

The servants in the Tower had tried to get the stain out of the wall, along with the fainter ones along the hall, with little success. Charred signs of her daughter's escape after the Brovettan attack were scattered throughout the Tower, most noticeably in the elevator. Varenov couldn't help a small smile at the thought.

"Ah, Lane. Where are you now, I wonder?"

A muted chime rang and Varenov turned toward the two Iandolan soldiers that stood near the entrance. She nodded once.

Favian charged through the door. He made it two steps before the guards seized him. "They've escaped from the Lyceum! They're gone! What did you have to do with this?"

Varenov's arms dropped and she straightened. "Who's gone?"

"Your daughter and her friend, Devon Alamort."

Varenov affected surprise. "When did this happen?"

"As if you don't know."

He attempted to pull out of the guards' grip. They looked to Varenov, who waved one hand.

Favian jerked forward, shot them both a glare, then adjusted his rumpled sleeves and focused on Varenov. "Are you claiming you had nothing to do with it?"

"This is the first I've heard of it." She motioned him into the formal sitting area, where she received guests, but neither of them sat. "You haven't answered my question. When did they escape custody?"

"Yesterday morning."

"Yesterday? And you're only coming to inform me now? What have you been doing since you discovered they were missing?"

"Attempting to find them, of course."

"And you didn't see fit to inform me or the Council?"

For the first time since his arrival, Favian appeared uncomfortable. "Proctor Gallean recommended it, but I countermanded the suggestion."

Varenov spun toward him. "You have that authority? I thought the Lyceum was run by consensus among the proctors?"

"It was. But after the attack by the Brovettans the college is in shock and in shambles. We are still dealing with wounded and the dead. Many of the students and proctors are traumatized. At our last assemblage, it was decided having a single leader would be more efficient, for the time being. I was elected Master Proctor."

Varenov wondered what Arrend, Devon's mentor, thought of that. He must be furious.

"I see. Why are you coming to me now?"

"Because we have failed to find them at the Lyceum or within the city."

"You were hoping to recover them before anyone knew they were missing, you mean."

Favian straightened, jaw set. "That would have been preferred."

A servant appeared and Varenov decided she'd made the…the Master Proctor squirm enough. "Bring us some Radimansque red, please." Then, to Favian: "Have a seat. I do not know where my daughter is. Or her friend—"

"Devon."

"Yes, Devon. The last I saw them was when you and I questioned them in the War student dormitory cellars. What do you know of their escape?"

Favian settled himself reluctantly in one of the scattered chairs, the wide oval window looking down on the city and the Flatlands beyond to one side. The servant returned and poured him a glass of wine, another for Varenov, which she ignored, and then retreated.

"The War students who were guarding the door said a woman in black leathers approached them...and that's the last thing they remember. They were found unconscious but unharmed outside the makeshift prison cells."

"A woman in black leathers. They couldn't be more specific?"

"Black hair, average height, a few scars on her face."

"Sounds like someone from the gangs. Did you ask them about it?"

Favian scowled. "Gallean went to them first. They claim to know nothing. As do the students set to guard the main entrances to the college. According to them, no one passed in or out that evening."

A tension in Varenov's shoulders eased and she reached for her wine. "If it was the gangs, they would hardly admit to it. And they likely know alternative ways to enter and leave the Lyceum. They know more about the city—especially the lower levels—than we do."

"This didn't happen in the lower levels. This happened at Mid-level."

"Still." She sipped and swirled the warm, thick red around her mouth before swallowing. "You'll have to inform the Council. My daughter and this Devon are dangerous. If the Iandolan gangs have them, that's one thing, but if what they know—if what they can do—falls into the hands of the Brovettans or any of the other Crystal Cities, we may have an insurrection on our hands."

"I agree. I'm...surprised to hear you say that, I must admit." Favian watched her, his look considering. "Perhaps you had nothing to do with their escape after all."

Varenov was spared from responding by the door chime. She stood as her clerk, Treant, entered and paused at the edge of the sitting area.

"The Council is set to begin in thirty minutes, Councilor."

"I am aware, Treant, thank you." She faced Favian, who had set aside his wine and also risen. "If you will excuse me, Proctor Favian."

"If you don't mind, I could accompany you to the Council chambers. That's why I'm here in the Tower. As you say, I need to inform you all of what has happened."

Varenov could not hide her shock. "You've been summoned? By whom?"

"I was *invited*. By Councilor Secora Arrum."

Favian turned away before Varenov could react, moving past Treant, who gave her a questioning look. She shook her head and followed Favian, Treant falling into step at her side, her two guards behind.

They rode the elevator in silence down to the fifth floor, her mind racing. Arrend had warned her Favian was politically motivated, but she had not fully believed it until now, even after her experiences with him in Brovetto, when he was a War Mage. The ill-advised raiding party he and the Iandolan Army had sent into Brovetto to quell the riots by force after they'd killed the Councilor at the time had been a disaster, one that she had stepped forward to mitigate. Relations between the two cities had always been tense, but Favian's raid had nearly pushed the two into outright war. Only her quick thinking had calmed the Brovettans down enough to broker a tentative peace. There had been concessions necessary, of course. Those in the raiding party had been demoted and reassigned. Favian and Gallean had been unwillingly retired to the Lyceum. Those in the army had been sent to training schools, their military careers effectively ruined. Some of them had simply vanished. And her diplomatic solution to the entire mess had garnered her this seat on the Council, one that had been promised to Havvelan Duprees.

Varenov had thought her hands washed of the whole event. Yet here was Favian again, invited to the Council by its titular head. What was his angle? And who was supporting him? Could it be Secora Arrum herself, or was she simply coerced into inviting him?

The elevator doors opened onto an opulent foyer, various clerks, attachés, and guards milling about. Tables were set up with light snacks and drinks, but Varenov's eyes snagged on Secora as soon as she stepped into the room. The Councilor stood near the doors to the Council chamber itself, engaged in conversation with Councilor Petrov Orrus and a merchant she recognized from Lambenesque.

"If you'll excuse me," she said to Favian, casting a significant glance at Treant. As she moved away, she heard Treant say, "So, Proctor Favian, how has the Lyceum dealt with their wounded and the dead?"

She didn't hear Favian's answer, her attention on Secora. The Councilor saw her approach, raising a hand to halt the merchant mid-sentence. "Councilor Varenov, is everything all right?"

"May I speak with you privately for a moment?"

"Of course. Gentlemen, I'll see you both in the Council chamber shortly."

Both men nodded and drifted away, Councilor Petrov glancing back with a frown.

Varenov drew Secora closer to the wall. "I have just been informed by Proctor Favian that my daughter and her friend have escaped the Lyceum."

Secora's eyes widened. "Weren't they under guard?"

"Yes, but because our resources have been stretched so thin there were simply War students watching them."

"They should have been made more secure. They are both a threat to our mage school, if what Favian has said is correct. The Prefect must be informed immediately." She scanned the room. "Arctus!" She motioned Arctus Mallora toward them.

"So you knew nothing of this? Why did you invite Favian to this meeting then?"

"Havvelan and Arctus requested it. They have a proposal that may affect the Lyceum and wanted the college's input."

Varenov stepped aside as Arctus arrived. He was the epitome of an army Prefect—clean-cut in his Iandolan maroon-and-white uniform, trimmed beard salted with gray, planar face with a fixed dour expression. He stood a hand taller than both Secora and Varenov. "Councilor Secora?"

"It appears that Lane Illea and Devon Alamort have escaped custody at the Lyceum."

"What! Why was I not informed immediately?" He caught the attention of two subordinate Prefects, who rushed over.

"Proctor Favian is here to inform you now," Varenov said. "Apparently, he was attempting to rectify the situation on his own first."

Arctus swore. "Proctor Favian, join us please." The words were couched diplomatically, but everyone in the room quieted as Favian complied, arriving with the two Prefects. "When were Illea and Alamort found missing?"

"Yesterday morning. We've been searching for them since."

"Why didn't Proctor Gallean send word?"

"With our army so drastically reduced after the Brovettan attack, I thought it best to use Lyceum resources to locate them. I ordered Proctor Gallean to find them himself. After all, we were told to hold them ourselves, using War students as guards. I remind you, half of the Council felt we shouldn't be holding them at all."

"Did you not see what they did to the quad at the Lyceum?" Arctus said. "They're dangerous. They need to be controlled."

"I agree wholeheartedly. Unfortunately, I wasn't given the support to do that effectively. When we hadn't located them this morning, I came here immediately."

Arctus swore again, more forcefully. He faced Secora. "You realize this only emphasizes the need for what I propose, don't you?"

Secora's lips thinned. "Yes, but I still feel it is premature. Go, handle this new situation. We'll hold off the discussion in the Council until you return."

Arctus headed away, the two Prefects in tow, already issuing orders. Their little group was now the center of attention in the room, hushed conversations already starting.

"What is Arctus going to propose?" Favian asked guardedly. "I remind you that the Lyceum is not under the direct control of the Army. We merely coordinate with them."

Secora waved aside his concerns. "It has nothing to do with the Army seizing control of the college. In fact, it's the opposite."

"What do you mean?" Varenov asked, her own concern rising.

"As the proctor pointed out a moment ago, the army has been significantly depleted, along with our city guard. We need to train replacements, fast, before Brovetto or any of the other Crystal Cities decide to take advantage."

"We still have our mages," Varenov said. "None of them would dare."

"Wouldn't they?" Councilor Petrov inserted himself into their group. "Have you forgotten that Brovetto managed to bring five of their own mages into Iandolo during this last attack? Who's to say they don't have more? Who's to say the other cities don't have mages of their own? I think our monopoly on mages has started to crumble."

Varenov couldn't argue.

He turned to Secora. "What's Arctus' proposal?"

"He wants the War and Mage colleges at the Lyceum to expand. And he wants additional training facilities—set up by the Lyceum—to be established at other locations."

"What about the other schools at the college?" Varenov asked.

"At the moment, our need for more soldiers and mages is more important than that of Historians and Scientists."

"And the Humanities? What about healers?"

Secora wavered, but Petrov leapt in. "With enough soldiers and mages, no one would attempt an attack. There would be no need for healers then, for there would be no wounded."

More of those in the room had drifted closer, listening in, many of them murmuring in agreement, including a few of the other Councilors, Varenov noted. Only Martov appeared uncertain, although he was difficult to read at the moment, his face haggard, eyes hollowed out with grief and betrayal. His own daughter, Terrial, had been the leader of the Brovettan mages, after all. According to the sole Brovettan mage remaining alive after the attack, after Terrial had been left for dead during Favian's failed raid in Brovetto she'd betrayed Iandolo and joined the Brovettan resistance, agreeing to train mages for them. She was adamant that Iridesque had only the five mages, that no others were trained, but how could they be certain?

And she couldn't bring that up now. It would only support Arctus' proposal.

"Would the Lyceum be able to shift toward more of a War college, Proctor Favian?" Secora asked. "Is that feasible?"

"Of course, Councilor. It would be no trouble at all."

Varenov nearly snorted. Of course not. It gave the Lyceum more power. "Do we really need auxiliary schools? Isn't it enough to bolster the Lyceum itself?"

"We need as many trained fighters as we can get." The increasing crowd parted at the new voice and Havvelan Duprees pushed through. He wore a tailored linen shirt, a vest with touches of embroidery and gold buttons, and pants of the finest material and cut, as befitted an influential merchant of fabrics. "After all, we need to replace those lost in both the army and the city guard, do we not? We can't rely on gangs of rogues as our sole source for protection."

"They did well enough pulling us out of the Warding," Varenov countered.

"But they aren't reliable. Even you must concede that, Councilor. Look at who your daughter has associated herself with. Devon Alamort had a warrant for his arrest on his head, did he not? And I believe he belonged to one of the gangs in the lower levels before he became a student at the Lyceum."

"I trust her more with him than with the Lyceum."

Havvelan stepped forward. "Is that so? And did I overhear correctly that your daughter and her friend are no longer under the protection of the college? That they've escaped? How interesting."

"That's enough, Havvelan," Secora said, a reprimand in her voice. "I believe all of the councilors have arrived. We should convene the Council and discuss all of this in more formal settings."

An Iandolan guard opened the doorway to the Council chamber and the councilors and their entourages began filing in. Varenov hung back, Treant and her guards making their way to her side.

"How much of that did you catch?" she asked her clerk.

"Nearly all of it. After Secora summoned Arctus, it was hardly a discreet meeting."

"An understatement. What were the reactions of the councilors regarding escalating the War college's role?"

"Gabrella and Iriarte are in favor of Arctus' proposal. Santigo appeared against it."

"Petrov is obviously for it. Secora and Martov are uncertain. We'll need to convince one of them to side with Santigo and I if we want to stall the decision today."

They filed into the Council chamber, the circular room sectioned off into eight areas—one for the entrance and then one for each Crystal City. In each area, a large desk for the Councilor and a clerk faced the center of the room, a tier of seats behind for the rest of the Councilor's escort. Behind that, on a raised platform, sat a gallery of seats for observers.

Varenov moved to the table marked with the green and gold colors of Luminesque. Ostensibly, each one of the Councilors represented one of the Crystal Cities. At the Founding, that had been strictly true, but over the years that had degraded. Varenov had been born in Iandolo, had been raised here, only moving to Brovetto as an attaché to Councilor Orland. When he'd been killed by the rebels, she'd stepped forward to act in his stead until a new Councilor could be named and sent.

But then Favian had come with his ill-timed raid, a retaliation for the Councilor's death, and she'd dealt with all of the fallout from that. She'd been given the Councilor's position officially upon her return.

Only two of the seats on the Council were actually represented by someone with strong ties to their respective city—Scintillesque and Radimansque. All of the others were controlled by someone with loyalties to Iridesque. Through political coups, collusion, and outright assassination over the last hundred years, Iridesque has been slowly seizing control of the Council, and from that, the interests of all of the Crystal Cities.

Varenov scanned the assemblage as the other councilors and spectators settled in. Havvelan had taken a seat in the gallery behind Opalesque, halfway around the room, a neutral location. Petrov broke away from Secora, who found her seat with a troubled frown. She stared at her desk in deep thought, until the room quieted and she gave a start.

Rising, she reached for a stone orb and rapped it twice against its wooden base. "I call this council to order. All Councilors are present. I'd like to start with a report from the army and city guard regarding recovery efforts and the disposal of the dead. Captain Mannert?"

The captain rose from the tier of seats behind Secora. Her hands shook. But that was to be expected. Two days before, she'd been a captain in one of the lower-level army precincts. Her handling of the alliance with the gangs in order to free the Lyceum and the Councilors from the Warding and halt the Brovettan seizure of the city had brought her to the attention of the Council. This was likely her first Council meeting.

"Councilors," she said, her voice cracking. She cleared her throat, her voice steadying as she fell into the familiar patter of a report. "Disposal of the dead proceeds, with pyres burning on nearly every level, particularly Mid-level. We expect to finish in another three days. Clean up and repair of damages will take much longer, but most of the main streets have been cleared. Looting continues and is difficult to police with our city guard and soldiers spread so thin, but the majority of the local communities have taken this into their own hands and appear to have it under control."

"What about the gangs who allied with you during the attack?" Secora asked. "Can we ask them to help?"

"That's who I meant when I said 'local communities,' Councilor."

"I see." Secora waved a hand. "Continue."

"Not much more to report. The number of wounded is still overwhelming. Most levels are requesting the aid of more healers."

"I believe we've already ordered all of the healers in the city into the streets." She turned to Favian, also seated in her tier. "Would it be possible to send fifth- and sixth-year students into the field?"

Favian stood. "I believe the sixth years have already been pressed into service, but I will discuss sending the fifth and fourth years with our Humanities proctors as well."

"Very well. Anything else, Captain Mannert?"

The captain glanced toward Varenov, making Varenov's hand clench where it rested on her desk, but Mannert said, "No, Councilor."

"Then the Council thanks you for the update, Captain."

Mannert sat, eyes flicking toward Varenov once more.

Treant leaned toward Varenov. "What's that about?"

"I have no idea."

The door to the Council chamber opened and Prefect Arctus entered, moving without hesitation toward Secora.

"Ah, Prefect Arctus, a timely arrival. Captain Mannert has just given her report on the state of the city and mentioned our depleted army and city guard. Perhaps you'd like to make your proposal now?"

Arctus halted beside Secora's desk. "Very well. It's rather simple. During the Brovettan attack, we lost over a quarter of the Iandolan Army and nearly a third of the city guard. We are now severely undermanned at a time when we do not know Iridesque's intentions. Are they readying another force to reinforce this one? I'm certain those behind this attack sent word of their success as soon as the Warding went up and they managed to seize control of the city. A force is likely already on its way.

"We need to supplement our own forces as quickly as possible, bring our army and the city guard back up to its former strength. This includes mages. Because of this, I propose that we shift the main focus of the Lyceum to recruitment and training in the War and Mage colleges, with an accelerated program. I also suggest auxiliary colleges be set up around the city."

Murmurs arose, although Varenov knew that nearly everyone had already heard this outside in the foyer. She watched the other Councilors intently.

"What about the gangs that helped us with the Warding and after?" Councilor Santigo asked. "Could we ask them to supplement our forces?"

Captain Mannert stood abruptly. "I've spoken to Carbolen, their leader, about this already. He's willing to help quell some of the looting and other deviant behavior on the lower levels, but that's it. He and the other gangs do not want to become part of the army or the city guard under any circumstances."

"What about asking citizens to volunteer?" Iriarte asked.

"We need trained soldiers, not bakers and butchers wielding rollers and cleavers," Arctus answered.

"Be careful of your tone, Prefect," Gabrella said. "Those bakers and butchers held off the Brovettans long enough to bring down the Warding. We would not be here today without them."

Arctus dipped his head. "Of course, Councilor. My apologies. But we need hardened men and women, ones who follow commands, not untrained citizens or...unpredictable miscreants."

Iriarte frowned. "Then where do you expect to find these new soldiers, if not the citizens?"

"We'll recruit, of course, but with the intent to train and discipline. We'll target the young, the apprentices and second sons and daughters. Perhaps initiate a draft or conscript criminals from our jails in exchange for lightened or expunged sentences."

"I don't think we're at that extreme yet, Prefect," Martov broke in forcefully.

Varenov seized the opportunity, standing. "I agree with Councilor Martov. I'm not certain we even need this escalation of the college's duties. Did not the captured mage and the rest of the supposed delegation from Brovetto claim that there was no other force coming from Brovetto? That they acted alone?"

"And you believe them?" Petrov asked. "Traitors all and an illegal mage at that?"

"Do we have reason to doubt them?" Varenov faced Arctus. "I assume we've sent out a scouting party along the wayfare to warn of an approaching army."

"We have."

"And?"

"We have seen no evidence of one coming along the wayfare from Iridesque."

"Then there is no imminent threat."

"But you must admit there is a threat, Councilor Varenov," Gabrella said. "Iandolo has been attacked with force by Brovettan soldiers three times within the last few months, this last attempt nearly succeeding in an overthrow of the city. That cannot be ignored. Brovetto is out of control."

"Can the Lyceum handle such a drastic change in their War and Mage colleges?" Santigo asked.

"Most certainly," Favian said. "We only need the approval of the Council."

Secora seized the stone orb. "Then I call an official vote of the Council. Those in favor of allowing the Lyceum to increase the role of the War and Mage colleges, including additional schools outside of the Lyceum grounds, please stand."

Varenov sat immediately, along with Santigo, while Secora, Petrov, Gabrella, and Iriarte stood.

Martov wavered, then pointed at Arctus. "I will stand on one condition—that the prospective soldiers are only found through recruitment, not draft or conscription."

"Very well," Secora said. "Would anyone like to change their vote based on the amendment?"

No one moved except for Martov, who stood. Varenov swore beneath her breath.

"Then the proposal has passed." She dropped the orb onto its holder. "Proctor Favian, please coordinate with Arctus regarding the needs of the Lyceum."

"Of course, Councilor."

"Let's move on, then. Councilor Iriarte, you had a trade agreement you wanted to discuss?"

* * *

The rest of the formal Council meeting was a blur, Varenov going through the motions of argument and agreement with the various proposals by rote. Her mind lingered on the Prefect's proposal and the increased power it gave to the Lyceum, along with the hints of further escalation that Martov had halted with his amendment. Thoughts of draft and conscription were premature. It did not bode well for future debates, especially regarding Brovetto. She had accepted the role of Councilor as a representative of Luminesque because she thought she could lessen the tensions between the two cities, between its rebellious populace and Iridesque itself. And she had…for a time.

Only when Secora rose toward the end of the session and said, "I now ask that all except the Councilors and Prefect Arctus leave the chamber," did her attention snap back toward the Council.

"Do you know what this is about?" Treant asked, already gathering up his notes as everyone in the gallery and tiers began to file out.

Varenov noted Captain Mannert hesitate, frown in her direction, then shake her head and move toward the door.

"I suspect it's to discuss Iridesque's response to this attack." She caught Treant's hand and nodded toward Mannert as she rose, the other Councilors and Arctus already gathering in the center of the chamber. "Perhaps you could touch base with Captain Mannert. Discreetly."

Treant didn't react, but edged toward Mannert in the throng as he made his way to the door.

Varenov joined the others, who remained silent until the Council doors were shut by the soldiers standing guard outside.

"I assume this is about our response to Brovetto's attack," Varenov said immediately. "I remind everyone that not all in Luminesque condone these actions. All three of the recent attacks have been planned and enacted by rebels."

"Rebels who appear to have the support of a significant portion of the Luminesque Army," Petrov protested. "I believe we've verified that in all three attacks, the men were indeed trained soldiers, not simply men dressed in their uniforms. At this stage, we must accept that all of Brovetto is in rebellion—including its governing officials and soldiers. You've lost control of your city, Varenov."

"But what of the delegation sent when they sued for peace?" Varenov faced Arctus. "You've questioned them? What did they have to say for themselves?"

"They claim they knew nothing of the intent to activate the Warding and the subsequent attack on the city. All of them allege that they were tricked, that they came with the full intention to settle for peace."

"And you believe them?" Secora asked.

"I do. Whoever is truly in control in Brovetto now, they sent this delegation in an attempt to 'clean house.'"

"They were getting rid of obstacles," Martov mused.

"The entire delegation was caught in the Warding. If it had held, they would have been trapped. The traitor mage has admitted that she intended to sacrifice herself for the cause by setting off the Warding. She never intended to be released. I don't think they knew *how* to release it."

The entire Council considered this in silence, until Secora said, "This was blatant defiance of the Council. Some kind of retaliation is necessary. What are our options?"

Arctus stirred. "We could send a segment of the Iandolan Army, with mages, but it would leave Iandolo vulnerable."

"Vulnerable to whom?" Gabrella asked. "Only Luminesque has challenged us in recent years. None of the other cities have risked our wrath."

"But there have been rumors of dissent from all of them. It's grown in the past few decades, with the failure of the lucent continuing and the resultant disruptions in trade."

"The only reason Luminesque is in open rebellion is because of the food shortages," Varenov added, her tone harsher than intended. "They were reliant on lucent mining, but that's now been depleted. They have nothing to trade now. They're starving and we've done nothing to mitigate that!"

"You sound as if you sympathize with them," Iriate said.

"I do! Not with the insurgents, but with those in Brovetto who have nothing and have nowhere to go. I lived there for a time, remember? I know their plight. I've seen it, up close and personal."

"And what do you propose we do?" Gabrella asked. "*Give* them everything?"

"Enough to tide them over. Or find a viable alternative, something that will give them a purpose, a life."

"All of the cities are struggling," Secora said. "Even Iandolo. No one has anything to give. We've discussed this before. There are no alternatives, unless you've come up with one since our last meeting?"

Varenov bowed her head and pinched the bridge of her nose. "I have not."

"Then I propose we return to our reprisal. Prefect, how long until you can gather the resources and men to send the army to Brovetto?"

"If I pull men from the pyres, I can march within two days."

"The citizens can manage the pyres. Are we in agreement then? A retaliation is in order?"

All of the other Councilors nodded, Petrov adding, "We cannot appear to be weak. Not at this stage."

Secora glanced at Varenov. "And you, Councilor?"

Varenov straightened. "I will not order an attack on the city I represent."

"So noted. We have six in favor, however. Prefect Arctus, you may begin your preparations."

"And what are we going to do with the captured delegation and mage?" Gabrella asked.

No one spoke, until Petrov cleared his throat. "They are traitors. I'd suggest a public execution."

Varenov was heartened to see both Santigo and Martov protest immediately. Even Secora and Gabrella appeared unsettled by the idea.

"It would be a vivid and memorable example to the rest of the cities—" Petrov said.

Secora raised a hand to halt him. "I don't think that is necessary at this time. Are we agreed?"

Only Petrov and Iriarte dissented, but with five in favor, the execution proposed was tabled.

"Then we will convene again in two days' time," Secora said.

They filed out, Secora and Petrov remaining behind. Prefect Arctus motioned his contingent to him as soon as he hit the foyer, the rest of the Councilors drifting toward their own escorts. Varenov didn't see Treant, but her guards were waiting.

As the elevator rose toward her floor, Varenov exhaled slowly, then brought her hands up before her. They shook and she squeezed them into tight fists and forced herself to relax. She needed some wine, perhaps even one of the aromatic candles from Scintillesque that always helped her think. Events were already moving faster than she had anticipated. Drafts? Conscription? Executions? She'd expected the call for retaliation—she'd come to expect nothing else from this Council—but this push for additional War colleges was a step beyond that.

When the door to her quarters opened, she found Treant and Captain Mannert waiting, the sky beginning to darken with dusk in the oval window behind them. She nearly ordered them out, too drained to deal with anything more.

Instead, she drew in a steadying breath and forced a smile. "Captain Mannert. I suspected you needed to speak to me."

"I'll make it quick. I know you've had a long afternoon."

"Treant, can you tell the servants to bring us something light to eat and something to drink?"

"Wine, I assume?"

"Most definitely."

Treant disappeared through the doors to the left and Varenov crossed the room to the window, taking a moment to look down on the glittering city below and the Flatlands beyond. From this height, at this time of day, the streets and buildings of Iandolo appeared flawless, the lucent and stone structures at Mid-level interspersed with circular fields for crops, rectangular gardens, and the rippling waters of cisterns and fountains. No sign of the dead lucent that permeated the lower levels, the rust and decay of machinery dying. Nothing like Brovetto, where nearly all of the lucent was dead, where buildings even at the highest levels were collapsing in on themselves, leaving shards of black lucent jutting into the blue sky. Cisterns were half full, the few viable farming areas shrinking each year.

It had been bad seventeen years ago, when Varenov had left. She couldn't imagine what it was like now.

Mannert drifted up behind her.

"What did you need, Captain?"

"I have a message from Carbolen. Lane and Devon are gone."

Varenov spun. "What do you mean gone? Were they recaptured? Carbolen was supposed to protect them."

"Not recaptured. They slipped out of Carbolen's lair, with one of Carbolen's Regulars and two of their friends."

Varenov took a moment to absorb this, then found herself chuckling. "They didn't trust him," she said to herself. "So they fled. And now, when Favian or the others ask if I know where they are, I can tell the truth and say I don't know. They could be anywhere."

The thought was sobering. She glanced out the window, into the distance, at the broken and shattered Flatlands.

Treant and the servants returned. She listened to them setting trays on the table, the sharp scent of cooked meat and roasted vegetables filling the room. It should have been enticing, but Varenov was no longer hungry.

"Was there anything else?"

Mannert hesitated. "He also wanted me to warn you."

"Of what?"

"He suspects someone on the Council is working with the Brovettans."

Chapter Three

Pain shot up from Lane's ankle and she stumbled, but after a quick glance at the others she realized no one had noticed. Raven, Dalton, and Devon were ahead, Nic already disappearing into the next shallow ravine cut into the barren land. Dalton and Devon were paying closer attention to each other, helping each other along, Dalton obviously still in pain. Only the two tuller guards bringing up the rear were behind her and they were more focused on whether anyone was trailing them.

Lane hefted herself up over the lip of the crack in the earth and plodded after Dalton and Devon, careful where she placed her feet. Barren wasn't exactly the best description of the Flatlands—there were pockets of dry, prickly brush and thorny scrub, some with vividly-colored flowers—but since they'd left the base of the plateau that held the city of Iandolo it had mostly been dry, dusty earth in every shade of tan, red, and yellow imaginable. And yet creatures lived here: small rodents that chittered at them when they approached, then scampered for cover with tiny tails rigid in warning; mottled snakes that left strange, S-shaped tracks in the grit; and ugly, black insects the size of Lane's fist with wicked tails. Except for the rodents, Maupin claimed nearly all of the animals were poisonous—their bite, their sting, even their skins. The plants were no better. Lane had gotten scratched by one with finger-long thorns and it was still red and throbbing. Some of the leaves of the bushes were coated with oil that burned the skin.

She looked ahead and was relieved to see the base of the plateau they were heading for only a short distance away, the stone cliffs rising almost vertically into the air. Birds circled in the air, hundreds of them, coming to light in the crevices and crags. Their cries were faint, but Lane could hear them now.

She wondered how many of them were poisonous.

Behind, Iandolo glinted in the harsh sun, enough she had to shade her eyes to see it. Even as distant as she knew it was, its plateau stretched across half the horizon. Above it rose the twenty-four tiers of Mid-level and below, then the three needle-thin towers, the highest of which rose another twenty levels above Mid-level. The blues and greens and purples—with the occasional touch of red or yellow—appeared bleached out at this distance, three fingers of glass jutting up from a pedestal of slate-gray steel and umber rock. Lane could see two wayfares branching away from the city, the roads at the same height as the plateau itself, one headed to Brovetto, the other to Bolnis.

"Beautiful, isn't it?" one of the trailing guards said as she scaled the edge of the ravine Lane had just left. She had flowing brown hair, dark arresting eyes, and a thin but easy smile.

"As long as you don't know who lives there."

"Isn't that the truth." She pointed toward the smaller plateau behind them. "We're almost there."

Lane turned her back on Iandolo and trudged after Dalton and Devon.

Two hours later, they crawled from a wash, the channel clearly cut by water, and stood at the base of the plateau. The rock thrust up from the ground, as if shoved upwards from below by an unseen hand. The earth around its base created a sloped incline riddled with boulders three- or four-times Lane's height in diameter.

Ahead, Maupin and his followers were already entering a hollow between two such boulders, the space inside dark. Lane slowed and caught movement from higher up—a flicker, nothing more—but someone knew they were coming. Had probably seen them approaching a few miles out.

It was significantly cooler in the shade and only became cooler the deeper into the plateau they moved. Light filtered down from cracks in the stone debris overhead, creating shafts of sun at odd intervals, enough Lane could see they were following a well-worn path. But then the texture of the rock changed and she realized they'd passed inside the plateau. Instead of boulders stacked upon each other, with the group crawling through the cracks, the walls were now vertical, the path actually a crevice with no visible ceiling overhead. Maupin and a few others lit lanterns; Devon flicked his lucent alight. Water dripped down from above—startling her as it struck her head—although not enough to make the walls or floor slick. Ahead, she could hear Nic, Dalton, and Devon chatting, the sounds bouncing off of the walls, as well as a few short bursts of conversation from Maupin's group farther in.

She smelled the tuller camp before she saw it, first the smoke, then some kind of roasting meat. Her stomach clenched and she picked up her pace, closing the distance between herself and the others.

All four of them halted as they stepped out of the crevice onto a ledge overlooking the base of a wide irregular shaft that reached all the way up to the open sky. A pool filled the lowest point, surrounded by lush brush and tall, spindly trees, a few bowing out over the water. At one end, a makeshift dock had been built, with two single-person boats tied to it.

Farther back from the water, men, women, and children were scattered around a central fire with an earthen oven at one edge. The elongated pit held multiple skewers, some with bird, snake, and what looked like lizard carcasses sizzling above the coals. Flat stones near the edge held filets of fish roasting on some kind of broad leaves and a woman was removing loaves of flatbreads from the oven.

Lane's stomach growled and Devon elbowed her with a grin.

"What?" she said. "We've had nothing to eat for the last few days except dry biscuit, some cured jerky, and skrill. Of course I'm hungry."

"It looks like they've anticipated our arrival," Maupin said, standing with Raven on the steps from the ledge down to the hollow. The others had already gone ahead. "I hope you're willing to experiment."

As they descended to the cookfire, people coming forward to greet them, Lane noticed tents and a few crude huts farther back from the pool, interspersed among more vegetation. "They live here." She scanned those gathered. "How many of them are there?"

"I'd say close to a hundred," Dalton said.

"I don't understand," Lane said. "I thought the Flatlands were deadly, that no one could survive out here."

"Most of it is."

Lane turned at the new voice to find the rear guard who'd spoken to her earlier holding out one of the leaves with fish in it.

"I thought I'd start you all off with something easy," she said, eyeing Dalton, Devon, and Nic. Raven had moved off with Maupin. "There's enough here to share."

Lane took the leaf, still warm from the fire. The guard—a few years older than Lane—led them to a set of stones they could use as seats, closer to the fire. As they settled, a couple of the children ran up to them, close, then shrieked and raced off.

"Forgive them. We don't get many newcomers here."

"I'd never have guessed," Nic said. He reached for some of the fish, stripping it away from the bones. Lane frowned at him, but the guard laughed.

"My name's Picall, and this is called trout. We catch it in the pool there. It's sweeter than anything you'll have had in the city."

Devon and Dalton waited until Lane had taken a piece, all of them commenting on the flavor. Picall nodded and took part of it for herself, motioning to the rest of the camp.

"Most of the Flatlands are deadly. Not just the wildlife, but the stone itself. There are sections where, if you stay longer than a few days, you'll start getting sores all over, then you'll cough up blood and die. Even here in the tull you have to be careful. The water in that pool is clean, but don't drink from any others you run across."

"Why's that?" Nic asked.

"At best, you'll get stomach cramps and shit yourself. At worst, you'll die."

"So we shouldn't eat, touch, drink, or breathe anything out here."

"Pretty much."

At Nic's dumbfounded look, Picall laughed, nearly spitting up her fish. She shook her head as she covered her mouth and recovered, swallowing before she spoke again.

"It's not as bad as that, although from your perspective I can see why you'd think so. I was born here. I've only been to the city on a few recent excursions. It seems more dangerous to me than the tull."

"Hardly."

Lane glared at Nic. "You're missing the point."

Picall grabbed the leaf and the remains of the fish from Lane. "I'll bring back something different." She headed back to the fire, placing the leaf and fish bones in an urn on her way.

Dalton shifted in front of the other three, closing off their group from the rest. "What do you think?"

"About what?" Lane asked.

The former soldier waved around at the tull. "All of this. Maupin and the rest."

"It's all so…odd, isn't it? There's no lucent, hardly any metal. Everything's wood or cloth. They use leaves as plates. That urn is fired clay. It's a little unsettling." Lane shifted on her stone.

"That's because you're from the towers," Devon said. "If you'd been forced to live in the lower levels, you'd see it differently. They're using what's available, whatever they can scrounge up or bring back from Iandolo, like the lanterns. Same for Dalton."

"It's more than that," Dalton said. "There's something else off about them. I can't place it."

"You were a War student. You're trained to be suspicious."

Lane caught Dalton's gaze and saw the same unease she felt there, then noticed movement behind him. "Picall's coming back."

The tuller had two flat trays made of wood, heaped with sliced meat and a couple of the poisonous insect bodies, although without the tail. She presented one tray to Dalton and Devon, the other to Nic and Lane.

"This is lizard meat," she proclaimed, pointing to some shredded pieces that were a bland grayish color, "and this is snake."

"Aren't these insect things poisonous?" Nic said, picking one of the fire-blackened bodies up with two fingers.

Picall plucked it from his hand. "We call them scorps. The poison sac is in the stinger. Take that off and they're a crunchy snack." She bit into it with relish.

Nic frowned. "You're enjoying this far too much."

They sampled all of it, although Lane found the lizard and snake too tough. She'd rather have the skrill. The scorp shell got caught in her teeth and she didn't think it had enough meat to warrant a second bite.

As they were finishing, Picall laughing at their reactions, Devon said, "Company."

Maupin and Raven were approaching.

"I'm glad to see you settling in," Maupin said. "I've spoken to the others and they've all agreed to let you stay. But not without some conditions."

"What conditions?" Lane asked, wary.

Raven answered. "They'll want us to help around the tull—hunting, fishing, farming."

"We don't know how to do any of that."

"I'll teach them," Picall said. "I can take them out hunting tomorrow. We'll start with lizard."

"I'll leave it to you then, Picall." The tuller leader turned and headed back toward the fire. Raven stayed behind.

Picall took the two trays and followed him. "I'll find you all tomorrow, bright and early."

Only then did Lane notice that the shaft had been enveloped in shadow. The sky was still bright overhead, but the sun had shifted below the height of the plateau, the light inside now dim and diffuse—a premature dusk.

"They've given us a tent," Raven said. "I'll show you."

* * *

Devon threw himself at the lizard, arm outstretched. As he slammed into the ground at the height of the plateau, he felt the lizard's textured tail slip out of his grip and he cursed, then spat as dust and dirt from his lunge got into his mouth.

He heaved himself up and dusted himself off, Nic laughing from a short distance away. Dalton merely shook his head; Picall wasn't even paying attention, her lithe form shifting from rock to boulder to ground as she hunted. It was their fourth day at the summit and so far Devon hadn't managed to catch one lizard. He was beginning to think Lane had the better idea: after the first day, she'd decided to fish instead.

He watched as Nic grew tense, eyes fixed on something to his left. He shifted position, the motion slow—

Then with a flick of wrist threw a knife.

With a cry of success, he pounced and held up a dead lizard at least the length of his arm in triumph. "Another one! That makes three today."

Devon retrieved his own dagger. He'd flung it and missed, startling the lizard. His lunge had been a last-ditch effort to snag it alive. His throwing skills had suffered horribly during his tenure at the Lyceum. He used to be able to hit the center of a target at twenty feet; this had been half that. Granted, targets didn't move when they caught sight of you, but still. The lizards weren't exactly thin. Even Dalton had managed to catch a few.

He took a moment to stare out at the Flatlands from this height. The horizon shimmered with heat, but far off to the East, toward Brovetto, he could see storm clouds headed towards them. They'd have maybe another hour before they hit.

Hefting the weight of the dagger in his head, he turned his back on the others and began a slow walk away from them, searching the ground for the telltale signs Picall had drilled them in that first day—two parallel three-clawed marks, sometimes with a central line down the middle if they were dragging their body or tail. But at this height, the wind gusted enough that such tracks didn't remain around long, and the ground was often scoured down to rock regardless, with nothing to leave tracks in.

Devon had found he had better luck looking for furtive movements out of the corner of his eye.

He caught a flicker and stilled. The lizard sat on a flat rock, sunbathing, but its snout was in the air, its tongue tasting the air. It had already sensed him, but it wasn't certain he was a danger yet, otherwise it would have skittered away.

Devon scanned the surroundings. The lizard was in a shallow wash carved out by rain. He could see where the water drained down into a crack in the stone at the far end. Dry scrub lined either side, but he'd have a clear shot if he eased himself a little to the left.

Moving slow, he positioned himself, raised his dagger, and threw.

The blade sank into flesh an inch above the lizard's hind leg, not a killing blow. It began to thrash and Devon bolted toward it, charging through the brush and falling on its writhing form, wrapping his arms around its body. It hissed into his face, tongue flicking Devon's cheek, claws raking his arms, but Devon hung on with an intense, "Oh no you don't, you bastard. You're mine!"

He rolled, reaching for his dagger, still stuck in the lizard's hindquarters, then again as it almost slipped free.

Then he slid over the edge of the wash into the crack.

He didn't have time to react, striking the far wall with shoulder-numbing force, then plummeting ten feet before hitting stone debris. An avalanche of rock began, carrying him down a gradual slope and into a small cavern. He clutched at the lizard instinctively, body curled up tight, until he came to rest on his side, feet upslope.

He gasped, unaware he'd been holding his breath, and shifted, but it caused another cascade of stone. Only then did he realize the lizard wasn't moving. Its head hung at an odd angle, its neck snapped sometime during the fall.

Moving cautiously, he righted himself, still holding the lizard with one arm. He retrieved his dagger, then looked around.

The cavern was dim, but enough sunlight came from the crack above he could see the stone scree ended at the edge of a puddle, the remnants of the last rain. The cavern obviously flooded during storms, the stone at the base worn smooth.

But it was the far wall that caught his attention.

Stepping carefully around the puddle, he reached up and touched the wall. It wasn't stone. It was crystal, a pale rose in color. A jagged formation of rough lucent made of hexagonal columns broken off at different heights, each about the size of Devon's fist in width, the nearest columns cracked and murky in places. Imperfect. Raw. Not like the lucent in the city at all.

"Natural," Devon murmured to himself.

He'd always thought of the lucent in Iandolo as natural, but that was because he'd never seen it in any other form. Now he realized that all of it must have been molded somehow.

Palm flat against the nearest crystal, he closed his eyes and tried to sink himself into it, as he'd done with the lucent locks to pick them, or the Warding when they released it. He merged with the structure instantly, sensing the geometric forms within. But unlike the Warding or the lock— or even the dead lucent of the Lyceum's Tower—the structure here was elementary.

"Devon! Devon, are you down there? Are you all right?"

Devon pulled back from the crystal and stepped aside, his foot kicking one of the small shards that littered the floor here. He reached down and picked one up, a hand in length but only about two fingers in diameter. Its edges were sharp.

"I'm fine, Dalton! A little beat up, but fine. Hang on."

He shoved the crystal in his pocket and headed back to the slope of stone, stepping carefully until he could see sky above. Dalton, Nic, and Picall were leaning over the edge, their relief evident even half-silhouetted.

"Can you climb up?" Picall asked.

"I think so."

"What are you carrying?" Nic asked.

"My lizard."

"Just drop it!" Picall called. "We've caught plenty today!"

"Like hell."

When he was within arm's reach of the lip, Dalton reached down and hauled him halfway up, Nic grabbing his other arm while Picall took his lizard. He sprawled out in the wash, all of the scratches and bruises throbbing. His shoulder ached where it had struck the wall. Nic and Dalton stood over him in concern.

"That was fun," he said, shading his eyes with one hand.

"We don't have time for this," Picall said, reaching down to pull him up. "That storm is moving in fast. We need to get down to the gorge."

* * *

When Lane pushed through the opening flap of the tent to get out of the rain, she found Devon sitting on his pallet, his notes scattered around him in disorderly piles, his green lucent lantern throwing shadows against the canvas walls. Another crystal rested in his lap. Dalton lay with an arm over his eyes, snoring lightly, while Nic lounged on his side, fiddling with his knife and watching Devon.

Lane wiped the rainwater from her face and headed to her own space. "Where's Raven?"

"Off on watch with Maupin," Nic said. "Where have you been?"

"Fishing," she said in disgust, using a towel to dry off whatever she could. "Apparently, the fish bit more when it's raining. And then we had to gut them. I never had to gut my own food in Iandolo. Did you know they use everything here for something? And I mean *everything*."

"You could be out hunting lizards and snakes and scorps with us."

"I'll take the gutting, thank you."

Nic leaned toward her and made a show of sniffing the air. "You don't smell particularly fishy."

"Because afterwards I scrubbed myself raw with that soap they make."

Nic lay back down and began tossing the knife, doing tricks. "Devon caught his first lizard today. He killed it by falling on it."

Devon shot the ex-gang member a glare. "I crippled it with my dagger first, *then* I fell on it. And then I found this." He handed Lane the crystal without really looking up from his pages. "Careful, it's sharp."

She held it up to the greenish light. Its ends were jagged and rough, not smoothed out like the lantern, and its interior was murky, with a few cracks. "It's flawed. Does it do anything?"

"It's raw," Devon said, taking it back. "And no, it's just a piece of crystal. For now."

Lane had heard that tone in Devon's voice before. She squatted down, began looking at the pages spread out before him, even picking a few up. "So what are you looking for?"

"I don't know yet."

The pages he'd discarded were all notes about the double pyramid structure—the Source and Outcome, Devon called them—and the sigils mages used to create their constructs. His current focus were the notes his mentor Arrend had made regarding the Wardings, along with his own additions.

She began sifting through the sigil notes. "What are you trying to do?"

Devon leaned back and massaged his temples. "I'm not certain. But something's tugging at the edges of my mind, something about this crystal and the lucent and the Wardings."

Lane was only half listening, her attention caught by sigils. "Did you need these?"

"I don't think they're relevant."

"Can I borrow them?"

Devon waved a hand dismissively.

Lane gathered up all of the pages and retreated back to her own pallet, spreading them out around her. They were mixed up and out of order, a result of their sudden exit from Iandolo and the fact that Raven had been the one gathering them up at the time. Lane sorted them using the numbers Devon had scrawled in each corner, but then realized he'd been approaching it from a mathematician's point of view. Knowing what she knew from the mage school—what little Favian had let her learn, anyway—she resorted them into new stacks, focusing on those sigils that produced fire effects, then light and air, earth and water. But some of the effects didn't appear to fit it any category.

At the Lyceum, if she'd brought this up, she knew the mage proctors would simply scoff and say she was overthinking it. The sigils were just sigils! You learned the pattern, then trained until you could reproduce the desired effect with no conscious thought. That was it. The focus wasn't on the sigils, it was on coordinating your movements with the other War and Mage students, memorizing the formations to make the army an effective unit. Research involved figuring out new formations or newer and deadlier combinations of the sigils already known. Unlike the Sciences, where graduation required that each student produce a challenge of seven questions that the selected Board could not easily solve, Mage students merely had to demonstrate mastery of the sigils and army formations on the yard, usually through a series of duels or mock battles with their fellow War students.

She held up the master diagram that showed the double pyramid drawn three-dimensionally, with various nodes annotated by Devon. He'd applied some kind of coordinate system to the Source pyramid, another to the Outcomes pyramid, nodes color-coordinated somehow, although she didn't see the pattern. Not that it mattered. She wasn't interested in the geometry of it, not yet. She was looking for something more general.

Setting the master diagram in the center before her, she pulled out all of the pages relating to the base sigil and stacked those below it. What she was looking for was in the secondary sigils. She'd caught a glimpse of it when the papers were scattered before Devon, but now…

She sorted the secondary sigils again, trying different groupings. After multiple attempts along the same lines as fire and earth and light, she realized that wasn't working at all. There were too many sigils that didn't fit any of those variations. So it had to be something else.

Maybe she didn't have enough sigils yet.

Scanning the notes, she realized that those in Devon's set were all from the Lyceum, from when they were illegally practicing in the lower levels— ones Devon had seen from his dormitory window being used in the practice yards, or those Lane had heard about from other Mage students.

"But we know a bunch more now."

"What was that?" Devon asked.

She glanced up and realized Nic had fallen asleep. Rain still pattered against the tent, gusts of wind rustling the canvas, but otherwise the tent was quiet.

"Nothing. I'm just—" She cut off when she realized Devon was staring at the crystal, not really paying attention to her. "Do you have any more paper? And something to write with?"

Devon motioned toward his pack without looking. "In there somewhere."

She rifled through the satchel until she found what she needed, then returned to her seat. Following Devon's pattern of description, she wrote out pages for all of the sigils they'd learned since being kicked out of the Lyceum—the fire spells she'd work out on her own while trapped in her rooms in the Tower, the cantrips they'd seen the Brovettan mages using, the lightning spells they'd improvised on the quad after freeing the Warding.

When all of the sigils were done, she laid them out in a long arc, then began pairing them up in different ways. Picking out those that had fire effects, she noted the similarities and differences in the sigil's pattern, then broke that set apart and tried another, such as lightning effects. Each grouping had some nodes in similar locations, although never exactly in the same place.

She began taking notes, using her own rough sketch of the double pyramid. This area contained all of the similar nodes for the cantrips, this area here the ones for air. One of the four faces of the Source pyramid on the bottom began to fill out, some of her areas overlapping. But what were the other nodes in the sigil for then? There had to be a pattern. If she'd learned anything from Devon over the past year it was that there was always a pattern.

Tentatively, she began trying other aspects of the effects. Instead of focusing on fire, she looked at the size of the effect. Her fireballs were about the size of someone's head, but the sheets of fire that rained down from above during the battle on the quad were much larger. And what about the direction of the effect? Some shot straight forward, like the cantrips, and moved in a straight line; others came down from above and targeted a specific area, like the lightning.

Working slowly, trying grouping after grouping after grouping, she slowly began to piece together the Source.

And then it clicked.

"Shards," she muttered, sitting back. She picked up her sketch, stared at her collage of markings, some scratched out, others dark because she'd gone over them two or three times or more. "There is a pattern."

She turned toward Devon, but he was flat on his stomach, face turned away, asleep.

How long had she been working at this?

She listened. The rain had stopped and the grotto was quiet. She knew someone was awake, on guard—there was always a watch, both here, at the entrance, and above on the plateau—but she heard no one else.

She must have been at it for hours.

She glanced at the sheet again. If she was right, if this part of the Source selected intensity and this one shape, this face direction and this other type...

"We could produce almost any variation of effect we want, up to a point."

Nic snorted and rolled over. She waited until he'd settled, then flicked Devon's green lucent lantern off and crawled onto her pallet, stacking Devon's notes and her own to one side.

"I could test it out," she said into the silence.

Except she couldn't. Because magic didn't work in the Flatlands.

Who had Maupin said she should talk to? Girard? Julian?

"Gillian."

* * *

Varenov stood back as the city guards opened the cell door that contained the sole Brovettan mage captured after the release of the Warding. She had only fleeting memories from that chaotic time, as the Council and the Iandolan Army regained control of the city, but she did not recognize the diminutive girl that lurched awkwardly upright on the cot when the door opened and glowered at the guards as they stepped aside. Her hands were bound behind her back, but when her gaze settled on Varenov it was defiant.

"Do you want us to come in with you?" one of her personal guards asked.

Varenov shook her head. "No. She's bound." And she didn't want anyone to overhear some of her questions. "Close the door behind me. I'll knock when I'm finished."

She stepped inside, the girl—she appeared to be twelve years old, although Varenov thought she must be older—shifting backwards on her cot.

Varenov waited until the door had closed, motioning to her guards that she was fine through the small window before turning back to the girl.

"My name is Varenov. What's yours?"

The girl didn't answer.

Varenov took another step forward and the girl flinched and turned her head away, revealing faded bruises along the line of her neck, beneath her long black hair.

Varenov's jaw set and she clasped her hands behind her back, drawing in a deep breath and releasing it slowly. "I have a daughter a little older than you who's also a mage." She caught a flicker of interest from the girl, so continued. "She's Brovettan, like you, as well. She was training at the Lyceum when your group first attacked us."

"The Lyceum is full of liars and traitors."

Varenov raised an eyebrow at the vehemence of the words. "Is that what you were told? Of course it is. Because you were trained by Terrial."

"They abandoned her in Brovetto, left her behind when the soldiers she was with were attacked by the rebels and she was injured. They didn't even try to save her."

The contingent led by Favian and Gallean, Varenov realized, the one sent to deal with the insurgents who'd killed the previous Luminesque Councilor that had been ambushed and was forced to retreat. Except, Favian's story was different.

"They thought Terrial was dead," Varenov said.

"They were too busy running away. They never even checked."

Varenov wondered how much of that was true and how much Terrial had exaggerated with each retelling. But it didn't matter. The girl was talking. Carbolen had warned her that someone within the Council had been working with the Brovettans. If so, she needed to know who.

"And then what happened?"

The girl clammed up, mouth pressed into a thin line, and for a moment Varenov thought that's all she would get from her. But then she said, "Then she joined the rebels."

"And they accepted her," Varenov said, nodding, "because she said she could give them mages."

The girl nodded. "She did. She found me and three others and she trained us and when she thought we were ready she began to plan. But when she approached the rebel leader, he wouldn't agree to it. It was too violent, too bloody, too risky. Terrial didn't like that. So she took her mages and left. Some of the rebels went with her. And then she approached the leaders of the city, brought us to them. They had no problems with the violence."

"It was the city government that attacked us then, not the rebels?"

"Some of us were rebels," the girl said defiantly, but then she backed down. "But it wasn't the main group."

"It wasn't John," Varenov said, to herself. Relief washed through her, a tension she'd held in her gut suddenly releasing. She sagged, her strength nearly giving out, but she caught herself. A throaty chuckle escaped her. "Not John at all."

The girl was watching her warily and she composed herself, wrapping the cloak of the Council around her once again.

"They couldn't have done this on their own," she said. "Not even the Brovettan government. They must have had help from within Iandolo. Who helped you get into the city?"

The girl turned sullen. "I already told the guardsmen everything I know. The mages came in through the waygates, like every other citizen. I don't know how the soldiers were brought in. I came with the treaty delegation."

That matched up with the reports Prefect Arctus had provided the Council. He hadn't mentioned that Terrial had broken off from the main force of rebels they'd been dealing with for decades in Brovetto, but then he wouldn't. They were all insurgents to him, all the same group.

And the Council had just sent him to Brovetto to deal with them. All of them, whether they were complicit in the recent attacks of not.

A new worry settled into her bones, but there was nothing she could do to warn John and the other rebels. They'd have to manage on their own.

She eyed the girl, but there was nothing else she could think of to ask. Pressuring her for more information would be useless.

She turned to go, but the girl asked sharply, "What are they going to do with us? With me?"

Varenov pinched her lips together, thinking about Petrov's talk of an execution. "I don't know yet. We haven't decided."

The girl's hope visibly deflated. "I just want to go home."

Varenov turned back. "You agreed to set off the Warding, knowing you'd be trapped inside. Why?"

"Terrial promised to let everyone out as soon as they'd seized control of the city."

Varenov drew breath to tell her that they suspected Terrial had no idea how to release the Warding once it was set, but sighed instead. "And what do you think we should do with you?"

"I just want to go home," the girl repeated.

Chapter Four

"Yes, I'm Gillian. Who are you?"

Lane stood at the entrance to a small room cut into the side of the cliff. On the ledge outside, herbs and a few vegetables grew in clay pots around a small table and chair. Beyond that, Lane could see the edge of the pool, the tents and huts of the village, and a swatch of the land the tullers farmed through the trees.

Her focus shifted to the austere woman who'd straightened from tending a small fire and kettle to one side of the room. A table lined with pots and pans and various other cooking utensils was shoved up against the wall, its surface covered with carrots, potatoes, and the carcass of a lizard. A second table sat next to it scattered with bunches of drying herbs and stoppered jars and urns. In the center of the room sat a third table with two benches, a cup already set up in one corner. The room looked mostly natural, with another entrance leading deeper into the plateau on the far side. Tall woven baskets and a few larger urns rested against the opposite wall, along with shelves of books.

"My name is Lane. I came with a few of my friends about a week ago—"

"Ah yes, I remember. I recorded it when you arrived, as Historians do."

She turned back to the kettle, now steaming, and poured its contents into her cup. Her hand shook and Lane noted her gray-speckled hair and the age lines around her eyes and mouth. Her back was rigid, her stance poised. She certainly reminded Lane of many of the Historians she'd encountered in the Towers and at the Lyceum.

She sat down at the table and raised the cup to her lips with both hands, blowing on it before sipping. "Well, what did you want?"

Lane started, then entered, settling at the table across from Gillian. It suddenly felt like she was back at the college, speaking to a proctor.

"I'm a mage…or I was a mage…it's complicated, but when we were leaving Iandolo, in the sublevels, I tried to use a sigil and it didn't work. I've tried a few times since we arrived here and…nothing. Maupin said I should ask you about why magic doesn't work here."

"Is that so?" Gillian took another sip, eyeing Lane from across the rim. "A little presumptuous of him, don't you think?"

"He said you're a Historian. I don't understand—"

"I *was* a Historian. Ages ago. I worked for the Council for twelve years, traveling from city to city with envoys and delegations, even some of the army battalions sent to quell unrest or deal with a situation the local forces couldn't. Then I worked at the Lyceum for another seven years, before I couldn't stand the politics and came here." Her eyes narrowed. "You're too young to have graduated from the Lyceum. What's your story?"

"I—I was expelled. For learning sigils and sharing mage secrets with a friend." Gillian's eyebrow rose. "It wasn't like how it sounds! The proctors weren't teaching me the right sigils, they were trying to force me out. I was desperate—"

"No need to explain," Gillian said, cutting her off. "I left because of politics, remember? I know what they can be like. In fact, I applaud you for trying to circumvent them. Pity you were caught." She sat back, some of the stiffness easing out of her shoulders. "You're the Councilor's daughter, aren't you? And your friend is the mathematician?"

"How do you know about us?"

"We don't become blind, deaf, and dumb when we come here, you know. Historians are insatiably curious. Just because I left Iandolo doesn't mean I'm not interested in what goes on there. I have the scouting teams bring me back whatever they can gather from the streets while they're there, especially regarding the Lyceum." She rose. "Would you like some tea? It's a special blend of my own. It has a little more kick than the usual."

Without waiting for Lane to answer, she poured a cup and set it before Lane, then drifted toward the bookshelves. Lane leaned over and sniffed the tea. It had hints of lemon and honey and something else she couldn't identify. She took a sip, the water still hot enough it burned her mouth and throat as she swallowed. But it tasted better than any tea she'd had before.

"Did you know the Lyceum has thousands and thousands of books in its Library, most of which haven't been read in decades? Some of them in hundreds of years. Only the proctors have access to them, of course, but most of the proctors don't care unless they're researching a question one of the Science students has brought forward in a challenge. A few do their own research there, like me, but not as many as you'd think. By the time most of us become proctors, we're already weary of research. That spark of interest that began it all has died."

She pulled a book from the shelf and returned to the table, dropping the massive tome with a thud that shook the teacups.

"What does this have to do—?"

Gillian held up a finger, cutting her off. "My interests lay in the history of the Founding. Who were the Founders? Where did the Crystal Cities come from? Who built them? How? How did we get to...all of this?" The Historian waved an arm around vaguely, encompassing everything, then caught Lane's hands in her own. "It made the other History proctors nervous. No one had taken a serious look that far back in ages. So, like you, I did my research discreetly."

She dropped Lane's hands and opened the book at random, then began searching through it. "The most ancient books are nearly impossible to decipher, using words that are unrecognizable. Some even refer to us descending from the heavens in ships, coming to rest on this earth to make it our home, even though it was not our intended destination." Gillian snorted. "As if boats could ever ply the skies. I'm not interested in folklore or children's stories. I want facts." She clicked her tongue in triumph, turned the book around so it faced Lane, and pointed. "Like this."

Lane pulled the text closer and singled out the section Gillian had noted. The script was strange, basic, with no flourishes or accents, unlike most of the material written today. The letters were blocky, although still obviously written by hand.

"*For those programmed to genetically interface,*" she read, sounding out the unfamiliar words with care, "*with the modified crystals of the planet—and for those genetically predisposed to interaction with the crystals—we have established a keyboard based on a diamond-shaped Zyrchovskian lattice for greatest flexibility. Enforcers can access the system with a simple hand gesture, as long as they are within network range of the local crystals.*"

Lane leaned back. "I don't understand half of these words. What does it mean?"

"It means," Gillian said, tapping the book, "that the reason your magic doesn't work here is because we aren't near any worked lucent. As soon as you descended beneath Iandolo, you went outside of 'network range,' and thus lost your ability to do magic."

"I...lost it?" Lane reached for the tea, held it with both hands as she took a gulp to keep herself from trembling. "I always thought the magic was part of me. That it was inside me."

"Oh, it is. That's what 'genetically' means, I think. It's not gone. But it also requires the crystals...the lucent...to work. Once you return to Iandolo—or any of the other Crystal Cities, I'd imagine—you'll be able to do magic again."

Lane was only partially reassured. She drank some more, noticed her fingers were beginning to tingle, and set the tea aside. "But that doesn't make sense. There's no lucent on the wayfares, but when the army marches on one of the other cities, the mages can do magic on the road."

"Are you certain?"

"I heard the fifth and sixth years talking about it in the dormitory at the college. And what about here? Devon has a lucent lantern with him. Doesn't that count?"

Gillian pulled her book back to her side of the table sharply. "I didn't say I could answer all of your questions. I don't remember offering to answer any of them, in fact."

"No. No, you didn't. I'm sorry to have bothered you." Lane tried to stand, but found she couldn't even shift forward. Her arms rested like leaden stone on the table, yet her body felt weightless. The edges of her vision wavered slightly. She frowned. "I...I can't seem to move."

Gillian's eyes widened and she reached for Lane, lifting one of her hands. It hung limp from the wrist. Lane could barely feel it. Even the tingling had stopped.

"Oh, for shard's sake," Gillian said in disgust. She rose and snatched up Lane's cup of tea, looked into it, then tutted.

Lane's heart thudded hard in her chest. "What did you do?" The shimmering in her vision expanded. "What did you *do!*"

"Hush, don't panic. It's nothing. The tea was stronger than I thought, that's all. Don't fight it, just let it happen. It's rather pleasant, once you let yourself sink into it."

"Sink into it!"

Gillian's shoulders sagged as she set Lane's cup on one of the side tables. "It's something I use to relax. It looked like you could use it. But I forgot how potent it can be the first time."

She turned, but Lane could barely see her through the vivid colors flashing in front of her eyes. She whimpered.

"Don't worry," Gillian said, leaning in close and patting her hand. "It should all be over in about an hour."

* * *

Varenov strolled toward the market set up on the edges of the square outside the entrance to the three towers in a rough arc surrounding the fountain at its center. She glanced at the statue of a young woman as she passed—head lifted, one arm outstretched—and the circle of stone behind her, water pouring through its center in a transparent, shimmering wall, but her mind was on the Council.

Arctus and the Iandolan Army had left for Brovetto three days ago, leaving Iridesque exposed and vulnerable. Entire levels were bereft of city guard, who'd been transferred to the waygates and main thoroughfares to replace the soldiers who'd accompanied Arctus. Most of those levels were now being policed by Carbolen and his gangs. Varenov had little faith in the gang leader, but she admitted, grudgingly, that there had been no significant incidents since the army's departure.

Meanwhile, Iriarte, Petrov, and Gabrella continued to push for a draft and conscriptions, even as the Lyceum converted to into a War college, accepting any and all volunteers of a certain age into their ranks, the Sciences, Arts, History, and even the Humanities schools appreciably reduced. Two other War colleges had also been created, both at Mid-level and under the supervision of Master Proctor Favian and Proctor Gallean.

Thankfully, Martov and Santigo continued to defy the others in the Council and with Varenov's vote had managed to stave off any kind of draft or conscription. But she could sense the frustration of the others increasing with each vote. Neither Martov or Santigo appeared to be wavering as yet, but it was only a matter of time. The Council was divided and tensions were high.

As she entered the market's arc, she forced herself to let her anxiety go, pausing a moment to breath in the faint breeze, scented with charred meats, perfumes, and fresh flowers. Her ever-present guards fell into step to either side as she began to idle down the curved lane created by the tents and carts, brimming with produce and wares. Unlike the other markets at Mid-level she'd attended, there were no garish hawkers shouting for customers' attentions here. These vendors were merchants, their displays elaborate, intended to capture the interests of those that lived in the three towers or nearby. Varenov sampled wine from Radimansque and Scintillesque. A glasswright from Opalesque displayed exquisite glassware that captured and refracted the sunlight. A merchant from Lambenesque had scented candles of the finest tallow and one from Incandesque had elegant jewelry made from various shades of lucent.

She was fingering fabric from Scintillesque when someone stepped up beside her.

"Did you notice these pieces over here? They're made from dead crystal. I find them rather macabre, although I hear they are the newest fashion with the younger elite."

Varenov glanced up. "Ah, Havvelan." Her eyes darted to the two guards behind him, keeping a discreet distance. Her own sent her a wordless question but she waved them back. "What brings you to the market? Shouldn't you be fawning after Secora or Petrov?"

Havvelan gave her a wan smile. "Aren't we defensive today."

"I came to the market to escape the Council and politics."

"You can never escape politics. I would have thought you understood that by now. When you stole the Council seat from beneath me seventeen years ago, you implicitly accepted that as part of your life."

"I did. But your continued resentment is old and tiresome and I have better things to do with my time."

She shifted away from the table, but Havvelan stayed with her.

"I must say, you and Martov and Santigo have created quite an alliance on the Council, strong enough to stop Petrov's push to increase the size of Iandolo's army."

"It's not an alliance. We simply all agree that such an increase is unjustified at this moment."

"Yet our forces are spread so thin. It's difficult to protect our own citizens."

"Protect them from what?"

"Themselves."

Havvelan wandered away and Varenov halted, watching him retreat. "What did he mean by that?"

Her guardsmen shrugged.

Two tents away, someone shouted, "Thief! Seize them!"

Varenov spun as her guards stepped closer. A Radimansque merchant of fine metal pointed at a man, woman, and their teenaged daughter, his eyes blazing, as the three turned back in surprise. Two men nearby grabbed hold of the man, another capturing the woman's arm.

All three were Brovettan.

Varenov swore and began to push forward. But those in the market were beginning to gather, far more than she had thought were present a moment ago. They appeared as if from thin air, expressions already ugly, clothes rough and worn. Not from the towers, not even from Mid-level.

Two more seized the daughter and dragged her back.

"What is the meaning of this?" the Brovettan man bellowed. "Unhand us! We've stolen nothing!"

"Shut up, traitor." One of the men punched the Brovettan in the stomach. He doubled over, his wife giving a shortened scream, cut off when the man holding her clapped his hand over her mouth. Her terrified eyes latched on to Varenov's as she struggled. The men with her daughter had already vanished.

"Stop this!" Varenov called out, trying to push through the crowd that had formed around them. Her guards began to force an opening for her, yanking men and women aside by brute force. "Stop this at once!"

The merchant reached into the Brovettan's lavish coat pocket and pulled out a bronze bracelet, raising it high so the crowd could see. "See! A thief! Not only did they attack our city, imprison our Council and Army within the Warding, and butcher our citizens, now they are stealing from our very hands!"

The Brovettan had straightened. "That's not mine," he said hoarsely, still gasping. "I didn't—"

The man hit him again, hard enough his knees gave out. His wife began to scream, the sound muffled. Before the Brovettan could recover, the merchant kicked him onto his side. "You think you can steal from us! You think you can take what isn't yours!" He kicked him again and again. "This is Iandolo! This is Iridesque! *We* control the Crystal Cities! We *are* the Crystal Cities!"

The Brovettan's wife wrenched free from her captor and screamed, loud and shrill, and bolted. The crowd surged after her, bringing her down within seconds. Varenov lost sight of her, of the man, as the latent fears from the Brovettan attack unleashed throughout the marketplace, men and women lunging for the hapless victims. Varenov howled for them to stop as those gathered edged out of control. Within moments, tents were collapsing, tables and carts overturned. Those near fixated on any Brovettan face in the market, including other merchants. Screams and bellows of rage erupted as some of them fought back, aided by a few Iandolans.

Varenov's guards closed in around her and she stopped attempting to get to the Brovettans' side. She couldn't see them anymore, not through the mob that had turned on itself.

"We need to get you to safety," her head guard said, already dragging her toward the space between two tents.

Varenov couldn't answer. She found she was trembling, her chest numb with shock. A high-pitched whistle of the city guard pierced the chaos, but the mob was out of control. She clung to her guard's arm, the second guard behind, beating back anyone who came within two paces.

Before they made the edge of the tent, it collapsed sideways, hundreds of pieces of pottery shattering as they hit the ground. Her guardsman angled her left, to the next tent, already stove in on one side, but a cluster of fighting blocked their way. They dodged further out into the market lane, where the mob had turned into a brawl between citizens and the city guard. Everywhere they turned there was blood and violence, the debris of the market strewn about. There was nowhere to go.

"Councilor Varenov!" someone called. "Over here!"

Varenov fixated on the voice, saw a group of ruffians holding off the mob on either side, another man motioning them forward.

Her guards hesitated.

"It's Carbolen," Varenov said. "Follow him."

They hustled her to Carbolen's side, his gang members retreating from the market behind them, keeping everyone at bay. On the far side of what had been the market arch was a line of trees, separating the towers' square from the nearest buildings, but Carbolen didn't stop, escorting Varenov and her guards into the streets beyond, heading toward Mid-level.

Before they'd gone past three streets, the rough group of mostly children and teens drawing the attention of passersby, Carbolen cut into a narrow alley and knocked on a door. It opened a crack, then wider as the woman inside recognized Carbolen and let him in. Varenov, her guards, and the rest followed, crowding into a storeroom filled with crates and shadows, lit by only a few lanterns.

The Brovettan's daughter from the market sat to one side, as pale as any Brovettan Varenov had ever seen, although otherwise untouched.

She spun on Carbolen. "What is the meaning of this? Why is she here? *How* did she get here?"

Carbolen ignored her. "Toral, report."

"We managed to grab the daughter but not the wife," the woman who'd let them in replied. "Both she and her husband went down. We don't know whether they're dead or alive yet."

"Then find out. You are my Eyes, aren't you?"

Toral snapped her fingers and three of the gang members departed.

"What of the other teams?"

"We managed to halt brawls at two other locations. At a third, a riot started but we got the Brovettans there out."

"And the others?"

"Leinn hasn't reported in yet."

Varenov stepped forward. "What is going on?"

Carbolen faced her. She'd last seen him after the Warding had collapsed and they'd retaken Iandolo from the Brovettan forces. The Council had conferred with Carbolen and Captain Mannert to determine what had happened, how they'd been freed, who had participated, and what Devon and Lane had had to do with it all. After that initial meeting, while parts of the city were still being retaken, the Council's only contact with Carbolen had been through Mannert. The gang leader preferred to stay hidden in the lower levels.

Which is why it surprised her to see him here, at Mid-level.

"Why are you at Mid-level? What just happened?" she asked again.

Carbolen smiled. Varenov assumed he thought it disarming. "I'm more often on Mid-level than you'd think, Councilor."

"Explain why you're here now."

He dropped the grin. "We heard a rumor there would be attacks on Brovettans at various places throughout the city today—markets, bars, other areas where Brovettans frequent more so than others. Mostly places where the city guard is thin or nonexistent in the lower levels. But one of the targeted markets was here at the Tower Plaza."

"So you came to stop it?"

"We came to try, but as you saw, we arrived too late. We had time to grab the girl, but that was it."

The Brovettan's daughter's chest hitched and tears began to stream down her face. "What—what happened to my parents?"

"You saved her?"

"You were there. You saw what happened."

"I'm not certain what I saw."

Carbolen shifted closer to her and she straightened. "Someone is organizing groups within Iandolo and encouraging them to incite riots. They've been told to target Brovettans in particular, to play on the current fear and hatred of them inspired by the recent attack. It doesn't take much prompting to turn a crowd into a mob, especially regarding Brovettans." A thought flickered across the gang leader's face. "Why were you at the market today, Councilor?"

"I needed a break from committees and sessions. Why?"

"No one suggested you come down today?"

"No." But then she remembered running into Havvelan. He'd departed rather suddenly. Had he known what was about to happen? Had he led her toward it? "Havvelan was there in the market moments before it began."

"The merchant whose place you took on the council?"

"Yes. But I doubt—" She halted, hearing her own hesitancy in her voice.

Carbolen turned away. "We don't know who is behind the attacks, but they aren't going to stop after today. They were too successful. We'll keep our Eyes open—" Toral nodded. "—and let you know if we find out anything else."

"Try to warn me of any future attacks if you can. Or warn Captain Mannert."

Carbolen looked back. "She gave you my warning?"

"Yes."

He motioned toward the Brovettan's daughter. "You should take the girl. I'll send a messenger once we know what happened to her parents."

Varenov approached the young girl, crouched down in front of her. Before she could say anything, the girl lurched forward and crushed her in a fierce hug, the pent-up sobs coming out in a torrent. Varenov held her tight, stroked her back, and let her cry.

When the girl had calmed down, she stood and motioned to her guards. But at the door, she paused.

"Why are you doing this, Carbolen? Why are you helping?"

"Because I believe that it's the same person who helped the Brovettans in their attack. They're trying to tear this city apart. I won't let that happen." When Varenov opened the door, he added, "Be careful, Councilor. The Council has become a dangerous place."

Her guards checked the alley, then led her and the girl back toward the three towers, bypassing the area where the market had been set up. As they approached from the side, Varenov attempted to shield the girl from the sight of the torn tents and scattered debris among the abandoned carts, all being patrolled by city guards and a few Iandolan soldiers now, even though they were too distant to see any blood or bodies.

Once inside the central tower, she headed toward the elevator, but saw Treant approaching fast from one side.

She knelt beside the girl. Her tears had stopped and her face had hardened, already recovering from the trauma. Varenov wondered how much she'd seen of the attack on her parents before Carbolen's men had spirited her away. "What's your name, child?"

"I'm not a child."

"No, you're not. I apologize. I have a daughter a few years older than you. Her name's Lane."

Treant arrived, but said nothing.

Varenov waited and eventually the girl softened.

"Eri. Eri Cantell."

"Very well, Eri. One of my guards is going to take you to my quarters here in the tower. You can stay there until we find out what happened to your parents."

A stricken look crossed her face, a crack in the façade, but she rallied, chin lifting. "Very well."

Varenov stood and motioned to her second guard. "Take her. I'll be there as soon as I can." Then she faced Treant. "What is it?"

"There's an impromptu Council meeting going on right now in the Council chambers. Only four members are there, but the others—including yourself—have been summoned."

"Regarding the events on the plaza?"

"And the other attacks throughout the city. We're only now getting word on some of them."

They were already moving to the elevators.

"How many attacks were there?"

"Five that we know of, including the one in the plaza."

They exited at the fifth floor, Varenov stalking across the foyer to the chamber doors without pause. She could already hear raised voices.

"—attacking their fellow citizens!" Martov was bellowing when she pulled open the doors. "This cannot be allowed! We must find the perpetrators and deal with them harshly!"

"After what has happened over these past few months—even beyond that—can you blame the Iandolans—the *true* Iandolans—for their actions?" Gabrella asked. The two were standing within inches of each other, spitting in each others' faces. Santigo and Petrov stood back a pace. "How do you know which Brovettans to trust? How do you know we can trust any of them?"

"Because some of these Brovettans have lived within our city since they were born!"

"And that means they are automatically trustworthy? The Brovettans have been hammering at us for decades. They could have sent anyone here during that time to undermine us."

"So what do you suggest? Shall we round them all up and kick them out? Send them back to Luminesque?"

"If that's what it takes to keep true Iandolans safe."

"May I remind you," Varenov said loudly as she approached, cutting them both off, "that the Brovettans that attacked us were *not* representative of all of Luminesque? They are rebels, a small percentage of the Brovettan population. Not all Brovettans should be punished for the actions of a few."

"But how are we to single out which ones are the rebels?" Santigo asked. "How are we to find them, if there are any remaining in Iandolo?"

"That's what our city guard is for."

"No!" Gabrella spat. "No, I refuse to place all of my trust in the city guard, especially now that it has been stretched so thin. We don't even have enough to cover the streets. Look at what happened in the plaza. They killed seven people, Varenov! It was brutal and insane."

Varenov wondered if two of those seven were Eri's parents. "I know, I was there."

That stopped Gabrella short, but she muttered, "If it can happen there, then it can happen anywhere, at any time."

"Ah, good," Secora said as she and Iriarte entered, "we're all here now. I have an update on the riots. It appears nine broke out at various times this morning throughout all levels of the city, most concentrated between Level Twelve and Level Twenty."

"Where the majority of our Brovettan citizens live," Varenov added, emphasizing the word 'citizens.'

"Yes. Apparently, there were at least three other near riots at other locations, but they were halted before they could become serious."

"By whom?" Santigo asked.

"By the city guard and," Secora glanced toward Varenov, "members of our own citizenry."

"This cannot be allowed to continue," Iriarte said with vehemence. "Our own streets are no longer safe. We need to seize control of the situation."

"And how do you expect to do that?" Varenov asked. "Don't you see? These 'riots' were planned. You don't have mass rioting on the same day on multiple levels, all targeting Brovettans, without some organization. We need to find the people responsible for it."

"And what do we do in the meantime?" Iriarte countered. "Cower within our quarters?"

"I believe Councilor Martov had an excellent suggestion earlier," Petrov said.

Martov looked confused. "And what was that?"

"Round them all up."

Martov spluttered. "That's absurd! I meant that as hyperbole. We can't round them up and kick them out. They're citizens!"

"I didn't say kick them out," Petrov said. "Why not round them up and seclude them in particular sections of the city. For their own protection."

Iriarte stepped forward. "We can keep a guard on them. That way they'll be protected from everyone else. And if there are any rebels among them, they'll have a harder time striking at the rest of the city. They'll be contained!"

"Protected," Petrov said.

"Right, protected."

"True citizens won't be able to complain," Gabrella added. "Anyone who does is likely helping the rebels."

Varenov was horrified. "You can't possibly be considering this. It's a flagrant violation of the Brovettans' rights. They are citizens! They have the right to live in any of the Crystal Cities. They have the right to travel freely from one to another. They have the right to travel anywhere *within* a city…unimpeded! It's stated clearly in the Founders Pact!"

"But these are exigent circumstances—"

"No, they are not," Martov cut in. "Under no circumstances is it lawful or moral to incarcerate citizens—for their own protection or otherwise. As long as I'm on the Council, I will not allow it!"

Secora sighed. "Who else is opposed to this idea?"

"I am," Varenov said immediately.

"As am I," Santigo said.

Varenov breathed a sigh of relief.

"Then, with three opposed, the motion fails. We will find some other option. For now, I will instruct the city guard to begin investigating who was behind these coordinated riots."

* * *

Back in her quarters, hours later, Varenov stood staring out her observation window at what she could see of the city below. It appeared so far away, yet what had happened in the plaza below still shook her. It felt as if her entire body were vibrating. Not even wine had helped.

Someone knocked at the door. She listened as Treant stood to answer it, heard him approach.

"It was a courier with a note," he said, handing it over.

She tore the envelope open, unfolded the small sheet within, let her arm fall to her side as she leaned her forehead against the glass.

"What is it?" Treant asked.

"Eri's father was killed by the mob. Her mother is still alive, although they aren't certain she'll survive her injuries."

Treant bowed his head, asked uncertainly, "Shall I fetch her?"

Varenov straightened. "Yes. We should go see her mother, just in case."

* * *

Havvelan Duprees scrawled in the massive ledger that, when open, filled up a sizeable portion of his desk. The rest was cluttered with an assortment of oddities, all ostentatious and opulent. A single lucent lit the room, centered on the desk, the shelves on either side in half-shadow, the rug beneath half-lit. His personal guard stood in the shadows near a set of chairs near the door.

The scratch of the quill paused and Havvelan turned a sheet of paper over and to one side, then began entering the orders from the next to the ledger. His merchant house was the largest in Iandolo, made so by his father, who started as a simple tailor with aspirations. Havvelan had taken the resultant fabric empire and expanded it into jewelry and metals, not to mention the illicit repurposing of machinery and lucent.

When the door to the study opened and two servants entered, he didn't stop, finishing recording the report as the first servant set down a tray of sliced ham covered in melted cheese with a side of fresh cut roasted beans. The second servant set a sealed envelope to one side with a quiet, "A delivery, sir. Just now."

Both servants departed.

Havvelan glanced at the food, but reached for the envelope. He broke the seal and removed the small card inside, then smiled.

"It would appear," he said to his guard, "that the time has come for a change within the Council."

Chapter Five

"Here's your tea," Gillian said.

Lane stared at the cup the Historian had placed beside the books she'd been reading, her stack of notes on the sigils and the double pyramid structure to one side.

Gillian chuckled. "The look on your face. Don't worry. I didn't make this batch as...potent as the other."

Years of etiquette from the towers forced Lane to reach for the tea and take a sip before setting it aside.

"I don't get it," she said in frustration.

"Don't get what?"

She waved at the text before her. "I'm trying to find information on the Source and the Outcome, what this book calls the 'Zyrchovskian lattice.' I want to know if my theory about how it works is correct, since I can't test it out myself here. But half of these words mean nothing to me and the other half that are familiar are being used in ways I don't understand. Like this: '*Any object powered by lucent will function with a continuous charge unless that object is taken outside the network range. After that, it will remain powered until its battery has been depleted or until it is once again brought within network range.*' Battery? What's that? I know what 'charge' means—when you bully your way into a fight or get arrested—but neither makes sense here.

"And then it's followed up with this: '*The exception, of course, is if someone is carrying a node, in which case the node will provide access to the network outside of the usual range.*'" She gave Gillian a bewildered look. "So magic won't work outside of network range except when it does, when you have this node? Whatever that is. Which is even more frustrating. They don't explain what any of this is, they assume that you already know!" She flipped the book closed and sat back with a grunt, arms crossed over her chest. "I just want to know how it all works. It's clear the mages at the Lyceum don't."

Gillian didn't react except to say, "You should have more tea."

Lane rolled her eyes.

Gillian left her to stew for a moment, then leaned forward. "Yes, it is frustrating, even for those of us who've been studying the old texts for our entire lives. Much of it doesn't make any sense. But that's the allure of it, isn't it? The mystery. Because at one point it must have made complete sense to someone, otherwise why would it have been written down?"

When Lane didn't respond, she leaned back again.

"Did you know that when the Crystal Cities were founded, they were all considered equal? Each one had a representative on the Council, the structure formalized under what we call the Founders' Pact. Everyone was working together—to create the cities and the wayfares—because they were trapped here in the Flatlands with no way out. And we all know how inhospitable the Flatlands are. Hard to imagine all of the cities working together as one, isn't it, with all of the hostilities between them over the last few hundred years? But apparently, it's true. Everyone working together to build something. Something that would get them home. Not that I know where their home is."

She paused in contemplation, sipped more tea, then sighed. "But something went wrong along the way. Politics, corruption, human nature. The Cities certainly aren't equal now. Iandolo has seized control, the Council subverted so its members have Iridesque's interests in mind. Whatever those original Founders were trying to build here failed."

"Is this supposed to make me feel better?" Lane asked.

Gillian smiled. "No, that's what the tea is for." She stood. "You keep reading. I'm certain the answers you seek are in there somewhere. I'll go see if I can find anything else that might help you."

* * *

"Would you put that damn crystal aside," Dalton said. "Lane is off... doing whatever it is she's been doing lately, and Nic is with Picall. We finally have the tent to ourselves."

Devon ignored him. He held the pinkish chunk of crystal up to the green light of the lantern and rotated it. Its faces flared, the details of the flaws inside picked out in various degrees of clarity as it turned.

The lucent lantern flickered, like a candle flame, then steadied and held. Devon frowned at it. It had never done that before.

Behind, he heard Dalton sigh, then shift closer, the ex-soldier cozying up to his back. He wrapped his arms around his waist, resting his head on Devon's shoulder.

"What are you trying to do, anyway? I notice you've been studying Proctor Arrend's notes about the Wardings. Are you trying to create one?"

"Shards, no! The one we had to deal with was enough."

"Then what?"

Devon twisted. "Do you really want to know?"

Dalton kissed him, arms tightening. "I wouldn't have asked otherwise."

Devon let the sensation linger, then pulled a few of the notes closer. "You asked for it. I've been looking at the structure of the Wardings. They're all different shapes, because they were based on different shards of crystal, but they all have the same premise—potential set up around a central trigger."

"Like one of the snares Picall taught us how to make, to catch the hares."

"Exactly! The Wardings were intended to be used for emergencies, to seal up the location until the authorities could arrive to deal with the situation. All one of the mages had to do was trigger the snare and the Warding would expand."

Dalton touched his mostly-healed side with a grimace of memory. "It wasn't that easy to take it down."

"No, because we had to reset the snare. That's what Lane did, in essence. Reset the trigger."

"What does that have to do with your new crystal?"

"Structure."

Dalton thought about this a moment, then shook his head. "I don't get it."

"It's all about structure. The Warding, the snare, the lantern—all of it's about structure. You set the snare by building a specific structure. Same with the Warding. Even the lucent lantern is all about structure. Each one is different, bringing about different outcomes, but it's still just..."

"Structure."

Devon sighed. "Have you ever noticed that everything in Iandolo— everything about all of the Crystal Cities—is structured? Look at this." He pulled up a sheet of paper with two diagrams on them. "This first diagram is a rough sketch of Iandolo as seen from above. I drew it based off of my memory of Carbolen's maps of the city. All twenty-four of the levels are tiered, each smaller than the last, connected by the Spokes, the main thoroughfares leading to the waygates. And then there's Mid-level and the three central towers at its center. Look at the symmetry of the main streets, with the towers at the center.

"Now look at the wayfares and the other Crystal Cities here in the second diagram. There are six other cities, with Iandolo at the center. They form an almost perfect hexagon."

Dalton gave him a skeptical look. "Aren't these drawings a little too perfect? You drew them yourself. And you're a mathematician. Everything is symmetrical to you. I know for a fact that not all of the levels are perfectly circular. And Mid-level itself isn't flat, with the towers at its center. There are a ton of other shorter towers scattered all over it. I think you've smoothed off some of the edges here."

"It's not perfect, but remember, the cities were built hundreds of years ago. We've been altering them in various ways ever since."

When Dalton didn't look impressed, he pulled up sketches of the Wardings. "And look at the Wardings. All of them have inherent structures. This is the one at the center of the quad at the Lyceum. I know this is what its inherent structure looks like, because I had to trace it out to figure out how to bring it down. It mimics the shape of the lucent. Based on that, I sketched out what the other Wardings must look like. All angular, all precise."

"But they aren't remotely symmetrical," Dalton countered.

"No, but they're ordered. Just like the layout of the cities, of Iandolo, even the double pyramid Lane uses for her sigils." Devon waved a hand, frustrated. "Never mind. I don't know how to describe it. There's something there…something meaningful. It's all connected somehow. I can almost see it."

Dalton began to massage his tense shoulders. "Then focus on something smaller. Tell me about the lantern and the crystal."

Devon almost gave up, almost let himself relax into the sensation of Dalton's fingers digging into his muscles, working out the stress. Instead, he reached for the lantern. It flickered when he touched it again. And was its light a little dimmer? He couldn't tell.

"Even this lantern has structure. It's much simpler than the Wardings or even the lucent locks I used to pick as part of the gang. Flicking it is the trigger, turning it on or off. I can trace it out just like I did the Warding."

"So what about the crystal?" Dalton asked.

Devon picked it up. "There's a structure of course, it's crystal, but it's flawed."

"So fix it."

Devon stilled. "What do you mean?"

"Fix it. You pick locks, right? Brought down the Warding? So fix this crystal."

"It's…it's not the same thing."

Dalton stared at him expectantly, then gave him a gentle shove with his hands. "Fix it."

Devon held up the lantern in one hand, the crystal in the other. He set the lantern aside and focused on the crystal.

As he'd done in the wash where he'd found it, he sank into it, traced its edges, its cracks. Singling out one of them, he focused and *pushed.*

The crack sealed up with a faint tremble in the shard. Devon ran his thumb over the outside, above where the crack had been, but the face was smooth and the interior perfect.

He shifted to the next crack, then the next, moving around the crystal until all of the flaws had been smoothed out. Each push made the shard vibrate, tingling in his skin, but within a few minutes the crystal was perfect.

But if he could fix the flaws, could he do more? He knew the structure of the lantern by heart, having studied it for the past week. Could he alter the crystal's base structure? It was already close to that of the lantern. All he'd need to do is move a few nodes…

Without hesitating, he pushed again. It was harder, but the nodes inside the crystal shifted with an audible hiss and click. This time, Devon felt the transformation shudder up through his fingers to his elbow.

"What did you do?" Dalton asked.

Devon didn't answer. Instead, he reached up and flicked the crystal.

Light burst from its center, tinged pink. At the same time, the green lantern flickered and dimmed dramatically.

Dalton sucked in a sharp breath. "You created a lantern?"

Before Devon could answer, a shout went up from outside.

Devon flicked both lanterns off, hands shaking at what he'd done, then scrambled after Dalton. They emerged from the tent to find everyone from the grotto running toward the ledge of the main entrance above the pool. Maupin, Raven, and a bunch of tullers were helping a ragged group of people down the stairs to the fire, some of them wounded.

"What the—" Devon took off toward the steps, but Dalton grabbed his arm and held him back. His face was set.

"Don't tell anyone here about what you just did," the soldier said. "Not until we know more about them."

"What do you mean?"

"I mean whatever *this* is all about. This isn't just a group of free thinkers living in the wilds. There's something more happening here."

"Fine."

Dalton's hand tightened. "Promise me."

Devon had never seen him this intense before. "I promise."

Dalton let him go and they made their way to the fire, arriving as Maupin, Raven, and the others stumbled into the center of the grotto. Maupin was calling out orders, some of the wounded collapsing to the dirt as soon as they halted. Men and women were dashing into tents, emerging with pallets and rags and water, some already beginning to tend to the wounds, dabbing at bruised faces and cuts. Lane arrived with Gillian, the older woman carrying a satchel. She knelt by each of those being seen, checked eyes and responses, rummaging in her bag and handing out small paper pouches. Some of those arriving were simply exhausted, slumping onto a stone or wooden seat or simply sagging to their knees where they stood. They were of all ages, parents with children, a few elderly, but the majority of them were in their twenties and thirties.

And they were all Brovettan.

Lane caught sight of them and approached. "What's going on?"

"I was hoping you'd know."

Lane shrugged. "As soon as Gillian saw them from her cavern, she snatched up her bag and headed here without a word." She scanned the area, then frowned. "They're all Brovettan."

"We noticed," Dalton said.

Nic came sprinting toward them from deeper in the grotto, where the gardens were. "What's happening?" he gasped, flushed and out of breath. Picall was behind him, her eyes on the activity before them. "We heard the shouting."

Before anyone could answer, a high-pitched wail came from one of the women. She clutched a man to her chest, rocked back and forth, his limp arm dragging in the dirt. Those tullers who'd been caring for him stepped back, heads bent, except for one who reached for the woman in comfort, resting a hand on her arm.

The woman flinched, wail wrenched short. She glared at the helper, looked down at the man in her arms, then glanced around those around her, most still tending to the other wounded.

When her eyes fell on Maupin, her face transfigured into pure rage.

She laid the body gently to the ground, leaned over him to kiss his forehead, two cheeks, and mouth, then stood and stalked toward Maupin. Halfway there, she raised one arm, pointed, and growled, "You did this! You convinced my husband that Iandolo would be safe! You brought us here! And now he's dead! Dead!" She shoved at Maupin, but he didn't move. She was at least fifty pounds lighter and a foot shorter than him. She began to pound her fists into Maupin's chest. "The gods-forsaken Iandolans killed him and for what? Because we were Brovettan? Because our skin is paler than yours? It's your fault! Your! Fault!" She sagged into Maupin and degenerated into body-wracking sobs.

Maupin hadn't reacted during the entire tirade, but now he drew the woman in tight as he scanned the newcomers and those tullers who'd come in with them. "Someone tell me what's happened in Iandolo."

One of the Brovettan women hovering to one side stepped forward. "It's the citizens. They turned against us, began attacking us in the streets, in the markets. They want us out! All because of what happened at the Lyceum with the Warding."

"But that was a band of rebels," Raven protested.

"They don't care! They think we were all in on it, that we helped them."

"It's true," one of the tuller guards who'd been in Iandolo said. "The attacks on Brovettans started a few days before we were set to return. We were headed back to report on it when this group found us and begged us to bring them back with us. They'd just been violently rousted from their homes on Level Fourteen. We...we couldn't say no."

Maupin pushed the now mostly calm woman back, handing her off to Raven. "You did the right thing bringing them here. Do what you can for the wounded and start preparing something for them to eat. Raven, Durran, and Ell, come with me. I want a detailed report."

The tuller who'd spoken up and one other followed Maupin toward his hut. Devon and Lane headed after them, but Raven saw and warned them off.

"I want to know what's going on," Lane said.

"We'll confront Raven later and find out," Dalton said from behind them. He was eyeing Maupin's hut, brows drawn down, arms crossed over his chest. Then he motioned toward the scattered Brovettans and tullers. "In the meantime, maybe we should help out."

Devon found himself carrying cups and a pitcher of water from group to group. Those that had just arrived from the heat of the Flatlands drank deeply. Most were distraught, sobbing, not always from their wounds. Up close, Devon could see it was mostly bruising from being punched or kicked, although he knew from his time in Carbolen's gang that even that could be fatal. Some were choking out stories to those patching them up, all more or less the same. They were at market, picking up fresh greens for their soup, when suddenly someone shouted some kind of slur at the Brovettans and their cohorts began beating them—with hands and feet, or bully sticks or knives. A few reported entering a shop, but being denied service. One woman reported the shopkeeper had appeared terrified, had warned her to run, but it was too late. Men had entered and dragged her into the street.

"So it isn't everyone in Iandolo," Lane said later, when all of the Brovettans had been fed and led to tents or pallets set up beneath the stars. They'd regrouped in their tent, Picall included, sticking close to Nic.

Devon sent the ex-gang member a telling look, but he merely gave a wild-eyed shrug. "Of course it's not all of them. That's not how these things work."

"And you would know how?" Lane asked.

"Because he was part of the gangs," Nic answered. "Not everyone in the lower levels is part of a gang. In fact, the gangs probably make up less than a quarter of those that live there. But do you hear about those other three-quarters? No. You only hear about the gangs."

"Or think about the Lyceum," Devon added. "You were bullied the entire time you were there, but not by everyone. In fact, you could probably count the real bullies, like Quinn, on both hands. Everyone else stayed out of it, didn't get involved."

"I'm surprised that shopkeeper even gave that woman a warning," Nic said. "She was braver than most."

"Based on what I heard," Dalton said, "the resentment against Brovettans is growing though. Everyone agreed that at first it appeared to be only a few people causing minor problems for them. Now they're invading the Brovettans' homes, throwing them out."

"And what is the Council doing about it?" Lane demanded. "My mother wouldn't sit by and let this happen. She represents Luminesque!"

"They aren't doing much," a new voice said.

All of them turned as Raven ducked into the tent, alone for once. Devon couldn't remember seeing her without Maupin at her side since they'd arrived. She didn't look happy.

"We have some questions," Dalton said from his seat next to Devon.

"I thought you might." Her eyes fell on Picall, who fidgeted.

"Should I leave?" the tuller asked.

"No. They're going to find out anyway. May as well face them now."

"Find out what?" Dalton asked. He'd tensed and Devon leaned into him in an attempt to get him to relax.

Raven sighed. She began pacing back and forth in front of the tent's entrance. "Why do I always fall for the dangerous men?" she muttered to herself.

Devon's green lantern flickered, but no one except Devon appeared to notice.

Raven halted and faced them. "Here's what I know. Iandolans began attacking Brovettans in the city ten days ago. The Council denounced the attacks, but they're hard-pressed to do anything about it, since a significant portion of what remained of the army has headed off to Brovetto in a retaliatory strike and show of force. That's left the streets thin on city guard, since they've been charged with protecting the waygates and other key positions.

"Apparently, Carbolen has been using the gangs to keep the racial attacks to a minimum in the lower levels, but even he can't be everywhere. The Lyceum has been converted into a War and Mage college, almost exclusively. They're training city guard and soldiers, but not fast enough to counter this."

"They should make Carbolen and the gangs official city guardsmen," Lane said.

Raven barked a laugh and shook her head; Dalton looked horrified.

"Carbolen would never accept," Raven said. "He'd lose his autonomy."

"And can you imagine the gang members as city patrolmen?" Nic asked. "Give them an edge and they'll steal a mile."

Lane frowned in annoyance. "All right. So what is the Council going to do?"

"At the moment…nothing."

There was a moment of horrified silence, then Devon said, "They can't do that."

"According to word on the street, the Council is deadlocked. They can't agree on what to do."

Dalton leaned forward. "What is Maupin going to do?"

Raven drew in a steadying breath, let it out in a rush. "He's going to get as many of the Brovettans out as he can. Those that want to, anyway."

"And send them where?" Dalton asked. "He can't keep them here. There's not enough room." When Raven hesitated, he added, "What did that woman mean earlier when she said, 'You brought us here'? What are the tullers really up to here?"

Raven glanced at Picall, who squirmed, then stiffened in pride.

"We smuggle people into Iandolo."

"Brovettans," Raven said. "They smuggle Brovettans into Iandolo."

"What?" Lane asked. Dalton was nodding his head.

"You don't understand," Picall said viciously. "You don't know how bad it is in Brovetto. It's a hundred times worse than what you call the lower levels. In some areas the buildings have collapsed. Towers have fallen. Nearly all the lucent is dead. People are starving because the crops in the city have begun to fail. The soil cannot take any more. It's as dead as the lucent. And no one is willing to trade with them because they have no more lucent. The mines are depleted, and they cannot mine enough of the other metals to compete with Radimansque. They are trapped!"

"You've been there?" Nic asked.

"No. But I've heard the stories from those that pass through here. I've seen the desperation in their eyes."

"Wait!" Lane reached out and grabbed Devon's arm, her eyes wide in sudden realization. "Did you...did Maupin smuggle in the Brovettans that attacked us? Did he smuggle in the rebels?"

Picall ducked her head, looked away.

Anger cut through Devon's chest, but it was Dalton who lurched upwards with a guttural, "I'll kill the bastard!"

Raven stepped in front of him, there was a brief struggle, and then she had Dalton pinned to her chest, her arm wrapped around his neck, one of his arms behind his back. He gasped, breathing hard, the other arm raised, hand grasping at air. "Let go of me," he said through clenched teeth.

Devon had surged to his feet, along with Lane. Picall had flung herself backwards, as if she thought he'd been after her. Nic had placed himself between the two.

Raven gave everyone a hard stare. "Everyone calm down," she said. "Maupin didn't know he was smuggling in rebels. He certainly didn't smuggle in the entire group that attacked Iandolo at the gates or that took the city after the Warding went up. His operation isn't that big."

"What about the group that hit Carbolen and the gangs at River Street?" Devon asked.

"And the mages?" Lane added. "Did he smuggle in Terrial and the others?"

"He admits that it's possible. He doesn't know for certain." When no one reacted, she added, "He brings in families mostly. He doesn't do a background check on everyone, for shard's sake!"

Devon glanced over at Picall, her hand clenching her hunting knife, ready to defend herself. He thought of all they'd done with the tullers since they'd arrived here. His anger still boiled deep, but the tension in his body eased. "Let him go," he said. After a moment, he added a sharp, "Raven!"

Raven whispered in Dalton's ear, "Don't do anything stupid," then released him.

Dalton staggered forward, but caught himself, turning as he rubbed his throat with one hand. Regular and ex-soldier glared at each other, but no one made a move.

"So now what?" Lane asked.

The lantern dimmed suddenly, died, stuttered back to life but at a fraction of its previous strength.

"When did that start happening?" Nic asked.

Devon and Dalton shared a look. "This morning," Devon answered.

"Lucent never works for long here," Picall said.

Devon frowned. But there were more important issues at stake at the moment.

"You said Maupin intends to get as many Brovettans out as he can?" he asked.

"That's his intent, yes."

Devon looked at Lane, Dalton, and Nic, their expressions an amalgam of anger and indecision. "We always intended to go back eventually."

Lane considered, then gave a minute nod.

Nic merely said, "I'm with you, wherever you go."

Dalton waved a hand. "I'm tired of lizard."

Devon faced Raven. "Tell Maupin we're willing to help."

* * *

"Why did you ask me to come here?"

Varenov glanced over the broken remains of the bakery on Level Twenty with a frown, the scent of flour and yeast and freshly baked bread still heavy in the air. But mixed in with it was the metallic stench of blood and the ashy tones of smoke. Shelves had been torn from the walls, splintered wood littering the floor, interspersed with linen towels and shredded woven baskets. A space had been cleared for her, by Carbolen and his men, she assumed. The room was dimly lit by two lanterns set on the counter. Varenov wondered why he hadn't used the lucent. It should be functional at this level; they weren't that close to the hub.

She focused on Carbolen again. The gang leader stood inside the door to the bakery's back room, a couple of his men flanking him, much as Varenov's guards were flanking her. "This was a Brovettan bakery, wasn't it? This was another riot?"

"It started last night, late," Carbolen said. "We received no advance warning this time, it appears to have been spontaneous, except for one thing."

"Which is what?"

"Let me show you."

Varenov turned toward the door, but Carbolen halted her.

"Not that way. I don't want you to be seen." The gang leader grabbed one of the lanterns and motioned her toward the back.

Varenov hesitated, then followed, stepping between Carbolen's gang members, who snatched up the second lantern and fell in behind her guards.

The next room was a workspace, ovens lining one wall, massive tables overturned, flour and sugar and blood spilled in fans across the floor. The scent of greasy ash was sharp here, the walls of the far corner stained black by smoke. A body lay crumpled against it, charred beyond recognition, and Varenov gagged as she realized it wasn't burnt bread she was smelling, but flesh. One hand covering her mouth, she swept through the room to the next, the living quarters. Two more bodies lay here, a woman and child, cowering together on a bed, beaten and partially burned.

Tears stinging her eyes, she stumbled out into an alley. The area behind the bakery was clean, except for the noisome trickle of water down the center, leading to a drain, but as they began to wind through a maze of odd niches and narrows behind the buildings, the path became choked with rank debris. Moisture dripped down from above, as they were deep enough inside the level to be beneath the level above. Varenov found it claustrophobic; she was used to Mid-level and the openness of the towers. Aside from an occasional backlit upper window in one of the buildings or a strip of dim lucent overhead, Carbolen's lanterns were the only source of light. Somewhere nearby a dog barked and, at one point, Carbolen halted as a back door farther ahead opened, an Iandolan man stepping out to toss the contents of a bucket into the alley. He caught sight of Carbolen, eyes widening, then made some kind of gesture with his hand—as if to say he hadn't seen a thing—and hurried back inside.

How could people live this way? When she'd left the tower to come down here, it was early morning. The sun should be out, and yet here it appeared to be late evening. There should be more light; there should be more activity, more noise.

Varenov had started to get irritated when Carbolen's pace slowed. He shuttered the lantern, the darkness only broken by lucent over the streets ahead. Two figures, both young, stood in the shadows at the end of the narrow—lookouts. At one of their footfalls, one of them spun, a short blade visible in one hand, then relaxed. She urged them forward with a tilt of her head, then tapped her companion's shoulder to warn him they'd arrived.

Before moving forward, Carbolen turned to Varenov. "The city guards haven't discovered the bakery yet, but they have cordoned off the street ahead. The main riot started here, then spread out, targeting Brovettan shops along four streets. Twenty-seven dead, not all of them Brovettan. Some fought back, killed some of the rioters. That's not what you're here to see—we'll have to go to the roof for that—but go take a look."

One of her guards held her back, stepping forward to check it out first, then motioning her to his side.

They were at the mouth of an odd intersection. The street before them was clear, not much wider than the alley, but to the left, not twenty paces away, ran a main thoroughfare and the convergence of at least two other streets. A statue of a woman stood in the center, face lifted upwards, arms half raised, something draped over them.

Bodies were strewn around the base of the statue where they'd fallen, the city patrol sidling among them, rolling them to the side, checking pulses, taking notes. A few were speaking to citizens.

Carbolen tugged on her sleeve, drew her into a side door of the building on the left. They entered a narrow staircase, ascended to the roof, slid up to the edge, closer to the intersection, with a view of the statue.

Hidden by the building's ornate façade, Carbolen said, "Look. In the arms of the statue."

Varenov's brow furrowed as she stepped up to peer through a rounded cut in the stone. She focused on the statue. "I don't—" she began, then gasped and stepped back, arm reaching out for support. One of her guards caught her, steadied her. She swallowed against the numbness in her chest, then stepped forward again. "The body in the statue's arms…it's Martov."

It hadn't been a question, but Carbolen said, "Yes."

"What the hell was he doing here?" Varenov said, shock giving way to anger. "This is Level Twenty! And to be caught in a riot? He's not Brovettan. And I doubt he was participating as one of the rioters!"

Carbolen pulled her back from the roof's edge sharply. "Lower your voice." One of the younger gang members stepping forward to watch in case she'd been heard. "No, he wasn't here participating in the riot. And he wasn't caught up in one by accident either."

"Then what happened?"

"His body was placed there *after* the riot, but before the city guard arrived."

"After…?"

"Someone killed him and they're using the riot to cover up his death."

"That's insane."

"They're going to claim the Brovettans killed him."

Varenov drew breath to protest, but then the true ramifications struck. "With Martov dead, there's a seat open on the Council. The balance of power could shift, depending on who is selected."

"That's why I brought you down here. To see for yourself and to warn you."

She stared at him, her thoughts churning, fear bubbling up within. "I have to get back to the tower."

She turned, but Carbolen caught her arm. "Take the alleys. My men will guide you. Don't be seen."

She nodded, then followed the two youngest gang members down off the roof and into the back alleys, weaving in and out, guided by their lanterns. They reached the street outside the bakery, her guards loading her into the carriage she'd used to get down here.

The ride to Mid-level was a blur. She hadn't yet formulated a plan when she stepped through the entrance of the main tower and headed toward the elevator. All she knew was that she needed to wash and change. Her shoes and edges of her dress were filthy from the alleys and she reeked of smoke and garbage. And she needed to consult with Treant, possibly Santigo. They needed to agree on a replacement for Martov, one that at least two others on the Council could support. It would take four Council seats to select—

"Ah, Councilor Varenov. How fortuitous. I've been looking for you. Where have you been?"

Varenov sucked in a sharp breath and halted halfway to the elevator, turning toward Secora. The Iridesque Councilor approached, with Gabrella and Haavelan slightly behind.

Varenov's gut tightened in apprehension. "Out."

"So I see. I believe that dress is ruined."

Gabrella frowned down at Varenov's shoes, but Varenov ignored her, focusing on Secora. "What did you need?"

"I have sad news. Council Martov is dead."

Varenov feigned shock. "How is that possible? Where was his escort?"

"All of them are dead. The city guards report they were killed during a riot on Level Twenty. They're investigating the riot now, although apparently it covered multiple streets and they've found over thirty dead so far. The rioters appeared to have targeted Brovettan shops."

"Why was he on Level Twenty?"

"No one knows," Gabrella said, speaking up for the first time. "Although, I've heard rumors that he's been ranging far and wide in his grief over his daughter's betrayal and death, seeking out ever more questionable drinking establishments and such."

"It's not nice to speak ill of the dead, Gabrella," Secora said.

"No, it's not," Varenov said. "Arrangements are being made for a funeral, I assume?"

"Of course. The city guard is retrieving the body and Gabrella and Iriarte are taking care of the rest."

Varenov nodded. Martov's wife had died eleven years ago, and he'd denounced his daughter Terrial. There was no one else to attend to his passing except the Council.

She felt nauseous. None of them appeared grief-stricken; Havvelan could barely suppress a smile. "We should convene the Council shortly then, to discuss a replacement."

"Oh, that's not necessary," Secora said.

Varenov's throat closed in sudden understanding. "Why's that?"

"We tried to find you earlier, when we first received word, but you were nowhere around. The rest of us met and, after some discussion, agreed upon a replacement amongst ourselves. Only Santigo dissented."

"And who is the new Councilor? Someone from Scintillesque?"

Havvelan stepped forward, not even attempting to hide a grin.

"I think it's time for a change, don't you?"

PART II

THE
INTERNMENT

Chapter Six

"What do you mean there are additional War colleges now?" Devon asked. He and Lane were following Raven through a section of Mid-level Devon wasn't familiar with. It was about a third of the way around the hub from the Lyceum, a district of shops and larger merchant houses, some of which were massive, taking up entire blocks. The crowd was a mix of all of the Crystal Cities, the juxtaposed colors and fashions clashing in a chaotic synergy. Everyone appeared to be going about their everyday affairs as usual, although there was an undercurrent of unease that Devon felt in his gut.

"According to Maupin's scouts and informers," Raven said, "the Council decided that, with the Iandolan Army in Brovetto and a significant portion of the city guard slaughtered by the Brovettan group that attacked here, they needed some additional security. The Lyceum has been converted into a War college and they've started up two others on Mid-level. He wants us to check them out."

"But why send me?" Lane asked, tugging at the edge of her hood. "I'm the last person who should be out and about right now. I'm only going to draw attention."

"Not if you keep your hood up and your head down," Raven said. "Besides, there are other Brovettans around."

She motioned to a group of seven Brovettans as they passed on the left. One of them eyed them warily, hand rather conspicuously resting on a sword hilt. At least three of the others were similarly armed, even though they were in one of the wealthier parts of the city and these Brovettans were obviously wealthy themselves.

"Have you noticed they're all traveling in groups of five or more?" Devon asked.

"That's not exactly comforting," Lane said.

"None of us should be out here," Devon said. "I'm certain Favian and the rest are still looking for us after our escape from the Lyceum. And Carbolen's probably got his Eyes out for Raven as well."

Raven had changed her look since returning to Iandolo—cut her hair short and ragged, changed her clothes from the sleek black of the Regular into softer browns with a splash of color—but Devon thought it would do little to keep her from Carbolen's notice, even if Maupin and the rest of the group had taken up residence on the opposite side of the city as the gang leader. Apparently, Raven thought the same. She'd been on edge since their return.

"Maupin wants you here, Lane, in case there's anything we might miss related to the mages at this new college," Raven said, returning to Lane's original question.

"What are Maupin and the others doing?" Devon asked.

She glanced at him. "Making contacts. Feeling things out. Planning."

Devon frowned. Maupin had specifically asked Nic and Dalton to remain behind. Now he wondered if Maupin was using Nic to contact Carbolen and the gangs and Dalton to feel out the city guard and whatever portion of the army remained behind.

"They'll be fine," Raven said. "No one actively wants to kill them on sight, unlike us." Then she slowed. "It should be up ahead."

They turned a corner onto a side street and approached a massive square that had been cordoned off with barricades. Men and women in city guard uniforms were drilling large groups in the art of brawling, the younger men and women paired off and wrestling with each other until one of them gained an advantage and pinned the other to the ground. Farther distant, groups were training with mock swords or shields. To one side, lines of trainees poured in and out of a stone building with lucent columns that spanned the length of the square; it looked like it had once been a merchant house. Shouted commands, curses, grunts, and moans punctuated the clack of wooden practice sticks against shields and the occasional thud of a body thrown to the stone cobbles.

"There are at least three times as many students here as there were at the Lyceum," Devon said as they came up to the barricade. "And you said there were three such schools?"

"Two new ones and the Lyceum."

"If they eliminated all of the other schools at the Lyceum, then they could house this many War students there," Lane said. "It looks like they're using that building as the dormitory. Probably classrooms as well."

Devon watched the training for a moment. He didn't see many proctors, only city guard. "I don't think they're focusing much on studying. Not of books anyway. Look over there." Both Raven and Lane turned. "They're running formation drills, looks like groups of eight. That's something the War students at the Lyceum wouldn't be doing until at least third year. In fact, nearly all of this is training reserved for the last few years. They've skipped over all of the basics."

"No, they've skipped over the bookwork—learning the laws, the protocols, the ethics. They've moved straight to the violence." Lane motioned with one hand. "Look at who they've recruited. Most of the trainees are young, from the lower levels."

Devon's grip on the edge of the barricade tightened. "So they're already rough and ready to fight. They're just making them more effective." He scanned the makeshift yard again. "I don't see any sign of mages, do you?"

Lane stepped forward. "No one actively using sigils, no. But the formations you pointed out are designed to support mages on the battlefield." She faced him, her eyes half-shadowed by the hood. "If I were Favian, though, I'd keep the mages close at hand, at the Lyceum. They're too important to Iandolan's control of the Crystal Cities. And there won't be many of them. They can't simply grab people from the lower levels and make them mages."

Raven touched Devon's shoulder. "Time to go. We've caught someone's attention."

One of the guards training in hand-to-hand was headed toward them.

They began walking back down the street, but when the guard called out, "Hey, you!" they broke into a run.

There were few alleys here, no nooks or abandoned buildings to cut into like the lower levels. And there was hardly anyone around, probably because the street had been blocked off for the new school.

But the intersection ahead was more crowded.

"To the left," Raven shouted.

Devon snagged Lane's arm and pulled her left. The guard had leapt the barricade and was running after them.

They rounded the corner and cut into the much more crowded thoroughfare, weaving in and out of people who gave startled exclamations or curses. Devon glanced behind, Lane right behind him, the guard over two hundred paces away, but when he turned back, he slammed into an older man stacking fresh produce on a cart outside his shop.

They crashed to the ground, a tangle of arms and legs and scattered oranges. He heard Lane hit the ground beside him, looked over to see her already rolling onto her side and getting up. Her hood had fallen askew.

The grocer groaned and snatched at Devon's shirt.

"I'm sorry," Devon said, twisting and catching the man's arm. He pulled him halfway up. "I'm so sorry. I didn't see you."

The elderly man shook his head. "It's all right. It happens. But what's the rush—"

From his seated position, he caught sight of Lane. His gaze flicked toward the approaching guard and his expression darkened.

The hand still holding Devon's arm squeezed tight. "Under the cart." He flipped up the cloth draped down its side. "He can't see you right now."

Devon threw a warning look at Raven, already thirty paces beyond, then ducked into the proffered hollow, banging his head against the edge as he did so. Lane scrambled in beside him with a muffled curse.

The man dropped the cloth and they found themselves in shadow. Devon attempted to find a more comfortable position, until Lane's fingers dug into his shoulder. He stilled.

Outside the drape, the grocer cursed loudly, still apparently on the ground, and footsteps raced up to his side.

"What happened?" the guard asked, voice tense.

"They plowed right into me! Knocked me to the ground and then took off. Blasted thieves. That's how they do it, you know. Distract you and take whatever they want while you're not looking. And look at these oranges! I'll never be able to sell them now, they're bruised!"

Devon heard him crawling around on the ground, joined a moment later by the guard. A hand reached beneath the cloth and snatched an orange Devon hadn't even noticed a few inches to his right.

"Here," the guard said. "Now which way did they go?"

"Toward Mercer Street. That way." Footsteps charged away and the grocer murmured, "Damned new city guard. Don't even know the local streets." Small thuds echoed from overhead as he replaced the spilt oranges, then he rapped on the side of the cart. "He's gone. You can come out."

Devon edged out, then turned back to help Lane. "Don't forget your hood."

She glared at him, then tugged her hood into place and stepped out, brushing at her clothes. "Thank you," she said.

The grocer eyed them both. "Don't know what he was after and don't want to know. But some of us don't approve of how they've been treating you Brovettans lately. It isn't right."

Deven caught sight of Raven hovering around the next corner. "We appreciate the help, but we need to go."

They took off after Raven, Devon scanning the street for the guard, but he saw no one.

When they turned the corner, Raven was right there. "Just keep walking," she said, nodding toward where two guards stood across the way. They didn't appear to be searching for anyone, merely checking out a merchant's wares.

"I think the guard recognized me" Devon said. "That's why he came after us."

"Or we were paying too close attention to what was going on in the square," Raven said. "Don't get paranoid."

"Should we check out the other new school? Or the Lyceum?"

"Maupin would expect us to, yes."

But Raven was staring at something farther ahead, eyes narrowed. After a moment, Devon realized that most of the people on the street were headed in one direction, toward a single destination.

"What's going on?" he asked. "What's up there?"

"A Pulpit," Raven answered. "There must be some kind of announcement happening soon."

"Should we listen in?"

Raven didn't answer, merely joining the flow on the street, the crowd growing denser as they reached the area outside the Pulpit. They worked their way forward toward the raised dais that stood at the end of a shallow amphitheater, the stage a mere ten feet high. A backdrop of curved, nearly translucent green lucent rose up overhead, like a cowl, projecting the voices of those on the stage outward. Devon had studied the ingenious acoustics of it at the Lyceum.

Someone jostled him and he frowned at those around them. The general tone of those gathered was tense and unsettled, with a grumbling undercurrent of dissatisfaction. They were hemmed in, off center of the Pulpit itself, but close to the front. If they had to flee, they were in trouble. The crowd was now too dense to navigate easily.

"I know Maupin wants information," Devon said, "but perhaps we should have stayed at the outer edges, just in case."

Raven glanced around, met Devon's gaze. "Just keep the hood up, Lane." But she undid the clasps on her knives.

Someone appeared on stage and a murmur rose up from the crowd, then quickly died when they realized it wasn't anyone of importance. A group of soldiers fanned out along the stage edge, dressed in the colors of two of the seven cities—Luminesque and Scintillesque. Servants rushed forward and placed a riser and podium near the front, then retreated.

Lane gasped as her mother and another man stepped forward. As the man moved to the podium, Varenov halting behind him with a stern expression of disapproval on her face, Lane turned to Devon.

"That's Havvelan Duprees, Quinn's father, the one my mother supplanted in the Council when she returned. He's a Councilor now!"

Devon strained forward for a closer look. "I can see the resemblance to Quinn," he said. "Narrow face, thin nose, scheming eyes. Quinn must be ecstatic."

"I doubt she knows," Raven said. "She'd be with the army in Brovetto."

"Citizens of Iandolo," Councilor Havvelan said, raising one hand for quiet, even though nearly everyone fell into an expectant silence almost immediately. He was smiling, his other hand gripping the side of the podium. Devon could hear him clearly, even over a hundred paces away. "The streets have been uneasy since the brutal and vicious attack by the Brovettans nearly a month ago."

"Rebels," Varenov said sharply from behind him. "Brovettan rebels."

Havvelan didn't acknowledge her, merely lowered his hand. "The Council understands why you are uneasy. These are troubled times. Uncertain times. One of our own Crystal Cities used a Warding—something that's supposed to protect us—against us in the center of our own city. For a time, your own Council and the Army sworn to protect you was lost, captured within crystal, and you were forced to fend for yourselves as the streets were overrun with Brovettan forces. What they did while we were trapped was..." he shook his head "...hideous. Savage. Untenable. They tortured our own soldiers. They gutted any mages found and strung them from wires over our streets!

"We cannot allow such actions to go unanswered and so we have not. We've sent the Iandolan Army to Brovetto. Even now, they are rooting out those behind this most recent atrocity. They are leaving no stone unturned. Brovetto is feeling our wrath, their streets flooded with Iandolan soldiers and mages. Prefect Arctus has orders to raze the entire city to the ground, if necessary. They will pay for what they have done to our city, to our citizens."

The crowd responded with a cheer and a hubbub of conversation, those around Devon, Lane, and Raven nodding their heads, a few raising fists into the air in support. Devon could only pick out one or two who looked troubled, casting worried glances to either side as they shifted awkwardly where they stood.

"But that does not solve the entire problem, does it?" Havvelan continued. "Oh, no. It is only the beginning. As we have seen here in Iandolo since the Brovettans were beaten back, there is a renewed sense of mistrust and uncertainty in the streets. After all, there are Brovettans here amongst us, are there not? Some of them have lived here their entire lives, working among us, alongside us. Some you may even call friends. But are they truly? Is it not possible that they are, instead, aligned with the Brovettans from Luminesque? Is it not possible that they are helping them or, at minimum, sympathizing with them?

"Your distrust is evident in the recent attacks on our Brovettan citizens…but they are, indeed, still citizens. Most of them likely have nothing to do with the recent attacks. Most of them likely know nothing of what the Brovettans from Luminesque planned or are planning. Most of them simply want to live out their lives here in Iandolo—to work, to shop, to laugh, and to love. We cannot have our citizens being attacked on the streets, at random. We cannot have them being pulled from their homes and killed, simply because they are Brovettan. They are still citizens, after all.

"Therefore, the Council has decided that, for their own safety and protection, all citizens of Brovettan descent are to be sequestered in designated zones on Levels Twelve, Sixteen, and Twenty. City patrols will escort Brovettans to these established quarantine zones over the course of the next week. Brovettans within the city should gather up all of their essentials and report to these zones within that week. Food, water, and all other amenities will be provided in these zones. And rest assured that this is only a temporary measure.

"I implore all of the Brovettans within the city to abide by this request. The zones will be protected by the city guard. We hope to end all of the wanton and random attacks that have plagued our streets in the past few weeks, attacks that have killed one of our own Councilors. These attacks must stop. Anyone who resists relocation to one of the designated zones will be assumed to be working with the Brovettans from Luminesque. Any other Iandolan citizens who harbor or help Brovettans avoid relocation during this time will also be assumed Luminesque insurrectionists. Report any Brovettans you see outside the quarantine after next week to the city guard immediately. They will be dealt with. Again, I reiterate to our Brovettan citizens, this is for your own protection!

"Relocation will begin tomorrow."

Havvelan turned from the podium. He passed Varenov without a glance. Lane's mother looked nauseous, eyes drawn in despair, yet her jaw was clenched. The guards pulled back from the edge of the stage, those from Luminesque clustering around Varenov protectively before drawing her back into the shadows.

"My mother would never condone this," Lane growled.

"Keep your voice down," Raven warned as the crowd around them began to disperse. All three of them remained where they were.

"I don't think she did," Devon said. "We need to find Maupin, let him know."

"If there were only two members of the Council here," Lane said, "then it's likely the others were making this announcement in other parts of the city. Word will spread fast. He'll know before we get there."

"We'll inform Maupin. But first we need to check out the Lyceum and the other War college," Raven countered. "With the relocation to the quarantine zones beginning tomorrow, we don't have as much time to help the Brovettans as we thought. We're going to need all the information we can get."

* * *

"—relocate them to quarantine zones starting tomorrow," Raven said, finishing their report.

Devon glanced around at the small group of tullers gathered in the foyer of what had once been a theater, the lush carpet long since reduced to tatters, the floorboards showing through. The gilt paint had peeled and only traces remained of the mural on the domed ceiling—a hand with a pointed finger, the fronds of some kind of tree, a burst of sun rays. It smelled of mildew and rotten wood. The doors leading into the seating and stage area stood open, with stairs to the balcony to the left and right. Devon and his group had crashed in the balcony space, while the tullers were camped out on what remained of the stage or among the seating.

Most of the tullers looked shocked, one of them even murmuring, "Can they do that? Can they just...move people about like that?"

"They're going to try." Maupin stood and began to pace. "This makes things more complicated. Originally, I was simply going to contact people, discreetly, one by one, and move them out as quietly as possible in small groups. Now..."

"Now we're going to have to be less subtle," Raven said.

They stared at each other for a long moment, then Maupin said, "It will put us tullers at risk."

"They would have been at risk regardless," Raven countered, "as soon as the Iandolans realized Brovettans were missing."

He exhaled harshly. "We need to get as many of our usual contacts out as we can. Tonight. Before they start looking. Durran, Vash, Rennick, Raven—you'll each lead a retrieval team."

"Lane and I will go with Raven," Devon cut in.

Maupin nodded. "Ell, work with me. We'll create lists of those we need to grab, three or four to each list, preferably all on the same level and close together. The rest of you divide up, grab your weapons and whatever else you think you might need, and gear up. We'll send you out as soon as we have a list for you."

The men and women in the room began to move, separating into teams of four or five. Raven motioned to one of the men, who joined her, but Devon moved toward Maupin, who was leaning over a wobbly desk to one side with the tuller Ell, already jotting down names and locations on sheets of paper.

"Send Durran to Level Fourteen. He can handle the riff-raff there. Raven's group will do better at Level Twenty—"

"Where are Dalton and Nic?" Devon interrupted.

Maupin glanced up in annoyance. "I sent them to get information. They haven't returned yet. Send Vash to Level—"

"What information?"

Maupin straightened and faced him, about to snap something, but he caught himself and said in a carefully controlled voice, "Dalton was to get information about the army. I sent Nic to Carbolen." When Devon stiffened, he held up a hand to halt him. "He volunteered to go. Picall went with him."

Devon stifled his surge of anger, nodded, then retreated.

"Why?" he asked under his breath as he approached Lane. Raven and the tuller were talking to each other to one side. "Why did he do it?"

"Why did who do what?" Lane asked.

"Nic. Maupin said he volunteered to contact Carbolen. Why? He knows what Carbolen is like! He knows Carbolen likely has a bounty on our heads for slipping away like we did!"

"Maybe that's why he went."

"What do you mean?"

"He knows Carbolen better than any of us, except possibly Raven. And maybe he has something to prove."

"To whom?"

"To himself. That he can stand on his own. That he can contribute. Ever since he met you, he's been following you. And before that it was Carbolen."

Devon considered what Lane had said, staring at the doors that led out onto Level Ten. "Let's hope he can handle him."

Raven tapped him on the shoulder. "We've got our first batch of Brovettans. Let's move."

* * *

Nic stood in the middle of the street on Level Seventeen, Carbolen's level, and tried not to sweat. His hands clenched into fists but he forced himself to relax. Overhead, one of the few remaining bands of lucent that lit the streets at this level flickered, but held. Buildings to either side appeared abandoned, although Nic knew there were inhabitants, even here, close to the area Carbolen claimed as his own. He'd felt eyes on him already, but no one had attempted to approach. They were likely wondering why he was standing in the open on a thoroughfare that the gang used frequently.

"Because I'm an idiot," Nic mumbled to himself.

Devon had managed to get them away from Carbolen—not once, but twice—and yet he'd volunteered to return.

He'd turn and run, but he knew someone from the gang had already noticed him. Word had already been sent.

"Maybe he'll ignore me," Nic murmured. "It's the others he wants."

A figure appeared a short distance away, stepping out into the street boldly, then began to approach, four others falling into step behind him.

Nic swallowed, forced his hands to unclench again. There was only one person on this level who'd be so confident here, of all places.

"Carbolen," Nic said, and gave a nod.

The gang leader halted ten paces distant, his escort of four fanning out behind him. Nic only recognized one of them. "Nic." He eyed the buildings, the alleys to either side at Nic's back—his escape routes if needed. "Where are Devon and Raven?"

"Not here. They had other business."

"What kind of business?"

"That's what I came here to talk about."

"Is that so?" He took a step forward and all four behind him bristled, hands near weapons. "What makes you think I won't simply kill you outright out of spite, you traitorous shit? You and your friends were *mine*!"

A crossbow bolt sank itself into the cobbles at Carbolen's feet, spitting up stone shards. Nic had been expecting it, but still he started. Carbolen glanced down, then scanned the buildings again to either side with a sharper eye.

"Devon and Raven aren't here," Nic said, keeping his voice steady with effort, "but I didn't say I came alone."

Carbolen stared at him a long moment, then said, "What do you want?"

"The Brovettans."

"Which ones? Those that attacked or those being persecuted now?"

"The citizens being persecuted now. We may have a way to get them out of the city. We were wondering if you could help."

Carbolen's posture eased, which only made Nic tense up more.

"We're already helping."

"So I've heard. You're patrolling the streets in the lower levels, halting the attacks when you hear of them, trying to keep the tensions low."

"These are our streets. We're merely keeping an eye on our own interests."

"It isn't enough."

"You little—"

"How many people have died already?" Nic cut in, shouting to drown Carbolen out. "How many because you couldn't stop it? Because you weren't there or didn't arrive in time? Dozens? A hundred? More?" Carbolen remained quiet, fuming. "It's not because you aren't trying. It's because even if you stop the attackers one night, they can come back the next or the night after or a week later. As long as the Brovettans are there, they're at risk. The only solution is to get them out."

"That's going to be harder than you think."

Nic frowned. "What do you mean?"

"You haven't heard? The new Council, in its esteemed wisdom, has decided to force all of those of Brovettan descent into internment camps, starting tomorrow. For their own safety, of course."

Nic nearly turned around to ask Devon or Lane if that was possible, but caught himself. "Can they do that?"

"They're going to try."

It had always been hard to read Carbolen, but Nic thought he heard an angry edge to the words.

"That means there's an even more urgent reason to get them out," Nic said. "We'll do what we can, but we could use the gang's help."

Carbolen considered, the street eerily quiet. "Who is this 'we' you keep mentioning? It can't be just Devon and Raven and Lane. And what kind of help do you need?"

"I don't know yet," Nic said. "I'm not sure they know yet. But there aren't enough of us to carry it out alone. Not without leaving a ton of Brovettans behind. That's why they sent me here. If you aren't willing to help," Nic said, backing up slowly, "we'll find someone else."

He spun and walked away, trying not to run, listening hard for the sound of footfalls rushing him from behind. He angled for the nearest alley.

He'd almost reached it when Carbolen said, "Wait."

He looked back. Carbolen had pulled the bolt from the street, was inspecting it. No one in his group had moved.

The gang leader looked up. "Tell Devon or Raven or whoever they'll have my support."

Without waiting for a reply, he motioned to the other four gang members and vanished into the depths of the gang's lair.

Someone dropped to the ground three feet from Nic, hidden within the alley, and Nic's heart slammed hard in his chest. "Shards, don't do that, Picall! I'm on edge as it is."

"That went well," Picall said, easing the loaded bolt free of the crossbow she held. She twisted the weapon around in her hand. "I like this. We should have them at the tull. They'd be useful catching lizards."

"You mean you'd never fired one before!"

"Seemed pretty basic to me." She flicked Nic's nose and he swatted at her hand. "Let's report back to Maupin. He's likely already heard about the camps, so I'm certain the plans have already changed."

Chapter Seven

Lane followed Raven, Devon, the tuller named Unsel, and one of Carbolen's gang out of the ancient theater and into the streets. Her fingers itched to try sketching out a sigil, just to make certain that her magic had returned, but she didn't dare do it in front of anyone, especially if she tried one of the new sigils based on what she'd discovered about the magic structure at the tull. She hadn't truly been alone since they'd returned, although she'd considered sneaking off one night while the others had been sleeping.

But no, she wasn't that irresponsible. She knew nothing about this level—its dangers, its inhabitants—nothing except they were far deeper than she'd ever been except for when they'd fled. Before that, the lowest she'd ever gone was Carbolen's lair and she hadn't been comfortable there.

As they skirted the light, headed toward the nearest Spoke, uncomfortably distant for Lane's tastes, she scanned the shadows and buildings to either side. Most were in worse shape than the theater, with gaping holes in their sides, roofs collapsed, edges of doors and windows ragged and torn, as if gnawed on by gigantic beasts. That made her think of the skrill and she unconsciously edged closer to Devon. They kept to alleys and narrows when possible, clogged with debris. And rats. Tons of rats. Raven had already scouted out the surrounding area, but the farther they moved from the theater, the more they had to retrace their steps when they ran into an alley blocked by a collapsed wall or where the street had caved in.

"Where are we headed?" Devon asked as they moved. He'd produced a rose-tinted lantern, one that looked suspiciously like the shard he'd collected from the tull. It had a softer light than the green one.

Raven didn't pause. "Level Twenty."

"I already knew that. Where on Level Twenty?"

Raven referred to the paper Maupin had given her. "Looks like the Harrow district."

"Outer edge then. Exposed. It will take us half the night to get there."

"I know a few shortcuts." She glanced back at them all, her gaze falling on the gang member. She'd been keeping a close on her since she'd arrived to join their group. "We'll get there by dusk."

Devon didn't respond, and Lane had no idea where the Harrow district was.

She settled in for a long walk.

Before they reached the Spoke, Raven cut through a building, emerging from its blasted-out back wall into an area covered with mounds of brick, a thick support beam for the upper levels at its center. A ladder had been cut into its side and she began to ascend without a word, the others following behind. Two levels later, Lane's arms burning with the exertion, Raven helped her up into a spare room through a trap door, the gang member behind her. Before she could comment on how horrid the room reeked, Raven had hauled the gang member up into a chokehold, her knife at the girl's eye. The girl thrashed and choked, until she saw the blade inches away from her face, her body going limp.

Raven loosened her hold slightly, enough the girl could suck in a harsh breath.

"What did Carbolen tell you to do?" Raven asked, voice low. "Are you here to kill me when my back is turned? Make it look like an accident when we're retreating? Or are you simply supposed to gut one of us and run, no pretense?"

Still heaving in air, the girl gasped, "None of that! He told everyone to leave you alone. No one was to touch any of you."

Raven tightened her hold again. "That makes no sense. I know Carbolen, better than any of you. He wouldn't simply let me—let *us*—go."

The girl's face began turning purplish-red and she began to kick feebly.

Raven waited another five seconds, then released her, the girl dropping to hands and knees, coughing and spitting as she recovered. She shot Raven a hate-filled glare as she wiped at her mouth, her color returning slowly.

Raven pointed her knife and said, "Don't try anything," then stalked away.

The girl's gaze wandered over all of them, but then she picked herself back up, brushed herself off, wiped at her eyes. She was a few years older than Lane herself, although leaner.

Without a word, she followed after Raven.

"Was that really necessary?" Lane asked Devon as they moved in their wake.

"Raven thought so."

They cut hubward, ascended in an elevator, then stairs, a main thoroughfare, finally emerging onto Level Twenty beneath the edge of the level above. The sun set on the horizon in a fiery blaze, the clouds scudding through the sky a burnished gold. The Flatlands were laid out in streaks of umber and red and black shadows cast by the plinths.

"Elegant beauty, yes?" Unsel said. "Simple beauty."

Lane turned to him, surprised; he'd said nothing to either her or the others since they'd left the theater. "Yes."

He nodded. He was perhaps ten years older than Lane, with soft hazel eyes. Faint scars on one cheek marked an otherwise simple face. A few gray patches were scattered through his dark hair. He looked odd without one of the tuller spears in hand, only a sword.

"We're close," Raven said, tucking the paper back inside her belt pouch. She'd pointedly ignored the gang member since their confrontation. "This way."

She led them to a perfume shop off of a narrow side street among a tangle of such streets, all meeting at odd angles. Pale blue lucent lights stood at every intersection, slowly brightening as the sun sank, the buildings crammed in between, only a few stories high. A tiny bell rang when Raven shoved the door open.

"Oh, I'm sorry, we're closed," a Brovettan woman said from behind the counter, with a pleasant smile that faltered when she saw them. "What is this?" she asked, an edge of fear creeping into her voice. "Willett!"

"We're friends of Maupin," Raven said, as a man emerged from the back room brandishing what looked like a cooking knife.

The woman halted him with a hand on his arm. "Maupin?"

Unsel stepped forward. "He told me to tell you 'Little Wren is fine. She's found her wings.'"

The woman's hand tightened on her husband's arm. "You know the bags we keep beneath the bed, Willett? Grab them. And anything else you absolutely can't part with. We're leaving."

"What about the shop? Our wares?" he protested, although he was already moving.

"You heard the announcement today. We're not going to their quarantine zones. We're getting out."

The man returned and thrust a bag into her arms. "What about Nadia and Hern?"

The woman looked at Raven.

"Are they close?" At the woman's nod, Raven said, "We'll pick them up on the way. Come on. We have a few more stops."

Raven, the gang member, and Devon left first, Unsel and Lane herding the two Brovettans into the street before them. The woman directed Raven to Nadia and Hern's apartment, both entering and hustling the two out into the street while Unsel and Lane kept watch. Both Nadia and Hern looked confused, but they followed the woman's direction. They'd obviously thrown on a coat over whatever they were wearing and neither had a bag or satchel.

After that, Raven led them on a circuitous route out of Harrow into another district, picking up scattered singletons or pairs on the way. At each new shop or apartment, it played out in a similar way, Raven or Devon pounding on the door, Unsel giving some kind of code phrase, a different one for each person, Lane and the gang member on watch outside. Most of the time, the Brovettans dropped whatever they were doing and joined them, some with satchels already prepared, more than Lane expected. Then again, if her people were being attacked at random, she might have prepared an emergency bag herself.

Except these were her people, she realized. A sickening hollow formed in her stomach. She was Brovettan after all.

At two locations, they had to wait while items were gathered in a mad rush.

By the time they reached the last apartment—a family of five; three children ranging from six to twelve—a few of those they'd gathered were weeping. All of them were afraid, clutching their possessions tight. They huddled in a tight, conspicuous group outside the building, Raven and Devon inside with the family. Lane looked over their distraught faces, tried to reassure them with a smile and nod, but didn't feel it accomplished much.

"Hey, you!"

She turned at the voice, her hand unconsciously crooking, ready to start the base form of a sigil. Two men stood at the end of the lane, one of them wavering as if drunk.

"What are you doing there?" the one in the lead shouted. He began coming toward them.

"None of your business," one of the Brovettans said.

"You're all Brovettans," the man sneered, his friend coming up behind him. He caught sight of Unsel. "Well, almost all. What are you doing out? Shouldn't you be inside, packing up for the 'relocation' tomorrow?" He laughed, his friend joining in uncertainly. They'd stopped a short distance away from Lane, the Brovettans falling back behind her. Unsel and the gang member had stepped up to her side. They were young and wore finely-tailored clothing, sported a few rings, a necklace. Not from this level; from higher up. Merchant's sons or even a family associated with the towers.

His laugh cut off sharply as he spied some of the baggage they carried. "What's going on—?"

"You should leave," Lane said, cutting him off.

His eyes narrowed in suspicion. "You aren't preparing for the quarantine, are you? You're getting ready to run."

He pulled a wicked-looking knife from a sheath at his side, suddenly no longer as drunk as he had seemed.

"Haven't you people done enough," he said, falling into a fighter's stance. His friend fumbled for his own weapon.

Lane began her sigil as those behind her gasped and Unsel stepped forward, drawing his sword. Before Lane could complete her sigil, a hand fell on her arm. She glanced to the side, to see Devon shake his head. The family had emerged from the building behind him.

She turned back to the street in time to see Raven plunge a knife into the man's friend's side. He collapsed backwards, making enough noise that the man with the wicked knife spun and caught Raven's blade in the gut. He folded over her arm as someone behind stifled a shriek and someone else murmured, "Don't look, darling, don't look."

Devon, the gang member, and two others stepped forward to help Raven move the bodies into the house the family had just vacated. The Brovettans conversed with each other in low voices, even more on edge than before, and then Raven and the others were back.

"That was our last pick-up," Raven said. "We're going to take you to Maupin now. He'll help you from there."

The woman they'd first met reached out and gripped Raven's arm. "Thank you."

Others echoed her. Looking uncomfortable, Raven, motioned them hubward. More of those gathered carried weapons now, those without pushed into the center of the group.

Lane stalked up to Devon's side, trembling with anger. "Why did you stop me? I could have handled them both."

"I knew Raven had it taken care of."

"That's not the point."

Devon glanced at her as they passed beneath the overhang of Level Twenty-One above, what little moonlight there was fading away. Only lucent lit the darkness now, fading the deeper into the level they moved.

"You don't want to use magic unless absolutely necessary," he said. "Think about it. The moment you do, they'll know it's you. If we want to get as many Brovettans out as we can, as quickly as we can, we can't have them hunting for you. And they will come hunting, as soon as they suspect you're helping them escape."

"What's the point of being able to control magic if I can't ever use it?"

"Don't worry, you'll get to use it. Sooner rather than later, I suspect. This is only the beginning. Tonight was easy. Tomorrow will be harder. They're going to realize what's going on and after that it will be a fight getting anyone out."

* * *

"They're vanishing!" Havvelan shouted into the nearly empty Council chamber. "Disappearing overnight! Leaving everything behind—shops, merchandise, clothes, even food. All we find when we appear at their houses to escort them to the quarantine zones are empty flats and abandoned bedrooms."

Varenov sat rigid in her seat, watching Havvelan pacing the center of the floor. "What did you expect? That they'd go willingly into imprisonment?"

"It's not imprisonment," Gabrella said from her seat. "We've provided everything they need. It's for their own protection."

Varenov leaned forward. "You keep saying that. Maybe they don't need your protection."

"We're supposed to let them be attacked and killed in the streets?" Gabrella countered.

"We should be making certain the streets are safe, not punishing those we've sworn to protect."

Gabrella waved her hand in dismissal, focusing on Havvelan. "Does it really matter? How many are actually 'vanishing'? I know it's not all of them. My sources report the city guard has escorted hundreds of Brovettans to the quarantine zones."

"There were only a few the first day, but in the days since the numbers have increased. At this point, I'd approximate about two hundred have eluded our quarantine."

"That's all?" Santigo leaned back in his seat. "Why are you making such a fuss over so few?"

"I believe," Petrov cut in, "Havvelan is 'making such a fuss' because in a few more days it won't be 'so few.' It will be five hundred. And by the time the week is out, it may be in the thousands."

"Where are they going?" Secora asked, before Santigo or Havvelan could respond. "They can't simply be vanishing into thin air."

"The city patrols have spotted groups of Brovettans heading deeper into the lower levels, on back streets and in the shadow of the level above. They're usually being escorted by others, although we haven't been able to determine who is helping them." He turned toward Varenov. "You wouldn't happen to know anything about this, would you, Varenov?"

Varenov stiffened. "Why would you say that?"

Havvelan approached. "Because the Brovettans are your people, aren't they? You are their councilor, after all. And you've made it clear that you disagree with these zones we've established."

"Because these 'zones,' as you call them, are in direct violation of the Founders' Pact. You're forcing citizens to give up their rights under the guise of protection. It's illegal. It's evil."

"All the more reason for you to be helping them, if you believe so. You haven't yet answered my question."

Varenov stood, rested her weight into her arms on the desk, so she was facing Havvelan eye to eye. "No, I am not helping the Brovettans escape the city guard."

He held her gaze, searching, but Varenov didn't waver. Then he spun away. "Regardless, we need to find out who these people are and deal with them. They are clearly in opposition to the Council."

Varenov sat back down.

"All of our resources are being used to round the Brovettans up," Secora said. "Exactly how are you proposing we deal with them?"

"When is Prefect Arctus expected to return with the army?"

"Our latest information suggests not for another few weeks. He has run into significant opposition in Brovetto, but expects to quell it with a particularly heavy strike within the week. He feels he's on the verge of locating the rebels' main base of operations."

Varenov's hands clenched on the arm of her chair and she involuntarily glanced over toward where Treant would normally be seated. Cursing herself—she would never have betrayed herself so blatantly if she weren't so stressed—she looked back in time to see Havvelan watching her.

"Then we can't rely on the Iandolan Army to help us," the new councilor said. He hesitated, as if about to ask her something.

"What about the students in the War colleges?" Petrov asked.

Secora frowned. "But they're just students. They've barely begun—"

"I'm not suggesting we use them in any other capacity except as escorts for the Brovettans. Some additional muscle. It would free up some of the city guard to search for these others helping the Brovettans escape."

"If they're hiding out somewhere in the lower levels, it will be difficult to find them, even with additional city guard," Santigo said. "Is it even worth it? Why not just let them go? Who are they harming?"

"Because I doubt these men and women are simply citizens trying to evade the quarantine," Havvelan said. "Those disappearing are likely Brovettans associated with the rebellion. What other reason is there to run and hide? They need to be found and captured and questioned."

Both Santigo and Gabrella appeared unsettled by this, but Varenov suspected for different reasons. She felt nauseous.

"All those in favor of using War college students as escorts for the Brovettans so the city guard can investigate these disappearances?"

Varenov made a strangled noise.

"Varenov?" Secora's voice was mildly concerned. "Are you all right?"

She stood. "I'm surprised you bothered to call for a vote at all. You already know the outcome. The five of you will vote for the proposal, as you have done ever since Martov's death, while Santigo and I will dissent. The motion passes. I question whether I should even attend these Councils anymore. My voice is so rarely heard."

Secora appeared shocked at the outburst; Havvelan merely smirked.

She spun and strode out of the chamber, Secora recovering enough to call out after her. Varenov ignored her, thrusting the doors open with stiff arms and heading immediately toward the elevator, her guards falling into step hastily to either side, the others waiting in the outer chamber giving her an odd look.

Before she reached the elevator, Santigo emerged from the Council chamber and approached, waving his own guards back. Varenov hit the lucent button to summon the elevator with more force than necessary.

"Were you telling the truth about not helping the Brovettans?" Santigo asked in a low voice as soon as he was within range. He halted a few paces away, glancing back toward the room with the other Councilors.

"Of course."

Santigo faced her again. "None of the others believe you. They're all convinced you're behind it."

Varenov gave an unpleasant laugh. "Of course they don't. It's the way their minds work. After all, they're orchestrating the attacks on the Brovettans to begin with."

Santigo looked stunned. "What do you mean?"

Varenov mentally kicked herself. "Nothing." She hit the elevator button again. "Forget I said anything."

The elevator chimed and the doors slid open. She stepped forward, but Santigo grabbed her arm and her own guards bristled.

"What do you mean?" Santigo repeated, with heavier emphasis.

She considered his earnest expression, the worry that edged his eyes, his mouth, his forehead. Then she glanced toward the Council chamber as she drew him into the elevator. Both sets of guards joined them.

As the elevator began moving toward her floor, she said, "I have no proof, but the initial attacks on the Brovettans were purposely instigated by groups sent to foment distrust and outright hatred of the Brovettans. My sources have been investigating, but they've only been able to verify that the orders were spread by men and women associated with Council members. They haven't been able to determine which ones, although I have my suspicions."

"That's…that's a serious allegation."

"Which is why I never intended to share it with you. That was an accident. I certainly can't share it with the Council, not without incontrovertible proof."

"But why? Why would they do such a thing?"

"To give them a reason to propose these insane measures, of course. It's a means to an end."

"But…what end?"

The elevator halted and the doors opened. Varenov stepped into the corridor outside her apartment, her guards flanking her, but turned back.

"I think someone wants to destroy the Council."

The elevator closed before she could see Santigo's reaction.

* * *

Devon dragged himself up the stairs to the balcony of the theater on Level Ten, every muscle in his body aching. When he arrived at the top, he found Dalton sitting with his back to one wall, waiting. He couldn't help but smile.

"It feels like I haven't seen you in days," he said as he sank to the floor next to the ex-guardsman and rested a head on his shoulder.

"You haven't," Dalton rumbled, raising his arm so Devon could tuck himself in closer after a lingering kiss. "You taste like sweat."

"So do you. I assume you've been running up and down levels, leading Brovettans to freedom."

"That and meeting with Captain Mannert to get updates on what the city guard is doing."

"And what does she have to say?"

"That the Council isn't happy with what Maupin and Carbolen are doing. Our little groups have caught their attention. Starting tomorrow, they're going to use the untrained students in the new War colleges as the escorts for the Brovettans and shift a portion of the city guard into searching for us and the missing Brovettans."

Devon pushed back from beneath Dalton's comforting arm and warmth. "Those students are nothing more than bullies. Worse even than the gangs, since they have no discipline. They aren't used to following orders."

"Mannert agrees. She and a significant portion of the Iandolan soldiers under her—as well as some of the city guard—have reservations about how this is being handled. So far, she hasn't been willing to help us directly—mostly telling those under her command to look the other way, let the city guard deal with us—but now she's reconsidering."

"Who's reconsidering what?" Lane asked, mounting the last of the steps and then collapsing onto her pallet face down. She groaned, the sound muffled by her blankets. "I never want to climb a ladder or set of stairs again. Why aren't there more elevators?"

"There are," Devon said, "they just don't work anymore."

"Why not?"

"Some of it is mechanical," Dalton said. "Cables broken, tracks rusted out, that kind of thing."

"And the rest has to do with the lucent dying. It provides the power, so if it's dead, the elevator's dead."

Dalton slapped Devon's arm with the back of his hand. "What about the rose lantern?"

Devon shot him a glare and rubbed his arm. "What about it?"

Lane suddenly looked up. "Yeah, I've been meaning to ask you about that. When did you get it? I saw it when we went on that first outing with Raven and Unsel."

Devon shared a glance with Dalton, who merely shrugged. "I...I made it actually."

Lane shot up into a seated position. "You *made* it? What do you mean you *made* it?"

"Remember that shard I brought back from the hunt at the tull? I was messing around with it and its structure was so close to the green lantern that I just…shifted it slightly…and I ended up with a second lantern."

"It required a little more prodding than that on my part," Dalton muttered.

"So you're saying you can manipulate lucent crystals."

"I guess."

Lane chucked a stray metal cup at him. "And you didn't tell me?"

"You weren't around at the time. And then the first Brovettans arrived at the tull and it sort of got lost in everything that's happened since then."

Lane sat back, her incensed look faltering. "I supposed I shouldn't complain, since I haven't told you everything either."

"What do you mean?"

She bit her lower lip, then sighed. "The reason I've been so anxious to use my magic is because I want to test out some theories." She pulled her satchel close, dug around inside, and produced some pages. "While we were at the tull, I used your notes and what I already knew of the sigils to sketch out a different way to look at the double pyramid structure." She crawled closer, handed over the notes, and leaned over his shoulder, pointing as she spoke. "I think the faces of the Source each represent different aspects of the effect you want to produce. This one is direction, this one intensity, then size and shape, and finally type. So let's say I want to produce a ball of fire. I just pick the nodes from the appropriate faces for where I want it sent, how large and hot I want it, and then select a node in this area for fire. Based on the sigils we know of, I've sketched out different areas that represent fire, lightning, light, ice, cantrips, and water. Obviously, this isn't precise yet, and some parts of the pyramids are blank, but I couldn't do anything at the tull to flesh it out because magic didn't work there."

She'd said it all in a rush, her breath hot against Devon's neck, but now she sat back to catch her breath. Devon scanned her sketch, pulling out copies of his notes on the sigils and comparing the selected nodes for each sigil to the locations mapped out in the pyramids.

"Is this what you were doing with Gillian?"

"Partially. She didn't know much about the sigils or magic. Mostly I was reading. She had a ton of books she'd stolen from the Library."

Devon dropped the notes to give her a hard, mocking stare. "And you didn't tell me?"

Lane shrugged. "They were mostly about the Founders and the Founding. Nearly incomprehensible. At least, what didn't seem like outright fabrications."

"I still would have liked to have seen them." But he let it go, turning back to her notes. "It's not as simple as you're stating it. Some of the sigils are more complicated than this, and there are subtleties with the depth of the Source—it's not all happening on the surface—but still…"

Lane leaned in close. "I think I can do more than the Mage proctors at the Lyceum. More than Favian, even."

Devon held her gaze. "Have you tried any of this out yet?"

"No. Because you were right—the moment they hear of someone within the city using magic, they're going to think it's me. I haven't even dared do anything here on Level Ten, in case someone down here saw and reported it."

"Probably for the best." Even he noticed the disappointment in his voice.

"But what about the lucent?" Lane asked. She glanced around the balcony space, most of the chairs ripped out, the floor bare. She stood, grabbed one of the regular lanterns, and drifted closer to the walls. A moment later, she gave a small exclamation and tapped the wall. "Here. There's lucent right here, embedded in the wall."

Devon rose and joined her. The wall was painted, most of it flaked away, but woven into the design were thin threads and curls of lucent. "What do you expect me to do?"

"Fix it." At his barked laugh, she added, "You said you created that rose lantern from a shard of crystal. Lucent is just formed crystal. The Founders mined it, manipulated it. Why shouldn't you be able to fix it?"

All he wanted to do was curl up with Dalton and get some rest before they were sent out again to fetch more Brovettans, but Lane appeared reenergized. Dalton merely waved at him to try when he looked back.

With a sigh, he touched a band of lucent and sank himself into it, as he had the locks he picked or the crystal he'd formed into the lantern. It wasn't as easy as any of his previous attempts, as if the stone were literally dead, whereas before, with the active locks or the Warding, it had been alive. Moving sluggishly, he began to trace out the lucent's cloudy pathways.

"What's happening?" Lane asked, her voice close. "What do you see? Why are you frowning?"

"It's not the same. It's harder. Much harder. Like the lucent is resisting me. But I'm not really sensing anything…*wrong*. The paths are just…dark. Closed and lifeless." Even as he said it, some of the resistance faded, as if the lucent were adjusting to his presence. Like the Warding, he began to realize that the paths had a specific, directed flow, coming from a main source. "Wait." He began to backtrack it, his finger following his mind on the thread of lucent in the wall.

"Now what?" Dalton asked, also close. He must have gotten up and joined them.

"All of the paths lead back toward what must be a single source. I'm trying to find it."

He heard them moving about as he shifted down the wall, eyes closed. He heard a clang of metal, the rustle of cloth, a soft curse, and realized they were moving things out of his way.

Then the path stopped.

He opened his eyes. Beneath his finger, the lucent had a faint crack. He wasn't certain he would have noticed it if he hadn't been tracing a path. "The lucent's broken right here."

"Then fix it," Dalton said. "You fixed the cracks in the lantern crystal at the tull."

Devon concentrated, trying to recall what he'd done then, but it came naturally.

With a *push*, the crack sealed itself up.

He stepped back. Nothing happened.

"Did you fix it?" Dalton asked.

"That crack, yes. There must be others. This isn't like the lantern. This is much bigger." Without prompting, he stepped forward and began tracing again, making certain the paths around the crack were fixed before moving on. He found three others before he reached the section of lucent where all of the paths converged. Others shot out in multiple directions from this central location, but there was a significant crack at the base. It took more effort, but like the lantern, it healed, the lucent trembling beneath his fingers.

He glanced up, but the lucent threads were still dormant.

Then he flicked the thread.

Dark green light blossomed at the base, spread up along the threads, branched, curling out and around, like a vine, picking out finer details in the lucent. Leaves unfurled, lined with veins. Delicate white flowers emerged. Some of the vines lit and flickered, then died. Some held steady. Others remained dark.

Devon stepped back from the wall, Lane and Dalton at his side. Footsteps pounded up the stairs from below, a few tullers, Maupin, and Raven appearing at the balcony entrance. They halted at its edge.

"What did you do?" Maupin asked. "I thought all of the lucent in this place was dead."

Devon shrugged. "I just...touched it."

Neither Maupin nor Raven looked like they believed him, but the others spread out on the balcony to marvel at the tangled image. Devon wondered what it must have looked like with the paint fresh. But it was still beautiful, especially for the tullers, used to the stark natural beauty of the Flatlands.

Then Maupin said, "Turn it off. We don't want anyone from outside seeing it. We're already at risk bringing the Brovettans down to this level before taking them to the sublevels."

Devon moved forward and flicked the lucent again, the light fading. He didn't think anyone would be able to see it from outside, but better not to take chances. They were already housing the Brovettans in a warehouse blocks away, to keep them separated from Maupin's group, the theory being that if the Iandolan city guard discovered the Brovettans, they'd still be safe at the theater.

The tullers and Raven filed out, Raven casting a vague warning look backwards before following Maupin down.

"Do you know what this means?" Lane whispered. She grabbed Devon's hand, then frowned in concern. "Devon...you're trembling."

Devon swallowed. "It means that your mother was right. The two of us are the most dangerous people in Iandolo."

Chapter Eight

"Oh, lovely," Nic said. "Rain."

"Maybe it will keep the city patrol at home," Dalton said.

They stood in the lee of the Level Twenty-Four overhang, water pouring down from above in a sheet ahead of them onto the street. Lightning flared, thunder rumbling into the cavern of Level Twenty-Three shortly after.

"I doubt it." Devon started forward. "It's the last day of the round-up. Let's get as many of the Brovettans down below as we can today." He ducked his head as he went through the cascading water, then kept it tucked in the torrent beyond, running out into the streets. He could hear Nic, Dalton, and Picall behind him, their feet splashing in the puddles, someone cursing softly. The streets were nearly empty, rain rushing in the gutters and spilling from rooftops. It gave the lit lucent an oddly muted, hazy glow.

By the time they made it to the first building on their list, Devon was soaked to the skin. They stumbled into the foyer and stood dripping on the mosaic floor of the apartment building.

"What floor?" Dalton asked, shaking himself off like a dog.

Devon pulled the sheet from an inner pocket, the ink already beginning to run. "Third, apartment five."

They hit the stairs, Dalton in the lead, Picall behind, all of them on edge, ears straining. As the week ran down, encounters with the city patrol and groups of the War college students had risen. For every ten Brovettans they collected, another hundred were herded into the quarantine zones. Some had become desperate, fleeing to the lower levels on their own. Maupin had been forced to put out watchers for these stragglers, although often the city guard got them first. The army's presence on the lower levels, searching for Maupin's base of operations, had increased as well. Every group had a scout now to get them past these groups and into the upper levels, the scout turning back once they hit Level Twenty. After the agreement with Carbolen, Maupin's teams had focused on Mid-level and the six levels below, while Carbolen and the gangs had taken everything lower. Still, the number of Brovettans they'd managed to bring to Level Ten's warehouse had decreased dramatically. That first night they had escorted nearly a hundred below. Now they were barely managing forty.

Ahead, Dalton motioned the third-floor hall was empty. With Devon on his heels, he edged down to the fifth apartment, tapping the already ajar door open with his foot. "We're too late."

Devon swore as Dalton stepped into the apartment, the others joining them. The interior had been trashed, shattered furniture and scattered clothing strewn across the room amidst broken shards of pottery and glass. Blood lay in a puddle near the door, a handprint smeared along the wall.

"City patrol gathering them up for the internment camp or something else?" Nic asked.

Dalton had been picking through the debris. "City patrol." He motioned to the blood. "They resisted, probably because they knew we were coming for them today."

"What about the destruction?" Picall asked. "I doubt they resisted that much."

Devon glanced at her. She'd mellowed since arriving in Iandolo, scenes like this one hardening the spirit he'd seen at the tull. "My guess is that this was done by War college students supplementing the city guard. Subdue them, then demoralize them."

"That's what Captain Mannert said is happening. There are two city guardsmen and four to eight War college students per team. The guardsmen can't control them."

Devon quashed the seething anger in his chest and pulled the damp sheet from his pocket. "The next pick-up is two streets over."

They returned to the rain, but found the next three shops and apartments empty.

At the fourth, an apothecary, the door had been kicked open, the counters overturned, powders and dried herbs littering the floor amidst bowls, mortars, and pestles, some of the stoneware cracked. The back rooms were a shambles as well. Dalton checked out the back door, which hung open, then returned.

"No blood," he said.

"And this seems more destructive than at the other places," Devon added.

"Devon!" Nic called from out front. He and Picall were watching the street.

As soon as they emerged from the back rooms, Picall motioned to the front window. "Across the street. The leather shop."

Devon took her place. He picked out the leather shop easily enough, but had to squint through the rain to see the figure in the window. "A woman. Brovettan. She just waved. And now she's gone."

He glanced back at Dalton, who shrugged. "Let's check it out."

Dalton led, Devon a step behind, Picall and Nic fanning out to either side of the door. The rain had lessened slightly, although by now Devon barely noticed it.

When Dalton knocked, another woman—obviously not Brovettan by her skin—answered. She glared at Dalton, then Devon, mouth set in a hard line, then scanned the street.

"Let them in," someone said from behind her.

She hesitated, then stepped back. Devon noticed a wicked-looking carving knife in her hand.

Inside, huddled around a small table covered in leather scraps, dripping wet, were three Brovettans—a man, woman, and young girl of about seven—and three other non-Brovettan children.

The man stood. "Did you come for us?"

"If you live in the apothecary," Devon said.

"We saw the city guard coming. We fled out the back and came here. We've been waiting."

"Disgraceful, what they are doing to these people," the woman who'd answered the door said. She had a Lambenesque accent. "Get them out if you can."

The man herded his wife and daughter into the street, Dalton, Picall and Nic forming up around them. Devon lingered a moment.

"Why are you helping them?" he asked the Lambenesque woman.

"Because today they come for the Brovettans. Next week they may come for us. None of us are alone."

Devon nodded, then stepped outside.

"Where are the others?" the man asked, water dripping down his face.

"Taken," Devon said.

He glanced at Dalton. They were supposed to have collected twenty-five people on this run. Instead, they had three. He hoped Raven, Lane, and the others had had better luck.

They headed hubward, Picall scouting ahead with Nic, people beginning to emerge from their homes as the rain died down. They encountered two groups of city guard, but avoided them by taking another route. Then they were in the lee of the level above and Devon felt more at ease.

Hours later, they emerged on Level Ten near the warehouse. The Brovettan carried his daughter in his arms, the girl asleep.

"Are we almost there?" the wife asked.

"Almost," Dalton answered. "It's just around—"

Ahead, a group of city guard appeared, hunched over and sprinting down the cross-street at the intersection, weapons ready. Devon saw them at the same moment Dalton cut off and with a hiss of warning pushed the woman up against the wall of the nearest building. Dalton did the same with the man, his startled expression turning to fear when Dalton motioned toward the guardsmen. When his daughter began to rouse, he cupped the back of her head with his hand and smothered her protests in his shirt, whispering to her. Picall and Nic were ahead of them, also plastered against the wall, but as soon as the last guardsmen passed their street they all retreated toward the alley behind them.

"How did they find us?" Nic asked, staying at the entrance so he could watch the street. Picall sprinted toward the other end of the alley to check that end.

"It was only a matter of time," Dalton said. "You can't move as many people as we have without someone noticing. I'm surprised it took them this long."

The Brovettan woman was breathing hard, her hands clamped over her mouth. Her husband pulled her into his side with one arm and she began to calm, focusing on her daughter.

He looked at Devon. "What do we do now?"

Devon sent a questioning glance at Dalton.

"The guards are headed toward the warehouse," the ex-soldier said. "That was a raid formation. They're going to hit it. Hard, if they had that many men with them. And half of them were War college students. There are probably other groups, with reinforcements waiting behind."

"Is there any way we can warn the warehouse they're coming?"

"I don't see how."

Devon swore. He glanced at the Brovettans, then Nic and Picall, returning from the end of the alley with an all-clear signal. He focused on the tuller. "Do you know where Maupin has been taking the Brovettans below, in the mines?"

"I do."

"You and Nic take these three down there. Warn them they may be dealing with an influx of people tonight."

"What are you going to do?" Nic asked, already motioning the three Brovettans toward the street.

"Whatever we can to help Maupin's men and the Brovettans at the warehouse."

"Thank you," the woman said, before her husband dragged her to the alley's entrance. Nic and Picall scanned the street, then rushed the Brovettans across to the opposite side. The ex-gang member glanced back once, then vanished with the others around a corner.

Dalton rested a hand on Devon's shoulder. "Funny, isn't it? Three months ago we were killing Brovettans in the street."

"No. We were killing violent insurgents. These are simply…people."

Dalton squeezed his shoulder, then the two of them headed toward the back of the alley.

They were a street away when they heard the explosion, followed by shouting and screams.

* * *

Lane pulled away from the Brovettans she, Raven, and the two tullers who'd been part of their team had brought to the warehouse. This was always the hardest part for her, besides seeing the ravaged apartments or the violence in the streets. The Brovettans invariably attached themselves to her after vacating their homes, probably because she looked Brovettan herself, even though she'd been raised in Iandolo. She'd taken to leading the Brovettans to where they'd be staying before Maupin collected them to take them below to the mines, then the tull, and finally the harsh trek to Brovetto. But leaving them after they'd been shown their pallets on the floor had become more and more difficult. Most of them looked so lost and uncertain, even after her reassurances. Others were afraid, for themselves or for someone they'd left behind or hadn't seen in days.

And tonight had been particularly bad. They'd arrived at one apartment building in time to see the Brovettans they were to pick up dragged out into the street, two of the guards—War students, really—beating on the couple until the true city guard emerged and put a stop to it. Other homes had been ransacked. In one, they'd found the body of a Brovettan man, sword wound to the chest. He'd held a bloodied knife in one hand.

Raven found her a few moments later, sitting against a wall, head tilted back, eyes closed. Lane didn't even know she was there until the gang member nudged her foot, startling her.

"Where are the others?" Lane asked, rubbing at her eyes.

"Talking with Maupin and the other tullers. They're deciding how many they think they can handle taking down tonight."

Lane glanced around the warehouse. Lanterns lit the open space at odd intervals, Brovettans huddled near them, their pallets spread behind. Most were talking, or holding each other. A couple were playing dice games or cards. A few children raced each other back and forth around them all. Aside from a few low conversations and Maupin's men, it was quiet.

"How many do you think we've helped?" Lane asked.

"I'd say a couple hundred."

Lane snorted. "Not enough."

Raven squinted at her. "More than would have been helped otherwise."

"And how many are now in the quarantine zones? How many Brovettans—no, how many citizens—were here in Iandolo when this began? A couple thousand at least. Five thousand? More? What about them?"

"I'm certain a few of them have hidden or fled on their own," Raven said. "But most are in quarantine."

"And are they safe there?"

"I don't know."

Lane caught her gaze, let her anger show. "I don't think so. Look at what they did to that couple we didn't get to in time. They weren't resisting. Their hands were tied for shard's sake! And what about the dead man. What did he do? Try to protect his family? Himself? And now he's dead."

Raven remained silent. Then: "What are you going to do about it?"

Lane stared out into the warehouse. "I'm going to get them out. All of them."

The front entrance of the warehouse exploded inward.

Raven ducked down, shoving Lane to one side and covering her to protect her. Shouts erupted, along with screams, the sounds muted by the ringing in Lane's ears. Splinters and chunks of wood rained down. Dust billowed. Lane pushed herself up from the floor, coughing, as guardsmen surged into the opening. They grabbed those nearest and thrust them to the floor, kneeling on their backs, or manhandled them outside. The Brovettans farthest back had leaped to their feet, those nearer the front and caught in the blast crawling away or struggling to rise. A few of them weren't moving.

"Guardsmen," Raven said.

"We need to help them," Lane said, half-standing.

Raven pulled her back against the wall beside her. "Maupin's men and those from the gangs who were protecting this place are already fighting back. They can handle it. We need to get the Brovettans out."

At the entrance, through the haze and dust, shadowy figures had begun to fight, even as more guardsmen poured into the opening. Most of them were Maupin's men, although some of Carbolen's gang who'd been dropping off Brovettans were among them. A few of the Brovettans were shouting at their families, motioning toward the back of the warehouse, then scrambling to find a weapon and join in.

Raven snagged Lane's arm, then raced with her toward the center of the warehouse. "Brovettans! To the back of the warehouse!" She began shoving woman and children in that direction, others taking up the cry. Another explosion ravaged the front of the warehouse, bringing fresh screams, those in front of them stumbling, but moving faster once they picked themselves up. Lane helped a young boy stand, then faced the front. Another section of the wall had been breached, more men pouring in from that direction.

Then a group stepped through the opening, guardsmen in a tight formation around a single central figure, a young man around Lane's age. She recognized him from…from the Lyceum. He'd been a fourth year then, would be a fifth year now…

He raised a hand, crooked it, and began a sigil.

"They brought a mage," Lane murmured to herself. She spun toward Raven and shouted, "They have a mage!"

The mage finished his sigil, the rest of his formation kneeling down at the last moment. A pulse pushed out from the center, flinging those nearest back, knocking those farther out to the floor. The veil of dust was blown aside, making the combatants clearer. Maupin bellowed an order to retreat, his and Carbolen's men beginning to fall back.

Raven dragged Lane toward the back of the warehouse. "There's only one door and it's small. It's going to take us forever to get everyone clear."

Lane looked at the crush of people scrambling to get through the opening, then back at Maupin and his men struggling to hold the guardsmen as they retreated.

She spun, jaw clenched, and began a sigil, walking clear of the Brovettans and Raven, toward the back of the warehouse. "Time to experiment," she muttered, then finished the sigil.

An entire section of the back wall blew outwards with a thunderous clap of sound, far louder and more intense than she'd expected. Ignoring the new ringing in her ears, she turned toward Raven, who stood dumbfounded. "Get them out!" she shouted. "I'll get Maupin and the others."

She didn't wait for a response, merely faced the front of the warehouse again. The guardsmen had surged deep into the building, the tullers and gang members barely keeping them at bay. But the unexpected explosion had given everyone pause. In the moment of hesitation, Lane roared, "Maupin, get everyone back here now!"

She raised her hand, began to walk forward, focusing on the cluster of guards around the mage. The fifth year—Candor? was that his name?—stood rigid, eyes wide in shock, mouth agape. She ended the sigil with a hard gesture, the same pulse she'd used to break open the back of warehouse now focused on the group of guardsmen surrounding the mage. It hit them full force, shoving them so hard they slammed up against what remained of the warehouse wall. The mage was thrown out the tattered opening into the street beyond.

"Still too strong," she murmured under her breath, already on a new sigil. Then louder, "Maupin! Move!"

Startled out of paralysis, Maupin shouted out orders, abandoning any pretense of resistance and charging with the tullers and gang members toward the hole Lane had made in the back of the warehouse. Maupin headed toward her with a small group, the tullers falling into a protective wall to either side.

"What are you doing?" he asked from her right, one hand holding his side.

"I'm going to keep them from following us."

The men Maupin had been fighting had held back, uncertain what was happening, but now they began to take tentative steps toward them. Lane used another pulse, more measured, to shove them back toward the main entrance, knocking many of them off their feet, then sent a half-circle of fire in their wake. She felt more comfortable with the fire, since she'd practiced that on her own in the tower after being kicked out of the Lyceum. But this wasn't a fireball shot straight forward. She varied the direction, intensity, and shape to create an arched wall that crept slowly outwards. Then she followed it up with a variation on another sigil she and Devon had played with during their own illicit practice sessions.

A wavering wall of blue light began to shimmer into existence, cutting the front portion of the warehouse off from the back at a slight angle.

She turned. "We need to get the Brovettans out before it fades. Or before they realize it doesn't do anything except block their view."

"Right." He ordered two of the tullers to stay with her, then ran with the rest toward the back of the warehouse. Lane followed at a trot with her escort.

Brovettans were being herded through the opening and the door, but not as fast as Lane would have expected. "What's happening?" she asked as she ran up to the back of the desperate crowd.

"They were waiting for us," a Brovettan woman said. She spoke deferentially, her eyes darting towards the blue wall behind them. "A small group, because they thought we'd only be able to get through the one door."

Ahead, Maupin had shoved his way forward with a few others. He'd almost reached the opening.

Lane glanced back, then toward the side wall. She stepped up to it, drew the base sigil, then carefully repeated what she'd done before, but with what she hoped was on a smaller scale.

The wall blew outwards, a few splinters of wood flying up into her face in a backdraft. One arm raised, she stepped into the street beyond and saw the Brovettans who'd already made it through, along with Raven, Devon, and Dalton, attacking a squad of maybe twenty guardsmen. Over half of them were already laid out flat on the street. Another group of Brovettans huddled to one side, mostly children, while others were helping the rest escape the warehouse.

Lane raised her hand, but one of her escort said, "I don't think that's necessary."

Raven, Devon, and the rest were already subduing the last of the guardsmen, a few of the Brovettans more harshly than needed.

Devon stumbled back from the fray, panting, holding his arm.

Lane stepped up and steadied him. "When did you get here?"

"Dalton and I saw the guardsmen getting ready to attack. We sent Nic and Picall with our Brovettans to the staging area below, then came to see how we could help. We saw this group watching the back of the warehouse right before they attacked." He coughed, caught his breath. "I see you decided to use magic."

"How—?"

He motioned upwards.

Lane looked, then gasped.

Her wall of shimmering blue light extended above the roof of the warehouse at least twenty feet and, from the angle, out into the street and maybe even the buildings on either side.

She winced. "I haven't been able to practice. And I felt it necessary—"

Devon waved her into silence. "You don't need to justify it to me. You certainly don't need my permission." His gaze shifted to something over her shoulder. "And now we don't have time."

Lane spun as Devon shouted a warning to Maupin. Guardsmen were rounding the corner of the building in formation. Lane saw hand movements from near the center.

"Get down!" she yelled, dropping to the street. A moment later, another pulse rushed over her, tugging at her hair and clothes. Behind, she heard grunts and cries as the wave hit Maupin's men and the Brovettans, but she didn't look back.

Devon crawled up next to her. "We'll never get everyone out of here with those guardsmen dogging us the whole way."

Lane pushed up from the cobbles. "I'll take care of them. Get everyone else to safety."

Devon hesitated, then nodded, sprinting toward Maupin, Raven, and the others. Lane stepped forward, already starting the base sigil, but she had to abandon it to drop to the ground again as another pulse—larger this time—was flung at them.

"Why are you only using pulses?" she muttered to herself. Candor was fifth year. He knew more powerful sigils than that. But she thrust the thought aside as she stood and began her sigil again.

Her first volley shoved the guardsmen back hard, Candor frantically trying to complete a countermeasure before it struck. He failed, thrown back with the others, their formation disintegrating. She followed it with another, before Candor could recover, then another, the guardsmen shouting curses as they struggled to their feet, only to be thrown down again. Somewhere during her attacks, Raven and Dalton appeared at her side, both with weapons ready. But once the guardsmen had been pushed far enough back, she changed the sigil, falling back on fire again.

A wall of flame ten feet high erupted from the ground between her and the guards.

"That should hold them—" she began.

The wall grew long enough it intersected the warehouse and building on the other side of the street. Both wooden structures caught instantly.

Lane swore.

"I'm guessing you didn't intend that to happen," Raven said.

Lane raised her hand, but Raven grabbed her shoulder and pulled her back.

"I have to stop it!"

"No, you don't. Let the guardsmen and their mage deal with it."

Lane allowed herself to be dragged back, her hand falling to her side. The entire side of the warehouse was engulfed, flames reaching toward the level above. Behind them, the blue wall she'd created was fading into wisps. Warning whistles from the guardsmen pierced the roar and crackle of the fire, shouts going up on all sides. Lane felt sick, the taste of bile in the back of her throat.

Then she turned and fled with Raven, Dalton, and the Brovettans.

* * *

Varenov was sitting at her desk in her study, a book detailing the articles and rules of the Founders' Pact before her, when Treant knocked on the door but did not enter. It was a subtle signal they'd worked out to warn her that whoever had come to see her may have prying eyes. She scanned her desk swiftly, tucked a few personal letters she'd sought solace in the night before beneath a stack of official correspondence, then said, "Come in."

Treant opened the door. "Councilor Havvelan and Proctor Favian to see you."

"Let them in."

Treant stepped aside, Havvelan entering first, Favian on his heels. Havvelan's expression was flat and serious, with a hint of an underlying smile; Favian's was furious. Both halted a few paces from her desk.

She leaned back in her seat. "That will be all, Treant, thank you."

Her assistant hesitated, then stepped outside, closing the door quietly behind him.

Varenov motioned to the seats arranged before her. "You may as well have a seat. I can tell this is important."

"As if you don't know what it's about," Favian began, but Havvelan quieted him with a look.

They both sat, Havvelan with his elbows on the arms of the chair, hands steepled before him. He began without preamble.

"Last night, we sent a contingent of guardsmen, along with a mage, to a warehouse in Level Ten where it had been reported the Brovettans who were eluding our sweep were being sent. The intent was to arrest them all, including whoever has been aiding their attempts to avoid the quarantine zones."

"Internment camps," Varenov interrupted. "We're in close company here, Havvelan. You may as well call them what they are."

He dipped his head. "Very well. Internment camps. Regardless of what they are called, the guardsmen met resistance."

"Are you surprised? I'm astounded there hasn't been more violence moving the Brovettans to their new quarters. Although I hear the death count among them is fairly high."

"This was a different kind of resistance," Havvelan said.

"What do you mean?"

"Our mage ran up against your daughter," Favian snapped. "She practically burned down Level Ten!"

A surge of hope and pride welled up in Varenov's chest, which she quickly quashed. "My daughter? Are you certain? It wasn't one of Terrial's mages we missed after the Warding dropped?"

"It was your daughter," Favian said. "My mage recognized her. She's helping the Brovettans in this city, Varenov. And she's apparently learned some new tricks."

Varenov tapped her fingers on her desk. "And you've come to me because...?"

"We want to know where she is!"

Havvelan raised a hand and Favian drew back with a grumble. "We wanted to know if you had anything to do with it, since you've been so... vocal with your dissent about how we're dealing with the Brovettans during Council. But it seems clear to me that you are not involved. However, perhaps you know where your daughter may be hiding? You, after all, know her better than anyone else."

Varenov stood. "It should be clear to everyone by now that I have never had control of my daughter, nor have I ever been able to predict her actions. She attended the Lyceum against my wishes. According to her personal guards, she practiced as a mage even after being expelled, here, in our quarters. And then she escaped the Council's custody after bringing down the Warding. I've tried my entire life to protect her, but she refuses to be protected."

"Forgive me, Councilor," Havvelan said, "but it almost sounds as if you're proud of her."

Varenov placed her palms flat on the desk and leaned into them. "I have no idea where my daughter has taken refuge in this city. Now get out."

Favian shot a glance at Havvelan, but the Councilor merely smiled and stood. Both meandered to the door, but Havvelan paused at the entrance and turned back.

"You've missed a few Council meetings, Varenov. I thought you should know that the most recent attack in Brovetto went well. The insurgents' main base of operations has been destroyed. Prefect Arctus and the army should be returning to Iandolo shortly. He even managed to capture a few rebel prisoners."

Then he slid out.

Varenov held herself steady, then collapsed back into her chair. Treant entered a short time later, hesitating when he saw her tears. She didn't bother wiping them away, motioning him inside instead.

"Are they gone?"

"Yes."

Varenov's shoulders sagged as tension bled out of her. Treant moved to the table against one wall and poured out two drinks from the tray of alcohol there, setting one down in front of her before retreating to a chair.

"What did they say?" he asked, sipping at what looked like bourbon.

"That my daughter is helping the Brovettans who are evading the quarantine." She picked up her glass and caught Treant's gaze. "And that Prefect Arctus has crushed the resistance in Brovetto. He should be returning shortly. With prisoners." She swirled the bourbon, then tossed it back, savoring the burn as it slid down her throat.

Treant had stilled, absorbing the news. After a moment, he rose and retrieved the glass decanter of bourbon and poured her another, setting the decanter on the desk. Varenov wiped away fresh tears.

"What about John?" he asked carefully.

Varenov gave a half laugh, half sob. "I've heard nothing since these letters from before the first of the Brovettan attacks nearly a year ago." She pulled the letters out from where they'd been hidden, leafed through them. "I've read them ragged, memorized them. There's no hint as to why John has fallen silent."

"We've gone over this before," Treant said carefully. "Terrial and her mages broke away from John's group, taking a significant portion of the rebels with them, and allied themselves with the nominal government in Brovetto. Their attacks on Iandolo and the subsequent responses from Iandolo and the army must have forced John and the other rebels to lay low. He likely hasn't had a chance to send word to you."

"I know, I know. It's all very logical, makes perfect sense. But it doesn't help." She tossed the letters to the desk and placed her head in her hands. "Do you think he's—?"

"I don't know. *I don't know!* That's what's so tortuous about the entire situation." She sighed and reached for the second glass. "When John and I disagreed all those years ago and I returned to Iandolo to fight the Council in my own way, from within, I knew it would be difficult. But I never expected...this."

"We were making progress—significant progress. Until Terrial's attacks."

"Were we?" Varenov glanced down at the book open on her desk. "I've been doing a little reading. The Crystal Cities and the Council aren't supposed to be like this. It's not how they were initially founded. The power was shared. Each city had their own representative, one of their own citizens, not someone like me—an outsider put in place as a proxy. Each city was equal. No one city had any additional powers, any additional weight.

"But look at us now. Iandolo has become the center of all power. And based on what I've read, the degradation of the other cities' power base has been happening for decades. Councilors have been slowly replaced by those whose true allegiance lies with Iandolo, not the city they supposedly represent. When I was made Councilor for Luminesque, I think whoever has been orchestrating all of this thought I would be malleable, that I would side with Iandolo, with the majority."

"Who do you think is behind it?"

"I've been trying to figure that out."

"Havvelan?"

Varenov ran a finger around the lip of her glass. "I think Havvelan *wants* us to think he's behind it. But he's not."

"Secora? Petrov? Gabrella?"

"Why do you think it's one of the Councilors? And why those three? Why not Santigo or Iriarte?"

"It would have to be one of the Councilors, wouldn't it? To manipulate everyone into place? And it can't be Santigo. He's mostly blocked the recent attempts at power. It could be Iriarte, I suppose, but he doesn't strike me as being that canny."

Varenov snorted. "He's not. No, I agree, it must be Secora, Petrov, or Gabrella. Havvelan is merely a...decoy."

They sat in silence while Varenov mulled over the three possibilities. Then Treant said quietly, "Do you think John is one of Arctus' prisoners?"

Something deep inside Varenov's chest shuddered. "I hope not. If he was there, I hope he was killed. Imagine what they would do if they captured the leader of the rebellion after all these years."

Treant shifted forward. "And what do you want to do about your daughter?"

"She's going to take after her father, isn't she?" Varenov smiled, a strange mix of pride and sadness. She'd tried so hard to protect her, to keep her safe. Her only connection to John here in Iandolo and she'd somehow managed to drive her away. "We'll do nothing. Havvelan's visit today was a warning. They'll be watching me closely now. In fact, I think we should make a point of being seen—in the Council, in the tower, at the market. Make it clear we have no association with her and whoever she's working with."

Treant rose and made to retrieve the decanter, but Varenov stopped him. "Leave it."

He made for the door, but before he was halfway there, Varenov said, "Start researching the history of the other Councilors, Treant. Quietly. Find out when and how they each came to power."

Then he left.

Varenov sat in silence, hand drifting from the book to the worn letters...

And finally to the decanter of bourbon.

Chapter Nine

The sublevels had changed.

By the time Lane and the rest made it down in the elevator—the rest of Maupin and his crew along with the remaining Brovettans from the warehouse going first—she was exhausted. When the elevator doors opened, a group of tullers met them, weapons bared, lanterns held high, only relaxing when Raven stepped forward. A contingent broke off to lead them to a section barricaded off from the skrill, guards posted outside. Lane noticed gang members and Brovettans mixed in with the tullers on watch. Only the tullers carried the spears used to bring down the skrill though.

Inside, Brovettans were huddled around fire pits made out of loose stone. Pallets were strewn across the stone floor, some with blankets tented over them. Children ran among those gathered, men smoked pipes, men and women both were cooking or sewing or playing games of cards or dice or tiles. It felt like the warehouse, except above there was an overall atmosphere of despair. Here, there was conversation and laughter, even if subdued. The scent of roasted meat and grilled onions filled the enclosed space. Everything felt transitory, but still more settled than on Level Ten. Lane recognized some of the Brovettans as ones she'd gathered up a few days ago. A few even waved or nodded in her direction.

Their escort took them to Maupin, the leader of the tullers situated in the back corner of the main hall. He was arguing with Leinn, one of Carbolen's captains, but as soon as he saw her he broke off and approached.

"What you did back there—" he shook his head "—we wouldn't have made it out without you."

"How many did we lose?" she asked.

"As far as we can tell, only eleven—three tullers, five from the gangs, and three Brovettans."

"How did they know where to find us?" Leinn asked, angry.

"Considering how many runs we've been doing to pick up Brovettans—" Raven began.

But Leinn cut her off. "I didn't ask you, traitor."

Lane hadn't seen any overt hatred of Raven from the gang members they'd been working with on their runs after that first incident, although Raven had been careful to work mostly with tullers and their own crew, but obviously some of Carbolen's captains still held a grudge. Leinn's glare could have split stone.

Maupin glanced between the two, then said, "I assume some of the guardsmen followed one of our teams there. It's the easiest explanation. But it doesn't matter. The warehouse is compromised. I assume the theater is as well. I have some tullers watching it now. If they deem it safe, they'll retrieve our gear and bring it back here. Right now, I'm more focused on getting these Brovettans out of here and to the tull. If they found the warehouse, they may know we're in the sublevels as well."

"We've seen no one suspicious anywhere near the elevator to this level. The gangs have been watching. Besides, the sublevels are far easier to defend than that warehouse."

"I'd rather be cautious."

"What about the others?" Lane asked.

Both Leinn and Maupin turned toward her.

"What others?" the tuller leader asked.

"The other Brovettans. The ones already in the quarantine zones."

"What about them?"

Lane barely tamped down her frustration, knowing part of it came from exhaustion. "How are we going to get them out?"

The entire group was silent. Maupin looked surprised and confused; Leinn exasperated.

Maupin stepped toward her. "Lane—"

"You've seen what they've done to people while escorting them to the zones. Do you think it's going to be any better for them once they're inside? We can't abandon them there."

"Lane," Maupin repeated, his hand falling onto her shoulder. She tried to wrench free, but his grip only tightened. "Lane, listen to me. Let us deal with the Brovettans we already have, get them safely out of Iandolo. Then we can talk about the others."

Lane tensed up, then sagged and nodded.

Maupin released her, shot a glance toward Raven. "We're all tired. Let's get some sleep and we can deal with all of this after."

He turned to Leinn, the two bending their heads together in low conversation, Leinn shooting a look towards her. Lane bristled, but then Raven stepped in front of her.

"I didn't think you were serious," she said, steering Lane toward a pile of pallets and blankets set aside for whoever needed them. Devon and Dalton were already rummaging through them. Nic and Picall stood off to one side with lanterns; they'd obviously seen them arrive. "Back at the warehouse. I thought it was a whim, brought on by fatigue and what we witnessed on the run."

"It might have been then, but not now."

Raven handed her two blankets, gathered a few for herself, then they followed the others into one of the side chambers, smaller than the first, probably used for storage when this was an active mine. The floor had already been cleared of stone debris fallen from the ceiling and a few Brovettan families were scattered through the room. Nic and Picall led them toward a vacant section near the far wall.

"Maupin didn't intend to go after the ones already in the camps, did he?"

"No, I don't think so. He was focused on getting out his own people first, those that helped smuggle Brovettans in, and then whoever else we could manage before they found us or it became too dangerous. He isn't a rebel. The tullers aren't fighters. They're smugglers. What you're talking about—" She sighed. "Lane, there are thousands of Brovettans in those camps. We barely managed to smuggle out a couple hundred in a week."

Lane lay down on the stone floor, brushed some grit aside, then pulled one blanket up over her. The other was wadded up as a pillow for her head. "Those are Maupin's excuses. You've already talked to him about this, haven't you?"

Raven chuckled. "I forget that you're a Councilor's daughter. Yes, I've already brought it up. He doesn't feel it's worth the risk. He doesn't want to expose the tull. It's been exposed enough already."

"And what about you? What do you think?"

The ex-Regular stared at her from where she'd settled. "I think Maupin is right, we should talk about this after some sleep." She rolled over, so her back was to Lane.

Lane sank onto her back, staring up at the craggy ceiling, shadows shifting from the lantern flames. Her entire body ached—from the day's run, from the fight at the warehouse and the long trek down to the sublevels—but her blood sang and her skin prickled in agitation. It felt as if her magic were flowing through her, as if she'd released it somehow, even though she knew she couldn't actively use it down here in the mine.

She didn't think she'd be getting much sleep.

When someone nudged her shoulder, she nearly leapt out of her skin. But it was only Dalton.

"Whatever it is you want to do," he said, his voice barely audible, his face a pale shadow, "Devon and I will help you."

"Count me in as well," Nic said from where he lay.

Raven growled. "You people will be the death of me. Now shut up. I'm dead over here."

Lane hadn't realized they'd all been listening in, but some of the agitation eased. She yawned. She didn't know what they could do, but they'd figure it out.

* * *

"If we're going to do anything," Dalton said, "we first need to find a way in."

Lane stood with Dalton, Devon, Raven, Nic, and Picall in an alley across the street from the internment camp on Level Sixteen. Barricades twelve feet high had been erected across the end of the street, forming a tunnel between the abandoned buildings on either side. Broken windows looked down from above, lanterns lit along the entire stretch so there were no shadows. Guards waited at the far end, surrounding a door barred on the outside.

"If you needed any sign that these are prisons more than they are shelters," Devon said, "that's it. Bars on the outside? And there are only six guards."

"Look again." Raven nodded toward the roofline, where a pair of guards circled, on patrol. "Also, if you watch certain windows carefully, you'll see movement. They have guards inside the buildings."

Dalton nodded. "The street is a trap. Anyone who tries to approach probably has twenty different pairs of eyes on them, along with a dozen crossbow bolts. If they're following the same strategies as we were taught at the college, they'll have an entire squad on the other side of the barricade, with the barracks close by."

"They might even have mages with them," Lane said. "After the warehouse, I wouldn't be surprised."

All of them shifted restlessly.

"Let's circle the zone, see what we're dealing with," Dalton said eventually.

They split into two groups, each circling the compound in opposite directions. Lane, Nic, and Picall took the left, staying back from the zone by at least a street, approaching cautiously along alleys and narrows. Each street that led into the quarantine was set up similar to the first. All of the buildings along the boundary were vacant. Level Sixteen was a lower level, but it still had residents, even this close to the hub. Lane assumed the city patrol had evicted anyone they found in those buildings on the border of the zone, and probably for those a block outside of that. The three of them didn't run into anyone on their route, although there was shadowy movement in the buildings beyond, enough they kept weapons visible to deter anyone from approaching. Lucent lights flickered overhead at odd intervals here, most of it dark. When necessary, Lane brought out the rose lantern Devon had created and flicked it on. They only saw the mellow light of a regular lantern a couple times, usually emerging from the cracks around shuttered windows or through splits in the decaying walls.

They had almost traversed halfway around the compound when Picall halted and said, "What about the roof? We should check out what it looks like from the roof." She pointed up.

Both Lane and Nic glanced up. They were outside an apartment, the once ornamental stonework over windows and doors now cracked and broken.

"It couldn't hurt," Nic said. He approached the boarded-up door, yanking a few of the planks off before kneeling and dealing with the lock. The door swung open a moment later and he slipped through.

Within a few breaths, he was back, motioning them through the narrow hole.

The interior reminded Lane forcibly of the apartment she and Devon had used to practice the mage forms, before Devon had submitted his questions and they'd both been expelled from the Lyceum. The foyer was a shambles, with hints of what it had once been. Not as refined or elegant as the one they'd used, but obviously once a grand building. They ascended the stairs, glancing inside vacant doorways into the tattered rooms inside, glimpsing torn rugs, ragged holes in floors and walls, and jagged splinters of lucent. A few had decaying furniture and the signs of recent inhabitants.

When they emerged onto the roof, Picall motioned them into a crouch and they approached the edge, peering over the lip toward the quarantine zone across the street. This building was slightly higher than those that formed the boundary of the zone, but not enough for them to see into the streets of the camp beyond.

They could see the guards placed along the roofline in both directions. The majority were on the edge overlooking the zone, keeping an eye on the camp below, armed with crossbows. Occasionally, a pair would break off and do a circuit along the perimeter facing the rest of the Iandolo, but it was obvious their focus was on the Brovettan side.

While they watched, one of the guards brought his crossbow up and shouted, "Back off! You know you're not supposed to be on the outer edge. Go back to where you belong." They didn't hear a response, but he waited, crossbow tracking whoever it was on the street below. When he finally relaxed, crossbow lowering, he spat over the side and mumbled something indistinguishable to his partner. Another said something snide, based on the laughter it caused. They were all young.

Nic pulled back behind the shelter of the roof edge. "Devon's right, it's a prison."

"We knew that already," Lane said. "How are we going to get them out?"

Picall, still watching over the lip, said, "Use your magic and burn the entire barricade block to the ground."

Lane smiled, but shook her head. "That wouldn't solve anything. We'd probably kill more Brovettans than we'd save. We need to sneak them out."

Nic got an odd look on his face. "Let's go find the others, see what they found."

They descended and within another two blocks, spotted Raven loitering in a doorway of one of the buffer buildings. She slipped inside as soon as she saw them. They found Devon, Dalton, and Raven inside, in a room that had once been a dining room based on the torn wallpaper and mock fireplace. A gaping hole cratered the ceiling where the chandelier had been and the warped wooden floor was littered with plaster chunks and a heavy layer of dust.

"What did you find?" Lane asked as soon as she entered, stepping carefully. Some of the boards sagged beneath her weight.

"More or less the same as what we saw at that first street," Devon said. "There's a wider street about a third of the way around our side that they appear to be using as a supply gate, but it's heavily guarded."

"We took a look at the zone from the rooftop. Picall's suggestion." The tuller waved the contribution aside. "They've got more men watching the inside than out. Even if we do get in, we're going to have to be careful we aren't seen."

Devon frowned. "Raven infiltrated one of the block buildings. Tell them."

Raven shrugged. "As I said, there are guards stationed inside, watching the streets through the windows. They're in nearly every building."

"How can they have so many when they're stretch so thin?" Lane asked.

"They're thugs," Dalton said. "New recruits, not guardsmen. They're pulling them out of the new War colleges only partially trained."

"Even so," Raven said, "their boundary is secure. I could get in—alone—but there's no way I could get a group of Brovettans out without us being seen."

"What about…" Nic began, but faded out, brow pinched in thought.

"What?" Lane and Devon asked together, looking at each other in startlement. Lane smiled. It reminded her of when they'd been linked, acting in concert, Devon providing the sigils, her the magic.

Nic looked at them both. "Something Lane said. You're all thinking like War students. You need to think of it like a job. We're trying to *steal* the Brovettans. How would we do that?"

Devon and Raven shared a look.

"Come in from above or below," Raven said.

"Is that possible?" Devon asked.

Raven stepped a few paces away, deep in thought. When Nic started to speak, she cut him off with a sharp hand gesture.

Then she turned back. "We'd have to rappel down from Level Seventeen. Carbolen's domain."

"But the internment camp isn't below his lair."

"No, but it's close enough."

"We couldn't be near the border of the zone. The guards on the roof would see us. It would have to be done toward the center."

"And then what?" Lane asked. "We rappel the Brovettans back up? I don't see many of them being able to do that, let along do it silently. That would get us in, but we'd need another way to get people out."

"She's right," Dalton said. "We'll have to get them out from below. What's on Level Fifteen, directly beneath the zone?"

Raven began moving. "Let's find out."

* * *

An hour later, they stood at an intersection on Level Fifteen looking up at the ceiling sixty feet overhead. A few people walked on the streets, keeping to the edges, moving a little faster when they saw them. Most gave them a wide berth. A few halted and either retreated or slid into the next available alley or alcove, disappearing from sight. There were no guardsmen here, not even random patrols, like there would be farther out from the hub.

Lane watched it all uneasily, even though she'd grown used to the lower levels to some extent over the last few weeks, until Raven said, "There," and pointed.

A block away, but still beneath the quarantine zone as best they could guess, was a building that reached all the way to the ceiling.

"Let's check it out," Devon said.

They approached from the outer edge, the building farther hubward. Dalton and Devon led, Raven behind, but they encountered no one. The building looked abandoned.

"Another warehouse," Nic said, gazing up at the shattered windows and hollowed out door. "Like the one Went took us to."

He shared a glance with Devon, who shook his head. Lane wondered what that was all about, but didn't ask.

Dalton entered first, then waved them inside. The interior was nearly vacant, a massive, empty chamber. She'd expected four or five floors, but it was evident there had only been two. Most of the floor of the second had collapsed inwards. Chains dangled down from above, some with hooks, their source hidden in the shadows. Water dripped down as well. Hulking pieces of machinery took up most of the lower floor, covered in the debris. As they moved deeper into the building, toward what looked like a central support, Lane noticed most of the machines were long rusted out. Spaces where lucent had once powered the devices were vacant, picked clean. A few more industrious people had attempted to rip the machines apart, metal scattered across the floor.

Rounding the last machine, they found it wasn't a support at all, but a set of stairs zigzagging up into the darkness and two massive factory elevators, obviously intended to haul heavy equipment and materials.

Dalton stepped out from the open entrance to the first one. "It doesn't work."

"What about the other one?" Lane asked. "This would be perfect, especially if it goes all the way up to Level Sixteen."

Devon checked it out, Lane a step behind him, but she knew the answer before they'd even entered. The lucent button on the outside had been ripped out, along with the long bar of lucent on the inside.

Lane swallowed her disappointment.

"Looks like it might go all the way up to Level Sixteen after all," Nic said. He stood behind them, looking up the elevator shaft. If there'd been a ceiling to the car, it had long fallen in or been ripped away. Only a lattice of supports remained, with cables snaking up into the darkness.

"Let's find out," Devon said.

They attempted the stairs, but entire sections were missing, too large to jump across, the supports too corroded to risk jury-rigging something in its place. Picall made it up the highest, but the structure was shaking so much Lane's heart was in her throat until Nic convinced Picall to come back down.

Then Raven called out, "Over here. There's another set of stairs."

They followed her voice to the far wall, where there had once been an enclosed office with stairs against the wall, not as rusted out as the first. They ascended, grit from the railings flecking Lane's hand. The second floor was stable only near the walls, any place between supports too weak to hold anyone or already caved in. They circled around to the section nearest the elevators and raised the lanterns toward the ceiling.

"It definitely goes up to the next level," Dalton said, "but I don't see any way up there."

"It doesn't matter," Nic said. "The elevators don't work. Are you going to have the Brovettans rappel down the elevator shaft? We already said that wasn't viable from above. It's not viable from below either."

"We could create some kind of platform, lower it down with people on it," Lane said, trying to suppress the desperation in her voice. "At least coming down the people won't be exposed. They'll be inside a building, both above and here. The guardsmen wouldn't see them."

"How?" Devon asked. "With a winch of some kind? I don't know where we'd find one, let alone how we'd install it once we had it."

"We'd lower it and ourselves down from Level Seventeen," Raven said. "Rig it up and get ourselves out by using it to get down to Level Fifteen."

Devon looked skeptical. "How long would it take to rig it up? Would it even be possible?" He stared out at the elevator shaft. "The elevators would have been perfect."

Lane grabbed his arm. "The elevators—they're lucent-run."

"They were, you mean."

She shook him, eyes wide, heart thundering in her chest. "What about the theater…the vines and flowers. Can you fix it?"

She saw comprehension dawn in his eyes. Then he was headed toward the stairs, Lane on his heels, the rest trailing behind.

"Can he fix what?" Nic asked as they ran toward the elevators. "What vines and flowers?"

No one answered. Lane piled into the elevator behind Devon, leaned over his shoulder as he reached inside the vacant slot where the lucent bar that controlled movement up and down had been.

He must have found some lucent, for his face went slack, as it had when he'd been focused on the vines of lucent in the theater. Lane watched, felt the others standing behind her, Nic agitated and pacing.

Then Devon returned, pulling his hand free. "There's lucent all the way up to Level Sixteen, but the power source up there is missing, like the connections down here. I repaired what I could from here, but if we want to get it running, we're going to need some lucent to replace what's missing, both here and above."

"What do you mean, you repaired it?" Nic asked, exasperated.

"Devon discovered he can fix lucent," Dalton said. "That's why the vines and flowers in the balcony at the theater light up now."

Nic gaped. Picall looked confused, as if she didn't understand the significance.

Raven had stepped forward. "Is that true?" she demanded.

"Is what true?" a new, deep voice said.

Lane started, but Raven, Picall, and Dalton turned, weapons drawn, all three fanning out instinctively. Nic stepped in front of Lane and Devon, knife ready.

Carbolen stood ten paces away, arm's crossed, near one of the broken machines. Four gang members stood behind him, two obviously senior, the other two younger. Lane suspected there were at least two others on their flanks, probably four.

"Hello, Raven," he said, focusing on the ex-Regular. "I'd heard you were around."

"I'd intended to be long gone by now," Raven said.

"That would have been wise." His gaze flicked to Devon, Lane, and Nic. "All of my former members are here, it seems. I could clean house right now, restore the faith and fear in my gang that no one leaves alive."

The four behind him bristled and edged forward.

Lane shoved past Nic, stepping up near Raven, hand raised. "Let's see you try."

Carbolen stared at her crooked fingers, his gang members shifting nervously. Then he met Lane's gaze. "I heard about what you did at Maupin's warehouse. But you can relax. If I'd wanted you dead—any of you—I would have sent Regulars after you." He looked up and frowned. "Now, what are you doing here?"

When no one answered, he began to pace around, not following a particular path. Lane and the others shifted with him, their small group tightening up. No one lowered their weapons. Lane caught movement in the shadows to either side, shared a look with Dalton and Nic, who nodded; Raven was too focused on Carbolen to notice.

Then Carbolen halted, abruptly, gaze dropping to Lane. "You're trying to save the rest of the Brovettans."

"What of it?" Lane asked.

Carbolen looked mildly impressed. "I thought Maupin only intended to save his own network. Those that weren't hauled off to the quarantine zones immediately, anyway."

"He saved more than that," Raven said defensively.

Carbolen's eyes narrowed, then he smiled. "That's where you disappeared to, isn't it?" He glanced over them all. "You went with Maupin." He stepped toward Raven. His smile fled and his voice hardened. "And you. You went *with* Maupin, didn't you? Is that what this little rebellion of yours is about?" He stepped even closer. Close enough he could lean forward and whisper angrily, "You're mine, Raven. I made you. I can unmake you."

Raven didn't flinch. "I don't belong to anyone. And I made myself. You merely gave me the opportunity to learn."

Lane realized Raven had a dagger tip pressed into Carbolen's side, ready to gut him, although he hadn't reacted to the blade at all.

"We'll see."

Carbolen stepped back, careful to turn away from the blade. Lane doubted anyone else but herself and Carbolen even knew Raven had had it to bear.

"What's your plan?" Carbolen asked.

Dalton shifted, then said, "Find a way up and then siphon as many of them out as we can."

"And then what?"

"I haven't spoken to Maupin yet," Raven said, "but we thought he'd continue to smuggle them out through the tull."

Carbolen nodded, then pointed upwards. "This is only one of the zones. What about the others?"

"We haven't taken a look at the others yet," Lane said.

"I'll have my gang check out the other zones, see what we can find."

"Why do you care?" Raven cut in. "Why did you help Maupin with the other Brovettans? Why are you offering to help us now?"

"Oh, I'm not helping *you*. I'm doing everything I can to fuck with the Council. They started the war with Luminesque. I suspect they're behind the Brovettan attacks months ago—the mages and the Warding. I don't think it went as planned and now they're using the fear and uneasiness to seize even more control over the city."

"My mother would never do such a thing," Lane protested.

He switched his gaze to her. "No. I don't think she's part of it. Not anymore. She's been shut out."

Lane felt a twinge of shock in her chest. She hadn't thought of her mother much since their escape from the Lyceum. "What do you mean?"

"From what I've heard, she's practically the only voice of dissent on the Council now. The others simply overrule her." He waved a hand dismissively. "Back to the zones. This elevator is broken. Has been for decades. How do you intend to get in?"

Dalton stepped forward. "Leave that to us. If we get them out, can you and the gangs get them safely down to Maupin?"

He considered them all with a frown, although he lingered on Devon and Lane. Then he stared a long moment at the defunct elevator before nodding. "I can. And I will." He motioned to his men and turned to leave. "You realize this won't last, don't you?" he said, voice fading as they all bled into the shadows. "They'll notice those that go missing eventually. And then what are you going to do?"

They all waited silently until Raven signaled that she thought they were gone. Picall and Nic headed out into the warehouse to scout it out, moving in opposite directions.

"He's right, you know," Raven said.

"We'll worry about that later," Lane said, facing Devon. "Can you fix the elevator?"

"If I can find the lucent I need."

"Then go. Find it. I want to start getting the Brovettans out as soon as possible. I don't think leaving anyone in those camps for long is a good idea."

Chapter Ten

Devon scanned the outskirts of the market, Dalton a reassuring presence at his back. He'd tried to come alone, but Dalton had insisted.

"No one should be traveling alone," he'd said, "especially those from our group."

Even though Devon had protested, he was glad Dalton was here, though there didn't seem to be a significant number of guardsmen in the streets at Mid-level.

"Where are all the patrols?" he murmured, focusing on the flow of people around the stalls and tents that had been set up on the square. Iandolans in their usual garb, Bolnians from Radimansque, Kerpezians with colorful yet formal shirts and coats, even a few Wattian merchants in their more utilitarian farming clothes. But no Brovettans. A sickening sensation settled in Devon's gut. Yet the longer he looked, the more he realized those that were not Iandolan were on edge. Furtive glances were cast toward any sharp noise. And most stayed behind tables and carts, their wares set up as shields from the customers. Only a few appeared truly at ease.

Dalton pressed forward for a look. "I'd wager most have been stationed at the critical defenses of Iandolo—the waygates and spokes—and the rest guarding the internment camps." He rested a hand on Devon's back. "Where are we headed?"

Devon didn't answer, merely emerged from the edge of the cross street and headed on into the fray. He didn't bother looking to see if Dalton were keeping up.

Old instincts kicked in and he merged with the flow, picking up on the undertones of fear and uncertainty. At first glance, the market appeared the same as when he'd been here last, bustling and filled with the noise of commerce. But beneath that there was tension. The haggling had an edge, words and gestures sharper, vendors less patient. He slowed, to allow himself to listen to the bartering. Merchants weren't willing to negotiate as much. Customers had a desperate edge to their voices, most settling begrudgingly at the higher prices or turning away with stricken faces.

Devon shook his head and picked his pace back up, heading toward the southwestern edge. He skirted the fountain, noted that there were no children at play. Fewer food vendors as well, the scent of grilled meats less exotic and spicy, more mundane. The air was slick with the odor of fried onions.

He wound through the maze of paths beyond the fountain, searching now for Geral's tent. He heard the clanking of the tinker's metal pots and pans tied to the tent stakes first, followed the faint noises to a sparse section of tents, most with tent flaps drawn. He halted before stepping out into the area around Geral's space, caught Dalton before he could continue.

"Is this it?" Dalton asked, voice low.

Devon nodded. "The tent flap is shuttered."

"So he's not here?"

Devon glanced around. There were fewer tents in this area than there used to be, but he supposed that made sense. This was the edge of the square. And times were uncertain. Many of the merchants had probably left—either selling somewhere else in Iandolo or returning to their own city.

He stepped to the side of the tent, away from the flap, and said, "Geral?"

No response. He glanced at Dalton, who'd stayed back, then knelt, pulled the tent flap back, and looked in. "Geral?"

A hand latched onto his shirt and jerked him inside the tent. He landed on the rug thrown over the square's hard stone, flailed as a knee sank into his back. A blade nicked his throat.

"Don't move," Geral's voice growled from overhead.

"I wouldn't do anything rash if I were you," Dalton said a second later.

Geral cursed, but he didn't move. "I should have known you bastards would come in pairs."

"Geral," Devon gasped, voice barely audible, "it's Devon!"

"Devon?"

The pressure on his back released, the prick of the knife withdrawn. Devon rolled onto his back and gazed up into Geral's grizzled face, the tinker looking far more haggard than he had the last time Devon had seen him. Dalton stood to one side, his sword pointed to Geral's neck. Geral held up his hands, palms flat, although he still held his knife with one thumb.

He swallowed. "I…I didn't realize it was you."

Devon sat up, rolled his shoulders to ease the kink in his back. "It's all right, Dalton."

Dalton hesitated, then lowered his blade.

Geral sighed. "I thought you were a guard, here to take me to the quarantine zone."

"You're…Brovettan?" Dalton asked.

"My mother was, my father Iandolan. I don't know what the guardsmen know. I've been laying low here in my tent."

"Why not leave?"

"Where would I go? I've been here for nearly forty years."

Devon glanced around. Geral's tent was sparse. Where before there'd been piles of tins and pans and cups sorted into neat stacks by metal type, now there was a scattering of odd objects, all metal, but mixed in random heaps. All of the pillows that had littered the center of the tent for seating were gathered at one edge, forming a nest. The tent reeked of body odor and old food.

"I don't think you have to worry," Dalton said. "If the guards haven't come for you yet, they aren't after you. They must not know about your mother."

Geral's shoulders shook, face squeezed tight, as if he were about to weep. He brought a hand to his face. "I do take after my father."

Devon gave him a moment, then said, "I came for something I hope you have."

Geral composed himself, bustling around the tent, tossing some of the pillows to the floor for Devon and Dalton, another for himself, mumbling beneath his breath as he did so, berating himself. Then he settled down. Neither Devon or Dalton had moved.

"What is it you need?" He'd almost restored himself to the Geral Devon remembered, the fake innocent smile a little strained.

Devon drew a breath, then said, "Lucent."

Geral stared at him. "Lucent?"

"Do you have any?"

"Ha! Why not? Lucent." Geral stood and began to rummage through the pile of tins closest to his nest, metal rattling as it tumbled to the ground and rolled around. Geral gave a short cry of triumph and turned, holding up a stained burlap sack. He handed it off to Devon and sat again. "Haven't had cause to trade in lucent since…since the last time you were here. No one's interested. Not much there, I'm afraid. Most of it is dead or flawed and worth nothing. All of the good pieces got snatched up ages ago. Market isn't what it used to be."

Devon ignored his rambling, taking out pieces from the sack. Geral was right, they were worthless. He'd never have been able to trade them if the situation were reversed. Slivers of crystal barely the size of his finger, pebbles of green and purple threaded through with black, shattered pieces of rose petals, a leaf, a roughly cubic chunk of puke green the size of his fist.

He spread most of it out on the rug, Dalton kneeling down next to him.

"What are we looking for?" he asked.

"Something that looks like it will fit into the slots where the pieces are missing. Like this." He picked up an egg-shaped piece tinted a faint blue. When Dalton looked confused, he said, "A button."

Dalton nodded in understanding and began searching. Geral had fallen silent, watching them with furrowed brow. Devon took the puke green crystal, then a few smaller pieces.

Dalton plucked out a long piece a dirty yellow in color. "Slider?"

Devon nodded. He sifted through what was left, uncertain. He didn't know what he'd need on Level Sixteen, where the elevator ended. There may be missing pieces there as well. But they couldn't risk an infiltration to find out either. That would risk a rappel down and then back up, two additional chances at discovery. So he grabbed whatever pieces were of a decent size and set them aside.

"How much?" he asked.

Geral opened his mouth, but caught himself, then said, "All those pieces are dead, worthless." All of his fear and anxiety was gone, replaced by confusion.

"How much?" Devon repeated.

A flicker of Geral's old avaricious self returned and he scanned the pieces. "Twenty bright."

Devon barked out an amused laugh and was heartened to see Geral smile. "It isn't worth a tenth of that. You said yourself it was worthless."

"Worthless to me. Obviously not to you. Ten bright."

"Five. And you should count yourself lucky to get rid of all of this."

Geral waffled, greed vying with practicality, and finally relented. "Five then."

Devon handed over the bright and began placing the lucent pieces into his satchel. Then he stood, Dalton already at the tent flap.

"Why do I feel like I got the raw end of the deal here?" Geral asked.

Devon didn't answer. "Don't let the Iandolan guard control you, Geral."

"But—"

"Look around," Devon said. "You're destroying yourself out of fear. Don't let that happen. It almost happened to me."

Then he ducked outside, Dalton following. They stood for a moment, Devon frowning. "Something's changed."

"It's quiet," Dalton said. "I don't hear many people in the market."

They began to make their way back, the pathways eerily empty. Merchants stood behind their wares and a few customers drifted here and there, but otherwise the square was quiet. Not even the guardsmen were in evidence. Some of the tents had been closed up.

Then they heard a shouted roar, coming from the direction of the nearest spoke.

They glanced at each other, then headed in that direction at a jog.

Two blocks away, they ran into the back of an immense crowd, everyone jostling to get closer to the main thoroughfare ahead. Devon, the smaller of the two, began elbowing his way forward, Dalton falling behind. He heard the ex-soldier cursing, but kept moving forward.

Twenty minutes later, another roaring cheer swept through the crowd and Devon stumbled out onto the edge of the street, the spoke cordoned off by guardsmen on both sides. Marching toward the three towers at Iandolo's center was the Iandolan Army, rank after rank of them.

Devon drew back instinctively, but the crowd pressed too close. A moment later, he realized none of those in the cordon or the army were paying any attention to him.

Most of the soldiers looked exhausted, faces haggard, some with light wounds. The mages in particular appeared beaten. They were being kept in the center of the square formations, their battle armor less damaged than that of the soldiers, but clearly scarred in places. A few appeared burned. Devon watched for Quinn, knowing she would have wanted to be front and center, but didn't see her.

The formation ended and a line of horses clopped past, two Prefects on the outside, two master mages next, and then two soldiers carrying the staffs, one with the blue crystal at the top, the other one red.

Devon found himself staring at the crystals as they marched by. He remembered seeing them in the quad at the Lyceum when the sixth years were being called on to defend the waygate. They were being used as rallying points. He'd wondered about them then, but there had been too many other distractions at the time. But now…

They passed out of sight, replaced by another column of soldiers, no mages this time, followed by a line of Prefects on horseback with no master mages or crystal staffs.

Someone blundered into him from behind and he spun, hand reaching for his knife, but realized as the man stepped aside with an angry look that was Dalton. The ex-soldier swore beneath his breath and tried to retreat but, like Devon, was caught by the crowd.

"Don't do anything to catch their attention," Devon said, nodding toward the guardsmen in the cordon.

Dalton remained tense, pressed up against Devon from behind, but then he relaxed. "They don't look like they were with the army. All city guards, or the new recruits. I don't think they'll recognize me."

"And the soldiers are too exhausted," Devon said. But he was only half paying attention to them, watching instead the ranks filing past, scanning for mages…and for the crystals. The next six battalions were all soldiers, broken up by Prefects, but after that there was another battalion with mages.

Followed by a line of Prefects, master mages, and the crystal staff bearers.

"I think I know why the mages never have to worry about not being able to do magic when they're with the army," Devon said. He pointed toward the blue and red crystal staffs.

Dalton gaze followed his hand, but he shook his head. "I don't understand."

One of the guardsmen noticed him pointing as one of the lines of Prefects nudged their horses into a fancy strut. The crowd roared approval.

"Never mind. Not important right now. I need to talk to Lane." He let his hand drop and turned, pushing Dalton back into those gathered. Retreating proved nearly impossible, until they had managed to force their way back a block, causing ire and irritation the entire way. Devon might have had a few altercations, but Dalton's presence kept everyone civil.

When they broke clear, Dalton said, "This is going to make doing anything around the city harder. With the army back, the city guards will be taken off the waygates and repositioned, probably on the streets and the quarantine zones. They'll likely send the new recruits back to the War colleges. We'll have more experienced soldiers to deal with everywhere, and likely more of them."

"I don't see that stopping Lane, do you?"

Dalton didn't answer.

"Let's find the others. We need to see if this is going to work."

* * *

Devon swore as the rounded lucent he held slipped and dropped to the floor, rolling until Dalton stopped it with his foot. He handed it back and said, "*Is* this going to work?"

"I haven't had a chance to try yet."

He glanced toward Lane, who hovered behind them in the warehouse on Level Fifteen. Nic, Picall, and Raven were patrolling, Raven focused outside, keeping an eye out for Carbolen and the rest of the gang. No one wanted the gang leader to find out Devon could manipulate lucent. He already thought Devon was valuable; he didn't need additional incentive.

Turning back to the elevator, he slid the rounded lucent into the hole where the call button would have been and closed his eyes, sinking into the crystal.

The patterns inside the egg-shaped orb hadn't matched any of the lucent elevator buttons he'd stopped to investigate before coming to the warehouse, but based on those, he'd already altered the orb so they should. All he needed to do now was figure out how to attach it to the—

His fingers brushed the threads of lucent embedded inside the elevator's wall and he sucked in a breath, his fingers tingling. He heard Dalton asking what was wrong, but he shook his head and didn't answer. The orb wasn't positioned right. He twisted it around, until certain pathways lined up, the tingling in his fingers increasing.

He felt it when the orb locked in place, that tingling racing through his entire body. He held steady, then merged the two pieces of lucent, withdrawing his fingers as the orb adhered and pulled slightly back into the wall. It wasn't a perfect fit, but it would do.

"It isn't glowing," Lane said. She'd been pacing in the background, but had come forward when he gasped.

"But it's attached. It won't work—if it will work at all—until we repair the power source on Level Sixteen."

He moved inside the elevator, to the vacant slot for the control bar. He placed the dirty yellow piece Dalton had picked out into place. It was shorter than the original, but he didn't think that would matter. "This is going to take a little longer," he said, then slid into the lucent, tracing the paths. Most of these were dead, degraded, so he had to spend time realigning them. But like the outside button, the paths were simple, nothing as complicated as the lock boxes he used to pick. Not even as complicated as the elevator he'd rigged in the tower when he and Raven and the others went after Lane.

When he finished attaching the bar to the lucent inside, he sagged backwards, Dalton catching him. He blinked. After the tingling faded, he realized he felt drained. "How long was I working?"

"Almost an hour," Dalton said, letting him go once he felt steady. "You need to rest."

"I'm fine. Let me tackle the other elevator."

At the second, he had to pick through what they'd bought from Geral to find pieces that would work, but now that he'd done it once, it took less time. He traced out the system to both elevators one more time, repairing anything that seemed out of place, then sat on the floor and leaned back against the elevator wall. Dalton handed him an apple and a water flask.

"I've done everything I can do down here," he said, after taking a drink and a bite. "The rest will have to be done above."

"Then we should get moving," Lane said. She stood near the door, glancing out occasionally.

"Not right now," Dalton said. When Lane appeared ready to protest, he added, "Look at him! He can barely hold the apple without trembling. He needs to rest."

"You said yourself that the army has returned," Lane argued, "that they're going to be reinforcing the waygates and spokes, redistributing the city guard, likely increasing the watch on the internment camps. We need to get this set up now, before it becomes impossible without being discovered!"

"It will take a few days for the army to get situated. It can wait until—"

"Dalton," Devon interrupted, even though he did feel drained. He hadn't spoken loudly or forcefully, but it cut Dalton short. He looked back in concern. "She's right. The sooner we get this done, the better." He lifted an arm so Dalton could help him stand.

Reluctantly, Dalton pulled him up, bringing him in close so he could murmur, "Don't overdo it."

"I won't." He pulled back and faced Lane. "Let's find Raven and the others."

Nic and Picall joined them as they made their way to the front of the warehouse. Devon slid to the side of the doorless entry and peered into the street. He saw no movement.

When he turned back, he jumped. Raven stood behind them, a grin tugging at the corners of her mouth.

"There's no one watching as far as I can tell," she said. Devon was heartened to see a couple of the others startle. "Carbolen's kept his distance."

"What about the arrangements on Level Seventeen?" Dalton asked. "Are you ready?"

"Everything's in place."

"Then let's go," Lane said.

Raven hesitated, glancing at Devon, making him wonder exactly how bad he looked, but then she slipped through them and onto the street.

They worked their way up to Level Seventeen, noticing as they did so that on the outer edges of Level Sixteen there appeared to be more guardsmen on the streets—not just in pairs or in threes, but entire squads moving purposefully down the main thoroughfares. Most were city patrol, but there were groups of soldiers. Some of the soldiers wore their battle-torn uniforms, as if they hadn't had time to change. People moved out of their way, stepping into cross-streets or shops, watching them pass.

Raven shunted them into an alley as a group of twenty marched by, close enough Devon could see the anger on their faces, some still sporting untended wounds.

"It will take a few days for them to get situated, huh?" Lane said.

Dalton shifted uneasily.

On Level Seventeen, they headed hubward, deep beneath Level Eighteen above. Raven led them to the remnants of a building, only two walls standing, the roof caved in, debris in a heaped pile on the other side of the gaping mouth of the door.

"What is this?" Nic said, as they all stood outside on the street.

Raven grinned and stepped through the door.

Devon and the others followed, edging around the debris pile along the wall. Above, pieces of the upper floors jutted out over them, wood splintered where it had finally given way. Devon was careful to keep to Raven's path, the tangle of broken floorboards, brick, and shattered glass shifting no matter where he stepped. Behind, Dalton grunted as he misplaced a foot and started a small avalanche.

Then, ahead, Raven vanished.

When Devon arrived, he found that the floor had given way beneath street level, a scree of debris leading down into a lower chamber. It reminded him forcibly of the chasm he'd fallen into at the tull. Supporting himself with one hand against the wall, he half-stepped, half-slid down to where Raven waited.

Once they were all present, she shoved a dagger into a gap in the metal at their backs and twisted.

A panel popped out with a shower of rust and paint flecks.

Devon stepped through into the pitch dark area behind, pulling his lucent lantern from his satchel. When he tapped it, it illuminated a cavernous space barely seven feet high, stretching out in a wide tunnel toward the hub. Four rucksacks and a lantern were waiting for them to one side in the thick dust, Raven grabbing one rucksack and tossing the others to Devon, Lane, and Dalton, who'd stepped into the tunnel as well.

Nic and Picall had stayed outside.

"You know what to do?" Raven asked them.

Nic nodded. "Keep watch here until you're safely gone, then return to the warehouse and wait."

Without waiting for a response, he and Picall yanked the metal panel back into place. That was followed by tapping as they secured it.

Lane coughed at the disturbed dust, edged closer to Devon and Dalton, and pulled out the rose lantern he'd given her. She shuddered. "This isn't like the lower levels. Or even the sublevels. I can touch the ceiling here."

"We're between levels," Raven said, already lighting a regular lantern for herself. She stood, holding it out in front of her. "It's going to get a lot tighter than this before we're done."

She didn't wait for a response. Devon followed her, Dalton and Lane behind, the tunnel narrowing once, then again, until Devon was brushing the sides with both shoulders. He glanced back once at Lane, saw her jaw clenched, shoulders hunched, but she didn't protest, eyes hardened in determination. Sweat sheened her face, the enclosed space warm.

The tunnel branched, then the ceiling dropped so they were forced to crawl on hands and knees. Then Raven slid out into a slightly larger square room, a junction for multiple tunnels. The ceiling was high enough they could stand hunched over, but Raven knelt on the floor, feeling around until her hand snagged on something on the floor. Devon noticed the dust here had already been disturbed; Raven had been here before. A handle popped up and she heaved a hatch upwards.

They all leaned over the opening. Rungs of a ladder led down the chute below, toward an opening that looked onto Level Sixteen, onto a roof approximately forty feet below.

Dalton sucked in a sharp breath and pulled back from the hatch, swallowing hard. "That's the internment camp below?" His voice was strangled.

"We're over one of the tallest buildings in the camp," Raven said. "Near the center. The closest guarded wall is four blocks hubward. There are a few lucent panels still operational nearby, but I hope to be visible for at most fifteen minutes." She pulled her rucksack open and retrieved a harness and a length of rope. "You'll each find a harness in your rucksack."

"I don't—" Lane began.

"Watch me. I'll check yours when you're done and show you how it works."

Devon pulled the tangle of straps from his rucksack and tried to mimic Raven as she put it on, the others doing the same. Dalton got it on the first try, Raven only making minor adjustments. With Devon and Lane, she had to unhook and rearrange, tightening straps until Devon winced. Then she showed them how to attach the harness to the rope and control their descent.

"Got it?" she asked, securing the rope to the top rung of the ladder inside the hatch. When no one answered, she said, "Dalton first. Then Lane, Devon, and I'll go last."

"Why me first?" Dalton asked.

"Because you can secure the roof once you're down there. And I don't trust you to follow us down if you're last."

He appeared about to protest, then simply muttered, "Right." Stepping up to the hole, he knelt, then sat and swung his legs into the opening. With trembling hands, he attached the harness lead to the rope, then descended into the opening, using the ladder at first.

Devon peered down after him as he hesitated at the bottom. Then he snagged the lead with one hand, the rope with the other, and let himself drop. The rope pulled taut, creaking, rust flaking off of the rung. His first few drops were jerky, but then his descent began to smooth out.

When he was almost at the roof below, Raven said, "Lane, you're next."

It took Lane longer to gather herself together, but she followed after Dalton, the ex-soldier waiting for her below.

"Now you," Raven said, giving him a small shove.

Devon sat and attached the harness, tugging it hard to make certain it was secure. Then he climbed down to the last rung. Taking a deep breath, he gripped the lead, the rope—

Then stepped off of the ladder. He fell five feet before he remembered to clench the grip on the harness to control the fall. He jerked to a halt as it caught the rope, straps biting deep into his crotch and chest, and swung for a minute, staring out over the level from the height of the ceiling. A lucent panel lit the streets and buildings below off to his right, dimmed for night, another straight ahead had a faint flicker. Most of them were dead. Lanterns lit the roofs of the buildings that formed the encampment's walls, blocked occasionally by sentinels on patrol. The streets below appeared empty, which was odd considering it should only be late evening.

A noise from Raven above reminded him to let go of the clamp and he dropped another five feet. By the time he'd reached twenty feet, he'd started to get the hang of it.

Someone shouted in alarm. He twisted, then swore.

A block distant, on a building two floors higher than the one they were rappelling toward, level with Devon, a guardsman pointed toward him. Two others lurched to their feet, one bringing a crossbow to bear.

Before he could fire, Devon released the clamp, dropping almost ten feet before allowing himself to stop the fall. The jerk started him swinging. The guards were shouting, Dalton and Lane gesturing to him ten feet below, but when he released the clamp again it dropped him only a few feet before catching. Dalton and Lane were grasping at his feet as he struggled with the clasp, but it was jammed. A crossbow bolt slammed into the rooftop a few feet away. He yanked on the harness lead, then began fumbling with the latches on the harness itself—

And suddenly the tension in the rope let go and he dropped, freefall, slamming into Dalton and Lane, all three of them thrown to the rooftop. The rope snaked down after them, coiling atop them.

Devon stared up at the ceiling overhead. "She cut it," he mumbled.

Then another crossbow bolt hit the roof and all three of them were scrambling toward the little hut that provided roof access. Devon grabbed an armful of the rope and dragged it with him. Dalton slammed through the door first, Lane a step behind, and then all three were pounding down the stairs of the apartment building toward the street. Tenants emerged from their apartments to look, some darting back inside immediately, others emerging and staring after them as they descended, Brovettan faces startled. A few shouted at them, Devon's heart pounding too loudly in his ears to comprehend them.

When they hit the foyer, Dalton halted, all three gasping.

Devon tossed down the tendrils of rope and began grappling with the clasps of his harness, the others doing the same.

"What happened?" Lane asked.

"There were guards on one of the nearby roofs," Devon answered.

"What are we going to do now?"

"We need to get out of the building," Dalton said. "They know we're here now. They'll be searching. We need to find a place to hunker down."

"What about the elevator?" Devon asked.

"We'll worry about that later."

Devon stepped out of the last loop of harness and tossed it aside, Dalton already looking out the door. Devon helped Lane with the last of her harness.

"No one on the street yet," Dalton said. "Let's move."

They darted out into the street, turning right, away from the nearby building with the guards. Dalton cut into the next cross-street. Warning whistles pierced the silence, shrill but from behind. Dalton wove a jagged path away from them, toward one of the boundary walls, until Lane snagged him from behind and drew them all to a halt.

"We can't go any further," she said. "Not in that direction. They've got a people-free zone in the street nearest the wall."

"Right." Dalton began scanning buildings. "This way."

Devon noticed lantern light blooming in some windows as they moved, faces peering down at them from above. Shutters were pulled, curtains drawn.

Whistles and shouts from the wall behind began to answer those on the streets ahead. Dalton tried a few doors, found them locked. He swore. The whistles drew closer, from all sides.

They drew up along another tenement. Dalton tried the door, shook his head. Lane stepped out in front of them, hand raised, fingers crooked. Dalton drew his sword, Devon his knife.

"Here!" someone shouted.

Devon spun toward a Brovettan woman motioning them toward a walkway between two buildings, not more than shoulder's width across. With no other choices, Devon grabbed Dalton and Lane and all three ran after the woman. She ducked into the narrow as soon as she saw them approaching. Twenty paces farther in, she knelt down next to an opening set into the building at street level. When Devon arrived, she gestured him to crawl inside.

He shoved his rucksack and satchel in front of him and slithered into the hole, going into about four feet into darkness before the ground dropped away beneath him. Hands caught him and lowered him to a floor, pulling him off to the side as he heard Lane, Dalton, and the Brovettan woman emerge behind him. Terse whispers passed back and forth and someone moved something large back into place, and then the soft glow of a lantern lit the room.

Six Brovettans stood around them in a sparsely furnished apartment—the woman who'd called to them, two other women, an older man, and two children. Devon guessed the boy was around eleven, the young girl nine. Three of the adults held knives or makeshift weapons.

"Who are you?" one of the women demanded, stepping protectively in front of the boy and girl. "Why are you here?"

"Hush," the woman who'd saved them said, pushing the other woman's knife down gently. "It's obvious they aren't guards." She glanced at Dalton. "At least I don't think so."

"No, we're not," Devon said. "We're here to get you out."

Chapter Eleven

"Ha!" the mother barked, her stance hardening. "And how do you propose to get us out? You're children."

Before Devon could answer, they heard doors slam open overhead and the tread of dozens of feet on the floorboards. Someone screamed and there were harsh voices—accusatory and demanding.

The woman who'd called to them in the street gestured at the mother, then motioned Devon and the others toward the large wardrobe they'd shoved against the wall to cover the opening to the narrow. She opened the door and pushed them inside against the clothes hung there. "Stay here. Don't make a sound."

Then she closed the doors.

Devon held his breath, felt Dalton breathing against his neck. Lane squirmed into a better position, against the far corner. Dalton shifted to accommodate her, his bulk pressing Devon up against the back wall. His face was smashed into clothing, a hanger digging into his cheek. He tried to edge to one side, the space stifling.

Through the door, he could hear muffled arguments, cut short when the door to the apartment burst open. One of the women screamed and someone began to sob.

"How dare you—" someone protested, but it was cut short with a slap, a body hitting the floor. The older man shouted as the heavy tread of boots spread out in the room beyond. There was a scuffle, the sounds of fists hitting flesh, another outcry and heavier sobbing, and then silence except for a ragged groan.

Another set of footsteps, then a terse voice. "We're searching for someone. Have you seen any others besides those in your building in the last hour?"

Slow movement. Then: "If you'd taken the time to notice, we have no windows here. And none of us have been outside the building since the evening market."

A measured footstep and there was a hitch in the breath of whoever was sobbing.

"You'd be wise to keep a…calmer tone with us."

"I'll take whatever tone I see fit. Now get out. Whoever you're looking for is clearly not here."

A weighted silence. Devon could feel Dalton's tension against his back, muscles flexing. His own hand was clenched into a fist. The tiny space was getting hot.

Then the guardsman said something too low to make out and there was the scuffle of feet leaving the apartment. After a pause, someone raced after them and closed the door hard.

The door to the wardrobe opened and all three of them stumbled out. The woman who'd pulled them from the street stood before them, a welt rising on her cheek, a trickle of blood coming from a cut near her eye. The older man lay on the floor, moaning. The mother knelt beside him and rolled him over, already searching for wounds, her two children huddled in a back corner on a bed. The other woman had her shoulder pressed to the apartment door, listening. The guardsmen were still searching the apartments around them, their movements punctuated by protests, screams, and the sounds of shattering furniture.

"Don't say a word," the woman said, moving to one side to help the mother with the older man. All three of them stood there while they checked him over, then moved him to a second bed. He gasped as they shifted his weight, hand clutching his side, then settled once they'd gotten him situated. The mother went to wet down a compress, fussing over the other woman's enflamed cheek, but she shushed her and told her to start cooking dinner. The mother called the two children over and they began chopping some vegetables, their mother taking the long knife she'd threatened them with and slicing into a hank of cold meat. She kept one eye on all three of them.

The woman who'd saved them glanced at the younger woman at the door, who gave a curt nod, then motioned to the table. "Have a seat. We need to talk."

Devon sat first, then Lane and Dalton. The woman dabbed at the cut with a wince, then placed both hands on the table. "Who are you?"

"We're here to get you out," Devon said.

"So you've said, and we'll get to that, but *who are you?*"

"Devon Alamort."

"Dalton Trent."

"Lane Illea." Lane leaned forward. "We were part of the group helping to get Brovettans out before they could be escorted to the camps."

"I heard about that," the woman said.

At the side table, the mother muttered, "Not that it helped us at all."

"Quiet, Alsa."

The older woman grumbled something under her breath, but she was ignored.

The woman considered them all, focusing on Lane. "Illea. Are you related—"

"I'm her daughter."

"And she couldn't stop this?" She waved a hand to take in…everything.

"I'm certain she tried."

The mother snorted.

The woman turned back to Devon. "My name is Cerelle. The woman guarding the door is my younger sister, Sadie. This is Alsa, her two children, Tim and Eva, and her father."

Devon nodded in acknowledgment. "Thank you for pulling us off the street." Cerelle said nothing, so he added, "Is this what it's like here? Guards storming into your rooms, demanding answers."

"That was nothing."

"They beat my husband unconscious in the street when he refused to give up a loaf of bread he'd stood in line for at the market," Alsa said, slamming down plates in front of them with a tiny portion of sliced carrots, raw cabbage, and a chunk of meat made up mostly of gristle with congealed fat on one edge. "Then they hauled his body away. That was five days ago."

She retreated before any of them could ask her anything else, taking a plate to Sadie, then settling onto the bed with another to try to rouse her father.

"We were all dragged from our homes and brought here within the first few days of the quarantine zones' opening," Cerelle said. "Sadie and

I managed to stay together when they came to collect us, but our mother and brother were separated from us. I don't know if they're even in this camp. We were placed in this room with Alsa and her family. Since then, I've seen people beaten or killed outright in the street, for nonexistent slights against the guardsmen. I've seen them raid tenements and haul entire families away. None of those they take come back. We don't know where they are or even if they're alive." She leaned on the table again, moving in close. "So if you're lying about getting us out..."

"We aren't," Dalton said, a warning in his voice.

Cerelle backed off, still skeptical. "Then how do you intend to do it?"

"There's an elevator down to Level Fifteen," Lane said. "We need to find out where it is here on Level Sixteen."

"An elevator? One that works?"

"It would be in a warehouse building, probably abandoned," Devon said.

"There are dozens of abandoned buildings here." She crossed her arms, chewed on her lower lip in thought, then shrugged. "I don't know of anything offhand, but Sadie and I can start asking questions tomorrow."

"But—" Lane protested.

Cerelle cut her off with a look. "You won't be able to do anything now, not with the guards riled up looking for you. And I assume they're looking for you, not someone else."

"They caught us sneaking into the camp," Dalton said.

Cerelle nodded. "Then I suggest you eat and settle down until tomorrow."

"Is this all you have?" Lane asked.

"We were lucky at the market today." Then, barely audible, "Eat it. You don't want to offend Alsa."

She took her own portion and moved to help Alsa with her father and the two children. She called her sister back from the door with a look.

Devon began picking at the food, watching Cerelle and the others surreptitiously as he did so. Alsa muttered something under her breath, Cerelle answering, Sadie joining in, the mother casting a sharp glance in their direction now and then. The two children watched them with frank appraisal.

"Can we trust her?" Dalton asked, chewing on his gristle.

"She hid us from the guards."

Dalton grunted, picking at his teeth.

"We don't really have much choice," Lane said.

"There's that," Dalton answered.

They bedded down on the floor, using their packs as pillows. Alsa slept with her daughter in one bed, her father and the boy in the other. Cerelle and Sadie slept on the floor.

* * *

"Where are the new prisoners from Brovetto being kept?" Varenov asked. "I want to see them."

The sergeant didn't even look up from the heap of paperwork on the desk outside the open doors to the barracks and army offices. "No one sees the Luminesque prisoners except the Council and Prefects, per Prefect Arctus' orders."

"I *am* a councilor, sergeant."

The man glanced up and fumbled the quill he was holding, splattering ink over the report he was writing. "Councilor Varenov! I—I'm surprised—" He stood abruptly, gaze flashing back toward the room behind him, where others in the Iandolan Army were working or scurrying from desk to desk. All of them studiously ignored him. "I'm surprised to see you," he finally said, facing forward again, taking in Varenov and Treant and her personal guards standing slightly behind her.

"The prisoners?"

"Yes. I'm afraid that—"

"You did say that the Council was allowed to see them, yes?"

"Yes, but Arctus specified—"

"And I am a councilor, yes?"

"Of course," the sergeant said.

"Then take us to them."

The sergeant hesitated, then exhaled in defeat. "Let me gather up the keys."

He retreated into the room beyond, pausing to speak to an army courier, who nodded and raced off in the direction of the inner offices.

"We aren't going to have much time," Varenov said to Treant. "He's summoned someone."

"Arctus?"

"Most likely. I don't think Arctus intended me to be included in those with visitation privileges. You may have to discreetly wander off."

Treant nodded.

The sergeant returned. "This way."

They followed him into the section which held the cells. The doors were solid, a window of clear lucent in each, the rooms beyond utilitarian—a cot, a pallet, a pillow, a shelf with a few necessities, a chamber pot. Food and water were slid through a slot at the base of the door. As they progressed,

Varenov glanced in each window, catching a quick glimpse of whoever was inside. Most were lying on the cot, resting or reading, a few were pacing or exercising. Most who caught sight of her gave her a hard glare or indifferent stare. These men and women weren't drunks or thieves; those were housed in the city garrisons. These were murderers and rapists.

And rebels.

She spied the young mage who'd followed Terrial to Iandolo and set off the Warding. The girl looked thinner than before, paler. Her hands were still tied behind her back. She lay on her cot on her side, knees curled up to her chest. She didn't move when Varenov walked by. All of the fire Varenov had seen when she'd spoken to her months ago had died.

The next few cells held others from that rebel band of Brovettans that had attacked months before. The sergeant stopped at one of these cells and unlocked it, opening the door and stepping aside.

"Here you go."

Varenov moved to the door and bristled. "I'm not a fool, sergeant. I've been down here before. This isn't one of the new prisoners. Take me to those who were brought in within the last few days."

The sergeant scowled and closed the door, relocking it before moving down another three doors. He shot a glance back the way they'd come and unlocked the door slowly.

As soon as the lock clicked free, Varenov stepped forward and swung it open, afraid she'd see John inside, beaten, bruised.

It was a man, face a swollen mess of cuts and abrasions. His arm was in a sling and his body was bound in multiple places with bandages, some with blood stains. But it wasn't John.

She exhaled in relief, then stalked forward and knelt. The sergeant made a grunt of protest, but she ignored him. The prisoner reeked of sweat and infection. When she raised a hand to his face, she could feel the heat of the fever.

One of the man's eyes cracked open. It took a moment to focus, but then he recognized her, gaze shooting toward the door. A ragged moan escaped him.

Varenov stood abruptly and faced the sergeant. "Is this how you treat Iandolan prisoners?" she snapped. "Has this man even seen a healer yet? Look at these bandages. The seepage is already visible. Haven't the wounds been sewn shut? And what about his fever? There's obviously an infection somewhere. Explain yourself!"

The sergeant stiffened. "The healers haven't been by yet."

Varenov took a step forward, saw Treant slip by in the hallway behind, her guards shifting to try to cover his absence. "Why not? How long have these men been in here? The army returned two days ago, did it not?"

"Yes, but—"

"A healer should have been sent here immediately! We are not savages, we are the Iridesque. We treat our prisoners humanely, even those who may be traitors."

"I had my orders."

"What orders? Who gave these orders?"

"I did, Councilor Varenov."

Prefect Arctus appeared at the cell door, the sergeant sagging in relief.

Varenov shifted her attention to the prefect. "And what were these orders, Prefect Arctus?"

But Arctus spoke to the sergeant instead. "Did the councilor come alone?"

"No, Prefect."

"Then I suggest you find her assistant. He appears to be missing."

The sergeant ducked out the door. Only then did Arctus' full attention shift toward Varenov.

"You are cannier than I thought, councilor."

"Thank you. I take it you gave the orders to incarcerate the rebels without immediate medical aid."

"I did not. Those orders came from the Council itself. Councilor Havvelan, I believe. I gave the prisoners as much medical care as could be provided in the field."

"So the bandages they do have come from your men?"

"Yes."

Varenov was only partially mollified. "And the orders that I not be allowed to see the prisoners myself?"

Arctus shifted, crossing his arms over his chest. "Havvelan and the other councilors thought you might have certain...sympathies with the insurgents. They thought it better you not have contact with them." He glanced toward the prisoner. "Do you know this man?"

A prickle of tension threaded down Varenov's back. "No, I do not. Why do you ask?"

"I wonder what prompted you to come down here."

Varenov was saved from providing an answer when Treant and the sergeant reappeared in the hallway behind Arctus. The prefect turned, clearly suspicious, but Varenov shifted forward and snagged his attention again. "I demand that you send for a healer immediately, more than one, if the reports are true that you've captured over two dozen rebels."

"We found twenty-seven alive after the raid."

Varenov fought back a wave of nausea. She hadn't lied—she didn't know this man—but he clearly knew her. Or at least knew of her. She wanted to ask him about John, about what exactly had happened in Brovetto, but the prefect was too attentive.

"And you're giving them food and water? On a regular schedule?"

"We are. We are not savages, after all."

Varenov frowned. How long had Arctus been outside the door before speaking?

Then she turned back to the man. He'd rolled partially onto his side, his good arm reaching toward her. She didn't know why, but she couldn't afford to find out.

She faced Arctus. "I'll speak to Havvelan and the other councilors about the healers. I expect to see these prisoners in better health when I return."

She strode through the door without looking back, Treant falling into step beside her, her guards behind. He didn't speak until they were outside the barracks, the street noises at Mid-level sufficient to mask what they were saying.

"Did you find him?" she asked, picking out the carriage she'd brought from the towers waiting farther down the street. They headed in that direction.

"He wasn't in any of the cells as far as I could see."

"Then he's either still free, they're keeping him somewhere else, or he's dead."

* * *

"You can't go," Cerelle said.

"What do you mean?" Dalton demanded.

Lane felt the exhaustion and tension prickling off of him in waves. She felt it herself. None of them had slept well. "She's right," she said, to deflect Dalton toward her. Before he could blow up at her, she added, "This camp is for Brovettans. You and Devon won't blend in."

"We can use hoods—" Devon began.

Cerelle cut him off. "The guards won't allow it. The moment you run across one, he'll rip it off."

"It wasn't like that at first," Alsa said. "In the beginning, they left us alone. But then something changed and they brought in those other guards, the younger ones, the ruffians. We found out from others brought in after us that it was because some of the Brovettans were evading the guards."

"Because of us," Lane said. She felt sick. Everything they'd done to help those on the outside had only made it worse for those already captured.

"What do you expect us to do?" Devon asked.

Cerelle had already gathered up a folded cloth sack with handles and secreted at least two knives in a wrist sheath and a boot. "Stay here. Wait." She faced Sadie and the others. "What do we have to trade?"

Alsa eyed Devon and Dalton, then dug out a flat rectangular box from beneath the pallet on the bed. Back turned, body blocking their view of the contents, she opened it and pulled out a silver chain with a pendant attached. She laid it across her palm, chain dangling, then sighed heavily, folded it inside both clenched fists, and kissed her fingers, muttering something beneath her breath. Her shoulders shuddered, as if she were sobbing, but when she stood and handed it to Sadie, her face was impassive. "It was a gift from my husband."

Sadie passed it on to Cerelle, who tucked it carefully into a pocket. Then she took Sadie's hand. "I want you to stay here today. Watch over them. I'll take Lane with me." Sadie nodded.

Cerelle faced Lane. "Let's go."

"Are you certain? I can stay here if you think—"

Cerelle walked past her. "You need to see this."

Cerelle paused at the door, listening, then opened it, scanned the hall outside, and stepped through. Lane followed.

As they made their way down to a set of stairs, a few people peeked out their doorway, one or two greeting Cerelle or waving. One woman stepped out, taking Cerelle's hand, folding something into it as she muttered, "Bread, if they have any. Whatever else you can manage."

Cerelle tucked whatever she'd given her into a pocket as the woman retreated to her door and the two young girls watching from the small crack. She shooed them back and closed the door with a frowning look at Lane.

"She doesn't recognize you," Cerelle said as she continued toward the stairs, "but she won't say anything. I've had strangers in the building before. Hell, practically everyone's a stranger to each other here in the camp."

Lane didn't say anything, merely followed Cerelle up to the first floor and out onto the street.

The lucent panels overhead—those still active—were brighter than the night before and people were out, moving with purpose, heads bowed, eyes downcast. Cerelle was the exception, facing forward, head up. She motioned to Lane, then joined those headed toward the center of the camp, keeping pace with everyone else. Ahead, some of the Brovettans shied away and when they drew closer Lane saw three guardsmen around a corner, questioning two Brovettans on the street. The man already had blood dripping from a cut lip, a bruise beginning to appear on the side of his face. Lane had to clench her hand to keep from interfering. Farther on, more guardsmen had herded the tenants of an apartment onto the street, a few of the women sobbing, others clutching children close, the rest standing stoically in a protective barrier around them. The sounds of furniture splintering and glass breaking came from inside the building.

Cerelle glanced back at her and said, "Still searching for you and your friends."

A couple of turns later, they rounded a corner and Lane found herself before the remains of what had once been a gated wall, a manse within. It took up the entire block, but sections of the stone wall had collapsed long ago and whatever gates had once kept the rabble at bay had long since been torn down. But the arch that housed them remained, providing the entrance into the open area beyond. Cerelle entered, veering off to the left immediately. Where the manse had once stood were the ragged remains of a foundation and two partial chimneys.

Spread throughout the foundation and what was once the courtyard and gardens were carts surrounded by guardsmen. Brovettans were gathered before them, forming rough lines. The guards would let people step forward one at a time, those at the carts handing over a handful of mushrooms, a bundle of carrots, a sack of grain or flour. Cerelle had already chosen a line and Lane joined her.

"Why not get in the line for bread?" Lane asked. "That's what that woman asked for."

"It's almost gone. By the time we got to the front, there wouldn't be any left."

A short time later, the bread ran out, the guards pushing everyone still waiting back while men cursed and women wailed. The crowd pushed forward until a few of the guardsmen brought out clubs and began beating people, then they scattered.

Cerelle shook her head, but said nothing. Lane's fists clenched tighter.

When they finally reached the front of the line, Cerelle explained Lane was her sister and the guard let them both through to the cart with a shrug. At the cart, full of bundles of turnips, she said, "I need six bundles."

"Everyone gets one. You know the rules."

"I need six. I'm here collecting for families in my building."

"One only," the guard repeated. His voice sounded bored, but his eyes were latched onto Cerelle's. The three guards behind him stirred.

Cerelle leaned forward, removing something from her pocket—a locket, what the woman with the two girls must have given her. She thumbed it open, the two halves inside empty. "I need six."

The guard grunted. "I'll give you four," he said, reaching for the locket.

Cerelle snorted in disgust but handed the locket over and grabbed four bundles, handing two to Lane, before moving away quickly. She threaded through two other lines, bargaining at both, but only trading something extra at one. Lane kept quiet, but noticed that many of the Brovettans deferred to Cerelle—allowing her to cut in front of them or stepping back to let her pass. She spoke to some, items changing hands surreptitiously with a few. Even a few guards gave her a slight nod or casual hand signal.

Then Cerelle withdrew from the carts to the far side of the enclosure, where Brovettans were milling amongst themselves. Groups formed, then broke apart; others merely loitered about. The guards kept a close eye on them all, a thin tension hovering over the entire market.

Cerelle joined a group and immediately one of the men said, "Who's this?"

"This is Lane, my sister."

"Another sister, huh?" he eyed Lane with one eye. The other was surrounded by scar tissue and clouded white. "Are you the one they're searching for?"

"One of them," Cerelle said.

The one-eyed man swore. Some of those with him shook their heads and sidled away. "And you brought her here?" He started to back away, but Cerelle snagged his arm. He made a feeble effort to pull free, but she held on.

"The group needs to see her, to see them. They have a way out."

The one-eyed man's face scrunched up skeptically, but before he could answer four guardsmen on horseback charged into the market, pulling their steeds up sharply as Brovettans screamed and fell back. Iandolan Army soldiers on foot poured into the enclosure behind them, spreading out as the mounted prefect brought his horse under control. He paced it back and forth as those in the market settled, a wide area opening up between the Brovettans and the Iandolan soldiers, then halted.

"The Iandolan Army has returned from Luminesque, the leaders of the insurgency now under arrest. The rebellion has been crushed. There will be a trial for those captured, followed by an execution. Until then, the Iandolan Army is taking over the administration of the quarantine zones, the city guard returning to the streets. Patrols will resume. Citizens are to remain in their assigned buildings unless seeking food or supplies from the distribution centers. Loiterers will be apprehended. Curfew will begin an hour earlier and will extend an extra hour later. Anyone caught on the streets during curfew will be taken with force."

Those around Lane began to fidget, muttering beneath their breath. Most of those closest to Lane wore angry expressions, eyes hooded, jaws clenched. The air tasted of hatred and fear, bitter and acrid.

The prefect scanned the restless crowd. "You may have heard about the incident last night. To quell the rumors, I'll inform you that an unknown group infiltrated the quarantine zone. The search for them will continue until they are apprehended. If you know of their whereabouts, I'd suggest you report it to us immediately."

Then he signaled his men, who approached the wagons of food. The Brovettans parted before them, stumbling to get out of the way, but the soldiers shoved the city guardsmen back, taking their places. The guardsmen looked confused, making token gestures of resistance, especially the younger thugs who had obviously never finished attending one of the War colleges.

The prefect turned his horse about, the others on mounts doing the same. "City guard, you can return to your barracks for new orders. Those of you conscripted from the War colleges, return to your college."

Without waiting for acknowledgment, he nudged his horse through the market gate and out onto the streets, the other three horsemen doing the same.

"This is not good," Cerelle said.

At the carts, the soldiers were shouting orders, the Brovettans milling around, but falling into new lines under their direction. They began handing out food again, one portion per person. The city guardsmen lingered behind them, still uncertain, until those from the true city patrol began herding the disgruntled conscripts from the colleges away. None of them looked happy at the sudden change in orders.

"Why not?" Lane asked.

"Because we'd worked out a system," the one-eyed man said. "The city guard, especially the new recruits, may have been brutal, but they could be bribed. Not so much the Iandolan Army." He eyed Lane. "You have a way out?"

"Yes. We—"

"Don't explain it here. Too many listening in." He focused on Cerelle. "The group will meet in two days, at the foundry. Bring them, if you can."

He broke away, others near them either following or striking off in separate directions. Lane hadn't been aware that all of them were part of his group.

Cerelle waited, watching the soldier's movement intently, gathering up what they'd managed to get from the carts. Lane grabbed what she could.

"So you're part of this...group?"

"No. Their goals are different than mine. I'm trying to help make our lives easier here—get whatever food I can for those in need who don't want to risk coming here, make connections for those with services to offer to those seeking it, carry news back and forth so people are informed. That's it. I'm a facilitator."

"And what does this group want?"

Cerelle nudged her toward the market's entrance.

"They intend to fight back."

Chapter Twelve

"What is this man's name again?" Devon asked.

"Scerano." Cerelle handed him and Dalton hooded cloaks.

"I thought hoods wouldn't work," Dalton said. He slid his on and checked access to his weapons.

"They won't. But if we run into one of the patrols—one of the many, many patrols now that the army has taken over—it may give us a few extra moments to react. The cloak will hide your sword as well. None of us are allowed to have weapons."

They were all dressed in dark but ordinary clothing. Dalton carried his sword and a knife, Devon his dagger. Devon wasn't certain how many weapons Cerelle had on her, but he'd seen her pick up at least three. Lane, of course, carried nothing.

Cerelle looked them over, the rest of those in the apartment huddled on the beds, except for Sadie, who stood near the door. Apparently satisfied, she nodded to her sister, who stepped out into the hall, leaving the door cracked behind her.

"Remember, stay close. If we're separated, try to make your way back here."

"I don't understand why you couldn't show us where we're going," Dalton said. "We've had two days to memorize a map."

"Because Scerano would not approve."

Dalton grumbled, but he'd been grumbling about everything for two days. Being forced to wait in the apartment with Alsa glaring at his back while Lane and Cerelle scouted out the new patrol routes and gathered information and food hadn't sat well with Devon either. He was itching for some movement.

Cerelle checked the door, then motioned them into the hall, up the stairs, and out into the foyer, where Sadie waited for them.

"Everyone stayed inside," Sadie said. "I don't see anyone on the street either—patrols or otherwise."

"There shouldn't be a patrol on this street for another half hour. Go back to the apartment. I don't know if we'll be back tonight or not, but keep an eye out and ear open."

Sadie didn't respond, merely retreated back down the stairs. Cerelle scanned the street through the door's side windows, then led them out into the lucent-dimmed night.

They moved swiftly across the street to an intersection, Cerelle ranging far enough ahead she could scout out the area beyond. They kept to the buildings and shadows where possible. After a few turns and passage through an alley, they heard the tread of a patrol. Cerelle flattened them against a stone wall, four soldiers wandering past the intersection ahead. Cerelle waited another hundred breaths after they passed, then checked the intersection again before moving them along.

Half an hour later, they came up on a large building with almost no windows, the doors to the loading docks gaping holes in one side. They slid in through one of them, staying close to the wall, circling around to the left. In the pitch-black space, Devon sensed massive structures nearby, his hands brushing against curved stone crete walls. It smelled of soot and decay, with a strong undercurrent of molten metal and acid. He heard water dripping, the scuffs of their feet on the floor, their breathing, but nothing else. He desperately wanted to reach into his satchel and pull out his lantern.

When they were nearly halfway around what Cerelle had called the foundry, someone said, "Stop there."

Lane gasped. Everyone halted.

"It's just us, Scerano," Cerelle said.

A lantern flared, revealing a short, thin man with one milky eye, two others behind him to either side. They stood between two enormous circular stone vats, nearly thirty paces deeper into the building. Catwalks ran above the vats, along with a crisscrossing lattice of channels and chutes. A massive stone bucket hung over one of the vats, lip pinched into a V for pouring, amid dangling loops of thick chain. Devon caught subtle movement above, on one of the catwalks, and there were vague figures behind the three, deeper in the foundry.

"You won't mind if my men verify that then," Scerano said.

Cerelle didn't answer, merely waited.

A short time later, two men appeared to either flank, hemming them in from both sides. One of them nodded toward Scerano, who grunted and stepped forward.

"You said these people had a way out?"

"We do," Lane answered, edging out in front of them. "We're part of Maupin's group, the ones trying to get you out before the Iandolans grabbed you to place in these camps. Now we're trying to find ways to get you out of here before things get worse."

"They've already gotten worse," Scerano muttered. "Have you seen the streets since the Iandolan Army took over? Patrols have doubled, even during the day. We're halted and questioned even outside of curfew. I've lost five men already, arrested in the street for carrying weapons or loitering or whatever charges the soldiers feel like using if they're even remotely suspicious. The rationing has gotten stricter and the damn soldiers can't be bribed. People have started eating rats."

"I know. Cerelle has been taking me out, mostly to the market, but I've seen it."

Scerano didn't appear mollified, his gaze shifting toward Devon and Dalton. "Many of the people here blame you."

Dalton stiffened. "It had nothing to do with us. They would have come and taken over regardless, once they returned from Luminesque. We'd already seen it in the streets before we came here."

"Still, if you hadn't come, perhaps they wouldn't be so...vigilant."

"Does it matter?" Cerelle broke in. "They're here. The soldiers are here. At least they're not as brutal as the newly-recruited city guard we were dealing with before."

Scerano drew in a deep breath, then exhaled slowly. "True, but small comfort." His gaze shifted back to Lane. "How do you plan to get us out."

"There's an elevator down to Level Fifteen. We have people watching it down there. They can get you to Maupin, who can get you out of Iandolo if you want, back to Brovetto. We need to find the top of the elevator here."

"An elevator." Scerano remained silent a long moment. Then he stepped forward, the men at his side tensing as he said in a low, angry voice, "Do you think I'm stupid? That I wouldn't have searched for damned elevators within the first few days of being thrown in here? Or that the Council would be stupid enough to place us in here with a working elevator to another level within our reach?" His fury had only escalated as he spoke. He waved a hand in dismissal. "Bah! This is a waste of my time...or at worst a trap. Kill them. Place their bodies—"

"The elevator doesn't work," Devon said sharply.

Scerano's contempt centered on him. "And how does that information make the situation any better?"

"Because I can fix it."

Scerano's eye narrowed. He approached, his bodyguards on his heels, halting a few feet in front of Devon. Lane backed off; Dalton stepped in behind Devon protectively.

"There is only one inactive elevator that I know of that goes down to Level Fifteen. It's in an abandoned merchantile a block from here." He gave a thin smile, as if he were pulling the trigger on a particularly nasty snare. "It's powered by lucent."

"I know. I can fix it."

All expression fell from Scerano's face and he stilled. "No one can repair lucent."

"I can prove it."

Scerano searched his face. Then his hand reached for a pocket. Dalton's hand fell on Devon's shoulder, ready to pull him back, but Scerano withdrew a rounded metal object that fit neatly into the palm of his hand. He thumbed a latch on one side. The face sprang open, revealing a watch, the hands inside immobile.

"It was my great grandfather's. It's lucent-powered, but it hasn't worked for over seventy-five years. It's simply been passed down generation to generation, my great grandfather, my grandmother and mother, and now me." He thrust it forward in challenge. "Fix it."

Devon hesitated, then took the pocketwatch. The chain it had been attached to had broken off, only a few links remaining. The exterior was bronze, tarnished in blotches, but the interior glinted in the light of the lantern. The face was layered bronze threaded with blue and green lucent, with a single circular knob of red lucent at its center, the hands protected beneath a layer of glass. All of the lucent was clouded black. It was heavier than Devon had expected, and even without having ever held one before he could tell it was finely-crafted.

He ran a thumb over the lucent threads, then closed his eyes and sank into them.

It took him a moment to sort out what lucent was purely decorative and what had been woven into the mechanics of the watch. After that, it took only a few breaths to repair the fractured crystal within and clear up the black streaks. Nothing as complicated as repairing the elevator; all of the pieces were here already.

He felt the casing of the watch thrum in his hand. He'd closed it into a fist without realizing, but when he opened his fingers, he could see the decorative veins of lucent glowing and the tiny hands beneath moving.

One of Scerano's bodyguards swore beneath his breath, the words half awe and half fear. Scerano stared at the watch, then reached for it tentatively. Devon handed it over. Scerano held it with trembling fingers, ran his hands over it as if afraid his touch would break it.

Then he glanced up. His one eye was watery and when he spoke, his voice was ragged.

"We'll take you to the elevator."

* * *

"It's in better shape than I expected," Devon said.

Dalton watched as Devon dug through his satchel in the light of his lucent lantern, pulling out an occasional piece of lucent, eyeing it, then either keeping it or searching for another.

"Can you fix it?" he asked.

Devon glanced up at him with a thin smile. "Let's find out."

He knelt and slid one of his pieces of lucent into an empty slot, then closed his eyes. A moment later, his body stilled.

"I hate when he does that," Dalton muttered. "I never know if he's going to come back."

Lane didn't respond.

He, Devon, and Lane stood at the mouth of the open elevator shaft, its maw reaching down to Level Fifteen below, the cables that held the car below dangling a few feet away. Only the lattice of a steel gate kept anyone from stepping into the hole. Cerelle and Scerano were mumbling to each other to one side, Scerano's bodyguards and crew positioned at the entrance and various points about the merchantile. Unlike the floor below, this building was mostly empty, no machinery in evidence, only inch-thick dust on what shelving, tables, and desks remained. Dalton guessed it had once been the storefront for whatever was produced below. A few partial walls remained, sectioning off what had likely once been the display room and shop out front, along with some attached offices. The area housing the elevators had obviously been for storage.

Dalton's gaze fixed on Cerelle and Scerano. "Keep an eye on him," he said to Lane. "Let me know if he needs anything."

"Where are you going?"

"To find out if there's a plan."

He sidled over to the two Brovettans, who quieted when they saw his approach.

"Is he going to be able to repair it?" Scerano asked.

"He's working on it, but I'd bet on it. Have any thoughts on how you're going to get everyone out of here?"

Scerano shot a glance at Cerelle, who cleared her throat.

"We were just discussing that. We need to get the families with children out first. I'm going to start approaching some of the parents, a select few that we can trust, at least until we see if this is going to work. We'll expand from there. But the children will go first. They and their parents will be the least likely to be missed."

"And how will we get them here?" Dalton asked.

"My men will handle that," Scerano said. "You and your friends will have to stay here. We'll set up a guard in the building."

"It's not the most defensible position. There are too many windows and it's too open."

"Agreed. I'll see what I can do. But we don't want to draw attention to it either." He looked toward the elevators. "When will it be active?"

"If I know Devon, it will be ready sometime tonight."

Scerano nodded. "Then we should get to work."

He motioned to his bodyguards and headed toward the entrance, calling a few others to him.

Cerelle hesitated, then said, "I'll bring you some blankets and food."

Dalton did a circuit of the building after she left, noted that Scerano's men were already placing heavy dark tarps over the few broken windows. Most of those were up front, where the merchandise would have been displayed. He marked the positions of the guards and wondered how sound the roof was and whether they could position a watch up there without being noticed by the Iandolan soldiers on the other roofs. They were too far from the camp's borders to be seen by those patrols, but as they now knew, there were others deeper inside the zone.

He returned to the elevators to find Lane sitting, back against a wall. Devon had shifted position to the second door, hand resting on lucent, body unnaturally rigid.

Dalton settled in next to Lane. "How's it going?"

"He's nearly done."

They sat in silence, until Lane suddenly said, "Strange, isn't it? A year ago, I was desperately trying to learn the basic form as a third-year at the Lyceum, failing at every turn because I just couldn't seem to get it. I didn't realize the proctors were setting me up to fail. I knew if I couldn't figure it out, I'd be sent back to the towers, to my mother, and I'd do anything to prevent that."

"I was a sixth-year War student, ready for my two months of freedom after graduation before a life serving in the Iandolan Army."

"And then the Brovettans attacked."

"Only it wasn't exactly the Brovettans."

"No, I suppose not. Although we didn't know that at the time." She gave a horrid chuckle. "Back then, I denied I was Brovettan so vehemently! I didn't want to be associated with them. And now look." She waved a hand at their surroundings.

"Strange how your perspective changes," Dalton said. "I only thought of the army. That's all I'd ever wanted. Now—" he glanced at Devon "—it doesn't seem that important."

Lane slapped the back of her hand against his thigh. "Someone's coming."

He stood, although he didn't think anyone threatening could have gotten by Scerano's men. Lane scrambled up beside him.

Cerelle appeared, Sadie, Alsa, her father, and her two children shuffling up behind her. All but Sadie looked anxious and scared. Each of them carried a pack or bag, hanging loose or clutched tight.

Cerelle stepped forward. "They go down first," she said, as if she expected an argument. When Dalton merely nodded, she handed him her bundle. "Blankets and food, as promised. And there should be a few other families joining us shortly."

Before Dalton could answer, a horrendous shriek of metal scraping on metal pierced the relative quiet of the warehouse. Lane cringed and clapped her hands over her ears. Alsa gave a choked off scream and clutched her children close. The sound escalated for an interminable moment, then cut back to a low grinding sound as everyone spun toward the elevators.

Devon stood beside one, eyes wide. "We should probably find some grease."

Dalton swore, then motioned to Cerelle. "Check with the guards. See if any soldiers outside on patrol heard it."

Cerelle darted off, shoving Sadie in the other direction, although Dalton could tell that Scerano's men within sight had already reacted. A few slid out the merchantile's side door, presumably to scout out the nearby streets.

Alsa and her family tightened up, staring at Dalton in terror, until he motioned them closer to Devon and the elevators. Lane stepped between them and the rest of the warehouse.

"Do you think anyone heard?"

"You mean besides everyone within a two-block radius?"

Lane winced. "We should have thought of this."

"I didn't think we were bringing an elevator up tonight."

Behind them, the grinding sound increased until the elevator appeared, crawling upwards with a rattling shudder. It came to a halt, the bottom of the car two feet below the level of the floor.

"That's as far as it will go," Devon said.

"Test it out," Dalton said, "then get them on board if it's safe."

Devon gave him an odd look at the harshness in his voice, but he pulled the gate aside with a clang and climbed down into the elevator. It creaked under his weight, but after a moment, he reached up to grab Alsa's two kids and help the others down. They huddled together in a far corner, Devon crawling out.

Dalton had kept half an eye on them, most of his attention on the possible vectors of attack, but the warehouse remained quiet.

"Why did you bring it up?" Dalton asked, keeping his voice low. "You should have waited."

"I didn't think about it. As soon as the last of the lucent was repaired, it triggered the call."

Dalton tried to brush aside his irritation. "If any of the soldiers heard…"

He tensed as the side door opened, then relaxed as Scerano's men stepped aside, three figures approaching. Scerano halted and swore beneath his breath when he saw the elevator, facing Devon.

"You did it. Even with my pocketwatch, I thought it was a trick."

"It hasn't been used in a long time," Devon said. "The tracks need oiling or grease or something."

"I heard." Scerano snapped his fingers, one of his bodyguards stepping forward. He murmured something to him and the man headed away at a fast trot. "My men will handle that. Thankfully, none of the patrols were close enough to be of concern, according to my scouts. But they're keeping watch now, just in case."

He stepped closer to the elevator, ran his hand along the panel where newly replaced lucent buttons now glowed with a faint light, peered into the car. "It can carry nearly forty people."

"If it can handle their weight," Dalton said.

Scerano nodded, deep in thought. "And there's a second?"

"Once I get it working," Devon said.

Scerano stepped aside and Devon shifted forward to start work on the second panel. The old man watched a moment, then sidled closer to Dalton.

"As soon as Cerelle returns with more families—and my men have a look at the car—we'll send them down."

"We should wait—"

"No! We will *not* wait. We have been ripped from our homes, held here, beaten, starved, spat upon, and *degraded* long enough. Families have been torn apart. People have been taken, even killed. *We will not wait.*"

He stalked away, Dalton silenced by the ferocity in the old man's eyes and the intensity of his words.

Lane shifted to one side. "I guess we're not going to wait."

* * *

Three hours later, Scerano's men crawled out from the depths of the elevator shaft covered in rust and grease and cobwebs. Cerelle had returned three times with families in tow, Sadie twice. Sixty Brovettans hovered near the elevators in small clusters, most of them children. Parents soothed their kids with hushed words and tight hugs. Some were accompanying grandparents. Scerano moved among them all, speaking to the men and women and a few of the older children, drawing them aside, away from their families. Many of them listened intently, nodded, often glancing back at their wives or husbands or children. Their expressions varied—drawn and serious, angry, pensive. A few winced as if pained.

Dalton watched the elderly Brovettan with growing unease, heightened enough by the end that he caught Lane's attention. "Have you been watching Scerano?"

Lane frowned. "What's he been doing?"

"As soon as the families arrive and have had a chance to settle in, he talks to the parents—the mother, father, or both. Sometimes some of the older teenagers. None of them look happy with what he has to say."

"Maybe he's just offering words of encouragement."

"I don't think so."

Devon approached, looking haggard, the skin around his eyes bruised, face drawn. "The elevator is ready. I almost brought up the second, but Scerano wants some of his men to go down with the first group and deal with greasing the shaft below before we do that. You two should go with them, to deal with whoever is waiting down below."

"You aren't coming with us?" Lane asked, voice stricken.

Devon was already shaking his head. "I don't dare. If something goes wrong with the elevators, I don't want to have to rappel down from

Level Seventeen again. I need to stay up here until we know they're both working."

"Then I'll stay here," Dalton said.

"I need you to run the elevators. Take the Brovettans down, get them offloaded and into Raven's hands. Lane can take them down to Maupin with Carbolen's help. They'll want someone they can trust with them, a Brovettan. Then you can bring the elevator back up."

Dalton didn't like it, but it made sense. And he wouldn't be gone that long. "Very well. When do we head out?"

"As soon as you and Lane can get everyone loaded."

Dalton grabbed Devon's shoulders. "We'll take care of that. You go get some rest." He kissed him, then shoved him toward where they'd piled their blankets and packs. Devon didn't argue. Dalton watched until he collapsed to his side and pulled a blanket over himself, back to them, then faced Lane. "Let's get these people out of here."

Lane began speaking to the families, leading them to the elevator, Alsa and her family already inside, while Dalton climbed down and scanned the newly repaired panel. The bar of lucent that controlled the elevator's height didn't quite fit the original slot, a bit short at both top and bottom, perhaps why the elevator wasn't level with the warehouse floor here, but everything appeared active. He then helped the Brovettans down into the elevator, although some refused him with a suspicious look, preferring Lane or the other Brovettans help instead. Most of these were the older Brovettans.

He thought there were more Brovettans waiting to escape the internment camp, but then he noted that many of the men and women Scerano had spoken to were clasping their family members tight, kneeling and speaking to their kids, giving tearful hugs, and then pulling away and stepping back into the warehouse to stand with Scerano's men.

He frowned. But the last of the families were now on board, along with Scerano's workmen carrying their tools, and so with a last glance toward Devon, he touched the lucent bar and dragged its pulsing light downwards.

The car jolted and gave a short, piercing shriek, then settled into a shuddering rumble as they dropped. A few of those in the car cried out, some of the kids sobbing and they grabbed onto their older siblings or grandparents. Nearly everyone of middle-age remained behind.

As they descended, the sobs and sniffles faded, the car becoming eerily quiet. Dalton glanced around at all of their faces, the younger ones wide-eyed and fearful, the older stoic. The car smelled of sweat, fresh grease, and musty air. Time appeared to drag out as Dalton shifted uncomfortably under their gazes.

Then the opening onto Level Fifteen appeared, sliding into view as the elevator came to a juddering halt.

The warehouse beyond was dark. The only light came from the lucent on the elevator.

Dalton stepped out of the car. Behind, he heard Lane rummaging in her pack. A moment later, the pale light of the rose lantern Devon had made illuminated the area in front as Lane stepped to his side.

"I thought someone would be here," Dalton said.

Lane didn't answer. Ahead, a footfall sounded and then Nic stepped into the light. His hand twitched near where he hid his knife. He glanced at Dalton and Lane, then toward the elevator, where the Brovettans they'd brought with them were peering cautiously out of the car.

"Is it safe?" Nic asked.

Dalton's neck prickled. Someone—likely Picall or Raven—had a crossbow or other such weapon trained on him, ready to fire. "It's safe," he said, lifting both hands. "It took us a while, but we managed to hide from the guards and get the elevator fixed. This is the first batch of Brovettans."

Nic came forward and hugged Lane, nodding at Dalton, then stepped back. "There've been a few developments down here as well."

Behind him, a man Dalton didn't recognize drifted forward from the shadows cast by the hulking dead machines, his gaze fixed on Lane. He was flanked by Maupin on one side and a couple new faces on the left. Dalton's hand dropped to his sword, but then noticed Picall shifting forward with a few other tullers from the right, Raven and a few men from Carbolen's gang to the left.

There were too many tensions in the group; he couldn't sort them all out.

The man ignored them all, focused on Lane. Thin, tall, with a scarred face and what looked like burns on his hands and arms, he halted directly before Lane and stared at her confused face for a long moment.

Then he reached forward to grab her shoulders. "Lane. My name is John Senn. I'm your father."

Chapter Thirteen

"What happened?" Dalton demanded. He and Nic were offloading the Brovettans from the elevator into the hands of a mixture of Maupin's men, Carbolen's, and the strangers that Dalton assumed had come with this John Senn. "Who is he, besides Lane's father?" He glared at the man standing with Lane off to one side, John talking, Lane in shock.

"He arrived here at the warehouse two days after you rappelled down into Level Sixteen, along with Maupin and some of the tullers. It didn't take long for Carbolen to show up after that. He must have someone watching us. All three of them had an immediate talk. From what I could tell, Carbolen wasn't happy to see him, definitely some antagonism there, but as you can see, Maupin defers to him without any qualms."

The last of the Brovettans in the car exited and Dalton turned to Nic. "So who is he?"

"The leader of the Brovettan resistance. The real one, not the group that arrived here with Terrial and her mages."

Dalton stepped into the empty elevator, but paused to glare out at John Senn. Lane appeared to have gotten over her shock. "What does he want?"

"I don't know yet. All I know is that the Iandolan Army attacked their center of operations in Brovetto. They assume that one of Terrial's men captured during the Warding attack here in Iandolo revealed their contacts and the army worked out their base from there. Not many of the rebels in Brovetto survived, but those that did escape headed for the tull."

"And now they're here." He didn't like it. Something significant had changed, had shifted.

He reached for the elevator's control bar.

"Hey," Nic said, startled. "Where are you going?"

"Back up to Level Sixteen. Devon and the others are expecting me. We've got more people to bring down. Tell the others to be ready."

Although as the elevator began to rise and John Senn sank out of sight, he wondered how much longer that was going to last.

* * *

I'm your father.

The words roared in Lane's ears, like a strong wind across the roof of the Tower at the Lyceum, drowning out everything around her. She knew she and the man who claimed to be her father had shifted to one side, knew that he was speaking to her, but she couldn't hear him. The wind consumed everything. It felt as if it were inside her, rushing through her chest, through her arms, as if she were hollow.

Her mother had never talked about her father, had always sidestepped the issue, the consummate diplomat, somehow managing to twist her concerns and questions onto some other topic, until Lane had finally given up and stopped asking. In her head, she'd assumed her father was dead.

But apparently he wasn't. He stood before her, had put his hands on her shoulders, had drawn her to the side, talking the entire time. His voice was like the drone of bees, a hum that vibrated in her teeth, in her bones.

Where had he been? Why hadn't he come to see her mother? Why hadn't he come to see *her*? He'd obviously known she existed. Why had he come to see her *now*?

Her shock began to morph into anger.

"What do you want?" she asked, the words cutting.

John Senn, her father, halted mid-sentence. She hadn't even caught the end of what he was saying, the wind only now receding.

"What do you want?" Lane repeated, crossing her arms over her chest.

John Senn straightened, pulling back from her. She realized she was almost as tall as him, had the same Brovettan features, although her face was narrower, cheekbones sharper, like her mother's. But they had the same black hair, the same eyes.

"I don't want anything. Not from you." He drew in a steadying breath, let it out in an extended sigh. "I haven't seen you since you were born."

Something stabbed into Lane's chest. "You were there when I was born?"

"As close as I could get. Your mother wouldn't let me into the birthing room. It was too risky. Someone on the Council, or beholden to the Council, might have seen. But as soon as they moved you and your mother to her own rooms, I was there."

Lane's eyes began to burn, but she hardened herself. "For how long?" Her voice came out deep and rough.

John's shoulder sagged. "Only a week. We couldn't risk any longer. Even a week was too long, but we were young."

Lane swallowed the tightness in her throat. "And where have you been since? Why didn't you come to see me? Not once. It's been seventeen years."

"I've been in Brovetto, hiding."

"Hiding? From who? Me?"

He chuckled. "No. Never from you. From the Council. From the Iandolan Army. I'm the leader of the Brovettan rebels, Lane. Your mother and I... we've been part of it since nearly the beginning."

"That—that doesn't make any sense. She's a councilor. She's been fighting the rebels practically her entire life."

"No, she hasn't. She went to Brovetto with Councilor Orland as an aide, but when she was there she met me. I brought her into the rebellion. I showed her what the Council had been doing to Luminesque, to all of the provinces. I introduced her to the people of Brovetto that were suffering under the Council's policies."

"But—"

John reached for her, but she drew back. He let his arm drop.

"But she's on the Council now? Is that what you were going to say? When Councilor Orland was killed in that ill-timed and ill-planned attack by the Iandolan Army, your mother saw an opportunity. She'd never been comfortable with some of the rebels' more violent tendencies—the raids, the occasional deaths. She wanted a cleaner approach. She decided to infiltrate the Council itself, to become a councilor. She hoped to help the Brovettans by working through the Council." He gave her a grim smile. "But it meant she had to leave, to return to Iandolo. I couldn't come with her. It would expose her. And besides, what could I do here in Iandolo as her husband? I couldn't help the Brovettans. Not to the same extent I could help them being in Brovetto itself. And then there was you. She knew she was pregnant and a rebellion is no place for a baby. So we agreed I'd stay in Brovetto and she'd return to Iandolo. It...wasn't an easy decision."

Lane didn't know how to respond. It was too much information, too fast. Her entire body trembled. The wind had died, but now she felt as if she were about to fly apart, only her crossed arms holding her together.

The only solid part of her was the anger, so she grasped desperately at that.

"Why are you here now, then? What changed?"

John glanced around the darkened warehouse, at the mix of people helping the Brovettans off the elevator, leading them away, to whatever haven Maupin and Carbolen had arranged for them.

"The Iandolan Army hit Brovetto hard. They'd discovered the rebellion's main channels of operation, had found our home base. They attacked it and many of our satellite camps throughout Brovetto. They either captured or killed almost everyone in our group. I managed to escape, with a few others, but Brovetto wasn't safe anymore. We had to leave." He faced her again. "So we came here."

"Why?"

"Because Maupin was here. He's been smuggling people and other resources back and forth between Iandolo and Brovetto for years through the tull."

"So it had nothing to do with me."

"You and your mother being here was just a bonus. I didn't expect to find you so quickly. But then Maupin explained what was going on and I knew it was you."

"How?"

"Your mother and I have kept in touch, sporadically. She told me what happened at the Lyceum, about the attack by Terrial and her mages, the Warding, how you released it. And that she'd helped you escape the Council. She was…extremely proud of you."

Lane had to fight back tears, the effort so difficult she couldn't speak.

"I haven't heard from your mother since then. And I haven't managed to get word to her to let her know I'm still alive. She probably thinks I'm dead. But when Maupin said he had a mage helping him with the Brovettan evacuation, I knew it had to be you."

"Evacuation?" Lane said, the word ragged. "We're just helping them escape the camps."

"That's how it started. But it's become bigger than that now." He motioned to the group around them. "You aren't pulling them out one or two at a time anymore. You're rescuing them by the dozens. And together, we're going to make certain they all get out."

He patted her shoulder and this time she didn't pull away, although she couldn't keep her body from tensing at the touch. He didn't appear to notice, already turning toward Maupin and the Brovettans they'd brought down from the camp. He started asking questions as soon as he approached, his own men answering in clipped sentences, Carbolen's men watching him warily.

"He's more or less taken over since he arrived," Nic said from behind her. "I don't think Carbolen is thrilled about it."

She hadn't heard Nic approach and started, her heart shuddering. She realized her arms were still crossed, her hands gripping her biceps painfully, and forced herself to relax, to drop them to her side.

"Are you all right?" he asked.

"No, I'm not. He claims to be my father. He told me things about my mother that I don't know if I believe. I...I don't know what to think anymore."

"Because what he said can't be true?"

"No." Lane shifted and met Nic's gaze. "Because if what he says is true, then I've misjudged my mother completely my entire life."

Nic considered this for a long moment, both of them watching as the Brovettans were organized and led away by an escort of a dozen, split evenly between Maupin's men, Carbolen's, and the rebels.

"Then maybe you should talk to her," Nic finally said.

"Who?"

"Your mother."

Lane scoffed, but Nic grew serious.

"I mean it. Dalton has contacts to Captain Mannert. She can get in touch with your mother, arrange a meeting. But don't go alone. If the Iandolan Army is looking for anyone, they're looking for you."

* * *

Varenov stepped out of the carriage and onto the walk outside the tavern called The Stout Vine, Treant on her heels. She scanned the patrons at the outside tables eating plates of elevated pub fare and drinking flagons of ale and sipping glasses of wine. The Stout Vine catered to the intersection of those above Mid-level and those below, a mixture of both worlds, neither elegant like some of the finer restaurants closer to the three towers, nor serving the greasy food and watered-down swill of some of the bars Varenov had heard Martov visited.

"You said Mannert wanted to meet here?"

Treant stepped forward. "Yes, The Stout Vine."

"Why here? Why not simply come and see me in my quarters at the towers?"

"She didn't say, but she was insistent. She said she would meet us inside."

Varenov frowned. "Very well."

She passed through the arbor draped with grape vines that served as an outside gate, then into the interior through a heavy oak door that groaned as it opened. Inside, the lighting was dim, no lucent in sight, only lanterns hanging from overhead wooden supports, the light from the windows diffused by linens. Tables were scattered between a large hearth with fire blazing and a long bar. It smelled of woodsmoke and old pine.

She caught sight of Mannert standing at a secluded booth in the far corner of the room. The captain gave a small wave of her hand, then slid into one side of the booth.

Varenov hesitated, quelling the unease in her stomach before moving forward.

Before she could say anything, Captain Mannert said, "Have a seat," motioning to the side opposite her. She shifted over, waving Treant to sit beside her.

Varenov sat before realizing there was someone else at the table beside her. She cried out before she realized it was Lane.

She grabbed her daughter and pulled her into a tight hug without thinking, her throat burning with pent up worry and need. Lane tensed in her grip, then relaxed, her chest shuddering with a few suppressed sobs of her own.

Varenov finally relented and pushed her daughter back. "It's good to see you," she managed, voice barely a croak, "but you shouldn't be here." She turned on Mannert. "You shouldn't have brought her. What if I was followed? Havvelan has eyes everywhere and he's been watching me much more closely since I surprised them with that visit to the prison. He and the others have been searching for her, specifically. If they find her here, with me—"

"Mom, shut up."

Varenov cut herself off, then closed her mouth. Her heart was pounding in her chest. She couldn't help sweeping her gaze over the patrons closest to them, realizing as she did so that she and Lane were mostly sheltered from everyone else in the tavern. Lane in particular was hidden. If she acted as if no one were sitting beside her, no one else in the tavern would know there was a fourth person at the table.

She shifted her position, attention on Treant, and saw Mannert's tension ease. The captain leaned back. "Lane requested the meeting, helped me plan it. No one saw her enter—she came through a side door. And no one will see her leave. I'll make certain of that."

Varenov realized there were already drinks at the table, along with a trencher of fine marble bread, some kind of meat dip, butter, and knives. She reached a trembling hand for her glass, sipping without tasting. "I didn't expect to see you ever again after releasing you from the basement of the Lyceum." She gave a ragged laugh. "I certainly didn't think you'd want to see me."

"A man found me. John Senn. He claims to be my father."

Varenov choked on the wine, one hand slamming down on the table as she forced herself to swallow painfully, then coughed as she pushed the wine glass away from her.

"Are you all right?" Lane asked.

She struggled to catch her breath, one hand on her chest. "I'm fine," she wheezed, coughing again. Her throat felt torn. She met Treant's eyes. "He came to you? He's alive?"

"He survived the army's purge in Brovetto and came here."

Varenov bowed her head and closed her eyes, the hand on her chest closing into a fist. She hadn't seen him in years, but still, the relief was almost unbearable.

"Is it true?" Lane asked before she was ready. "Is he my father?"

She forced herself to look at her daughter. Lane deserved that. "Yes, he's your father."

She watched varied emotions cross Lane's face—stunned hope, disbelief, pain—all of it settling into anger, as Varenov knew it would. She was so much like John.

"You never told me he was alive. You never told me he was in Luminesque."

"I never said he was dead either."

"You never told me anything! You dodged all of my questions, or blatantly refused to answer. I could have gone to see him. He could have come here to see me. Why? Why did you say nothing?"

"Because if you'd known, you *would* have gone to see him. I wouldn't have been able to stop you. Then you would have seen how he lived, seen what he was fighting for, and you would have joined him. And I couldn't risk that. I couldn't risk *you*, Lane. Everything I did, everything I said, was to protect you—from the Council, from the rebels, from everyone. I didn't want you to get caught up in what your father and I were trying to do."

"So it's true," Lane muttered, more to herself than to Varenov. "Everything he said about you and the rebels is true."

Mannert gave Varenov an odd look, but Varenov no longer cared what the captain overheard. She'd kept the secret for too long.

"I've been using my position on the Council to support the rebellion in Brovetto, yes. Since the day I accepted it. The circumstances around Councilor Orland's death offered up too tempting an opportunity to resist. I had to take it, even though it meant leaving John behind. As a councilor, as a representative of Luminesque, I could sway the Council's vote toward policies that helped the people of Brovetto, that helped the rebels. I could stall votes, argue, cajole, whatever it took to keep those in Luminesque safe."

"Isn't that a betrayal of the Council?" Mannert asked.

"No," she said, too sharply. In a more even tone, she added, "Isn't it the job of the councilor to protect the province she represents? That's all I was doing. I've been doing some research into our history and the Founders' Pact. This isn't how the Council is supposed to operate. Someone has been subverting the roles of the councilors for years."

"And you mean to correct it?"

"If that's what it takes."

"So all of this time," Lane said, ignoring the interruption, "you've been working with my father, communicating with him, planning with him. And you never said a word to me."

Varenov reached for her daughter's hand, but she jerked away. "I didn't want you to be involved, Lane. John and I chose this life. You didn't." She gave a thin smile. "And even after all of my efforts, look at where you are? You rebelled against me and began studies at the Lyceum. Then you rebelled against the Lyceum. And now you're helping the Brovettans. Nothing I did made any difference. You're too much like your father, preferring action over words."

Lane stiffened. "Have you seen what you're doing to them?"

"Who?"

"The Brovettans. I've been inside one of the quarantine zones, mother. They're being beaten, starved, abused, even killed—men, women, and children. There are three or four families per apartment, if the families aren't being separated and torn apart. Rations are pitiful. The guards are corrupt...or at least they were, when they were using the city guardsmen and those thugs pulled from the new War colleges. Now the Iandolan Army has taken over. Most of the Brovettans fear to walk the streets, even to collect food. They'd found a way to survive before, but... It's not a quarantine zone, it's an internment camp."

"That's not how it's supposed to be."

"Of course not. Do you think the other councilors or the prefects would be telling you the truth? You should go see for yourself. You're a councilor, after all. They can't keep you away, can they?"

Varenov thought of Havvelan and Prefect Arctus and thought perhaps they could, but she said nothing. Instead, she asked, "What about your father?"

Lane flinched. "What about him?"

"Is he hurt? How many people managed to escape with him?"

"He's fine. I don't know how many came with him, but he's already trying to take control of our elev—" She cut herself off with a curse. "He's fine," she said again, then faced Mannert. "I'm done here. Time to go."

Mannert nodded, nudged Treant out of his seat, but Varenov grasped Lane's arm, squeezing tight. "Give him a chance, Lane. He didn't want this. I was the one who insisted on leaving."

She didn't leave Lane an opportunity to answer, pushing away from the table. While she, Treant, and Mannert collected themselves, Lane slid behind them to a side door and was gone.

"I'll make certain she's safely away from Mid-level," Mannert said, then followed her.

Varenov and Treant headed for the door, stepping out into the bright sunlight. Varenov blinked and shaded her eyes, then spotted their carriage.

"At least we know he survived the raids in Brovetto," Treant said.

"Yes, but now we have something new to worry about."

"What's that?"

"What he plans to do now that he's here."

Treant opened the carriage door and Varenov clambered inside, Treant situating himself across from her.

"What do you plan on doing about it?"

"Nothing at the moment."

She stared out the small carriage window at the streets passing by, the people.

Then she faced Treant.

"I think we should take Lane's advice and arrange an unexpected visit to the quarantine zone on Level Twenty. I want to see what conditions the Brovettans are living in."

* * *

"I'm a councilor," Varenov said, calmly, but with a razor's edge to the words. "I don't need permission from anyone, least of all Prefect Arctus.

I am the representative of Luminesque. The Brovettans are my charges. Open the gates."

She and Treant stood outside the quarantine zone, forced to disembark their carriage when their driver could not get the Iandolan soldiers to open the barricade for them. The driver stood behind them, back stiff with affront, with Treant and the two soldiers Varenov had brought along as escort. Varenov stood within an arm's length of the captain who manned the barricade. He gave her a cold stare, the fingers of one hand smoothing out his mustache. His gaze flicked toward Treant and the others, then back to her, and his hand dropped.

"What is it you want to do in the zone?"

"Look around. The Council has established these zones to keep the Brovettans safe, providing food and amenities. I want to see how everything is going. Consider it an unannounced inspection."

The five soldiers behind the captain fidgeted, until he finally sighed. "Very well. You may enter, but I will provide an escort while you are inside. There has been unrest among the inhabitants."

"What kind of unrest?"

But the captain didn't answer her, retreating back toward the barricade and his men. He muttered orders, one man running toward the nearest building, the others beginning to pull the barricade back.

Varenov turned back to the driver. "We'll leave the carriage here. Stay with it until we return. The rest of you, accompany me."

By the time they'd formed up around her, the barricade had been lifted and they walked through, the captain waiting on the far side with seven other soldiers. As soon as they were inside, the barricade was replaced.

"Are you to be our escort, Captain—?" Varenov asked.

"Pulvar. It's the least I could do." The captain's tone didn't suggest it was an honor. "What would you like to see first?"

"Food distribution."

He gestured with one hand, the motion subtle, but one of the soldiers took off at a trot. "This way, Councilor Varenov."

They headed out in the same direction as the first soldier, moving at a sedate pace. Varenov was instantly suspicious, but said nothing. Instead, she scanned the streets, noting there were few Brovettans outside. Those who were were headed in the same direction as they were, keeping their heads lowered, shoulders hunched. One or two stepped from the doorways of their tenements, saw the captain and their group, then quickly retreated back inside, closing the door silently behind them. Varenov noticed a young girl, no more than twelve, staring out at them from a tenement window, the right side of her face bruised. Her expression was vacant, face gaunt, her eyes sunken into their sockets. Before she could bring the girl to the captain's attention, the girl's mother—or so Varenov presumed—pulled her back and yanked the curtain closed. The terrorized look she shot those in the street cut Varenov to the bone.

They passed three groups of soldiers on patrol, the men stepping to the side, but watching them pass with hooded suspicion and anger. The same look they presented to all of the Brovettans in the zone, Varenov realized. No wonder that mother had looked terrorized. The pall of fear and oppression was like a weighted blanket, smothering the streets.

Then Treant tapped her arm, bringing her attention to the square that opened up ahead. Carts lined one side, Brovettans lined up before each. A few soldiers were shoving some of the men into line as they approached, one falling to the ground with a sharp cry.

"Get up!" one of the soldiers barked. "We must have order here! Get in line!"

He went to kick the elderly man, but then noticed Varenov's gaze. He and the others retreated.

Varenov shot Captain Pulvar a dark look, then went to the old man, helped him rise. "Is this how you treat all of the Brovettans here?" she demanded. "Look at him! He's skin and bones, can barely stand he's so weak, and yet your men are throwing him to the ground, threatening him?"

"We must have order," Pulvar said. "As I said, there have been incidents."

"Why? Because they're fighting back? Or are you instigating these 'incidents'?"

"If we don't enforce some order, they would charge the food carts. It would be chaos. There would be rioting and then no one would get their allotted food allowance."

One of the women in line snorted and muttered something under her breath.

Varenov turned on her. "What did you say?"

The woman cowered, then glanced at the captain and straightened. "I said no one would riot over the food. Half of it is rotten as it is."

Varenov spun on Pulvar. "Is that true?"

He clenched his jaw but said nothing.

Varenov took the woman by the arm. "Show me the carts."

They strode to the nearest, the Brovettans closest falling away before them. Even the soldiers handing out the food stepped back a pace. The apples appeared edible, seconds obviously, but with few pock-marks and scabs. Varenov's anger faltered.

"These look fine."

The woman made a noise in her throat. "They obviously knew you were coming." With one arm, she raked the top layer of apples aside, exposing those beneath, bruised and maggot-eaten already. Varenov reached for one. Her thumb sank into its side as she picked it up. She could smell the sickening sweetness of the rot before she brought it near her face.

"This is what you're feeding them?" She stalked toward Pulvar, standing a few paces away. She thrust the apple into his face. "Eat it."

"What?"

She edged closer, forcing him to step back. "I said, eat it."

He spluttered a moment, then caught her gaze.

Reaching up, he took the apple from her hand. She let it drop, so the juice dripped from her fingers.

The captain glanced at the apple, turned it slightly, so the best side faced him, then met her eyes again.

He bit into it. The sound not a respectable crunch of teeth through flesh, but a soft mealy mush.

Pulvar managed one bite, then bent over and spat the pulp to the ground, dropping the apple with a splat. Varenov could see the maggots wriggling in the remains.

Over his crouched, heaving body, she said, "The Council said to send the seconds and thirds to the zones. Even Havvelan didn't protest that. But these aren't even fourths. I doubt a distiller would consider these for mash. What about the rest of these carts?"

She moved through the rest, shoving the top layer of onions and potatoes to the side, revealing the layers beneath. Some of the onions had sprouted, the base of their roots as soft as the apples. The potatoes were no better, either already half-rotted or dusty white with some kind of mildew. Varenov swept the gathered soldiers with a baleful eye, took in the condition of the Brovettans themselves. Gaunt and starved, all of them. Most of those present were men, only a few women, all of them sporting yellowed bruises, thinning hair. She'd seen no children on the streets.

She stomped back to where Captain Pulvar had recovered, watching her with outright hatred now.

"Where is the meat allocation?"

"It's in a separate building."

"Take me there."

The captain gestured the escort into formation, Varenov motioning Treant toward the woman who'd shown her the rotten apples. Treant sidled over and made certain she accompanied them. Pulvar didn't appear to notice.

Varenov smelled the building before they turned a corner and saw it, the reek of blood and offal staggering. The building was deeper toward the hull, tables set up outside with portions of meat of various types set out, flies buzzing over it all, blood dripping to the cobbles. A group of Brovettans waited to one side in a cluster, held back by more soldiers. Through the open doorways into the interior, shouts mingled with the bleat of sheep and the clatter of knives against butcher's blocks. Varenov could see only vague shadows inside, but the stench that rolled out through the doors forced her to cover her mouth with one hand.

A man with a stained butcher's apron suddenly appeared and dumped the contents of a bucket on the table, disappearing back inside without a glance. She scanned the meat, already swarmed by the flies—all of it thick with fat and gristle, cut into portions for a child. Some of it had an off color; none of it looked appealing.

"What kind of meat is this?" she asked through her hand.

"I wouldn't know," Pulvar said.

She faced him. "I want to see inside."

Before he could protest, she rounded the table and entered, pausing a few paces inside so her eyes could adjust. Near the front, butchers worked, knives skinning and deboning with precise movements. Others carved haunches and flanks down to portions without finesse, using cleavers. No carefully sliced filets here. She forced herself to move deeper inside, where she found vats of offal and blood and fat near the slaughtering area, carcasses strung up to drain. The air grew hot and heavy, sticky with blood. It coated her skin. Stomach heaving, she pressed deeper still, to where the animals were housed, cows and goats and sheep milling about in their own shit, their skins coated with excrement, flies attacking their eyes and the sores on their flanks, some of them clearly diseased. A few were struggling to get up, their hindquarters paralyzed. She saw at least three already dead, rats gnawing at the bodies.

She tasted bile at the back of her throat and bolted for the opening, aware that only Treant, the captain, and her own bodyguards had entered with her. Outside, she bent over, one hand against the building, and dry heaved, thankful that nothing came up.

A hand fell onto her back and Treant asked, "Are you all right?"

She nodded, swallowed back the acid taste that coated her tongue, and rose.

"This is what you're feeding them?" Her voice cracked, her rage matching his hatred. "Diseased animals? Butchered in these conditions? Do you even bother to pull the rats off or are the rats part of the menu?"

"This is what we are sent."

Varenov moved toward Pulvar. She reached for him, hands trembling, but she didn't trust herself and closed them into fists, forced them to her side. She halted a few paces away. "And nothing inside you prompted you to protest? No qualm, no waver of decency, urged you to demand better?"

"After what they did to this city, it is only what they deserve."

"None of them did this!" Varenov spat. "The ones who did were captured. They sit in the city prison. I know this. I've been there."

The captain said nothing.

They glared at each other until Varenov said, "I want to see Eri Cantell."

Pulvar's hatred broke in confusion. "Eri Cantrell?"

"She and her parents were assaulted in the initial riots at the marketplace beneath the towers. Her father was killed. Her mother was badly beaten. I was her ward, until her mother recovered. I believe they were taken from their home and sent here, to this zone. I want to speak to them. I want to see how they are faring in the zone."

The captain's anger returned. "We don't keep records of who is here or where they reside."

"I know Eri."

They both turned to face the woman who Varenov had pulled out of line, still standing near Treant and her guards.

"Take me to her."

Pulvar protested, but the woman had already struck out and Varenov followed, gesturing Treant and her two escorts to her side. She heard the captain shouting orders behind her, his soldiers scrambling, but Varenov ignored them.

"Where are all the children?" Varenov asked the woman as they walked, moving swiftly.

"Most keep them at home and don't let them out. The soldiers separated a few of them from their parents, to punish the parents, and now no one lets them run free." She shot a glance behind them, clearly terrified of the captain, then whispered, "Some of them have been smuggled out."

"How?" Varevnov asked, then thought of what Lane had almost revealed. "No, don't answer that. I don't need to know. What else can you tell me?"

"The soldiers have become suspicious that people are missing. They're investigating. It's only a matter of time before they find out what we're doing. The rest of us here, those that are staying behind, we expect we're going to have to fight to help the last of us escape. We've already started preparing, but we don't know when it will happen. Soon though." She sucked in a sharp breath. "The captain is coming."

Varenov looked back to see Pulvar and a contingent of men double what he'd brought before running toward them. He must have summoned reinforcements while she was inside the abattoir. "Take me to Eri, but don't say anything else. As soon as we're there, slip away if you can. And don't come back out. He'll come after you."

The woman only managed a nod as the captain and the others overtook them, forcing them to halt.

"What are you doing?" she asked.

"You aren't allowed inside the zone without an escort," Pulvar said, barely containing his anger.

"I'd forgotten." She turned to the woman. "Eri Cantrell lives where again?"

"Down there, second tenement on the left, fourth floor. She and her mother share the third apartment with two other families."

Varenov absorbed this without comment, merely scanning the indicated street before facing the captain again. "Shall we?"

He gestured her to move. "After this, you're leaving."

"Of course. I'm going to need to speak to the Council. And Prefect Arctus."

Pulvar didn't seem particularly concerned. "Who do you think gave me my orders?"

The interior of the tenement was clean, the building in surprisingly decent shape, considering how close to the hub they were. Only half of the lucent lighting worked, supplemented by oil lanterns. Those who were outside of their rooms, congregating in the halls or the lobby, quickly retreated upon sight of the captain, doors closed and locked. They proceeded to the fourth floor. Pulvar tried the third apartment door.

"Locked," he said, then motioned some of his men forward to break it down.

Varenov forestalled them with a look. "Allow me."

She knocked.

The door cracked open, a matron peering out. "What do you want?"

"I'd like to see Eri Cantell and her mother."

She gave Varenov a rough once-over, caught sight of the captain standing at her shoulder. "I suppose you'll just break it down if I don't let you in."

She swung the door open, Varenov stepping in before the captain, gaze sweeping the cramped room containing three beds, a table, and a cupboard with a meager supply of plates and bowls. Two elderly men watched them from chairs around the table.

"Where are they?" Varenov asked the matron.

"The door on the right."

Varenov pushed past the table, catching a glimpse of the other room to the left. A man stood protectively at the door, sheltering a woman and two older boys inside. All of them were as gaunt as those at the square.

When she halted at the door to the room on the right, another young man stood abruptly, shoving Eri behind him, both protecting the woman lying in the bed. "You can't have her!"

"I'm not here to take anyone. Eri, it's me, Varenov."

Eri gasped and hope lit her eyes, dying almost instantly as she caught sight of Captain Pulvar stepping past her.

"This is the girl?" he asked with a frown. "And her mother?"

"It is." Varenov stepped toward Eri and the man, the girl breaking into silent sobs. "Eri, what's wrong?"

"It's mother," she gasped between hitching breaths. "She's ill."

The young man pulled Eri close, her cries muffled in his shoulder. Varenov brushed past them and knelt, reaching for Eri's mother's forehead. Her skin was yellowed and slick with sweat, the heat palpable even before she touched flesh. The woman's eyes were sunken in their sockets and she reeked of sickness.

"She's burning up with fever." Varenov shifted her hands to her neck, her chest. "And her neck is swollen, breath shallow. She needs a healer immediately. Treant, fetch the carriage."

"Halt where you are!" Captain Pulvar barked, and the Iandolan guardsmen who'd accompanied them up the stairs suddenly tensed.

The captain turned on Varenov. "No one is fetching any carriages. These Brovettans are staying here. The only people leaving are you, Councilor Varenov, and your escort. I should never have let you enter in the first place. Sergeant! Get them out of here!"

The Iandolan soldiers shoved forward, the matron crying out in the outer room, a scuffle breaking out, men swearing, the mother in the other room screaming, the father slamming the door shut. Varenov's guards blocked the door to the inner room, drawing swords, cutting Treant, Varenov, the captain, Eri, and the young man holding her off from the others. The Iandolan soldiers drew weapons, the sergeant shouting orders down the hall to those waiting outside.

Then everything grew still.

Varenov stood, but Captain Pulvar slid a dagger from its sheath and held it to her neck before she could move away from the bed.

"I will kill them all unless you leave peacefully. Tenants, bodyguards, and assistants."

Varenov's hands were clenched into fists again. Her bodyguards kept their eyes trained on the Iandolans, although one of them shot a hard glance back at the captain. Treant stared at her in shock.

She lifted her chin slightly, the captain's blade following. "We'll leave. Without trouble."

Stepping forward, she paused next to Eri, held protectively by the young man now. "I'll send a healer."

Eri nodded.

Edging around them, Captain Pulvar staying close behind her, she motioned Treant to leave in front of her, her bodyguards ahead of him. They eased out into the outer room, the matron and the two elderly men huddled up against one wall, one of the chairs splintered. A gash in the woman's forehead trailed blood down her chin.

The Iandolan soldiers retreated before them, down the hall and out into the street, where they were immediately surrounded. Captain Pulvar issued orders and they marched past the slaughterhouse and the square to the barricades. Brovettans peered from windows, alcoves, and alleys, Iandolan soldiers clustering at corners and keeping the streets clear.

When they reached the barricades, already open, Varenov made certain Treant was through, then faced Pulvar. His men were already resetting the barricades.

"I'll be sending a healer."

"They won't be allowed in. We have healers of our own here."

Varenov doubted it—doubted if they did that the healer would be sent to see Eri's mother.

She retreated to the carriage, Treant already inside, one guard settling inside with them, the other remaining outside with the driver. They lurched into motion.

"What can we do?" Treant asked.

Varenov ground her teeth together, then faced him.

"Contact Mannert. I need to speak to her."

Chapter Fourteen

Lane waited as the elevator settled, not quite even with the floor on Level Fifteen, and Devon and Cerelle ushered the latest batch of refugees from the quarantine zone out into the warehouse.

"That's the last of the elderly and the young," Devon said as they shambled uncertainly toward where Carbolen's gang were clustering them in smaller groups to be taken to one of the several safe houses he, Maupin, and Lane's father had established on the various levels.

Lane hadn't been present during that discussion, but with the arrival of John Senn and the other rebels from Luminesque, it became clear that funneling everyone out through the tull to the safety of Brovetto was no longer an option. There was no haven in that Crystal City any longer.

Instead, Carbolen had identified areas deep within the lower levels, near the hub, in dead zones and other abandoned areas, where they could remain hidden, at least for a while. His gangs took them there, then helped protect the areas from discovery. Maupin's men worked on settling them in and getting supplies to them. Lane knew of at least three such locations, but there were more.

She wondered where these new refugees would be taken and if it was better than the internment camp they'd fled.

"Who will be coming down next?" she asked.

Cerelle stepped back into the elevator. "No one else tonight. Scerano wants to meet with the others to discuss what happens next." Devon moved to join her, but she gently shoved him back, nodding to someone behind them. "You've got a meeting of your own."

The elevator lurched into motion, pulling her up out of view, as Lane turned to see what she meant.

Raven and Nic stood behind them.

"We've been summoned," Nic said, with distaste.

"By whom?" Lane asked, although she already knew.

"John Senn," Raven said.

* * *

Raven led them all down to Level Ten, the small group joining another set of refugees from the Level Twelve quarantine zone briefly before they cut away to wherever their new safe house would be. Carbolen had found a narrow twist of tunnel between Level Eleven and Twelve that allowed those in that zone to escape.

The zone on Level Twenty had been more difficult.

A moment before they arrived, Lane recognized the streets they were on. "Wait," she said, "we're headed toward—"

"The theater, yes," Raven said, rounding a corner.

Before them stood the theater Maupin had used as their initial base of operations on their return.

"Whose idea was this?" Devon asked. "Wasn't this compromised when the Iandolans discovered our warehouse?"

"According to Maupin's tullers, they never saw any activity here from the city patrol or the army. Maupin thinks it's safe."

"What about you?"

Rave hesitated. "I wouldn't use it, but I've done some surveillance and it appears fine. He and Senn have twenty men on patrol and I'm certain Carbolen has at least that many as well."

They approached the main door, Raven slipping inside first, Nic bringing up the rear. The foyer was dark, but light glowed through the doors leading to the audience seating area and stage. Movement near the stairs to the balcony caught Lane's eye, two watchers posted there, another two on the other side.

They stepped across the ragged carpet to the main hall.

A large square table sat on the stage, seats placed on all four sides. Senn was already in deep discussions with Maupin and a few tullers at one corner. Both of the men glanced up as Raven led them down between the remaining seats.

"Where's Dalton?" Devon asked. "I thought he'd be here."

"He's coming," Raven said.

Before they arrived, Carbolen stepped onto the stage, entering from the right, flanked by Leinn, Toral, and a slew of gang members. They fanned out on that side, while Maupin's and Senn's men tensed, shifting position.

"I'm here," Carbolen said, taking in the table, the theater, the number of men Maupin and Senn had on stage. His gaze fell on Lane and the others as they circled behind the table toward the back.

"Thank you for coming," Senn said, pushing away from the table. "Did you bring your maps?"

"What is this about, Senn? I've already agreed to help with the Brovettans—find them housing, try to keep them away from the city patrols and the army's eye. What more do you want?"

"A diversion."

Carbolen's eyebrows rose. "A diversion?"

Senn rounded the table, motioned to the chairs on one side. "Have a seat." Behind him, Maupin and the tullers took seats at one edge, Senn's men settling to the side to their right, closest to the audience.

Carbolen hesitated, then strode forward and sat, Leinn and Toral taking the seats to either side. The other gang members spread out behind him. "Talk fast."

"We've been funneling Brovettans out of the internment camps for days now. Using your tunnels and the elevator, we've managed to bring out nearly all of the elderly and the youngest children. We're about to start with the rest, but we both know that we won't be able to continue this indefinitely. The Iandolan soldiers are already suspicious. They've noticed the decreasing numbers, but they haven't been able to verify it because it's only been children and the elderly. Once those between start disappearing, they're going to investigate."

"So we pull out as many as we can before they discover the tunnels and the elevator. Everyone knew the risk when we started this."

Senn began to circle the table. "Unacceptable. The Brovettans should never had been imprisoned like this. What the Council did is unconscionable. Immoral. Illegal according to the Founders' Pact. But they forsook any pretense of following the Pact decades ago." He'd rounded to the side of the table that remained empty and now leaned his weight into both arms. "I will not leave any Brovettans inside those camps."

Carbolen produced a dagger and fiddled with it, resting the tip on the table's wood. "That's not my problem."

Senn slammed his palm flat, making everyone jump. "It is! All of this is everyone's problem! Because if we allow them to incarcerate the Brovettans on the pretense that they're all insurgents, then who's next? What if the guilds in Lambenesque demand a better trade agreement for their food and livestock and Iridesque disagrees? Iandolo can't survive without that food. They'll send their army, their mages, and if that doesn't intimidate the farmers guild, they can simply declare them rebels. Then they can seize the foodstock—the rice and carrots and beef—and if the farmers resist they'll arrest them and throw them into more camps like these."

"The other cities would never allow it."

Senn shoved away from the table. "Like hell. How many protested their treatment of the Brovettans? And even if they did—let's say Scintillesque's guilds protested the arrests of their fellow farmers in Lambenesque—what can they do? If they do anything significant except complain, Iandolo will simply declare them insurgents as well.

"No, if we allow them to get away with it now, with the Brovettans, then there will be no stopping them. It's what they're counting on."

Carbolen spun the dagger by its tip but said nothing.

Senn drifted back around behind him. "You've been waiting over seventeen years to take down the Council after they betrayed you, Captain Ben Coral." Carbolen stiffened. "After all this time, after building up your army of ruffians, are you going to let this moment slip by?" He leaned in close, mouth next to Carbolen's ear, although his voice was loud enough to carry. "The Council has exposed its throat. Seize the opportunity. Slit it now, before they realize their mistake."

Senn pulled back. Carbolen's dagger had stilled. Lane found herself holding her breath, fingers twisted into knots behind her back.

"You mentioned a diversion?" Carbolen finally said.

Lane exhaled, head bowed.

"You thought he would say no?" Raven asked, voice pitched low.

"He could have. After all, Carbolen isn't after the entire Council, only whoever was behind his demotion and the failed attack on Brovetto seventeen years ago."

"He may have reached the point where the particular traitor doesn't matter anymore, as long as whoever it is goes down with the rest," Devon said.

At the table, Senn had retreated toward his own men. "We know we can't get everyone inside the camps out in the slow trickle we've been using so far. To save the last of them, we're going to need to pull all of those remaining out all at once."

Leinn snorted. "And how do you propose we do that?"

Senn smiled. "We attack the barricades."

Leinn laughed, the sound sharp. "Have you seen how many guardsmen they have on the gates? And those are only the ones we can see. Who knows how many are actually inside the buildings they're using as their walls."

"Not as many as you think," Senn said. "We've been watching their shift changes and patrols."

Toral shifted forward. "Eyes can only see so much, unless you have someone on the inside."

"Actually, they do," someone said.

All of the various escorts reached for weapons as Captain Mannert and Dalton entered from the left. Mannert moved toward the fourth side of the table, Dalton catching Raven's attention and motioning them to join them. Raven, Devon, and Nic drifted forward, Lane a step behind. Dalton gave Devon a brief kiss before settling into one of the chairs, Raven into another. Mannert remained standing behind the third.

"I thought your allegiance to the army wouldn't let you interfere," Maupin said.

"Except to look the other way, if possible. That was our initial agreement, yes. But I've had a change of heart."

"Captain Mannert has had more than a change of heart," Senn said, rounding the table behind Maupin. "She's the one who has been helping us pull Brovettans out of the Level Twenty camp."

"How?" Carbolen asked suspiciously. "We couldn't find an access point."

"Deliveries come and go," Mannert said. "I was in charge of some of them. And not all of the city patrol or soldiers are comfortable with what's been done to the Brovettans." She sat. "It worked well, until the army returned and took over. It's more difficult now. And I'm afraid the number I managed to smuggle out was negligible."

"What's changed? Why are you here now?"

Mannert faced Carbolen. "The army has changed, Captain. I thought with their return and the orders to seize control of the Brovettan camps that the situation would improve, but it's only gotten worse. The men and women Prefect Arctus has put in control are more vicious and brutal than the city patrols and ruffians they'd pulled from the War colleges to run the camps initially. It's caused a split in the army, although those who oppose the camps keep quiet."

"Like you."

Mannert tensed at the accusation, then forced herself to relax. "Yes, like me. Until recently."

"So I ask again, what's changed?"

Mannert hesitated, then said, "I've been ordered to help."

"By who?"

"My mother," Lane said.

Everyone turned to face her and her heart stuttered in her chest. But she kept her eyes on Mannert.

"It was my mother, wasn't it? She went to see the camps."

Mannert merely nodded.

"Then have Varenov release the Brovettans," Carbolen said. "She's a councilor after all."

"It doesn't work that way and you know it," Senn said. "She's doing what she can without exposing herself."

"You know this how? Have you been in contact with her?"

Senn had halted behind Maupin. "I haven't. But I know my wife. Varenov would never stand by and do nothing."

Everyone remained silent for a moment, then Lane stepped forward. "So what's your plan for getting the Brovettans—all of them—out?"

"We attack the barricades, on all three camps, at the same time."

"Who attacks them?" Leinn asked.

"All of us. Your men, Carbolen, mine, and Maupin's. The Brovettans on Level Twelve and Sixteen are already coordinating their own assault from the inside. There's a reason most of those able-bodied have remained behind."

"That's not enough to take down the barricades," Leinn said, "even with the Brovettans flanking them. How—"

"That's the diversion," Carbolen interrupted. He fixed his gaze on Senn. "The attack on the barricades is simply to buy everyone time to get all of the rest out through our tunnels and the elevators."

Senn didn't answer, began moving around the table toward Mannert. "It won't be easy. But we have Captain Mannert here to help us."

The captain leaned forward. "Level Twelve has the least number of soldiers assigned to it. The assault on the barricades might even work there, depending on how many you send. But the main goal is to distract while the Brovettans escape through the tunnels. Same for Level Sixteen, except there are more seasoned soldiers there. Thankfully, the elevators on that level can handle more Brovettans faster than the tunnels on Twelve. The real problem is Level Twenty. Captain Pulvar is, unfortunately, competent. And the men surrounding him are mostly loyal to him. Factor in that there is no easy escape route for the Brovettans to use and I'm not certain how we'll get them out."

"Careful planning," Senn said. He was now standing to Dalton's right. He faced Carbolen. "Your maps?"

Toral glanced at the gang leader, who nodded. She swung the satchel over her shoulder to the table, pulled out a sheaf of papers, and began spreading a select few of them out across the table. "These are for Levels Twelve, Sixteen, and Twenty, the areas around each of the camps, altered to indicate the current barricades and what information we have about the changes made inside."

"Careful planning won't produce an escape route," Carbolen said as she worked, "not for hundreds, no matter how detailed our maps. If we couldn't find it before, it isn't there."

"We aren't looking for an escape route," Senn said. "We're going to create our own."

"How?" Maupin asked.

"With our own personal mage." And Senn turned to Lane.

Her heart faltered and she took a step back, then halted.

Devon shifted between her and Senn. "You have no right to ask this of her!"

She reached out and caught his arm. "No, Devon, it's all right." She faced her father, chin up. "I'll do it."

* * *

Lane sat cross-legged in one of the rooms she and the others had claimed on the second floor of an old tenement on Level Twelve, near the warehouse and the elevators. The rooms were empty and non-descript. Even the dead lucent embedded in the walls was utilitarian; no branching trees or curling vines with delicate flowers here. The paint on the walls was peeling, the floorboards scuffed and creaking. One section had been torn up in the far corner where someone had searched for something underneath. Devon had fixed a couple of the lucent lights, which cast the room in soft shadows and pale green light. Idly, she traced the base sigil in the air before her, the familiar shape of the double pyramid manifesting before her as the potential inside her chest surged forward, waiting for direction. She held it, hand crooked, then waved it away, the tingling fading with the pyramid. Then she did it again.

"You don't have to do it, you know."

Her hand clenched, cut short mid-sigil. She glanced over her shoulder at Nic standing in the doorway.

"Whatever Picall is teaching you, it's working," she said. "I didn't even hear the floorboards creak."

Nic shrugged and stepped inside, settling down next to her. "I doubt it has anything to do with me. Wherever you were, you were in there deep." He hesitated, then asked, "Thinking about the raid on the camps? It's almost time to head out."

"Honestly, no. Thinking about my mother, my childhood, my...my father." The last word caught in her throat and she gave a curt laugh. "That's the first time I've called him my father out loud. It's...strange."

"What is? Everyone has a father. Some of us even know who he is."

Lane gave him a sidelong look, suddenly realizing she knew nothing about Nic's past, only that he was a gang member. "Do you know yours?"

"Not really. I know his name—Carl—and I know he was a right bastard. He used to beat on us when I was little. He didn't even need to be drinking to do it, although he was often enough. One night, when I was six, he beat my mother to death in our little flat. Before he could turn his rage on me, I ran. One of Carbolen's gang found me huddled behind a heap of trash deep inside Level Eleven."

He said it all without any emotion.

"That's...terrible."

Nic waved a hand. "That's the past. No use mulling on it endlessly. Turns out Carbolen's gang wasn't much better. Same fear that if you did something wrong, someone would retaliate. But the retaliation wasn't as random."

"I always thought the towers were a prison, that my mother was my jailor, but now I'm not so certain. She's spent the last seventeen years on the Council, secretly working with my father and the Brovettans—the real rebels—trying to make the lives of those in Luminesque better. Having me there, a constant reminder of what she'd lost, must have been hell for her. And a risk. If anyone found out about her, about who my father really was—"

"But no one did."

"No. No one did." Silence for a moment. "So much of what my mother did when I was younger makes sense now though."

Someone was approaching, the boards in the outer room creaking.

"Everyone ready?" Raven asked as she appeared in the door. She was back in her Regular outfit—dark clothing, glints of metal and leather where daggers and other weapons were hidden. She'd even cut her hair short. Devon and Dalton were behind her. "Where's Picall?"

Nic stood, helping Lane up. "She's already with Maupin and the other tullers on Level Twelve."

"Then it's time to go."

They descended to the street, Raven and Dalton taking point, Nic behind, a formation that had become unspoken ritual.

As they headed toward the warehouse and the elevators, Devon asked, "Are you ready?"

Lane clenched and unclenched her sigil hand a few times. "I'm ready."

As they passed the warehouse, Devon and Dalton broke off, the guards shadowing the doorway letting them through. They'd spent the last three days organizing the coordinated attacks. Cerelle would be waiting with the bulk of the Brovettans above—those that couldn't or wouldn't fight—while Scerano would lead the attack on the barricades from the inside. They'd bring down as many as they could in the elevators as fast as they could once the attack started. After a certain time, Scerano would retreat with the rest of the Brovettans while the attack from the outside, led by Leinn and a slew of Carbolen's gang members, intensified, hopefully keeping the Iandolans at the barricade. No need to follow the Brovettans after all, they were already all trapped inside the camp.

Lane, Raven, and Nic, meanwhile, would be hitting the camp on Level Twenty. They'd selected a wide dead-end alley that cut into one section of the buildings that served as a wall for the camp. Carbolen would lead the majority of his gang members on a frontal assault on the barricades here, while Lane created a passage for the Brovettans to escape through at the end of the alley. It was significantly far from the main attack, so if the Iandolan soldiers noticed the escape route, they'd have to divide and fight on two fronts. Captain Mannert had spread the word to the Brovettans on Level Twenty to be prepared to run and intended to be inside the camp when the attack started. She and a select few of the Iandolan soldiers who didn't agree with the current policies of the Council and Prefect Arctus would help protect the Brovettans on the inside.

Everyone who managed to escape was to be taken to the lower levels and the hidden areas Carbolen and Maupin had established for them.

By the time they reached Level Twenty, Lane's entire body was vibrating with tension, her skin itching. Raven led them to where Carbolen and his gang were amassing for the attack, a square only a few blocks from the barricades. Only a hundred people were present, scattered across the square, idling around the benches and the statue of a falcon at its center. Raven hesitated at the square's edge, until Nic said, "There," and pointed.

"Not too many here yet," Raven said as she halted ten paces from Carbolen's back.

He turned and gave her a cold look. "They'll all be here. None of the gangs dare defy me. Unlike you. Besides, we still have time. You, Nic, and Lane need to get into position. Do you need a map?"

"All I need is our escort."

Carbolen stilled, then relaxed and nodded. "Toral?" The gang's spy leader stepped forward. "Is your team ready?"

"Of course."

"Then accompany Raven, Lane, and Nic to the alley."

Toral raised a hand and twenty of the surrounding men broke away to join her. She sauntered up to Raven, halting a step away. "Lead the way, Regular."

From behind, Lane saw Raven's hand twitch toward a blade near her back, fingers touching the handle, but she let them slide away without a word, spinning and catching Nic's eye as she passed. Lane couldn't decipher what it meant.

Then they were all moving down streets, any citizens who saw them slipping quietly into doorways or shifting to the far side of the road. Only those clearly headed to the square to join Carbolen didn't falter, giving Toral a nod as they passed.

Only when they were close to the alley did Toral step forward, a curt word sending four scouts out in front of them to scan the street and the surrounding buildings. As soon as they returned with an all clear, they entered the dilapidated tenement across from the alley at the back, threading through the halls and rooms until they were near the front door.

Lane peered through one of the side windows. The alley across the way was shadowed, but clearly empty. It cut in between two brick buildings, ended in a brick wall, once some kind of loading dock. Or perhaps it was part of a building facing the street on the other side of the wall. The brick was a slightly different color, the outlines of a wide door clear even in the darkness.

She pulled back to let Raven look. The Regular spent no more than a breath scoping it out before asking, "Can you get through?"

"Not without making some noise."

Raven glanced over her shoulder. "Hopefully Carbolen can distract them enough they won't notice."

"Hopefully Captain Mannert doesn't leave us all high and dry," Toral said sharply.

Raven straightened. "She won't."

Two of Toral's scouts returned, one reporting, "Only the usual patrols on the roofs. Four men visible a couple of buildings down to the right, another four farther away to the left."

"Any sign of mages?" Toral asked.

"Not here."

"Mannert said they have them," Raven said. "It's just a matter of where they are when we strike."

Toral didn't answer.

Lane shook out her hand, opening and closing it, paced back and forth a few times.

Nic sidled closer. "Relax. Raven and I intend to stick close, protect your flanks, like we did with you and Devon at the Lyceum."

Lane gave him a weak smile.

A hollow thud bit the air, then another. Everyone tensed as two more followed.

"Time to move," Toral said.

Raven wrenched the door open, stepped out onto the street, then motioned them all forward. Lane raced across first, focused on the alley, on the brick wall at its end, aware of the faint shouts and screams coming from blocks away where Carbolen had attacked the barricades. She'd already started the sigil before reaching the alley entrance, let it lose the moment she stepped inside.

The brick exploded inwards, as if a gigantic hammer had smashed it from this side. Clouds of dust billowed outwards, choking as Lane forged into it, covering her mouth with her arm, blinking at the grit. She could hear stone raining down as the building settled, but she couldn't see to the far side yet.

"It's a storage room!" Raven shouted. "We aren't through to the far side yet. Toral, get your group moving!"

Raven latched onto Lane's arm and hauled her forward. They stumbled over a heap of brick, climbing it into the cavernous storage room beyond, Nic at their heels. Toral was shouting orders, gang members racing past on either side, securing the site. Something struck Lane hard on the shoulder, but she ignored the pain, coughing as they cleared the worst of the dust to see another brick wall before them.

"Lane—" Raven began.

But Lane had already completed the sigil.

The second wall burst like the first, the room beyond smaller as they all raced into the dust and falling debris. The third wall exploded out into the street beyond.

They stumbled over the threshold—

But the street beyond was empty.

"That damned Iandolan scumbag—" Toral began.

The door to the apartments across the way swung open. Mannert appeared briefly and shouted, "Rooftop!"

At the same moment, a crossbow bolt sank into the doorframe, splinters flying. Mannert vanished, but left the door open.

"Toral," Raven said.

"Already on it." The spymaster waved and five men broke left, another five right, slipping along the base of the building, then kicking in doors and entering those on either side.

"Wait here," Raven said, pulling Lane back, Nic stepping forward protectively.

"No need." Lane faced the doorway where Mannert had been, then completed a sigil, one that traced a pattern similar to something Terrial had done in the Lyceum quad.

Shimmering light shot up from the ground, framing a pathway from the breech to Mannert's building, curving up into an arch over their heads. Everything on the other side of the wall was visible but blurred and distorted.

"A shield," Lane said, as Raven took a tentative step forward, "like the one Terrial placed around herself, Devon, and I during the fight at the college. It should stop the crossbow bolts. And anything else they may throw at us."

Raven glanced back at her, then toward Toral. "Let's get these Brovettans out of here."

Raven raced to the far door, Mannert already shoving people through into the shield's tunnel. Toral's men split, half urging the terrified Brovettans across the street and up into the holes created in the storage room. The others retreated, to lead them out of the internment camp and into the city beyond. The Brovettans stumbled along, some sobbing, mothers clutching children close, a few with satchels or suitcases or sacks. Toral stood beneath the crumbling entrance to the storage room, bellowing directions and shoving them up and over the piles of brick. "Faster! Run, you bastards! We don't know how long we can keep them busy!"

Lane stepped out a gap between the shield she'd created and the brick wall, stumbling as debris shifted beneath her feet.

"Where do you think you're going?" Nic said, following her.

Two bolts slammed into the barrier she'd created with sharp cracks and her heart thudded hard in her chest. But she swallowed and stepped out from the wall, hand raised, looking toward the roof where three men gazed down into the street, two frantically reloading their crossbows, the third glaring down at her.

Nic swore and stepped in front of her.

"Where's the fourth guard?" she muttered to herself.

One of those with a crossbow finished reloading and aimed it straight at her and Nic, the other soldier barking an order Lane couldn't make out.

Nic shoved her hard toward Mannert's end of the tunnel. "Move!"

"Wait," Lane said.

Abruptly all three on the roof spun to face something behind them. The first soldier shot his bow, then swung it as Toral's men appeared, blades already drawn.

Lane turned in the other direction, saw fighting on the rooftop farther down the street, then focused on the shield as Raven and Mannert stepped outside and approached. Mannert had a cut along her cheekbone, trickling blood down her to her chin.

"What happened?" Raven asked.

"Toral's men took out those on the roof," Lane answered, "but I only saw three of them. Didn't she say there were four?"

"Let's hope they caught the other one inside the building," Mannert said. Lane pointed to her cheek and she wiped at it with one hand, smearing the blood. "It's nothing."

"We shouldn't be out here," Nic said. "We're exposed. What if there are more of them?"

A hollow boom echoed through the street, bouncing oddly off the ceiling overhead and the buildings to either side. It came from the direction of the main barricades.

All four of them faced that direction.

"That sounded like some kind of explosion," Nic said.

"It was," Mannert said. "They have a mage."

Nic swore and Lane stepped forward, toward the barricade, but Raven grabbed her arm, fingers digging in hard.

"You can't," she said. "You need to stay and protect the Brovettans."

Lane drew breath to protest, caught the look in the ex-Regular's eyes, then nodded.

Mannert faced Raven. "You have this under control?"

"For now."

"Good. Then there's someone I need to check on." Mannert began to walk away from them, long, purposeful strides.

"Who?" Lane asked.

Mannert didn't turn. "A friend of your mother's!"

She broke into a trot, then veered hard to the left, down an alley, and vanished.

The three were silent a moment, until Raven asked, "Any idea what that was about?"

"Not a clue."

Lane faced the tunnel, shadowy figures running down its length toward freedom inside, light streaming down its sides like water.

"I wonder how Devon and Dalton are faring on Level Sixteen."

Chapter Fifteen

"Go, go, go!" Devon yelled at Dalton, who slammed his hand onto the elevator bar and slid it downwards, the elevator jolting into motion, the sobbing Brovettans crammed into the car shrieking as they were thrown into each other. Dalton gave him a last grim look through the lattice of the gate as he disappeared, then Devon shoved back from the press of bodies behind him and turned.

"The elevator will be back as soon as they unload below!" he bellowed, although no one was listening to him. Brovettans pressed up against him, all of them jostling for a better position. Men and women, faces filled with desperation, glistening with tears and sweat. The warehouse echoed with moans and prayers and gasping shrieks.

"Please!" Cerelle shouted from the gates of the second car. "Stand back! Calm down! We'll get to you as soon as we can!"

She shot a look of horror at Devon, then continued to try to calm the mob.

A man stumbled into Devon, breath hot in his face, reeking of onion, as he cried, "You have to let me on next! I have a wife! A child! A little girl of four!"

Devon pushed the man away. "We intend to get everyone."

"For the Founders' sake!" the man pleaded, others already scrabbling forward, pulling the man away. "A daughter! Her name is Hallie!"

Hands tugging at his arms, his shirt, Devon leaned his head back against the elevator shaft wall, closed his eyes, and tuned the ocean of voices out.

Beneath their uproar, he could hear the fighting. An entire squadron or battalion or whatever Dalton had called it had found them almost immediately after the attack had begun at the barricades. Scerano and nearly all of those that had agreed to fight at the barricade from inside the walls had already left. The sudden appearance of the soldiers had startled them all. Those fighters that had been left behind immediately roared a warning. Some of those waiting inside the building to use the elevators had grabbed up weapons and joined them in an attempt to hold them off.

Everyone else had panicked.

A hideous shriek yanked Devon out of his calm as the other elevator returned and Cerelle barked, "Stand back! Stand back or we won't be able to get the gates open!" She shoved people back, hands scratching her arms, her face, and then suddenly her sister, Sadie, appeared, blade drawn, and began slashing. Someone cursed and another screamed, but those near the front jerked back out of her reach.

Cerelle didn't wait, pulling the gate to the side with a clang. As soon as it was secured, her sister stepped aside and the mob surged forward, people pummeling each other in their attempt to get on the elevator. A man punched a woman in the face, blood streaming from her broken nose. Farther back, someone stumbled, hand grasping onto a shoulder and they screamed for help, but no one noticed as the fingers pulled free of the shirt and the person was dragged under.

Devon felt bile at the back of his throat.

Then he felt the wall rumbling at his back as his own elevator returned.

\To the side, Cerelle shouted, "We're full! We're full! Stand back!" and Sadie waded into the fray again.

The elevator ground to a halt and the tide of bodies shifted toward Devon.

"Get back!" Dalton roared, before Devon had a chance to reach for the gate. The ex-soldier stood in the middle of the elevator, sword drawn, rage in the lines of his face. Blood matted his hair, smeared his forehead. "Get back or no one gets on board!"

Those closest lurched backwards, startled, their panic stuttering. Devon seized the opportunity and pulled the gate open, Dalton edging forward. He glared around at them all, flicked a glance toward Devon, then stood to the side.

"Now enter."

As they surged forward, he roared, "In an orderly fashion!"

They crowded forward, still pushing, still driven by fear, but they weren't fighting each other.

"Are you all right?" Dalton asked, standing vigilant at the edge of the door.

"I'm fine," Devon said. "Hot, sweaty, nauseated, but fine." He wiped at his forehead, skin feeling gritty, throat dry.

Dalton scanned the rest of those in the warehouse as he stepped back to reach for the panel. "Only twenty more trips."

Devon elbowed people back from the entrance and closed the gate without a word.

* * *

Captain Mannert slipped into a vacant tenement as a squad of her fellow Iandolan soldiers raced down the street, headed toward the main barricades, the sergeant snapping orders as they passed. She glanced both directions, caught sight of a group of Brovettans cutting across the street into an alley. She frowned. Word had been spread about the attack tonight, but she supposed that not everyone would have heard. Then there were those that would refuse to heed the advice. And those that couldn't...or wouldn't.

Like those Varenov had asked her to check up on.

When the street cleared, she stepped out and strode purposefully down the block, catching flickers of movement down an alley or in an upper story window. But even so, the street was eerily quiet. She'd been here enough to know what it should feel like—tense and desperate and fearful, but populated. There should be soldiers on the street, Brovettans traversing to the market or the butcher, shoulders hunched and eyes averted.

She passed the square, the wagons of produce abandoned. A covey of youths raided what was left, tossing the worst of it to the ground. One of them cried out and pointed. The rest turned and tensed, faces defiant, half-rotten apples clutched to their chest. For a moment, she thought they might charge, but they held.

She gave them a half-assed salute and moved on.

Three streets and five blocks further on, she hesitated before a building. She'd seen no soldiers after the square and only a few solitary Brovettans. It gave her hope that most were at the rendezvous with Raven, Lane, and the others.

Looking up, she saw a curtain fall back into place and sighed.

Mounting the steps outside, she paused in the foyer. She thought she'd heard the creak of floorboards, but when she leaned back to scan the first-floor hall, she saw nothing. All of the apartment doors were closed. Still, she took the stairs slowly, drawing her sword before she'd hit the second floor. At the third, she leaned over the balustrade down to the foyer, but the lower floors were empty.

Something distant exploded, felt as a thump in her chest more than heard. The building shook slightly. She was closer to the barricades here than she'd been earlier.

"Third apartment, fourth floor," she murmured to herself, moving down the hall.

The third door was ajar. She toed it open, hinges creaking. The interior was a mess, clothes and food and trinkets scattered across the floor and table, chairs askew, as if someone had left in a hurry, grabbing whatever they thought was important at the last minute. She stepped inside, heels crunching spilled rice underfoot, headed toward the door on the right.

It was open. Inside, an older woman lay on a bed, a younger girl kneeling at her side, hunched over her. The woman's breath was ragged and strained, her lungs filled with fluid.

Mannert lowered her sword. "Eri Cantell?"

The girl's shoulders tensed, her visible hand clutching the blanket on the bed. "I heard you come in. What do you want? The others have left, all of them. They didn't believe the rumors until they heard the sounds of the attack on the barricade, then they snatched up what they could and fled. Even Nils." Her voice caught. "He said he loved me. But he wouldn't stay."

"Why didn't you flee with them?"

Eri faced her, her eyes bloodshot, the flesh beneath bruised. "I won't leave without my mother."

Mannert stepped into the room, but Eri bolted upright, a knife flashing in her hand. Mannert could smell the death in the room now, the suffocating rankness of sweat and disease.

She held up her free hand, slid her blade back into its sheath slowly. "I'm not here to hurt you. Varenov sent me."

The intense hatred and grief in Eri's eyes faltered. "Varenov?"

Mannert took another step forward, both hands free now. "Yes. She wanted to make certain you and your mother made it to the rendezvous."

Eri's hand began to tremble. "So it's true? We can get out of here?"

"And get your mother to a healer, yes."

Eri began to sob and Mannert grabbed her wrist and lowered the forgotten knife. She held Eri close, the girl's body shuddering, then gently pushed her aside to check on her mother.

The stench of sickness nearly gagged her, the woman's clothes sodden and limp, her skin yellowed and feverish. Mannert grimaced. She didn't think a healer would help; she was too far gone.

But she'd promised to get Eri out.

Leaning forward, she hauled the stick-thin woman up by one arm, tucking herself under and wrapping her other arm around the woman's waist. She weighed practically nothing, but it wasn't the weightlessness of starvation. This was different. It was the weightlessness of death. She'd felt it with others before—her own father, hauling fellow soldiers off of the streets after a battle.

"Let's go," she said, already moving toward the door.

"I don't think so."

Mannert halted at the rough voice, an Iandolan army sergeant stepping into the doorway to block their way, sword pointed at her chest. At least two other soldiers stood in the outer room.

"Eri, get behind me," she said. Then, "Step aside, sergeant. I need to get this woman to a healer."

"I don't think so."

Mannert straightened. "I outrank you. Step aside."

His sword didn't waver. "Captain Pulvar said that if you came here, you were to be treated as a traitor."

Mannert met his gaze. "I think it's clear this woman is sick. She needs a healer."

The man's sword shifted and sank into Eri's mother's chest without a sound, pulling free with a gout of blood and recentering on Mannert before she could suck in a shocked breath. Eri's mother stiffened and then sagged in her grasp.

"I think she's beyond a healer's help now," the sergeant said.

Then Eri screamed, the sound penetrating. Mannert heaved her mother's body at the sergeant, reached for her own blade. He stumbled back with a curse, then shoved the body aside with enough time to counter Mannert's first swing. Swords clashed, the vibration shuddering up Mannert's wrist into her arm. The sergeant advanced, Mannert stumbling back toward the bed. She yelled, "Eri, run!" but the other soldiers were already forcing their way into the room, treading on Eri's mother's body as they came. Eri screamed and screamed, Mannert's ears ringing as she parried and thrust, the sergeant blocking and countering with ease. The room was too crowded and confined. The other soldiers seized Eri and began dragging her toward the door. Mannert swore and scored a shallow cut on the sergeant's upper arm, but his next thrust shoved her back into the bed and she tumbled.

Twisting as she fell, she hit the headboard with her right shoulder and slammed into the floor. Her arm went numb, sword falling from senseless fingers, but still she rolled, left hand reaching for her dagger.

A boot heel pounded into her chest, her breath expelled in a ragged gasp, spittle flying. Before she could heave in another, the same boot settled onto her throat, pressing hard.

She choked, scrabbled at the sergeant's leg, rocked her body, but the booted foot didn't budge.

Her vision began to narrow as she stared up at the sergeant's face. He wasn't grinning or smirking, she noted. He wasn't angry. His face was implacable.

Her struggles grew lethargic, her chest burning with an intense, tingling fire.

And then everything went dark.

* * *

"Keep moving! Don't crowd or no one will get through!" Lane shouted at the press of Brovettans in the narrow rooms of the tenement Mannert had chosen for them to hide in. People were shoving to get to the door and the shield tunnel she'd created beyond, most of them breaking into a ragged run as soon as they passed through. She and Nic were trying to control the mob. Raven was at the other end with Toral. "Back off! You're pushing too hard!"

"Where are they all coming from?" Nic asked. "It didn't seem like we had this many an hour ago."

"We didn't."

"None of us believed it was happening," an older man crushed up against Lane said. He winced in apology. "But word spread that it was real."

Lane twisted and shoved him through the door, the man falling to his knees. The next person through helped him up and then both ran for the far side.

"Shar!" a woman four deep in the crowd yelled. "Shar!" She turned to Lane. "My daughter! I was holding her hand, but she slipped away. Now I can't find her. Shar!"

The men and women around her pressed forward. Lane let another woman with five children clutching her dress through, then a young couple and two younger men, and then the woman was grabbing for her.

"My daughter! You have to help me find my daughter!"

"We can't," Lane said, prying her hands free from her arm. "You'll have to find her on the other side."

"I can't leave without my daughter. I won't!"

She stumbled as someone squeezed around her, those nearest already getting angry. "She's blocking the doorway!" someone bellowed. "Shove her through and let's get on with this!" Cries of agreement rose on all sides, people surging forward. The woman was forcibly heaved through the door, screaming, "Shar!" and then a half dozen broke through, pushing the woman to the side. Lane lost sight of her, but she could still hear her screaming her daughter's name.

Before she could react, Nic said sharply, "Lane!" and pointed beyond the shield. "We've got company."

She let the next few people through and stole a glance outside. In the crack between the shield and the front of the building, she saw an entire complement of soldiers marching toward their position.

She swore and pulled back. Then motioned to Nic. "Keep them going through, as fast as you can."

Without waiting for a reply, she swung through the door, between the shield and building, and into the street. On the far side of the tunnel, Raven emerged with Toral and four of Carbolen's gang members.

They converged in the center, before the tunnel.

"I thought we'd have more time," Toral said.

"Someone warned them we were here," Raven said.

"Time to pull out then."

"No," Lane said. "There are too many Brovettans still inside."

Toral snorted. "What do you intend to do? We've only got twenty of Carbolen's men here. There are over a hundred soldiers headed toward us. They span the entire street."

"You have me." Lane turned toward the building she'd just vacated, already starting a sigil. "No need to be quiet now. Nic! Get everyone away from the door!"

She didn't wait, sigil complete. Brick exploded out into the street with a blast of wind and grit, the entire façade of the building and the one next to it falling away. Stone rattled against the top of the tunnel, people inside screaming as dust billowed upwards in a thick cloud. Striding forward, Lane slammed her hand against the tunnel and released it, the entire shield shattering into shards of light like glass that danced upwards and winked out. Inside, Nic huddled with the rest of the Brovettans crowded into the now exposed rooms, while behind, the Iandolan soldiers were suddenly shouting orders.

"Run, you fools!" Lane yelled, then spun to face the soldiers.

The Brovettans still within the camp hesitated a moment, then broke for the jagged hole in the storage rooms that breeched the outer wall. Nic raced toward Lane, brushing brick debris from his hair and shoulders.

"A little more warning next time," he growled as he halted by her side. He scanned the army. "What are they doing?"

"Setting up a formation," Raven answered. "Toral, get as many of the Brovettans out as you can."

Toral cut back towards the storage rooms, shouting orders at the Brovettans and gang members alike. The four gang members stayed with them.

"What kind of formation?" Nic asked.

Raven shook her head. Lane watched, wishing she'd paid more attention to Devon's notes on the War students practice sessions in the quad. But she hadn't been interested in that. She'd focused on the notes on mages.

The soldiers had split into three groups, a block marching slightly forward from the others. In the center, she caught site of a flicker of gray amongst the Iandolan maroon and white.

Her chest seized in understanding and at the same time the soldiers in front parted in a well-practiced move. She could already see the hand gestures completing as she shouted, "Mage! Scatter!"

She'd barely taken two steps to the side when the cobblestones before them exploded upwards in a jagged path, cutting through their small group and into the mass of fleeing Brovettans.

Lane was thrown to the street as if punched from the side, her ears throbbing from the concussive force of the attack, hands and arm scraped up by the stone. Muffled screams filled the street. She groaned and rolled onto her elbows, chest bruised. Bodies were flung to either side of a shallow trench where the spell had landed, including two of the gang members. Others were picking themselves up, the Brovettans in the clear already recovering and sprinting for escape in desperation. A few paused to grab those that had been caught in the blast but were still moving. Nic lay a few feet from her. She could see him breathing, so she twisted and sat up.

The Iandolan soldiers were marching forward, still in formation.

Lane started a sigil.

As she finished the base form, the soldiers parted and she caught the end of the Iandolan mage's next attack. Same as the first.

Her hand snapped out a counter.

Cobblestones exploded again, slamming toward the Brovettans, but then a second set of explosions raced toward it, the two meeting twenty feet from Lane. The blast peppered Lane with pebbles as she shielded her face with one arm. On the other side of the street, Raven and one of the gang members were thrown to the ground again.

But Lane had already spun toward the soldiers. "Enough of this," she said, climbing to her feet. She completed a base form, shaped the secondary, and released it.

Fire rained down from overhead in sheets, but a shield appeared above most of the soldiers before it struck, shunting the flames off to one side, into a building. It caught instantly, only a portion of the flames missing the shield and hitting the edge of a formation. Men and women screamed and flailed, falling away, but Lane had already started another attack. Streaks of lightning lanced though the billowing plume of black smoke into one of the formations in the back, behind the shield, the jagged flashes blinding, the thunder deafening in the enclosed street. Bodies flew, the taint of ozone and burnt flesh harsh on the air.

Lane began blasting the front ranks of the soldiers with fire, trying to bore her way through to the mage behind. The first three men were enveloped in the conflagration, fell where they stood, the formation beginning to crumble, but suddenly daggers of ice dropped from the air, shattering on the cobbles like glass. One grazed her neck and with a harsh cry she twisted her latest attack into a defense, a wall of fire rising before her.

She glanced back, hair blowing in the currents from the flames before her and the raging inferno of the building to one side. Ice pelted the street behind, only a thin band of safety between fire and ice in the middle. More bodies littered the street, but Toral, Raven, Nic, and the gang members were herding Brovettans across. Raven was shouting, but between the ragged winds of the fires and the cracking ice, Lane couldn't hear her.

Something tickled her neck and she reached up with one hand, felt her shirt matted to her skin, her fingers coming away bloody. The ice had cut her more significantly than she'd thought.

Then the ice daggers halted. She spun back around, let the wall of fire abate.

The soldiers had regrouped and reformed. Now there were two block formations, side by side. They began to advance again, smoke from the building roiling above them.

Lane raised her arm, fingers crooked, began the base form—

But the smoke from the fire abruptly shifted, the black clouds billowing and spilling unnaturally down into the street.

They swept over her, heat and ash searing into her lungs, embers burning her skin. She lost the form and dropped to the ground. Arm covering her mouth and nose, coughs wracking her body, tears streaming from her eyes, she rolled onto her back and managed to finish a form, wind sweeping down and then up, thrusting the thick plume of noxious smoke toward the ceiling of the level overhead.

Through blurred sight, she noted the two formations were almost upon her.

Still coughing uncontrollably, she levered herself up onto her hands and knees.

Then Raven and Nic seized her from behind, lifted her by both arms, and dragged her back, heels scraping across the cobbles.

"You're bleeding!" Nic yelled.

"Ice," Lane managed, her voice hoarse and gritty. She let them pull her halfway back to the Brovettans, then began to struggle. "Let me go."

"We need to get you out of here," Raven said, but halted.

"The Brovettans—" She broke into hacking wheezes, bent over where she sat.

"We aren't going to be able to save them all," Raven said. "There are too many of them. We're going to be overwhelmed."

Lane shook her head. "I'll hold them off."

"With what?" Nic asked in exasperation.

"A shield."

She crawled to her feet. "Go." Her hand was already creating the form. She heard Nic and Raven retreating as the sheet of light began to form before her, stretching from building to building, cutting them off from the advancing soldiers. Its shimmer distorted her view, but she could still make out the two formations enough to know that they'd halted.

The one on the right parted and a vague form stepped forward. The mage. Lane watched the amorphous figure intently as it halted, considering the shield.

Then movement caught Lane's eye. The second formation broke as well, another figure moving forward.

"Two mages?" she muttered to herself. "Why would they have two mages here?"

The only reason would be that they'd been expecting her.

The two mages consulted. She could see them gesturing, but the shield blurred them too much for her to pick out what they intended.

She glanced back. Brovettans were still running from the blasted front building to the ragged hole of their escape route, although the numbers had thinned. It was no longer a mob of hundreds of bodies.

She turned in time to see the two mages break apart, moving to either side of the street. One began what had to be a form, although she couldn't see which one. She braced herself.

Explosions echoed down from overhead. She looked up in time to see a trench gouging a path through the ceiling, like the ragged path that already marred the cobblestones. Metal shrieked as it bent and twisted. Lucent shattered.

Then an entire section of the ceiling gave way.

Lane screamed an incoherent warning as it began to fall. She began to run, watching in horror as realization struck some of those caught in the street, others oblivious. Nic spun toward her, confused. Raven looked upwards and dodged toward the building to the left.

Light debris began to hit the street, pattering against Lane's head and shoulders—small chunks of metal, broken threads of lucent—followed by entire panels. Nic hunched down and began a sprint for safety with the rest of the Brovettans, but something struck him, hard, and he stumbled, ran a few more steps, and then collapsed. Raven darted from the protection of the gaping hole Lane had torn in the brick storage building and grabbed his shirt. She hauled him under cover as heavier debris slammed into the street all around them.

Something glanced off of the side of Lane's head and she went down to her hands and knees with a gasp, vision blurring. She blinked, focused on Nic and Raven, the ex-Regular crouched down, checking Nic—obviously unconscious—then glancing out toward Lane.

Toral suddenly appeared behind Raven.

Before the ex-Regular could react, Carbolen's spymaster raised a wicked-looking club and bashed her in the back of the head with a satisfied smirk.

Lane screamed and reached for Raven as she dropped, but an entire support beam crashed into the street before her, chipped stone and rust pelting Lane's face. She choked on the dust, saw Toral and two other gang members grabbing Nic's and Raven's limp forms and disappearing into the shadows of the storage rooms beyond.

Then something heavy slammed into her back and crushed her to the street. Her head hit the cobbles, hard, and sound dampened, her sight doubling, tripling. She fought it, tried to raise her head, crawl forward out from beneath the weight pressing her down.

But with a strangled groan, unconsciousness took her.

* * *

"They've breached the building!" Sadie shouted. "They're inside!"

Devon swore as the mob of people before him surged forward in a panic, even though there were no elevators available.

"Stay back! Stay back! There's nowhere to go!"

He gasped as he was crushed up against the gate by a woman who groaned in pain and a hulking man shouting incoherently, spit flying from his mouth. Over the moans and screams of those behind them, he could hear fighting and men bellowing orders.

At his back, through the bars of the gate, he felt the rumble of the elevators returning.

"It's coming," he growled at the man, "but you have to step back." He gave the man a hard shove and twisted to his side, the woman now clutching at the gate beside him. "Help me with this," he said.

She nodded.

Dalton came into view, face drawn and haggard, and as soon as the otherwise empty elevator came to a stop, Devon and the woman shoved the gate to the side hard.

Those pressed up against it fell into the opening before Dalton had a chance to step forward and control them. Those behind didn't wait, trampling those that had fallen, Dalton roaring unheeded orders, reaching to drag those on the floor to the side and then upright. Devon clutched at the half-open gate, refusing to move it further. The woman clung to it beside him.

An explosion ripped through the building, the blast deafening, and one entire wall of the storage area fell away, Iandolan soldiers pouring into the gap, swords swinging before anyone inside had a chance to react. The mob's eddy shifted as those closest attempted to flee, the soldiers cutting into them indiscriminately.

To the side, Cerelle's elevator had arrived, both her and Sadie trying to control the panicked Brovettans to no avail.

Devon turned back to Dalton, the ex-soldier yelling, "What's happening?"

"They've breached the building. And they've brought a mage."

Another explosion ripped through the building from the same direction, the entire structure shuddering. Sheets of dust poured down from overhead. Devon sucked in a lungful and began coughing, his eyes tearing up. He scanned the Brovettans crowding forward, realized the Iandolans were already halfway to the elevators.

He spun back to the gate, to Dalton, to the woman. He locked eyes with her, then jerked the gate farther back and shoved her into the mass of people that filled the gap almost immediately.

Through the gate's lattice, he yelled, "Dalton, take as many of them as you can. Have them stand on top of each other if you have to. We don't have much time."

Dalton had been shoved into the corner. "What are you going to do?"

"We should have time to get one more car load."

Dalton was already shaking his head. "No! Get on this elevator, Devon. Get on here now!"

"It's already too full! Go!"

Dalton began struggling forward. "Get on this elevator now!"

Devon snaked his arm to the elevator button on the outside, sank into the lucent, and activated it.

"Devon!" Dalton surged forward as the elevator began to lower. "Devon! Get your ass on this elevator! Devon!"

"Unload them and get back up here as fast as you can!"

People were still trying to get on, even as it lowered. Devon began grabbing them and pulling them back, the moans of despair and panic as it vanished rising. A few of those closest cursed and spat at him, before shifting their focus to Cerelle's elevator. The current of the mass of people eddied again in her direction and some of the pressure against him released.

Another explosion rocked the building, more than dust falling from overhead now. Devon ducked, one arm over his head for protection, then began fighting his way toward Cerelle and Sadie.

"Cram them in and then go!" he yelled as he got closer.

"It's almost full," Cerelle answered.

The crowd around them was breaking, people realizing they weren't going to make it, the Iandolans too close behind. Despair was overtaking fear.

Devon reached Cerelle, standing before the elevator entrance, Sadie on guard beside her.

"Time to go," Devon said.

He shoved both Cerelle and Sadie into the mass of the people packed into the elevator's car, jerked the gate in front of him, then slammed his hand onto the button.

Cerelle's eyes shot wide. "What about you?"

"I have to keep them from following!"

And then they were gone.

Devon twisted back to the chaos of the room before him. The Brovettans were hemmed in, the Iandolans slicing into their ranks with abandon. It wasn't a fight; it was a slaughter. Nausea brought bile to the back of Devon's throat, but he swallowed it down, concentrated on the vibration on the elevator shaft at his back, his hand still on the button, his senses half sunk into the lucent. Another explosion and the entire corner of the building collapsed to one side, dust billowing over them all, obscuring the madness.

As soon as the vibration in the stone beneath his hand halted, the elevator on Level Fifteen, he sent a surge through the lucent. Crystal fractured, pathways cut, the glass going dead. When he took his hand away, the lucent had gone dark.

He began shoving his way toward the second elevator. Someone struck him in the face with an elbow, another crushed his foot with their heel as they scrambled for safety that didn't exist.

He'd almost made it when another explosion hit the building. Only this one was inside.

He was flung up against the elevator shaft with enough force he heard something crack in his chest, beneath his shoulder, then he fell to the floor. His ears were ringing, sounds muffled. From his side, he peered out into the room, bodies strewn in all directions, a pile of debris in the center where a section of the ceiling had caved in. Iandolan soldiers were already filtering into the gap, stepping over bodies. There was no resistance. There was no one left to resist. Those Brovettans left were either dead, unconscious, or moaning from serious wounds.

Someone shouted and pointed toward him.

Shifting onto one hand and hip, Devon reached for the soft glow of the elevator button, pain piercing through his chest at the movement. He grit his teeth, vision fading to yellow, but touched the button.

The elevator had already started back up.

"Sorry, Dalton. I thought there'd be enough time."

He sent a pulse through the lucent, felt it go dead beneath his touch.

Then he collapsed onto his back, another bolt of pain making his vision waver. He coughed, felt something wet against his lips, his cheek, but then there were shouts and the tread of boots, and suddenly three Iandolan soldiers stood over him, two with swords pointed at his chest.

He managed to chuckle, even though it felt like it tore something deep inside.

"You're too late," he said, voice cracked and thick with fluid. "They're already gone."

One of them spat to the side. Then they reached for him, hauled him up.

He couldn't stop the scream.

PART III

THE EXECUTION

Chapter Sixteen

Devon wavered in an out of consciousness as they dragged him from the storerooms that held the elevators on Level Sixteen and tossed him into the back of a wagon with a slew of others. Pain washed over him, fluid and viscous, and he moaned. He pried his eyes open, Iandolan soldiers shouting orders in the chaos on the streets. Six Brovettans lay flat on the wagon bed, one or two groaning, clutching an arm or a leg. Three others were seated on the benches along both sides. A man with straggly hair matted with blood leaned over him. "Bet ya cracked a rib."

The wagon lurched into motion and Devon's vision washed away in a haze of yellow.

When it returned, sunlight blinded him. He raised a hand to shade his eyes, his entire back screaming at the abuse. The wagon jostled with motion and the muted sounds of a busy street filtered over him. Most noises were dulled, as if his ears were packed with cloth, but certain sounds came through clear, piercing and loud, like a child's shriek or the clang of a bell. Behind it all was a high-pitched whine, like a dog's whistle, and a rhythmic gurgle that he finally recognized as his own labored breathing.

When his vision cleared, he found the straggly-haired man starting down at him. Beyond, he could see the towers.

"They're takin us to the barracks."

"Maybe you," Devon managed, then broke into a coughing fit that sent splinters of pain through his chest and into his arm.

"What's that mean?" the man asked.

Devon curled into a fetal position, which seemed to ease the pain, although not the aches that twinged throughout his body.

"What's that mean?" the man asked the woman sitting beside him. She didn't respond, face blank, one cheek scraped up, grit embedded in the cuts. He turned to the man on his other side and repeated the question. When he got no answer, he reached down and shook Devon's shoulder. "What's that mean?"

Devon jerked back from the agony of his touch, teeth clenched against another scream, breath seizing, then devolving into short, sharp pants. But he remained conscious.

The wagon halted and soldiers ordered everyone out of the back. A moment later, others tramped up into the bed and began picking up those that couldn't move on their own, starting at the back. The first soldier checked a woman and announced, "Dead," moving on to the next. They yanked the unconscious man up and handed him down to those waiting, dragging him inside the police barracks. The next two received no better treatment.

When the soldier reached Devon, he slapped Devon's face. "You conscious?"

Devon coughed and nodded. "I'm awake."

"Then get up or we'll haul you out ourselves."

Devon didn't know if he could move, let alone stand, but he'd seen the way they'd handled the others. He propped himself up on an elbow, then crawled toward the end of the wagon as the soldiers retrieved the rest. Once there, he swung his legs over the edge and pushed himself upright and stood. His entire body with sheathed in sweat from the exertion and his vision pulsed in syncopation with his heart. He found holding his right arm crooked across his chest eased the pain a little.

"Good," the soldier said. "Now follow us."

He followed, his steps slow, breathing ragged. Inside, the station and barracks were a madhouse, soldiers and sergeants and captains shouting orders, rushing in all directions. It wasn't like the city guard station where his mentor, Proctor Arrend, had found him. Even amid all the chaos, Devon could sense the order. The city guard station had been more relaxed, less rigid. Even so, if he hadn't been focused on simply remaining upright, he might have attempted to slip away.

After a brief pause, they began to lead or drag those from the wagon down a hallway that led to cells. Devon began to follow, until someone said sharply, in a voice Devon recognized, "Not this one."

The noise in the outer room of the station house quieted.

Devon turned to find Proctor Favian, Councilor Havvelan, and a prefect standing inside the entrance.

The soldier who'd unloaded the wagon stepped forward. "These are all men captured on Level Sixteen, fighting in the quarantine zone. My orders were to take them into custody."

Favian stepped forward and repeated, "Not this one. This is Devon Alamort, a former student of the Lyceum."

The councilor's gaze settled on Devon. "The one working with Councilor Varenov's daughter?"

"I'm certain he knows about these traitorous attacks on the quarantine zones. I'd wager he was one of those who planned them. We already know Varenov's daughter was involved in the attack on Level Twenty. Where you find one, you find the other."

"What do you want us to do with him?" the prefect asked Havvelan.

The councilor considered. "I'll take him to the tower with me."

"Very well."

The prefect motioned the soldier to proceed with the other prisoners as he began arranging an escort for Devon. Favian stood behind Havvelan with a smug expression, the councilor watching the Iandolan soldiers as another group of Brovettans—battered and bruised, most unconscious—were herded into the station's outer room.

"What did you and your friends intend to accomplish?" Havvelan asked.

"We wanted to give the Brovettans their freedom."

Havvelan faced him. "After what they did at the Lyceum with the Warding?"

"None of those in the quarantine zones were part of that and you know it."

"So you say. The citizens of Iandolo believed otherwise."

"Because you lied to them."

Havvelan turned away. "It doesn't matter. None of this matters. The Brovettans you've released today have nowhere to go. We'll find them, one way or another, and when we do, they'll no longer be kept in zones, they'll be prisoners."

"I don't think it will be that easy. And for now, they're free."

Havvelan frowned in irritation, but before he could answer the prefect returned.

"I have an escort assembled. If you're ready?"

"Of course."

The prefect led Havvelan and Favian through the main entrance, six soldiers forming up around Devon. He would have scoffed at the attention, if it wouldn't have hurt so much. Taking a steadying breath, he followed the others.

A carriage waited outside, Havvelan, Favian, and the prefect already climbing inside. Devon pulled himself up with a pained hiss, then collapsed into the space next to the prefect, facing Havvelan and Favian. As soon as the door was closed, two of the escort hopped up onto the footrests and the carriage lurched into motion, Devon gritting his teeth to keep from crying out at the flare of pain in his chest.

"What have you done with Varenov's daughter, Prefect Arctus?" Havvelan asked.

"Don't discuss it!" Favian cut in. At Havvelan's raised eyebrow, he motioned toward Devon. "Not in front of him."

"He's not in any position to do anything about it," Havvelan said.

"Don't underestimate him."

"Just because he slipped through your fingers doesn't mean he'll be able to slip through mine."

Favian winced at the reminder, but pressed his lips together and said nothing.

Havvelan turned back to the prefect. "Varenov's daughter?"

"My men have taken her to the tower, as you asked, although I repeat that I think that unwise."

"You've taken precautions, I assume? She's bound, cannot use her mage abilities?"

"Of course, although she's been unconscious since our mages quelled the riot on Level Twenty."

"And what about the other two quarantine zones?"

"Resistance fell as soon as we brought the mages to bear. I'm afraid nearly all of the Brovettans escaped from Level Twelve, and at least three-quarters of those on Level Sixteen. Far fewer on Level Twenty, even with Lane Illea helping them."

"She did significant damage. From the reports, she created significant barriers and had far greater control over her magework than our own mages. I thought you said her powers weren't advanced enough for us to worry about, Favian."

"They shouldn't be," the proctor said defensively. "Based on what we knew after the attack at the Lyceum, she had barely learned the base form and some fire sigils. All of the magework we saw at the Lyceum came from him."

They faced Devon, who was barely hanging on to the thread of the conversation, each bump and rut in the road sending jolts of pain through his body.

"I told you then, I can't do magework," he gasped. "I'm not a mage."

"But you know the forms," Favian said, leaning forward. "You figured out the structure. You bonded with her and taught her after your escape!"

Devon chuckled, even though it hurt and devolved into a rough cough. "I taught her nothing. She taught herself."

Favian reached for him, but Havvelan restrained him with a gesture.

"She's a fast learner then," he said. "Her defense of the warehouse you were using as a staging area before funneling the Brovettans into the sublevels was…wild. Uncontrolled and erratic. I believe eight buildings burned before we were able to get the fire she unleashed under control. The attack at the quarantine zone on Level Twenty was much more stable."

Devon glared and said nothing.

Havvelan shifted his attention to Favian. "She couldn't have advanced so quickly without help. Didn't you say she and Devon here worked together to build this mage structure? He must have had notes. She's using those."

"It's possible."

"And what about the college?"

"What do you mean?"

"Does the college have any of his notes."

Favian shook his head. "All we have are the questions Devon posed during his challenge. We don't have the solutions."

"That at least gives you a starting point."

"For what?"

"Discovering whatever it is that Lane Illea has learned."

Favian had gone still. "That challenge was sealed, by order of the board overseeing Devon's challenge. No one has access to those questions."

"We cannot have rogue mages out there with abilities our own mages do not understand. As a member of the Council, I'm ordering you to unseal that challenge and begin studying those questions." Havvelan turned back to Devon. "And if that doesn't elicit results fast enough, we now have Devon to help clarify the issues."

Devon swallowed back nausea as the carriage came to a halt. The door was pulled open by a member of the escort, but they weren't at the main entrance to the tower. Instead, a servant's entrance stood open a few feet away, those exiting the carriage shielded from view.

"The passage to the prepared rooms has been cleared," one of the soldiers said.

"Very well."

Prefect Arctus nudged Devon, who clambered down from the carriage with effort. The soldiers ushered him through back hallways, but he lost track of the twists and turns, lucent lights passing by overhead in a blurred haze.

When they finally entered a dimly lit room, he collapsed onto the bunk with a moan, breath coming in short hitches, skin sheened with sweat. Havvelan and Prefect Arctus stood over him; he vaguely recalled Favian being dismissed somewhere along the way.

"Lane Illea and the captain are already here," Prefect Arctus said, his voice fading in and out as Devon fought off unconsciousness.

"And the others?"

"We'll have them shortly."

Devon struggled to hear more, but the pain took over. As he sank into oblivion, he prayed that his destruction of the elevators had worked and that at least Dalton was safe.

* * *

"We're almost there!" Cerelle called from the floor of the warehouse, over twenty feet below.

Dalton continued to pace back and forth inside the elevator's car, letting his anger seethe, because he knew if he let the anger subside, then the fear for Devon would overtake him and he didn't want to see what form that would take. Better to be enraged at what his partner had done. Because he knew it was Devon's fault the elevator had died on its way back up to retrieve him. He'd seen it in Devon's eyes when he forced the elevator back down that last time.

"Get ready!" Cerelle called. "Back away from the opening. We're swinging the grappling hook now. Get ready to grab the rope."

Dalton slid behind the edge of the elevator's opening, beside the blackened bar of lucent that no longer worked.

As soon as he stopped pacing, the fear scrabbled forward, his chest tightening, tears burning at the corners of his eyes. He fought them back, sucked in a few deep, steadying breaths—

Then heard the clatter of the grappling hook as it struck the upper back of the elevator car, the length of rope attached to it already snaking back out the opening as it rattled to the floor. He dove for it, grateful for the distraction, but missed.

Leaning out of the opening, he shouted down, "Missed it!" his voice breaking. He cleared his throat and added, "Try again!"

He heard grumbling from below, but another warning came from Cerelle a short time later and this time he snagged the rope before it could slip away. Securing the hook to one of the metal loops that protruded from the elevator walls at about head height, he tested the rope's strength. It felt thin in his grip, thinner than the rappelling rope they'd used to get into the internment camp on Level Sixteen. He moved to the edge of the elevator's opening and stared down at Cerelle and the group waiting below, lit by lanterns.

Cerelle motioned with one hand. "Come on, quit stalling! We don't know how long it will take the Iandolan Army to get here!"

"Right."

Dalton sat down on the edge, legs dangling over. He heaved in a breath, then rolled onto his stomach, rope taut, and let himself slide out. The rope creaked as it took on his weight, but held. He began lowering himself down, his shoulders and arms already burning. This wasn't like rappelling; they hadn't had time to get the appropriate gear. As he began to sweat, the rope grew slick in his grip. He dropped faster, gasping, face throbbing with exertion, and then the rope began to slip through his grasp. He tightened it, but the rope burn was too much and with a cry he let go.

He landed hard on the crete floor, a jolt shooting up both legs into his spine, and fell onto his back. His breath whooshed out in relief.

He thought he had much farther to fall.

Cerelle appeared, glaring down at him. "Can you move? Because if you can't, we're leaving you."

He grunted and raised a hand for help, hissing at the sting when she grabbed it to haul him up. Both hands tingled and throbbed, hot like a fever. He ignored the pain, following in her wake as the entire crew that had remained behind to save him began a frantic retreat through the warehouse. "We have to go back for him."

"Not happening."

"He saved all of you! He got the elevators working. He—"

Cerelle spun on him. "He's the one who shoved me and Sadie into the elevator, then fried it once we were down so that no one could follow us."

Dalton flinched back from her, even though he'd known. He met her gaze, saw his own hurt and pain echoed there, his own frustration, and his shoulders sagged. "I know."

She glanced away. "Even if we could go back, when I left, the elevators were being overrun. We'd be walking into a death trap." She faced him again. "If he isn't already dead—"

"He's not."

Cerelle's lips pressed together, then nodded. "We need to help the Brovettans he saved first."

Without waiting for an answer, she continued after the others. Dalton looked back at the now dead elevators one last time, barely visible, then joined her.

When they stepped out of the warehouse, the street beyond was chaos. Carbolen's men were shouting at the Brovettans, who were yelling back, arms flailing, pointing toward the elevators, toward the level above. Some were screaming, others wailing or sobbing, a few clutching wounds or holding fellow Brovettans upright. Sadie stood to one side.

"Where's Scerano?" Dalton asked.

Cerelle shrugged. "Still up on Level Sixteen, as far as I know. Still fighting."

But Dalton could tell she didn't believe that; she thought him already dead.

Cerelle stepped forward and tried to shout over the cacophony, but her voice was drowned out.

Dalton sighed, then drew in a deep breath and bellowed, "Quiet!"

The word rebounded from the surrounding buildings, startled most of those before them into silence.

When he had their attention, he continued. "We don't have time for this! The elevators have been destroyed, which has bought us a reprieve, but not much. The Iandolan Army will be here shortly, are likely already on their way. We've established a few protected safe zones in the city on various levels, places where you can hide out for now, or you can head off on your own. We can't protect you if you're on your own. But if you want to go to our safe zones, gather together into small groups and Carbolen's men will escort you to them. We can't go all as one group, and we can't all go to the same zone, but you need to make your choice now."

A bunch of conversations broke out, but one of the Brovettans nearby took a step toward him. "How do we know these safe zones aren't worse than the quarantine zone we just escaped?" A slew of others shouted agreement.

"You don't," Dalton answered.

Cerelle shot him a glare as everyone began to grumble. "What he means to say is that these safe zones are only a haven for us, a place to hide, until we can find some other alternative—either leaving Iandolo or coming to some kind of agreement with the Council." She ignored those spluttering at the absurdity. "Where else are you going to go? Where else is it safe? Nowhere here in Iandolo. Scerano sacrificed himself to give you this chance. Carbolen and Maupin and their crews fought to get you free. Are you going to turn your backs on them now?"

No one moved, but the grumbling had decreased. A few of the Brovettans appeared abashed. But mostly they looked terrified.

Dalton singled out three of them. "You three, grab fifteen others and follow those two. Do it! You over there, same thing, but follow these two. Carbolen's men, divide them up and take them to your assigned safe zones. Remember, use back streets and different paths! We don't want to lead the Iandolans right to us. Be smart and move fast. Now go!"

As the Brovettans began to separate into reluctant groups, the first few already trotting out into the city, Dalton snagged Cerelle's arm. "You stay with me. You, too, Sadie."

"Why?" Sadie asked.

"Because I'm going to need your help. We need to find Nic and Lane and Raven. Then we're going to go after Devon."

Sadie and Cerelle shared a look, but neither protested.

Dalton watched as the group of rescued Brovettans and Carbolen's crew thinned, people scattering in all directions. A few broke away on their own and Dalton wished them luck. They weren't his responsibility anymore.

When it was apparent there would be no more trouble, he motioned Cerelle and Sadie after him, then headed away from the hub, toward the edge of the level.

"Where are we going?" Cerelle asked.

"To meet with John Senn. All of the key members of our little resistance were to meet there after the attacks and regroup."

"And where exactly is that?" Sadie asked.

Dalton didn't answer.

They ran from the area around the warehouse, the streets emptier than usual in this area. Dalton kept his hand near his weapons, but the typical nooks and shadowed corners were conspicuously vacant. He still felt eyes on them in the prickling of skin at the nape of his neck, but wherever they were, they were keeping distant. Only when they neared the edge of the overhanging Level Sixteen did the normal pedestrian traffic resume, along with carts and horses, hawkers and thieves. There, they slowed, Cerelle and Sadie falling into step on either side of him.

Before they reached the edge, sunlight flaring in from outside at a heavy slant, making Dalton blink, Sadie grabbed them both and hauled them into the lee of a set of steps leading up to a brownstone building. Seconds later, Dalton heard the shout of the Iandolan guards to make way as they raced down the street, still in formation. He noted the tight ranks, nodding slightly in approval, as the battalion swept past them.

As soon as they passed, the regular citizens began filtering back onto the street.

"Good eyes," Dalton said.

"Good hearing," Sadie answered.

Dalton grunted.

By the time they made it down to Level Ten, they'd seen four such battalions racing in various directions, even more sets of squads, most of them concentrated around Level Sixteen and Level Twelve. Still, Dalton approached the theater on Level Ten cautiously, eyes and ears open to anything untoward. By this time, exhaustion had begun to set in, so even though he was alert, he startled when one of the tullers stepped from an alley ahead and said, "Where are you headed, friend?"

Removing his hand from the hilt of his sword, raising it palm up before him, he answered, "The bountiful fields. I hear the flowers are bright this year."

The tuller relaxed and three other men and women stepped out of the shadows before them, two of them Carbolen's men. Two more fell in from behind.

"I recognize you," the tuller said, "but not them."

"They're two of the Brovettans we freed today."

The man nodded, then motioned them forward. "Go on in."

Dalton led Cerelle and Sadie to the back of the theater, passing two other sets of guards before they entered through a creaking door once used by stage hands. They wound through the back halls and staging area and emerged onto the main stage, Dalton pausing to take in who was already there. John Senn sat at one of the four tables, men and women—a mix of Maupin's and Carbolen's men, along with Senn's own crew from Luminesque—reporting to him or delivering messages as he scribbled on his own papers and consulted the scattering of maps that lay before him. He didn't see Maupin, Carbolen, Raven, Lane, or Nic, although Picall was there, hovering off to one side.

He headed toward Picall.

"Where's Nic and Lane?"

"They haven't returned yet." Picall eyed the two Brovettans. "Who are they?"

"Cerelle and Sadie. They organized the Brovettans from inside Level Sixteen's internment camp."

Sadie and Picall sized each other up. They were about the same age, Dalton realized. Both of them touched their weapons, frowned, narrowed their eyes, and straightened imperceptibly.

"What happened on Level Twelve?" Dalton asked.

Picall dragged her attention back to him. "The attack overwhelmed the barricades. The Iandolan soldiers were driven back into one of the buildings. We held them there until the Brovettans could escape, then fled. What about Sixteen?"

"We pulled out as many as we could. I don't know what happened at the barricades with Leinn and her attack."

Picall suddenly stiffened, picking up on his agitation. "Where's Devon?"

Dalton's throat seized. When he didn't answer, Cerelle said, "He sent us down in the elevators, but stayed behind to sabotage them so the Iandolans couldn't follow us."

"Is he—?"

"We don't know."

Dalton cracked his knuckles, eyeing Senn and the hectic movement of all of his men. "We need Lane."

At the front entrance of the theater, doors slammed open, followed by the heavy tread of booted feet. Carbolen emerged into the theater, half-lit by the few lanterns on that side. He paused a few paces inside, gang members spreading out wide behind him, filling the back of the hall. Leinn took her place a step behind and to his right as his gaze latched onto Senn.

The leader of the rebellion in Brovetto stood.

"That was a fucking shit show," Carbolen said, voice low and dark, but amplified by the acoustics.

He began walking toward Senn, straight down the main hall.

"We knew it wasn't going to be pretty," Senn said.

Carbolen reached the edge of the stage but didn't bother moving around to the stairs on either side. Instead, he leaped and heaved himself up, rising to his full height immediately in front of Senn, the two facing each other less than an arm's length apart.

"They had mages," Carbolen said. "Not just one or two. At least four. They were waiting for us."

"If that were true, you wouldn't have returned. Trust me. They've ambushed my men before, in Brovetto." They glared at each other for a long moment, Carbolen's hands opening and closing into fists slowly, Senn unperturbed, until finally Senn asked, "What happened?"

Carbolen hesitated, then turned and paced away. "We attacked the barricades as planned. At first it went well. My crew almost managed to breach them, but then they brought out their mages. After that it was a slaughter." He faced Senn again. Leinn and a sizeable number of his gang members had made their way up onto the stage. "We held as long as we could and then retreated. They followed us for a few blocks, but after that my men scattered with orders to regroup at the lair. I held back long enough to watch them refortify the barricades. Then they sent a few of their mages deeper into the camp with at least three squads for protection. The rest stayed behind to defend the barricades."

"Mannert warned us Captain Pulvar was competent."

"What about Raven, Lane, and the others?" Dalton said, edging forward. "Where are they? Did they get the Brovettans out?"

Both men faced him, but the answer came from the left end of the stage. "Not all of them."

Dalton spun as Toral emerged from the back stage shadows, Nic's arm draped over her shoulders. The ex-gang member was moving, but obviously needed the support. His legs were weak.

Picall cried out and raced to Nic's side, taking his weight from Toral as a few more gang members who'd accompanied the spy leader straggled in behind her.

"Report," both Carbolen and Senn said at the same time.

Toral faced Carbolen. "Lane blew a hole through the side of the building as planned, then set up some kind of shield to protect us from the few soldiers stationed nearby. We managed to get a significant portion of the Brovettans who were waiting for us there with Mannert out. But then two mages arrived with support. Lane held them off for a while, but they ripped into the ceiling. Part of the level overhead came crashing down around us and we were forced to run."

Dalton stepped forward. "Lane? Raven?"

"The last I saw of Lane, part of the ceiling had collapsed onto her. She wasn't moving. If she's not dead, then they have her. As for Raven—" Toral shot a look at Carbolen. "—she didn't make it."

A wave of nausea overwhelmed Dalton and he found himself braced against the table, palms flat, his knees weak. Cerelle was asking him if he was all right, but her voice was distant. "They're both gone?"

"We don't know that," Nic said. Picall had found him a chair. He grabbed Dalton's arm, the grip centering him. "We don't know anything about what's happened to them yet." He clenched his jaw. "But we're going to find out."

"Not right now," John Senn said. When both Dalton and Nic glared at him, he added, "The city is in turmoil. The streets are flooded with Iandolan soldiers searching for the Brovettans, for Carbolen and his gangs, for all of us. Anyone asking questions right now is going to be immediately arrested."

Dalton shoved back from the table. "So what are we supposed to do?"

"Lay low. Wait for it to calm down."

"That could take days."

Senn's voice hardened. "We have bigger concerns at the moment, such as protecting the Brovettans, keeping them hidden."

"That's your problem, not mine."

Dalton turned, ready to storm out, but Nic held onto his arm. "Where are you going?"

"Back to our flat."

Nic hauled himself upright with a grimace, one hand going to his side. Through gritted teeth, he said, "I'm going with you."

"Us, too," Cerelle said, Sadie and Picall nodding agreement behind her.

They headed for the side entrance, Nic managing to walk on his own, although someone always stayed close in case he needed the support. Dalton half expected Senn or Carbolen to stop them, but they passed through the layers of sentries around the theater unmolested.

When they reached the streets of Level Ten, they became more cautious, making certain that Cerelle and Sadie weren't seen whenever possible. Picall scouted ahead, reporting that the outer edges of the level were teeming with scattered groups of city guard and soldiers, so they worked their way hubward, where the lucent had almost entirely failed. Cerelle had grabbed a couple of the lanterns at the theater, which gave them enough light to find their way, with what overhead lucents still worked. They saw two groups of Brovettans being guided toward the safe zones Senn and Carbolen had set up, but they hid before being seen and let them pass.

At the hub, they ascended back to Level Twelve, then hunkered down in an abandoned storefront while Picall checked the streets leading to the flat, since it was close to the warehouse with the elevators.

She returned a short time later. "Good news and bad news. The warehouse is swarmed with soldiers, along with the streets within a few blocks surrounding the elevators."

"We expected that," Dalton said. "What's the good news?"

Picall grinned. "They appear to have already searched the apartments where you were staying. They didn't find where we stashed our stuff. If we can get there without being seen, I think we'll be safe."

"Then let's go."

Nic groaned, but dragged himself upright again.

They slid through the streets, lanterns covered, and made it to the flat without running into any of the Iandolan Army.

As soon as they entered the outer room, Nic collapsed to the floor while Dalton went to check on their things, hidden behind a wall panel.

"Let's see how bad this is," Cerelle said, Nic barely protesting as she pulled up his shirt and rolled him to one side. She sank back onto her heels; Sadie gasped.

Dalton stepped closer to get a better look.

Nic's entire side was an ugly purple-black bruise, the worst of it near his left shoulder.

"What happened again?" Cerelle asked. She began prodding the bruise, Nic hissing and flinching away.

"You heard Toral. Their mages brought the ceiling down on us. I remember starting to run, then something hit me. I managed to stagger a few more steps and then I blacked out."

Cerelle kept up her investigation, Nic bearing it with ill grace, then she sighed. "I don't think anything's broken, just bruised. Picall, dig out whatever you have stashed here and I'll see what I can do. Sadie, you're on watch."

Sadie vanished while Dalton helped Picall spread their supplies out on the floor for Cerelle to peruse. She shook her head. "There's nothing here that will help with the pain or the healing. The best we can do is wrap it and keep you immobile."

Nic rolled onto his back with a sigh. "Great." Picall sank down beside him. He caught Dalton's gaze. "So what are we going to do about Devon and Lane?"

Dalton shifted forward. "We need to find out if they're even alive first. But I'm not certain who we can contact without raising suspicions."

"I'd start with Mannert."

"If I can reach her. She's likely to be busy dealing with the search for us. Who else?"

"Not many we can trust. I can ask Arch at the Shandy Quad. He may have heard something. What about Arrend, Devon's mentor at the Lyceum?"

Dalton nodded. "I'll approach him. He may have heard something through Favian and the other proctors."

Nic winced. "That's not much of a start."

"I'm afraid we can't be of much help," Cerelle said. "Neither Sadie nor I have any significant contacts, aside from those we made within the Brovettan camp."

"And I know no one in the city," Picall added.

"If they are alive," Cerelle said, "then most likely they've been taken by the Iandolan Army. What do you intend to do then?"

Dalton drew in a steadying breath. "Rescue them. Although I don't know how we're going to do it with only the five of us."

"Six," Nic said.

Dalton faced him. "Six?"

Nic grinned. "Six. When Toral dragged me out of the rubble on Level Twenty, I was unconscious, but I faded in and out as she retreated. I heard her talking to her men." He propped himself up on one elbow. "Raven's not dead. Toral took her to the lair. Carbolen's got her."

Chapter Seventeen

Lane woke with a start, blinked up at the blurred ceiling overhead, listened to the low murmur of voices from the other side of the room.

"—lucky. Her left leg will heal on its own, as long as she remains off of it for a few weeks. The head wound is more serious. She's likely to have some vision problems, headaches, maybe even disorientation for the next few days, if not longer. All of the other marks are scratches or bruises, nothing more."

"No broken bones? No shattered vertebrae? She was struck in the back by a metal panel."

"Not that I can see."

"Pity."

Lane snapped her head to the side and glared at Havvelan—Councilor Havvelan. His gaze shifted from the woman who stood before him to her at the movement and he smiled.

"It appears your patient has rejoined us."

The woman turned, her furrowed brow at Havvelan's comments smoothing out as she approached the bed tucked up against the wall.

"How are you feeling?" she asked, reaching for Lane's forehead. Pain shot through Lane as she applied light pressure and Lane hissed and attempted to bat her hand away but discovered her wrists were bound together.

She brought both hands up into her field of vision, what felt like her entire body protesting the movement. Twinges plucked at her lower back and a hundred pins and needles pricked her arms and shoulders. She held her hands up long enough to see the twine tied there, so tight it had already dug into her skin.

She let her arms drop.

"Are those really necessary?" the healer asked.

"Certainly." Havvelan said, stepping closer. "You may go."

The woman faced him, hesitated, then nodded and left.

Havvelan stared down at her. "You've become quite the insurgent, haven't you?"

"I don't know what you're talking about." Her voice came in a low rasp, her throat dry.

A muted scream startled Lane halfway upright, white-hot pain firing down her right side. She gasped and fell back onto the bed, tears forming at the corners of her eyes. Her breath came in ragged hitches as she fought the pain back and, when it finally faded, she felt a dull, persistent throb coming from her lower leg. But that was nothing compared to the ache in her head, radiating out from the region where the healer had touched her. It caused her vision to appear glassy in the center, hazy at the edges.

Havvelan had glanced toward the scream. "That would be your friend Devon Alamort. He's being interrogated by Prefect Arctus as we speak. So far, he hasn't been extremely cooperative, but he has let slip a few things, such as where you two hid during those few months after your escape from the Lyceum. We never considered the sublevels, at least, not until after you'd already returned. I'm surprised you survived the wyrms that live down there."

"The skrill," Lane said. "They're called the skrill."

"Oh really?" Havvelan shifted toward a table to one side, where a pitcher of water and a few glasses sat. He poured her a cup and brought it to her, holding it out as he asked, "Who told you that?"

Lane's chest seized at the question and she met his gaze. He didn't know about Maupin or the tullers…or the tull for that matter. He was leading her with crumbs, hoping she'd reveal more than she intended.

She struggled into a seated position, the agony in her lower back intense. Her left leg felt leaden and unwieldy, wrapped in bandages from the knee to her ankle, but she refused to whimper or moan, teeth clenched hard to hold it in.

Once upright, she took the glass with trembling hands and drank, the water cool as it slid down her parched throat. She spluttered and coughed once, then drank a little more, letting the glass rest in her lap, cupped by both hands. She took in the room—bed, table, chairs, pitcher, and glasses. Nothing else. The ache in her head intensified.

"This isn't the city prison."

"No. I wanted something a little more private. And secure."

Lane held his gaze, tried not to show the sudden fear curling up in the pit of her stomach. "What do you want?"

Havvelan's smug smile evaporated. He grabbed one of the chairs around the table and sat.

"I want to know who helped you and Devon after your escape. I know it wasn't your mother. I kept a close eye on her during that time and she kept to the towers, immersed herself in the duties of the Council. I want to know where you were and why you came back. I want to know what prompted you and Devon Alamort to side with the Brovettans after their previous attack on Iandolo, one that you helped quell. I want to know how you managed to get them out of the quarantine zones. And I want to know where those Brovettans are hiding right now."

Lane considered him as another scream rose from beyond the wall. This time, it faded out into choked sobs.

"No," she finally muttered. "You aren't that stupid."

"What do you mean?"

She gave a half-hearted chuckle and shook her head, wincing as it increased the throb in her temples. "I mean, you aren't that stupid. You already know it was Carbolen who helped us after our escape. He hid us and then he helped us when you began your persecution of the Brovettans. And you already know that the Brovettans who attacked and put up the Warding were a splinter group of rebels who had nothing to do with the real rebellion going on in Luminesque. But you have no qualms using them as an excuse to fan the fear and hatred of those in Iridesque and the other Crystal Cities so that they'll feel justified in incarcerating the innocent Brovettans living here in Iandolo. And what is it all for? Is it because the Brovettans pose a real threat? No. They're fighting for their own survival. It's because you and the other members of the Council want to solidify your power. You know the Crystal Cities are dying, that the lucent is dying, and you want to make certain that you and the Council and those here in the upper echelons of Iandolo remain in power, in control, until the Cities' last gasping breath."

Havvelan rested an arm against the table, fingers drumming on the wood. "You are most certainly Varenov's daughter."

The door opened and Prefect Arctus and Favian stepped inside. Lane's heart leaped into her throat at the sight of Favian, but she tamped it down. An old reaction, from her time at the Lyceum, although she did wonder why he was here now.

"She's awake," Prefect Arctus said. "Did you learn anything from her yet?"

"No. She's as stubborn and clever as her mother. What did you learn from the Science student?"

"Nothing we didn't already know."

Havvelan turned to Favian. "And you?"

"He passed out before I could ask him anything."

Havvelan stood. "Then perhaps you should start with your own questions with her, before Arctus has his chance."

"I will." Favian stepped across the room and pulled the glass from her hands. "But first we need to redo her bonds. Her hands need to be tied behind her back."

"She can do magework with them bound before her?"

"It's unlikely, but I don't want to take any chances. She and Devon have surprised us before."

Arctus shifted forward, drawing a knife. He cut the cord near the knot, unwound it roughly, then twisted Lane around so he could bind them again behind her back. Nausea rose up and her vision faded to yellow when he turned her, enough that she sagged against the wall for support, but it had faded by the time the prefect finished.

She pushed herself back from the wall and glared at Favian, the proctor pulling pages out of his satchel and spreading them out on the table.

Once organized, he faced her and said, "Tell me everything you know about this."

She frowned, glanced at Arctus and Havvelan, then forced herself to stand.

The throb in her head became a hammer and she felt sick to her stomach, closing her eyes to steady herself and fight it back. Someone was speaking to her, but their voice was dampened and distant. When she pried her eyes open, it took a moment for the room to focus.

"—should wait," Favian was saying.

"No," she said, eyes locked on Havvelan. "I'm fine."

She turned toward the table, took a step, and stumbled into the chair as her left leg threatened to give beneath her. The movement covered her gasp of shock as she saw the double pyramid diagrams and notes scattered across the pages Favian had laid out. For a moment, she thought the proctor had gotten ahold of Devon's notes. Or her own. But as she caught her balance and took another step to the table, she realized these notes weren't remotely as detailed or as neat as Devon's or her own. The diagrams of the pyramid's faces were mostly empty, the handwriting jagged and scratchy. The main nodes weren't even labeled.

Scanning the rest of the pages, she realized the double pyramids there had sigils picked out for the secondary form, positions denoted in a specific order, with notes on the expected effect if done correctly. She saw ones for the ball of fire, the lightning, Paterni's wall—the blue wall of light that was taught to third years first after they'd mastered the base sigil—and even a cantrip, something they must have learned from watching the Brovettan mages that attacked the Lyceum. Many had sketches of hand positions.

She straightened. "This is the double pyramid structure that's the base for all mage sigils. It appears that these others are specific sigils, although I only know a few of them. You only taught me one or two before you expelled me from the Lyceum."

"Don't play naïve." Favian picked up the main diagram, the largest depiction of the double pyramid. "We know you worked with Devon on this structure. He presented it to us as part of his challenge, along with several questions. Based on those questions, we know he'd devised a...a lexicon for the forms. I want to know what that lexicon is. I want to know everything he knew—lexicon, sigils, forms. Everything he learned and taught you."

"I only know what you taught me at the Lyceum."

Favian gestured toward Arctus and suddenly the prefect's arm wrapped around her throat. She had time to take in a startled breath and then he tightened his hold, her airflow cut off as he lifted and bent her backwards. Her back screamed at the abuse, but it was the inability to breathe that caused her to panic, her heart thundering in her chest.

"You see, I know you're lying," Favian said, setting the page down. "When we sent the raid to Level Ten to halt the slow trickle of Brovettans attempting to escape the upcoming quarantine, we weren't expecting any kind of resistance, especially not from another mage. You caught us off guard."

Lane began to choke, mouth gaping wide, nostrils flaring. She desperately wanted to reach up and clutch at Arctus' arm, claw at it, but her hands were still bound behind her back.

"Our mage reported that the magework he ran into was raw, powerful, almost unchecked. We knew it was you, of course. It couldn't have been anyone else. Oh, we considered other sources—the Brovettans who attacked with the Warding may have had other mages, for example—but those we took prisoner after the Warding fell all claimed there were no others, that we'd captured or killed them all. So it had to be you."

Yellow spots began to appear in Lane's vision, pulsing in sync with her heart and expanding. She began to thrash, but Arctus' grip only increased.

"We assumed it was you and Devon, working in tandem using the bond, as you did during the attack to overcome Terrial. But now I don't think so." He tapped a finger on the table and looked at her. "Now I think it was only you. The magework at the Lyceum, when you were bonded, was controlled, precise. That was Devon's work. And then there's the much more serious transgression yesterday—the attacks on the quarantine zones. You were on Level Twenty. Devon was found on Level Sixteen. You couldn't have been working in tandem, could you? Not at that distance." He shifted closer, until he was only inches away from her. "It was only you. Which means you do know more than we taught you at the Lyceum. Much more."

Lane could barely see him, the pulsing yellow obscuring most of her sight. Her struggles had grown weak and she felt herself fading.

Favian's gaze flicked toward Arctus and the hold around her neck released.

She collapsed to the chair, arms and legs limp, nearly sagged to the floor but caught herself as she sucked in air, coughed, and sucked in more. Even then, her vision sparking and flaring, she nearly passed out.

Before she could recover, Favian grabbed her chin and forced her to look at him.

"Tell us what you know."

* * *

Dalton stood at the intersection of Barley and Wents Circle, the roundabout bustling with wagons, hand-drawn carts, and pedestrians. He shook his head. Three days before, all three internment camps had been attacked, three-quarters of the Brovettans being held captive disappearing into the city, and yet the streets here at Mid-level were business as usual. Granted, he saw no Brovettans among the crowds—and few Bolni, Kerpezians, or any of the other Crystal City denizens, honestly—but still, he would have thought there would have been some significant reaction to the uprising. Protests. An outcry. Even mild grumbling. Something.

Instead, the activity appeared normal. Perhaps a little more frantic, glances edged, faces more circumspect, but with a veneer of normalcy.

A group of four Iandolan soldiers walked past and he sank back along Barley Street until they were gone, then returned, scanning the center of the circle where benches surrounded a statue of a woman with hand lowered, head tilted slightly, as if she were tossing breadcrumbs to the birds.

"Where are you Mannert?" he mumbled.

No one had heard from Mannert since the attack on the camps. He'd scoped out her usual contact points—the bars around the barracks, a tavern he knew she liked, even the bakery where she typically bought bread. Nothing. Yesterday, he'd staked out the barracks itself, but didn't see her enter or leave. The circle was the last place he knew she frequented.

He needed to find her. He needed to know if she knew what had happened to Devon and Lane.

He waited another hour, the bench where Mannert usually sat remaining vacant. He would have waited longer, except a tie on a Kerpezian wagon loaded with baggage snapped and dumped cases and trunks into the circle. One burst open, the fine, colorful clothing inside spilling onto the muddy cobbles. Two more carts laden with furniture and more baggage drew up behind it, along with a carriage. Kerpezian servants instantly scrambled to repack the wagon, but traffic on the circle ground to a halt. An Iandolan merchant attempting to pass jumped down and began cursing the Kerpezian driver out. Kerpezian guards appeared, the Iandolan backed up by others on the street. The shouting escalated and Iandolan soldiers arrived, a Kerpezian noble—based on his clothing—emerging from the carriage.

As a heated discussion began between all four groups of men, Dalton noticed one of the Iandolan soldiers hanging out at the edge eyeing him. He straightened, searched his memory, but didn't recognize her from the Lyceum, even though she was close to Dalton's age.

The soldier glanced back at her sergeant, busy with the noble, then headed toward Dalton.

"Time to go," Dalton muttered to himself.

He headed down Barley, cut into the first cross-street, looking back as he did so. The soldier was still behind him, had cut the distance between them by half.

He cursed and picked up his pace. He didn't know these streets well; this was Mannert's domain.

Halfway down the next block, the soldier was still behind him, closing fast. He scanned ahead, saw an alley entrance, and took it.

Within seconds he realized his mistake. It wasn't an alley, rather a niche to a loading dock, the arched doors closed and latched. With another curse, he spun back toward the entrance, but the soldier was already there.

He tensed and drew his dagger. The soldier raised one hand, palm out, although her other dropped to the hilt of her sword.

"No need for that," she said. "You're a friend of Mannert's, right? I've seen you around—at the barracks and the pub."

"What of it?"

The soldier glanced back in the direction of the circle, then faced him again, taking a short step forward. "I don't have much time—they'll notice I'm gone—but I'm one of those who helped Mannert sneak the Brovettans out of quarantine on Level Twenty. I haven't seen her since the gangs attacked and liberated most of them. I think someone found out about her. I think they took her."

Dalton's tension eased, but he didn't lower his dagger. "Where?"

"I don't know. Not to the cells at any of the stations. We've looked. But she hasn't returned to her room at the barracks and none of the captains appear too concerned about it. I haven't dared ask around about her. But someone should try to find her. If you're a friend..."

Someone shouted from the street and she flinched, turned away.

"Wait!" Dalton lunged forward.

Within one step, the soldier had her sword drawn and pointed toward his chest.

He lurched to a halt, both hands up, palms out, dagger held only by his thumb.

"Wait," he said, and swallowed. When she didn't react, expression hard but curious, he said, "We've lost a few people—Devon Alamort and Lane Illea. Do you know where they are? If they're alive?"

She hesitated, the shout coming again from the street. "I don't know. Everyone captured at the quarantine zones were taken to the station. But there was one man who was singled out. They took him away in a carriage."

"Who took him?"

"Prefect Arctus and Councilor Havvelan."

The shout again, this time sharp and demanding. The soldier sheathed her sword and stepped out into the street with a quick glance back at him. He edged to the corner.

"Where were you?" a sergeant demanded.

She shook her head as she strode toward him. "I thought I saw someone suspicious, but it was nothing."

He looked over her shoulder, scanning the street. "We're to escort the Kerpezians to the waygate."

"They're leaving?"

The sergeant scowled. "Fleeing, more like."

They headed away, the soldier not looking back.

Dalton waited another ten minutes, fingering his dagger, then headed clockwise and hubward, moving purposefully, using main thoroughfares. No one bothered him and no one appeared to be following him.

The sun was beginning to set by the time he ducked into a tavern on the edge of the area surrounding the Lyceum. He paused inside the door, scanned the room as his eyes adjusted to the darkness. Only a few lucents were lit on the supports and near the bar. He caught sight of Nic at one of the side tables, an empty glass before him, another full one already waiting.

He slid into the seat opposite the ex-gang member as he took a sip. "Find out anything about Raven?"

Nic set the glass down and swallowed, wiping his mouth as he slouched back with a grimace. "Nothing. None of my contacts—those outside of Carbolen's reach anyway—know anything. The lower levels are chaos right now. The Iandolan Army is ripping them apart trying to find where the Brovettans have gone to ground. Everyone's scrambling to stay out of their way. They haven't touched Carbolen's lair yet though. Or many of the other gangs."

"Did you approach any of those you know in the gangs?"

Nic shot him a look. "Not yet. I could ask around about Devon and Lane, but who would you trust not to run straight to Carbolen with word that we're asking around about Raven?"

"What about Arch?"

Nic took another hard swallow. "Headed there next. Want to come?"

Dalton gestured to the two glasses. "I think I'd better."

"It helps with the pain."

He sat forward, tossed back the rest of the drink, then pulled himself up from the chair, one arm cradling his side.

As they headed back outside, angling toward the Lyceum and the Shandy Quad, Nic asked, "What about Mannert?"

"Nothing. She wasn't in any of our usual contact points. But I did run into a soldier who said she hasn't been back to the barracks since the attacks on the camps."

"So she's missing, too."

"Looks like it." Dalton let the little snake of worry squirm in his gut for a moment, then added, "She also said Arctus and Havvelan took someone from the station away in a carriage, a man they'd captured in the camps."

"Devon?"

"I don't know."

"But you think so." They paused at the edge of a street, Nic's breathing labored. "Where'd they take him?"

"The soldier didn't say."

"Which means he could be anywhere."

Dalton didn't answer. They'd reached the Quad.

The interior looked exactly the same as when Dalton had been a War student at the Lyceum—dark, loud, with scattered tables, a long bar along one wall, students milling about laughing and conversing. And yet it felt completely different. The patrons were young, the energy high and oblivious. No one appeared affected by the attack at the Lyceum months before, or the recent activity surrounding the Brovettans. No lines of worry or concern marred their faces.

Dalton's gaze fell to the table where he'd nearly bled out after bringing down the Warding. When he glanced back up, Nic was already at the bar, both of them drawing curious looks.

He cut through the crowd and joined Nic, already speaking to the bartender, a girl Dalton didn't recognize.

"—looking for Arch," Nic was saying. "Is he around?"

The girl—tall, with a narrow face and suspicious eyes—scoped them out as she poured. Her lip curled at Nic, but the scowl dropped when she saw Dalton. "He's in the back. I'll let him know you're here."

She passed the drinks off and ducked through the door behind the bar.

"What was that about?" Nic asked, then looked at Dalton. "Oh."

"What?"

"You've got your soldier stance on, all stiff and formal. She probably thinks you're city guard."

The back door opened and Arch came through. "I don't have time for—" He halted when he saw them, face going slack for a moment, then hard. "Let them behind the bar. I'll see them in the back."

The bartender squeezed by him, motioning them through the bar, while Arch eyed the customers. He let them by, then followed, closing the door behind him.

"My office."

They stepped through stacks of crates and boxes into the small room at the back, standing aside as Arch passed them. He moved behind the desk, pulled open a drawer, then slapped a dagger on the desktop.

"What in hells are you doing here?"

"We need your help," Nic said.

Arch's gaze snapped between them. "Half of the students out in the room probably recognize you from before. The other half are likely working for Carbolen. You must be desperate."

"Raven, Devon, and Lane are missing, among others," Dalton said.

"Missing?"

"Raven was taken by Carbolen," Nic said. "As for Devon and Lane..."

"Captured or dead, we don't know," Dalton finished. "They were part of the raids on the internment camps. We think Devon, at least, was taken by Arctus and Havvelan."

The tension in Arch's shoulders eased and he sank down into the chair behind the desk. "And what do you expect me to do about it?"

Nic leaned forward. "I know you have contacts in the upper city. Can you ask around to see if anyone knows what happened to Devon? If Arctus and Havvelan took him—"

"He's likely being held somewhere Mid-level or above." Arch spun the knife as he considered, then focused on them both. "Havvelan was a merchant until his recent elevation to the Council. He has many contacts and resources. I'll see what I can find out, but I wouldn't count on it happening anytime soon. I'll have to be circumspect and that always takes longer."

"What about Lane?" Dalton asked.

"If Lane is missing, then I'd wager Havvelan has her as well. They've certainly been causing an inordinate amount of trouble for the Council lately."

"So if you find Devon, you'll find Lane."

"I'd be surprised otherwise. Unless one of them is dead."

Even with the lurch in his gut by that statement, Dalton felt better. Arch was a smuggler, had dealings with the upper city, with its merchants. They'd know about Havvelan.

"Then what about Raven?" Nic asked.

"That I won't touch."

Arch began to rise, but Nic reached out, as quick as one of the tull's lizards, and clamped his hand down hard over Arch's, grinding it into the dagger trapped beneath. Arch grunted in pain, fell back into his seat as Nic's grip tightened.

"You know what Carbolen will do to her," the ex-gang member said. "I might have escaped, but only because I'm beneath Carbolen's notice. Not her. She was a Regular. She was his lover. He's been biding his time, but now that he's got her, he'll want to make an example of her. It won't be clean and it won't be respectful and you know she won't survive it."

Dalton reached forward and laid his hand on Nic's shoulder. The tension there trembled, then snapped, and Nic snatched his hand away, releasing Arch and stumbling back a step with a grimace of pain. He clutched his injured side, but glared at Arch.

"She pulled me from beneath the collapsed ceiling," he said, tone harsh, "and Toral took advantage of it to take her down. I can't let Carbolen have her."

Arch shook his hand as he glowered, flexed his fingers. But he said, "He's got her."

"Where?"

"The temple, in the dead zone. But I doubt she's still alive."

"He'll break her, then he'll parade her around in front of the rest of the gang. If he hasn't done that yet, then she's still alive."

"How will you get her out?"

"That's not your concern."

Dalton shifted forward, catching Arch's attention. "There's one more thing…"

"You've got to be kidding me."

Dalton leaned onto the desk, palms flat, nearly eye-to-eye with Arch. "We need you to set up a meeting with Proctor Arrend."

* * *

Dalton paced inside the tight space of the hidden room of Miriam's Blooms, the flower shop at Mid-level where Nic said he and Devon had once met up with Arch. His hand clenched and unclenched compulsively. Every breath was scented with faded roses and old sweat and a mustiness that caught at the back of his throat. Devon's green lucent lantern lit the interior.

Nic leaned up against the back wall, arms crossed, near the narrow door that led to the shop.

"You should stop," the ex-gang member said. "You're making it warmer in here and it's already stifling."

Dalton drew in a steadying breath and forced himself to a halt. "He's been gone five days, Nic. Both of them."

"Wearing yourself out isn't going to find them or free them any sooner. We're searching as fast as we can."

"Still nothing new from Arch?"

"Nothing we didn't already know. He's verified Havvelan took someone from the city guard, but not where they went. None of Havvelan's warehouses or storefronts have seen any suspicious activities. Havvelan himself has stuck to his usual routine as far as Arch can ascertain."

Dalton leaned against a wall with one arm and bowed his head. "What about Raven?"

"Picall has scouted out the dead zone where the temple is located. There's only one entrance that I know of and, while it doesn't appear to have a guard at the edge of the dead zone, she's certain there are at least three or four deeper inside, where they can't be seen."

"How does she know that?"

"She's counted how many go in and out, kept track of their faces. They're all Regulars, except for Leinn, Toral, and Carbolen himself."

"So there's something there he doesn't want to draw attention to, but still wants to protect."

"It's Raven."

Dalton didn't want to question Nic's certainty, not after how he reacted when Arch resisted helping them. Besides, he thought Nic was right. "Then how do you plan on getting her out?"

"Cerelle and Sadie are working on that."

The door leading into the courtyard behind the flower shop rattled and Dalton tensed, hand dropping to his sword. Nic pushed away from the wall and drew up beside him as the door rattled again, then opened.

Three shadowed figures, limned by moonlight, entered. The first was clearly Arch. The second was hooded, shoved forward by a man Dalton didn't know.

"You wanted to speak to Arrend," Arch said, pulling the hood from the second figure as the third turned to shut the door behind them, "here you go."

The proctor shook himself, blinked in the sudden light, and drew in a ragged breath. He took in the room with one glance, gaze settling on Dalton with a frown.

"I was told you wanted to speak with me. About Devon. Where is he?"

"We don't know," Dalton said. "That's why we came to see you."

"What happened?"

Dalton gave a quick run-down of what had happened at the internment camp on Level Sixteen, ending with, "He sacrificed himself in order to give everyone who'd managed to escape a chance."

Arrend nodded. "I should have known Devon would be in the middle of the fighting. And what about Lane?"

"We think she was captured to," Nic said. "Along with many others."

"Have you contacted her mother, Varenov?"

Dalton's shoulders sagged. "Our usual messenger to Varenov, Captain Mannert, is one of those missing."

"So you're left with me."

"And me," Arch grumbled.

"We wouldn't have—" Dalton began, but Arrend cut him off with a wave of his hand.

"I understand. I hold some power within the Lyceum, but little elsewhere. I'd only use me as a last resort as well." He paused in thought. "I should be able to get word to Varenov. It's not unheard of for proctors to visit the towers. Favian has been—" He halted abruptly, head jerking up. "Favian."

"What about him?" Dalton asked.

"You know he's seized control of the Lyceum? That he's in charge of the additional War colleges that have cropped up around the city?"

"Yes."

"He's been preoccupied with his newfound power, rarely seen at the college. He spends most of his time at the towers, hovering around the Council. That is, he has since the attack with the Warding. But that changed five days ago. The day after the revolt at the quarantine zones, he came back to the Lyceum and gathered up a few of the mage proctors. They evicted everyone from the scriptorium and sealed the doors."

"Why would they do that?" Dalton asked.

"According to the Historian who was overseeing the library that day, they wanted to unseal Devon's challenge, the one that got both he and Lane expelled. They forced him to retrieve it from the library vault, under protest, then kicked him out as well. He immediately came to me, not that I could have done anything to stop Favian."

"What do you think it means?" Nic asked.

"At the time, I thought nothing. Now that I know Devon and Lane have likely been captured—"

"You think Favian knows about it, knows where they are."

"And is likely questioning them himself. That's why he needed Devon's challenge. He's trying to get them to reveal what they know. He lost his chance when they escaped after the Warding."

"So all we have to do is follow Favian," Nic said.

"I'll follow Favian," Dalton said. "You focus on Raven."

"I don't think you'll have to follow him at all."

Dalton faced Arrend. "Why not?"

Arrend drew himself upright, almost defensively. "Because I've been keeping an eye on him since the Historian told me what he'd done in the library. The only places he's visited besides the Lyceum and a few taverns and cafes are the towers."

All of them fell silent.

"But that means," Nic began quietly.

"They're being kept in the towers, yes," Arrend finished.

Chapter Eighteen

"Where are the insurgents hiding the Brovettans?"

Devon hung forward in the chair where he was bound, his arms screaming in pain, tied behind him—behind the chair—holding up his weight. The rope ties had dug into his wrists, flayed the skin there off. His head hung forward, bloody drool trailing from his mouth to the floor. His hair hung ragged, blocking his view of the room. All he could see was the smooth stone of the floor, spattered with blood and spit. His entire face throbbed with his pulse, but he didn't have the strength to lift it, nor to sit upright to relieve his stretched arms. Not to mention how any movement set off the dulled but excruciating pain from his chest.

Havvelan's voice came from the left, where he knew a second chair had been positioned. A third sat across from it, on the opposite side of the door. But it was the steady pacing of Arctus' boots that held Devon's attention.

Right now, they'd paused to his right, just out of sight.

"Where are the insurgents hiding?" Havvelan repeated.

Devon had answered the question a hundred times over the last few days, but he drew in a ragged breath—something in his chest pinched—and said again, "I don't know." His voice was hoarse, yet thick with phlegm.

He sensed the hand flick from Havvelan and tensed.

Arctus grabbed his hair and snapped his head upright. Devon gasped and cried out, lightning pain licking down his neck, through his shoulders, then Arctus' fist slammed into the side of his head—once, twice, a third time.

His vision reeled, the glimpse of Havvelan sitting back sedately in the chair whirling, fading into a haze of yellow with spots of black. He sobbed, unable to control it, as blood pounded through every bruise and cut in his face. The ache radiated down through his neck, twinged in his shoulders, and stitched its way into his brutalized chest.

Through the roar in his ears, Devon heard the door open and someone entered.

"Again," Havvelan said.

Before Arctus could follow through, a familiar voice—Favian—said, "Wait."

Devon heard his approach, felt the proctor's hand roughly straighten his head in Arctus' grip, fingers pinching his cheekbones. Favian's breath was hot against his skin, but his vision hadn't cleared yet.

"He's barely conscious," Favian said in disgust, letting Devon go. Arctus let his head drop. "How do you expect me to make progress if he's never aware enough to answer my questions?"

"You have Lane to interrogate."

"She's not exactly cooperative."

Devon felt a surge of satisfaction. He might have chuckled, if he hadn't been fighting to breathe.

Havvelan stirred. "You're going to have to do something about that."

"Such as?"

"Be more…creative in how you apply pressure."

Favian didn't respond to the implication. "What have you found out from him?"

A rustle of cloth as Havvelan rose and approached. The haze in Devon's eyes had cleared enough he could see the shadowy shapes of Havvelan's feet.

"Nothing of substance. He persists in repeating the same lies." Havvelan's voice grew smug. "What he doesn't realize is that we already know the answers to so much. For example—" And here Havvelan's voice shifted to focus on Devon. "—we already know the gangs were behind the attacks on the quarantine zones. We know Carbolen was the ringleader… or should I say former Captain Ben Coral? We know they were hiding in the sublevels after they escaped your custody, Proctor Favian."

"None of that is particularly impressive," Favian said defensively. "Easy to deduce or discover from the gossip on the street."

"True." Havvelan shifted closer, knelt down beside Devon, so he was on the same level, his breath ruffling Devon's sweat-straggled hair. "But we also know where the elevators are that Carbolen is using to reach the sublevels. And we know one of their bases of operations is in an old theater on Level Ten. We know of at least two locations where they've taken some of the escaped Brovettans. And, of course, we know where Carbolen's lair is on Level Seventeen. So you see—" He grabbed Devon gently by the chin and raised his head enough Devon could look into his eyes. "—there's really no point in playing the martyr and refusing to answer. It's only causing you grief and pain that, in the end, you won't be able to endure."

Devon clenched his jaw—against pain, against rage—then forced himself to say through dry, split lips, "You can't make me reveal what I don't know."

Havvelan's face twisted in disgust. He sighed. "I suppose there's still something left in Captain Mannert. At least she's putting up more of a fight. She's certainly more entertaining." He leaned in closer. "And there's always Lane Illea to resort to…or perhaps Dalton Trent?"

Devon's entire body seized, his eyes flaring wide involuntarily, breath expelled as if Arctus had punched him in the chest. Every nerve and synapse buzzed with fear. For a horrifying moment, every slash, crack, and bruise in his body flared.

"No." The word trembled. "No, you don't have him. I made certain he got away."

Havvelan chuckled, his grip on Devon's jaw tightening. "You tried. According to the reports from Level Sixteen, when they hit that merchantile the elevators were working. And then they weren't. None of the architects who've scrutinized those elevators can explain how this happened. The mechanisms aren't broken. Old, decaying, but still functional if they were provided power. But the lucent is clearly dead." He locked onto Devon's eyes. "How did you manage to make them work with the lucent dead?"

When Devon didn't answer, his brow creased in anger and he thrust Devon away, standing. Devon's head dropped like a stone and he winced, but his heart thundered, frantic, and his stomach felt hollowed out, his soul empty. They couldn't have Dalton. He'd made certain they couldn't follow him!

"See if you can get it out of him," Havvelan said. "You might find him more accommodating now."

"That isn't exactly my purview," Favian answered.

"It is now. Arctus?"

The prefect who'd remained silent to one side bent down and whispered into Devon's ear, "We'll continue this tomorrow." The soft words sent a shudder into Devon's gut.

Havvelan and Arctus departed, Havvelan saying something about starting the preparations, not to wait any longer, before the door closed behind them. Devon began to think that Favian had left with them, until he heard a scuff and a shuffle of feet.

"There's no point in not cooperating," Favian said. Devon could see him moving at the edges of his vision, but he couldn't tell what he was doing. "You aren't achieving anything. It's only causing you pain. Havvelan is discovering everything he needs to know from the others."

"Others?"

"Captain Mannert. Lane. A couple of others captured during the quelling of the quarantine riots."

"They weren't riots."

Favian stepped close. "No, they weren't. But that's what Havvelan and the Council are calling them now, spreading the word through the streets of Iandolo, condemning those involved, those that started them." He grabbed Devon's shoulder and pulled him upright, so that he rested against the back of the chair and his arms fell slack.

Devon hissed, biting back the scream as the muscles of his shoulders eased back into place and the skin of his arms began to twitch and tingle as normal blood flow returned. The ropes binding his hands loosened and he felt fresh blood drip from his fingers to the floor. His hands felt leaden, unwieldy. Spikes shot up from his chest and lower back.

"The people have already started to believe it," Favian continued, as Devon panted out quick breaths to control the pain. "Even those who were involved. The power of a repeated lie. A bid for freedom becomes a riot, a revolt perpetrated by insurgents."

"They weren't insurgents."

"It doesn't matter. The people of Iandolo don't care. It's easier to believe the lie—even though they know it's a lie—and go about their daily lives than to question it. If they question the lie, then they'll feel compelled to become involved, to do something about it. No one wants to do that."

Favian had shifted around behind him, stood at his shoulder.

"Now, I need you to look at something." He grabbed Devon's hair, much as Arctus had earlier, and tilted Devon's head back. Devon's vision swam, grew dark again at the edges, but Favian slapped his cheek. "Ah ah ah, stay focused. I need you to concentrate. Now look."

Devon blinked, the room slipping and sliding beneath him, but with effort he managed to clear a rough circle amidst the blur. Favian had laid pages out on the cell's floor.

"What's...this?"

"Notes on the mage forms. Everything we've managed to construct using your challenge questions, what we learned from the Brovettan mage attack, and what we already know about the sigils. But your challenge hints that there is more."

Devon managed a weak chuckle. "You should have let me go through the challenge." He swallowed down a thick gobbet of phlegm and blood. "Then you would have learned all about it."

He felt Favian's fingers tighten in his hair, then relax. "Perhaps you're right. I reacted hastily back then. I plan to rectify that here." He let Devon's head fall, stepped forward to select one of the pages, and shoved it under Devon's gaze. "Explain your understanding of this diagram."

Devon managed to lift his head, blink his eyes into focus. The page contained the double pyramid, notations on the nodes to one side. The script was cramped and terse, appeared to crawl across the page. Devon had a hard time making it out.

He drew in a ragged breath and said, "No." Tiny spots of blood speckled the page.

The page trembled, then withdrew, but when Favian spoke he didn't appear upset. "I assumed that would be your answer. Up until now, I've been able to keep Havvelan satisfied interrogating you and Mannert and the others. I convinced him to leave Lane to me. But she is as stubborn as her mother. No amount of coercion on my part has forced her to explain how she has learned to manipulate the mage forms to do what she can do. It is more than simply learning the forms—she knows forms that even the proctors at the Lyceum do not know, forms that even the mages from Brovetto in our custody claim not to know. If she were still part of the Lyceum, I would be impressed with her creativity, but she is not. Again, perhaps I was hasty in expelling her along with you. But that is irrelevant at this point."

He faced Devon. "You heard Havvelan. He grows impatient. He wants results. I don't think I can protect Lane much longer. He has already indicated he wants more brutal techniques used against her. I'm not certain how long she would last beneath Arctus' ministrations. After all, she was raised in the towers. You have the advantage of being a survivor of the lower levels. You've seen brutality. You've experienced it, likely at the hands of your own gang leader, Carbolen. You've been hardened to it."

He stepped closer, knelt down. "Lane has not. Oh, I'm certain she'd put up a good fight…at the beginning. She'll convince herself she can withstand the pain. But she doesn't know what true pain is, does she? She's never been beaten in an alley to the point she pisses blood for a week. She's never felt her own fractured bones grinding beneath someone's heel. She can't imagine such exquisite, splintering pain. Yet you know she will resist. Do you want to see her bruised and broken?"

Devon held Favian's gaze, eyes narrowed with hatred, but said nothing.

Favian smiled. "I didn't think you'd cave to that." He searched Devon's swollen face, the bruises, the cracked lips, the sweat-matted hair. "What I described is only the surface of what Arctus and Havvelan are capable of." His eyes returned to Devon's. He reached forward and prodded Devon's shoulder, producing a flare of unadulterated pain that caused Devon to moan. "This is only the beginning. There are so many more levels beneath. They haven't employed them on you or Lane because they need information from you, information they can't get anywhere else. But Dalton, now… they need nothing from Dalton."

Devon's breath began to accelerate. He tried to control it, but it huffed between his teeth. "Leave Dalton out of this."

"It's not my choice. It's too late, regardless. But if you answer my questions…"

Devon's gaze flickered over the scattered pages of notes. His chest constricted, his breath harsh in his own ears. Maybe he could answer a few questions, enough to keep them from harming Lane or Dalton…

He swung back to Favian, hardened himself. "No."

Favian reached into a pocket, withdrew a cloth stained rust-black. "As I said, it's too late. They've already started in on Dalton." He peeled back the corners of the cloth and revealed a bloody, mangled toe.

Dalton's gut seized and he retched to one side, his mind screaming as his vision blurred again and he grew lightheaded. Favian lurched out of the way, dropping the severed toe to the floor, but the actions were dampened. Removed. Devon's stomached heaved again, but there was nothing left to vomit up. Pain wracked his body as muscles convulsed and at each surge he withdrew further.

Until Favian struck him across the face. The sharp, bright agony brought him back to his body, his vision sparking. Favian clutched at his jaw again. "Do you want them to stop before he loses other body parts? He's already down three toes and two fingers. I can bring them in if you need more incentive."

Devon choked on his own breath, but Favian's fingers dug in deeper. He brought the page with the double pyramid diagram back into Devon's line of sight. "Tell me what you discovered and Dalton won't lose a hand next."

Devon sobbed, his face flushed with heat, mouth sour with bile. The acidic stench hung on the air, overpowering even the slick scent of blood and the odor of sweat.

Favian released him with a disgusted grunt and Devon let his head fall forward. He heard Favian gathering up the scattered pages and squeezed his eyes shut. He regained control of his breath, his chest aching now with a different pain.

But even with his eyes shut, he could still see the severed toe.

When Favian opened the door, Devon pulled his head up and said, "I call the lower pyramid the Source, the upper one the Outcome. The nodes are labeled apex, nadir, primary, secondary, tertiary, and quaternary."

* * *

"What did you find out?" Cerelle asked as soon as Dalton and Nic walked into the abandoned flat on Level Fifteen. Both she and Sadie were sorting materials they'd gathered in their excursions, readying for whatever action they decided to take. "Did Arrend know anything?"

"More than we expected," Nic muttered, already settling in with a wince against the far wall where he'd created a nest out of blankets.

Sadie grabbed the unguent she'd mixed up to help with the pain and bruising and trotted over to him. "Lift your shirt."

Nic protested feebly before relenting to her ministrations.

"What does that mean?" Cerelle asked Dalton, ignoring the other two.

"Devon and Lane—if they're even still alive—are in the towers."

Cerelle's eyes widened.

From the side, Nic yelped and spat, "Careful!" Sadie muttered an apology.

"How are we going to get them out of the towers?" Cerelle asked quietly. "Do we even know where they are being held there?"

"No, but Arrend is going to try to contact Varenov. Perhaps she'll know. Or will be able to find out."

"Find out what?"

All three of them, Nic excluded, jerked toward the new voice, reaching for weapons, only relaxing when they saw it was Picall. The tuller raised a hand. "Sorry."

"Find out where Devon and Lane are being held in the towers." Dalton gave a quick run-down of what they'd discovered during their meeting with Arrend, then turned to Picall. "Have you discovered anything new?"

"Nothing regarding Devon and Lane. And nothing has changed with Raven's situation."

"Still at the temple in the dead zone?" Dalton frowned even as he asked. He didn't like where this was headed, knew the others wouldn't like it either.

"As far as I can tell. But there's something else going on in the lower levels."

That diverted him for a moment. "What have you seen?"

Picall had settled in around the stash in the middle of the room, pulled additional items from her satchel as she spoke. "Movement. The Iandolan Army and the city guard have been tearing the lower levels apart looking for the Brovettans, methodically searching the inhabited sections level by level. They've found some of those who fled on their own, but for the most part Carbolen and Maupin have been able to keep the Brovettans hidden, shifting them from location to location if the soldiers come too close. The larger camps are too deep in the uninhabited zones for the army to have gotten too close to yet, although everyone knows it's only a matter of time before they begin searching even there."

"So what's changed?"

"They've stopped searching. At least on some of the levels."

Something tugged in Dalton's gut. "What are they doing instead?"

"Pulling back, gathering at barracks or stations. Squads are being shifted around, men being pulled from the gates and the walls."

"Sadie and I noticed it as well," Cerelle said, "when we were out collecting supplies. Streets where we'd normally have to be careful were empty of patrols."

Dalton considered. "What levels?"

"Eight, Ten, Eleven, Fifteen, and Seventeen. There are a few others, but the concentration of soldiers isn't as heavy there."

Dalton faced them. "They're planning some sort of action, something that will happen in the next day or two at most." He scanned their supplies, knelt down and began picking items out and setting them to one side.

Cerelle crouched down across from him. "What do you think their target is?"

"I'd say they've discovered where a few of the Brovettan camps are, based on those levels. And Carbolen's on Level Seventeen."

"But how did they find out? Devon and Lane don't know where the camps were set up. Neither does Mannert."

"They captured more than just those we care about at the internment camps. They were bound to get some of Carbolen's or Maupin's men who knew the location of one of the camps."

"So what are we going to do?"

"Picall, you need to warn Senn, Carbolen, and Maupin, through whatever contacts you have, although they probably already know. Do that now, then get back here as soon as possible. We'll be ready by then."

"And what are we going to do after I return?" Picall asked, already headed for the door.

"We're going to go get Raven. Varenov and Arrend *may* be able to get us into the towers, after they manage to find out where Devon and Lane are being kept, but I *know* Raven can get us in. She led Devon inside when the towers were occupied by the rebel splinter group of Brovettans in order to get Lane. We need her if we're going to have any chance of getting Devon and Lane out."

Behind him, Nic groaned. "I knew I wasn't going to get any rest."

* * *

"There has to be another way in," Dalton insisted.

"There isn't," Nic answered, "and Carbolen knows it. That's why he's using the temple. You'll see when we get there." The ex-gang member stuck another knife into his boot and patted down the leathers he'd changed into, checking his other weapons.

Sadie, Cerelle, and Dalton continued their own preparations, Dalton's mind fretting. He hadn't seen the dead zone or the area containing the temple, so it was difficult to plan, but he didn't like the only option Picall had presented them for retrieving Raven. A frontal assault along the only possible approach was begging for disaster, especially with Regulars guarding the entrance. There had to be another option. Maybe once he was there—

The sound of footfalls approaching at a run interrupted his thoughts. The others had heard as well, Cerelle already falling back to one side of the door, Nic to the other. Dalton slid a dagger from its sheath—the room was too close for swordplay—and caught Sadie doing the same.

A moment later, Picall stumbled into view, catching herself on the doorframe, Nic reaching out to steady her. She was gasping for air, hand on her chest.

Dalton lowered his dagger even as his heartrate escalated. "Picall. What are you doing back? You couldn't possibly have warned—"

"Too...late," she heaved, coughed, then swallowed. "Army already...on move."

Cerelle's eyes widened. "That was fast."

"I hope Senn and the others were paying attention."

He would have continued, but Picall was waving her hand. "Think they might...be coming here." She drew in a ragged breath and exhaled, finally catching her breath. "They're on the way."

"Here?" Sadie asked sharply. "Do they even know about this place?"

"Doesn't matter," Dalton said. "Grab everything you can. Nic, go watch the street. Yell if you see anything. Move!"

They all began tossing whatever they could get their hands on into any available satchels or sacks, Dalton grabbing clothes and food, Cerelle and Sadie focusing on weapons and other utensils. Picall spent a moment more recovering, then grabbed a few of the full bags before laying a hand on Dalton's arm.

"We don't have time."

He looked into her eyes, hesitated a moment, then said, "Right. Cerelle, Sadie, take whatever you've got and go."

They abandoned everything else immediately, sprinting out the door with whatever they carried. Dalton scanned what was left, then swore and grabbed Devon and Lane's satchels, tucked into a corner. Pulling the straps over his shoulder, he ushered Picall out, the tuller adjusting satchels so that nothing interfered with her weapons.

At the end of the hall, she drew Dalton to a window and pointed.

Three blocks distant, beneath one of the few working lucents overhead, squads of soldiers were moving down the street, headed directly toward them. Their formations suggested they had mages within their ranks.

He urged her down the stairs, meeting up with the others below. "They're only a few blocks away. Stay close to the building. Take the first cross-street."

Nic nodded, slipping out through the door, the others a few paces after, Dalton bringing up the rear. The lucents were dead overhead here—one of the reasons they'd chosen this building—so the area was cloaked in shadow, although there were enough random panels of lucent working nearby that they could see to move without resorting to Devon's lantern. Behind them, between their building and the soldiers, Dalton caught a few of the local residents scurrying across the streets, sliding into doors, and shutting windows. Some of the sources of light began to blink off.

Nic cut into the next street, also shadowed, but pulled up short at the next corner. "They're on the parallel street as well."

"Head away from them, but cut across as soon as you feel it's safe."

Nic nodded, the others trailing behind him, jogging across open spaces or any place lit by lucents, all of them keeping their eyes on the streets. They were noticed by more of the locals, but as soon as they saw the approaching soldiers they scattered. A few obvious scouts and runners took off at a dead sprint, no doubt to warn nascent gangs of what approached. No one this deep on this level wanted the attention of the Iandolan Army.

Two blocks distant, Nic angled across the street in a particularly heavy patch of darkness and they turned left at the next street.

Before they'd gone another block, the dull *whump* of a not-so-distant explosion rolled over them, bringing them up short. A rumble followed, punctuated by metal twisting, crete grinding, and glass shattering as a building collapsed in on itself. Dalton felt the shudder through his feet.

"Look," Sadie said, pointing.

Behind, partially lit by lucents, a cloud of dust rose above the intervening buildings and hit the level overhead, billowing outwards.

"Was that our building?" Nic asked.

"No," Dalton said. "Not close enough. Judging by the direction and distance, I'd say they just destroyed the warehouse with the elevators we used to retrieve the Brovettans from the internment camp."

"So this is retaliation," Cerelle said, a hint of disgust in her voice.

"A show of force," Dalton countered. "It's how the Council operates. Look at what they did following the attacks on the waygates and the Lyceum."

"Are they after us or not?" Nic asked.

"They would already have overtaken our building. If we don't hear another explosion, I'd say they're not."

All of them stilled, listening intently. After a few minutes, Nic exhaled and leaned back against the building, one hand holding his side. "I don't think they know we're here."

Picall had shifted to the corner behind them. "But they're still coming."

They all joined her. What lead they'd had was narrowing; they were now only two blocks behind.

"What could be their second target, if not us?" Cerelle asked.

Silence as they all considered. Then Dalton met Nic's gaze. "The elevators," they said simultaneously.

Cerelle looked confused. "We just heard them blow those up."

"Not those elevators," Dalton said. "The ones we used to escape Carbolen down to the sublevels. The ones we've been using from various levels to get the Brovettans out of the city, to the tull."

Cerelle and Sadie traded a horrified look. "We have to stop them."

Nic snorted. "There are five of us. Against at least twenty times that."

"And they have mages," Sadie added.

"If we don't stop them, how are we going to get our people out?" Cerelle asked. "We'll be trapped in Iandolo." Her hand clenched in frustration as she turned a hate-filled gaze on the approaching soldiers.

"We'll find another way," Dalton said. "Besides, that's not our problem, it's Senn's." When Cerelle didn't budge, the soldiers edging closer, he reached out and gripped her arm. Her muscles were knotted with tension. "It's suicide to try to stop them now. It won't accomplish anything. We need to go."

She spun on him. "And where are we going to go?"

He glanced at Picall. "You said the soldiers were grouping on Level Seventeen, right?" Picall nodded. "Then they're going to hit Carbolen. We should head up there."

"We aren't going to help Carbolen, are we?"

He met Cerelle's gaze. "No, but he's going to be distracted."

Realization hit and some of the tension in her eased. "Raven."

"It's likely our best chance of success."

"Or another form of suicide," Nic said. "But I'm game."

The others all nodded. With the advancing soldiers only a block away, they headed down the street, still angling away from their flat but hubward, Picall and Nic taking the lead. Before ascending to Level Sixteen through a maze of interconnected buildings, they heard another explosion, distant, Cerelle halting abruptly and looking back. Dalton thought he might have to say something to get her moving again, but she turned with a jerk and sharp gesture, nearly running Picall and Nic down.

Level Sixteen was quiet, but as soon as they emerged on Level Seventeen through a trapdoor in the floor of an abandoned tenement, they heard fighting. Nic signed a warning and they hauled themselves up out of the tunnel in silence, Dalton shielding the light from Devon's lantern until all of them were above. He flicked it dark and pulled himself up into the darkened room, slats of light from outside outlining boarded up windows on one wall. He could vaguely see the others huddled there, peering out.

"Assessment?" Dalton asked in a hushed voice as he came up behind Nic.

Nic glanced back at him. "They're attacking the lair. Hard. I'd say they've infiltrated at least the outer layer, but the halls and buildings and streets are all designed to be traps. It will take them awhile to get to anything significant. Thankfully, we aren't going there."

He motioned to Picall, who slipped out the vacant doorway and into the hall beyond. She reappeared a moment later and signaled all clear.

They exited onto the street, the fighting from the lair much louder out here, punctuated by explosions that made Nic wince. He shared a look with Dalton, clearly indicating he hadn't factored in mages in his earlier assessment. The group picked up their pace, circling the heart of the fight through desolate streets. They met no one, saw no furtive movements.

Then they hit the dead zone.

The edge was abrupt, the street before them simply caved in, along with half of the building to one side, rooms gaping wide, steel supports bent downwards, edges jagged. Fifty feet away, a block over, the buildings were still intact, but they were pitted and gutted, appearing structurally unsound. Dalton shifted to the edge to look down, the collapse cutting through at least two levels. Above, ragged holes appeared in the ceiling up into Level Eighteen, although the damage above was less severe.

"This way," Picall said, and stepped into the building to their left without hesitation. Nic was the first to follow her, Dalton bringing up the rear reluctantly.

They edged out into the unstable edges of the dead zone, the structures around them shifting and groaning as they moved. They traversed the lip of the drop-off, the ledge only three feet wide, then another tenement, the entire building shuddering beneath Dalton's feet. When they could see out into the emptiness of the zone, lucent lights reflecting off of brittle edges and odd angles, his stomach flipped and roiled. At one point, something nearby broke free and tumbled into the depths, clanging as it hit obstructions on the way down.

But then Picall slowed and waved Dalton forward, to a gaping hole in the side of the building they were in. She pointed outside. "That's the temple."

A hundred feet away, an island of intact structure remained atop a plinth of metal supports that stretched down into the darkness below. Its main building had odd architecture—not a tenement or warehouse, more like the theater they'd used as a base on Level Ten. Two stone towers rose from each end, a steeply pitched roof in between, covered with a few remaining tiles between ragged holes. Tall, narrow windows interrupted the stone at intervals. It was surrounded by smaller, mostly collapsed buildings and a couple narrow streets on all sides. A narrow bridge ran from the edge of the dead zone to it, perhaps forty feet long. All of it was lit by flickering lucent from panels overhead or the edge of the zone beyond.

"Only one approach," he muttered. Glancing down at its support, he could see that there might have been a pathway up, but it would take decades to find it. It was nothing but twisted metal on the verge of collapse. He faced the others. "Ready?"

Nic and Cerelle nodded; all of them looked grim, anxious fingers touching weapons or twisting in fabric or the handles of satchels.

"We'll leave our supplies here," he said, shrugging out from under Devon's and Lane's bags. "Take only what you'll need to fight. You can find this place again, Picall?"

"Of course." She dropped her packs with Dalton's, the others doing the same, everyone making minute adjustments once free.

Then Dalton flicked the go-ahead to Picall.

They moved swiftly but with stealth, Picall pushing ahead, gestures picking out places to step, shadows to hide in, windows or gaps to avoid. They rounded the ragged edge of the collapse to the start of the bridge without seeing or hearing anyone. Dalton drew his sword as they paused, Nic and Picall peering through a rent in the side wall looking out on the temple's island, but when they looked back both shook their head and shrugged.

Pical had said there was no guard on this side of the bridge.

Dalton hesitated. They were up against Regulars. Who would they lose here? Was this really necessary? But he thought of Devon, of Lane.

He raised a hand, his other tightening on the leather grip of his sword, and motioned go.

Nic and Sadie went first, both smaller in stature and agile. Dalton and Cerelle followed, Picall staying behind with crossbow and bow ready. She'd cover them from the edge if she could.

Dalton's breath huffed, his hearing heightened as he scanned the far side of the bridge. As usual in combat, his heart sped up, but his chest and gut calmed. His mind focused. Nic and Sadie raced forward, leaping holes in the bridge and dancing back and forth to make it harder to target them. Cerelle kept pace beside him and slightly behind, leaving enough room they could both dodge obstacles and gaps without interfering with each other. Metal pounded beneath his heels. A few sections gave sickeningly beneath his weight, but held. He saw and heard nothing on the island ahead.

A cold certainty settled into his stomach, but he shoved it aside as they reached the first street, Nic cutting left to a shadow in the lee of the only wall that remained of a building, its lone door leading to a heap of rubble and debris. When Dalton reached him, he glanced back to see Picall already halfway across the bridge.

"Where are they?" Nic asked, breath coming in harsh heaves.

"I saw nothing on the way over," Cerelle said.

Picall arrived.

"Where were the Regulars stationed?" Sadie asked.

"I couldn't tell. They always vanished into the streets. I never saw them from the opposite side after that, on patrol or at any watch posts."

"So they could still be at the temple." Dalton ignored the skeptical looks. "Let's go."

Now that they were across the bridge, they proceeded cautiously, two scouting ahead, waving the others forward. They edged down the street, spreading out as they neared the main temple, the tower looming over them. The long center of the temple contained only the tall, narrow windows, no doors. The only entrance Dalton could see cut into the side of the tower, an arched alcove at the top of a series of rounded steps.

They came at the door from both sides, crossing the street in front in a crouched rush. Yet still no crossbow bolts rained down on them from the slitted windows above. Dalton took the lead, stepping into the alcove to the door, back pressed up against the stone to one side. He reached out and eased the door outwards, using it to shield himself, but no one came rushing out.

He peered around the door's edge into the dark interior, pulling out Devon's green lantern and flicking it alight. He tossed it into the room beyond, watched it rattle against the stone floor and skitter to a halt amongst scattered debris.

When there was no reaction, he drew in a deep breath and entered, sword ready.

It opened into a foyer, rotten tapestries hanging on the walls, floor covered in chipped stone and shattered tiles from the roof. Stairs headed upwards to the left. A table had collapsed to one side, its wood pungent. The entire room reeked of decay and stone dust.

Dalton shifted to the wide double doors opposite, already open, picking up the lantern as he passed, as the others trailed in behind him. The room beyond was empty except for a large stone altar at its center and heaps of decaying pews shoved to either side. Light filtered down from the wounds in the roof, but Dalton still held the lantern up high as he approached the altar.

This room didn't smell of must and rot. It smelled of blood and piss and shit and torture.

"She's not here," Nic said.

"But she was," Dalton answered, reaching down to touch a dark patch on the stone. He held up his hand so they could see the stain on his fingers. "And recently. The blood's still tacky."

"If it was her and not someone else," Sadie said.

"It was her," Nic snapped.

"Then she's dead," Cerelle said. "Why else wouldn't she be here?"

"No." The word held a hint of desperation. Nic stepped forward, between them all. "Not dead. He wouldn't simply kill her."

"Then what?" Cerelle asked in exasperation.

Nic's hand grasped at the air as he spun around. Then he pointed at Dalton. "Carbolen wouldn't kill her outright. He'd want to prove a point."

"That no one can escape, not even a Regular," Dalton said, recalling Nic's words earlier.

Nic nodded. "He's taken her to the lair, to parade her around."

The ex-gang member spun toward the door, but Dalton grabbed his arm. "Where do you think you're going?"

Nic turned on him, jerking his arm free. "To the lair. To get her."

"They're under attack by the Iandolan Army."

"Precisely. They'll be a little distracted."

They glared at each other, until Dalton relented. "Do you know an alternate way in? Because we won't make it through the army and Carbolen's men alive."

"Of course I do."

He stalked off, moving faster the farther away he got.

Cerelle shot him a questioning look, but before anyone could say anything, he motioned them to follow and jogged after Nic.

They headed toward the sounds of fighting, cautious until they'd left the edge of the dead zone, then picking up speed as the footing became more solid. Nic led, Picall not far behind. Cerelle kept attempting to catch Dalton's attention, her expression clearly saying, *This is insanity*, but he ignored her. He'd never seen Nic's eyes so haunted or intent.

When the noise sounded as if the confrontation was on the next street, Nic ducked into an alley, heading to the far left side, where he inserted his dagger into a seam and shoved the handle hard. A section of board popped free, revealing a doorway behind. He paused long enough to listen, then slammed his shoulder against the door until it gave.

Without waiting, he stepped into the building beyond.

They sprinted through rooms and hallways, the outer edges of the lair a maze. Dalton struggled to keep up. Inside, the sounds of the fighting were muted, even the explosions from the mages muffled. They paused at a hallway as a group of gang members raced by at the far end, shouting, backtracked at another when they turned a corner and found the room beyond packed with soldiers and gang members in an all-out brawl. Blood smeared a few of the corridors, bodies lying to the side or propped up against walls. An explosion shuddered through the stone surrounding them, deafeningly close, dust and chunks of the ceiling falling down on them as they raced to the far side.

Then Nic led them around a corner and Dalton recognized where they were. Carbolen's main hall lay ahead, on the right. Part of a wall to the left had collapsed inwards, partially blocking the corridor, but Nic was already halfway over it. A scattering of gang members saw him at the last moment, one of them calling out a warning, but then he was on them, blade slashing. Two fell before the others raced off. Picall dropped one of them with her crossbow, but Nic shouted, "Leave them," and they entered the gang's main hall.

It was as Dalton remembered it—wide and open, the gang's paltry belongings strewn around its edges, cots and hammocks strung up along the walls between the supports. The dais rose from the floor at the far end, chairs and settees arranged like a room upon it, a table at its center, littered with papers and whatever trinkets Carbolen needed or found appealing. A few gang members were rooting through the bags and chests and clothing strewn about. They started forward when Nic entered, but backed off and huddled warily into corners when Dalton and the others stepped inside.

Raven, body so bloodied and bruised Dalton barely recognized her, was strung up spreadeagled against the wall, beneath the giant purple lucent orb that lit the room.

Behind him, Dalton heard Sadie gasp, Cerelle curse. All of them stood in mute shock, until another explosion rattled through the hall.

Nic lunged forward, storming up the dais. Dalton's gaze traced out the ropes that bound her as he followed. "There!" he shouted. "To your left! I'll get the ones on the right. Cerelle and Sadie, catch her once she's lowered down far enough. Picall—"

"Already watching the door."

Dalton fought the knots holding Raven up, tempted to cut them, but knew the fall might kill her, if she wasn't already dead. Her body was limp and she hadn't moved since they'd entered. Spitting curses, he heaved a breath of relief as the knot finally gave, then snatched at the rope so he could lower her slowly. On the far side of the dais, Nic was doing the same, Sadie and Cerelle waiting below.

Cerelle grabbed for her as soon as she was close, Sadie on the other side. "She's alive!" she called out and Dalton felt his entire body go weak.

Then another explosion rocked the hall. "Move!" he shouted.

Picall walked toward the doors, crossbow cycling between those in the hall and the door. Cerelle and Sadie supported Raven between them, the ex-Regular still showing no signs of life. Nic and Dalton brought up the rear.

Once in the outer hall, Nic began to lead them out. "We need to get her back to the safe house on Level Fifteen."

"No," Dalton said as they scrambled through the lair as fast as Cerelle and Sadie could go with Raven's weight. "We need to get her to Arch. He knows a healer."

Chapter Nineteen

Dalton kicked the door to the Shandy Quad open and shouted, "Arch! Are you here?"

The interior was quiet. It was early, but not early enough to account for the locked door. The Quad should be open. There should be customers scattered about the tables and at the bar. But then, the streets had been unduly quiet on their way up here. Those out had stayed clear of their group as soon as they saw Cerelle and Sadie supporting Raven. Yet they hadn't encountered any city guard or Iandolan soldiers on their way here. They'd kept to the back streets on the lower levels and came up by the hub, but once they reached Mid-level, Dalton had expected to run into some kind of trouble with the guard.

They must all be supporting the army on the lower levels.

"Arch!" he shouted again, as he motioned Cerelle and the others inside. Cerelle and Sadie guided Raven to one of the lower tables, eased her onto it. She moaned, the first sound she'd made since they'd lowered her from the lair's wall.

"Keep your cursed voice down," Arch said as he emerged from the back rooms. A blade glinted in the half light of the bar, but he lowered it as soon as he recognized them. "We're closed."

"Call your healer." Dalton motioned toward Raven.

Arch scanned them all, then snatched a lantern from behind the bar and approached. He sucked in a breath and swore as he ran the light over Raven's body.

"Where is everybody?" Nic asked. Dalton noticed he'd drawn one of his own knives.

"Word came the lair was under attack. All of my help scrambled out of here. I stayed behind to shove everyone else out and close down."

"You didn't join them?"

Arch shrugged. "Rumor has it, not just the lair's under attack at the moment."

"What have you heard?"

"Movement on some elevators and a warehouse on Level Fifteen—"

"We were there," Cerelle said, and Arch nodded.

"—a theater on Level Ten—"

Dalton, Nic, and Picall traded looks.

"—and a few compounds on Levels Eight and Eleven where they suspect the escaped Brovettans are hiding." He gestured toward Raven. "You can't keep her here."

"What do you mean?" Nic took a step forward, brandishing his knife, but Arch didn't flinch.

"What I said. I assume you took her from Carbolen. His men will likely be coming through here, if not to return to work than to get help with the fallout from this attack. I am one of his contacts. I doubt you want them to find her here."

"Where do you suggest we take her?"

"Anywhere but here."

Dalton grabbed Nic and hauled him back before he could lunge forward. He stepped into Nic's space instead, coming in close to Arch. "Look at her," he said softly. "We can't take her to one of the healer sanctums. They're going to ask questions about how she got those wounds. They obviously aren't from a fight or an accident. They'll likely summon the city guard. None of us can afford that kind of scrutiny. And you know if you shove us out the door and we don't find help, Raven will die. She's practically dead already."

Arch held Dalton's gaze, sweat beading his brow. His head tilted back slightly, jaw clenching. Then he exhaled harshly, breath reeking of alcohol, and said, "You're going to be the death of me." He swung around toward the bar. "Pick her back up. I meant it when I said we can't keep her here. You two—" He pointed at Cerelle and Sadie. "—do you have cloaks with hoods? Put them on. You all just walked two Brovettans into my bar in broad daylight. I'll be surprised if I don't catch hell for that from someone."

He continued grumbling as he rooted around in the back room, Dalton and Nic sliding Raven from the table while Cerelle and Sadie slipped on cloaks and ducked into the hoods. Picall remained by the door, occasionally checking the street outside.

When Arch reappeared, he'd gathered up a satchel. He tucked a few more items inside as he straightened up the bar, then paused, as if reconsidering.

"Where are we headed?" Dalton asked. He didn't like the way Raven's weight rested on his shoulders. Too light. Too empty. He didn't know how she wasn't already dead, with the number of cuts he'd seen on their way over here. Her tattered clothing was saturated with her own blood.

Arch grunted. "The only place I can think of at the moment: my own apartment."

* * *

"What in all of the living hells do you think you're doing, Arctus?"

Varenov didn't keep her voice low, even though she, Treant, and her guards had just emerged from the elevator into the outer room of the Council chamber. Dozens of conversations abruptly fell silent as she stormed across the hall, directly toward where Arctus stood with Havvelan and Councilor Secora, Treant racing to keep up. Merchants and sycophants and hangers-on stared as she drew to a halt before the three.

"Or should I say, what have done, since it's already well underway?" Her gaze shifted to Havvelan, scathing and contemptuous. "How much of this should be laid at your feet, Councilor?" Then Secora. "And yours? Was this a Council decision? If so, I wasn't made privy to it, which means it cannot possibly be legal."

"Your input wasn't deemed necessary," Havvelan said calmly.

Varenov stared at each of them individually, but focused on Secora at the end, the leader of the Council stiffening. "So the Council met and agreed upon military actions on citizens within Iandolo itself without all of the councilors present? Not simple actions, such as individual arrests or the taking out of a cell of a dozen criminals, but an attack on multiple groups of hundreds of people on several levels. People who, let us not forget, we illegally incarcerated ourselves within 'quarantine zones,' against the express wishes of several councilors. Have you forsaken the Pact completely? Have you forsaken your own ethics?"

Secora spluttered.

"A majority of the councilors agreed that these actions were necessary," Arctus said. "A formal vote of the full Council wasn't needed. The outcome was clear. And a certain amount of discretion was necessary so that no one warned those we intended to target and allowed them to prepare."

Havvelan shot Arctus a black look. "What the prefect means is that we felt expediency was required. We didn't have time to convene the full Council."

"And what required such swift action? You sealed the waygates after the attacks on the quarantine zones. No one can get out without the Council's express approval. Those that escaped are trapped in Iandolo."

"No, they were not. We discovered they had an alternate route out of the city, down to the Flatlands." Murmurs and a few gasps rose from around the room and Havvelan straightened, voice rising slightly. "Part of our actions today will seal that escape route. We also learned of the whereabouts of some of the escaped Brovettans, but those that are aiding them move them frequently. We wanted to take advantage of our information before another move was made."

His voice lowered again as he faced Varenov, the tight smile he'd presented to everyone else in the room slipping. "Now, if you'd like to discuss this further, I suggest we retire to a more private location. I can give you all of the details and the reasons behind them."

Varenov drew breath to protest, but hesitated. Anger still flared along her arms, prickled in her shoulders, but that did not mean their disagreement needed to be projected to everyone in the outer hall. "Very well."

Havvelan turned to Secora. "If you'll excuse us, Councilor Secora, I believe Prefect Arctus and I can handle Varenov's concerns."

"Of course, Councilor Havvelan. Let me know if I can be of assistance."

Secora drifted toward the Council chamber, those nearest attaching themselves to her the moment she drew close, casting glances backwards.

"Should we move this to your own chambers above, Varenov?"

The suggestion surprised her. She would have thought Havvelan would prefer one of the smaller rooms surrounding the Council, or perhaps even his own suite, but she nodded. "I believe everything is in order."

She shot a look toward Treant, a pace away, who gave a discreet nod. She couldn't recall leaving any documents or personal correspondence in view.

Havvelan motioned toward the elevator, letting her and Treant take the lead.

"You realize that no matter what your reasons and no matter how many informal votes of support you have from the councilors, a formal vote during a Council session is required," Varenov said as the elevator opened and the four of them stepped inside, her and Treant first, Arctus and

Havvelan behind. She turned as the doors closed, her guards still outside. "Anything else is illegal and subversi—"

Her voice caught as Arctus drew a knife from a sheath in his belt and stabbed Treant in the left side, the blade slipping in without a sound. Treant gasped and Varenov reached for him, but Havvelan latched on to her arm, his grip bruising. Treant looked at her, mouth working without sound. The board and stylus he always carried slipped from his arms and hit the floor, papers scattering everywhere. He slumped, but Arctus caught him.

"What do you think you're doing?" Varenov demanded, not liking the high-pitched tone of her own voice, the panic and terror there. Her breath came in sharp heaves she couldn't control. "What have you done?"

Havvelan reached with his other hand and touched the lucent bar that controlled the elevator, drawing it upwards, but not as high as Varenov's own floor, not even as high as his own newly-assigned quarters in the tower.

"I'm afraid that the Council has decided to charge you with treason, Varenov."

"Treason?" she spat. She wrested her arm from Havvelan's grip as the elevator began to move. "On what grounds?"

"That your daughter was part of the little insurrection at the quarantine zones. I believe she led the force that blasted through a building in the zone's wall, allowing the Brovettans being kept safe there to flee."

"I've not had contact with Lane since you and the others incarcerated her at the Lyceum after she brought down the Warding."

"I don't believe that and, more importantly, neither do the other councilors. Especially once they saw all of your correspondence with one John Senn, leader of the rebellion in Brovetto and, if I were to wager on a guess, Lane's father."

Varenov's throat closed off and she nearly staggered as the elevator drew to a halt. She managed to swallow and whisper, "John?" Her voice cracked.

Havvelan stepped into the hall beyond, a corridor Varenov had never seen, even though she'd lived in the tower for seventeen years. It was lined with doors, three on either side. As they moved forward, she saw two similar corridors around the curve of the central elevator shaft.

"He's here in Iandolo now," Havvelan as he led the way down the corridor. Behind, Arctus dragged Treant's body into the foyer and dropped it, returning to the elevator to retrieve the assistant's board and papers. "Although I think you know that already."

He paused in front of one of the doors, opening it with a shove, gesturing Varenov inside.

Varenov refused to move. Inside, she could see a cot and a table and chair. Nothing more. "What is this?"

"Your new accommodations."

From one of the rooms behind her, someone moaned, the sound breaking into ragged sobs at the end.

* * *

When Varenov emerged from the elevators into the hall outside the Council chambers, Arrend sighed in relief and pushed himself away from the wall where he'd been lurking, trying to remain inconspicuous. He'd managed to gain entrance to the tower by claiming he was in search of Favian, relaying important Lyceum business. Most of the Iandolan soldiers knew him from the college since they'd trained there. But he could hardly ask them the whereabouts of Councilor Varenov under that pretense, so he'd been obliged to wait for her appearance.

Except she immediately stormed across the hall to face off with Havvelan and Arctus. Arrend had been forced to listen, slipping back to his position against the wall as it escalated and drew the attention of everyone in the room.

When Councilor Secora broke away and Varenov and Havvelan made for the elevator, Arrend sidled discreetly towards them, managing to catch Varenov saying, "—formal vote during a Council session is required—" before the elevator doors closed.

He thought it odd her escorting guardsmen remained behind.

He watched the bar indicating where the elevator was headed above the entrance, frowned when it halted only a few floors above the Council chamber's floor.

The councilors had quarters much higher than that.

He pressed the lucent button to recall the elevator, then glanced around the hall. As soon as Varenov and Havvelan left, all of those gathered had broken into frantic conversation, most of them watching Secora. The head of the Council appeared distracted and troubled, only half listening to those who were speaking to her.

The elevator doors shushed open behind Arrend. Without thinking, he stepped inside and glanced around.

Against one wall rested a stylus, a drop of black ink beneath its tip.

A foot away from that lay a spatter of drying blood.

He took a startled step backwards, out of the elevator, before the doors could close on him. Breath tight in his chest, he glanced around the hall, but no one appeared to have noticed him. His gaze fell on a few of the soldiers scattered about the room, his first inclination to report to someone in authority, but he couldn't do that, could he? Even Varenov's personal guards had vanished.

Agitated, his hands twitching with indecision, he took a tentative step toward Councilor Secora, then paused. Based on the conversation the entire hall had overheard, Secora was compromised. She'd clearly agreed with Havvelan and Arctus. She'd be unlikely to believe him or, even if she did, come to Varenov's aid. If what Havvelan had said about the Council leaving Varenov out of the vote were true, he doubted any of the councilors would.

Which left...no one.

He straightened, hands clasped in front of himself to still them, then turned and called the elevator again. When it arrived and he stepped inside, the stylus, ink, and bloodstains were gone. He stared at the clean floor a moment, then pressed the lucent bar and lowered it to the ground floor.

* * *

Arch led Dalton and the others through a few back streets to the rear of a nondescript building with a wooden staircase zigzagging up the back floors. Potted plants dotted the levels as they climbed—vegetables and tiny fruit trees, mostly—the entire edifice creaking unsettlingly at every step. The bartender ushered them through the fourth-floor door, keeping an eye on the alley below, then closed it behind them, lighting a standard oil lantern to illuminate the austere outer room. Dalton was mildly surprised at how uncluttered it was, considering the state of the Shandy Quad's back bar and the rooms behind. Even Arch's tiny office there was stacked with crates and boxes and scattered papers. Here, everything was neat and orderly: a table and chairs in the center with a setting of plates and utensils and a cup; a hutch to one side, with decanters and additional glasses and a smattering of odd sculptures and trinkets; a set of stacked trunks against the far wall, near a battered but clean fire pit. Through a door slightly ajar, he could see a smaller room and the corner of a bed.

"Where should we put her?" Dalton asked, pausing just inside the doorway. Arch was drawing shades across the single window overlooking the alley.

"On the table."

Cerelle stepped forward immediately and snatched up the setting, clearing the table as Dalton and Nic eased Raven down onto it. She moaned again as Arch retreated to the bedroom, returning a second later with a pitcher filled with water and a bundle of rags.

"Do what you can to clean her up," he said, setting them on the table. "I'll go fetch Mindell. And don't leave this apartment, especially you two." He eyed Cerelle and Sadie, then left.

The five of them stared at the closed door a moment, then Cerelle motioned to the rags. "Hand me some of those."

Dalton reached for them and said, "Picall, watch the alley."

They spent the next hour carefully washing Raven's wounds, pulling and cutting matted clothing from scabbed-over cuts, leaving it in some of the deeper cuts for fear it would cause more significant bleeding that they wouldn't be able to stop. Dalton's initial fear turned to nausea and anger the longer they worked. Raven's skin along her arms and legs had been flayed in long, thin sections over days, based on those that had started healing and those that appeared fresh. Her fingernails had been yanked out, the skin beneath raw and livid. Dozens of incisions had been cut into her stomach and back, salt pressed into the wounds, crusted around their edges. Multiple fingers had been broken, along with some of her toes. Many of the cuts were infected, red and hot to the touch, leaking pus or a clear fluid once they'd cleared away what had dried on the surface.

But the worst wound, the most disturbing, was that Carbolen had removed one of her breasts, the flesh seared closed.

Sadie gasped at the discovery, Cerelle grabbing her hands and pulling her in close. Dalton tasted bile at the back of his throat, but swallowed the acid down and continued working. Raven's breath came in short huffs, interspersed with whimpers and occasional moans at their ministrations, but her eyes never opened.

Nearly two hours later, Arch arrived with Mindell, Dalton's angry demand to know where they'd been cut off by Arch's furious look. Mindell, face more drawn and aged than Dalton remembered from before, paid none of them any attention, moving immediately to the table, setting two bags to one side. He ran his hands over Raven's body, mumbling and cursing to himself, then he snapped his fingers at Sadie and Nic. "You two, pull everything out of my satchels. Find the green ceramic container and grab one of the unused rags. We need to deal with the infections now, before they spread further. But before that…" He placed one hand on Raven's forehead—her face was the least damaged, Dalton noted—and the other over her chest, closing his eyes. Nothing appeared to happen, but a moment later Raven's breathing smoothed out and all of the tension in her body relaxed.

"What did you do?" Cerelle asked.

He waved a hand negligently. "Put her into a deep sleep. I also assessed her wounds and her will. She's strong. She's fighting. Most of the serious wounds are on the surface, nothing too deep except some internal bruising." His brow creased in bitter anger. "Who did this to her?"

"Carbolen."

His lips thinned, but he said nothing, simply began to work.

Dalton drew Arch aside. "What took so long?"

"I couldn't find him. He'd gone down to Level Seventeen to help with the wounded. I had to drag him away. Physically. It's a madhouse down there."

"At the moment, I'm finding it hard to be sympathetic to Carbolen and his gang."

Arch glanced at the table. "Understandable."

They watched Mindell work in silence for a moment, Nic and Sadie applying poultices and unguents as instructed, Mindell prodding and stitching and mumbling to himself. Picall remained at the window watching the street, her expression fraught. Cerelle paced off to one side, hands tucked up under her armpits, shoulders hunched.

"Do you think she'll—"

"Mindell knows what he's doing," Arch cut in. "If there's a chance, Mindell will pull her through."

Dalton nodded. "We'll have to change our plans."

"Why's that?"

"Because Raven was supposed to get us into the tower and from what Devon told me about it, it wasn't easy. I don't think our ex-Regular is going to be up for it. And I don't think it's something she can simply explain to us. We needed her to lead us there."

"So what are you going to do?"

Dalton shook his head. "I don't know."

Arch shifted toward the door. "Might be best to wait for the dust to settle on this little skirmish the army has initiated."

"Maybe. Where are you headed?"

"Back to the bar. It's where anyone looking for me will expect to find me."

* * *

Dalton traded pacing duties with Cerelle for the next several hours, when the Brovettan didn't spell her sister at the table with Mindell. Dalton tried to relieve Nic, but the ex-gang member refused.

Six hours later, Mindell pushed back, wobbled slightly, but caught himself.

"That's it," he said, his voice paper-thin. "I can't do any more for her. Not right now. She'll either make it through the night or she won't."

Cerelle shifted to his side, her touch causing him to flinch. "You need to rest," she said, and guided him into the back bedroom. Dalton heard rustling as she put him to bed.

He stepped toward Nic. "You and Sadie, too. Cerelle will watch over Raven."

Nic nodded, touched Raven's head, her black hair, then staggered to a chair. Sadie grabbed her satchel and curled up on the floor at his feet. Cerelle noticed from the bedroom door, retreated back inside, and returned with blankets that she laid over both of them.

Dalton drew in a deep breath, but regretted it. The room reeked of blood and fear-sweat and the stinging scent of Mindell's unguents.

He needed to leave, to escape these rooms, the images of Raven that replayed in his head, along with thoughts of Devon and Lane, who they were no closer to now than they'd been before.

Cerelle approached and laid a hand on his arm. "Go. You're fidgeting like a twelve-year-old. Take Picall. I'll watch over Raven and the others."

"You're exhausted."

"So are you, but will you sleep? Neither will I. Now go, before I change my mind."

Dalton turned, Picall already waiting anxiously at the door.

They left, night already settled deep across Iandolo. The alley was empty, most of the street beyond as well. At the end of the first thoroughfare, Picall asked, "Where to?"

"Level Seventeen. We need to retrieve our bags from the dead zone. And I want to check out what's happening with Carbolen and the gangs." He couldn't keep his disgust leaking out at the gang leader's name.

They skirted where the fighting had been and grabbed their bags where they'd left them, undisturbed as far as either of them could tell. The streets at each level were shockingly quiet, although they did have to evade more patrols than they'd seen earlier. They could still hear fighting near Carbolen's lair, not as intense as before, so they retreated with the bags to Level Fifteen and left most of their items in the flat, also apparently undisturbed. The army had never been after them. While there, they scouted out the warehouse and the elevators down to the sublevels. Both buildings were gutted, nothing left but debris and a few remnants of walls. The elevators were gone, merely a gaping shaft that Dalton assumed dropped all the way to the mines.

Dalton's entire body ached with exhaustion, but he was still restless, muscles twitching, mind skittering from his last sight of Devon as the elevator dropped, packed with bodies, to the blood dripping from Arch's table as Mindell worked, to Raven's body strung up in Carbolen's lair.

Picall turned from the elevator's pit. Dalton couldn't imagine what ran through her mind. "Where to now?"

He drew in a ragged breath, felt the hard stone of frustration and anger and pain building up in his chest. "Level Ten."

She didn't question him, simply followed as he led the way toward the hub.

They descended, found Level Ten in chaos, buildings burning, people scattered in the streets, terrified, although no one appeared to know exactly what was happening. The Iandolan Army had raided an abandoned section of the level toward the southeast, but something had happened and they'd pushed farther outwards. Bands of soldiers had begun attacking at random, targeting tenements and homes, claiming those inside were harboring Brovettan fugitives. People were dragged into the streets and beaten. Iandolans had protested, especially when only a few Brovettans had been found, but the raids escalated. Some had finally fought back. It became a riot, bands of citizens and soldiers roaming in search of violence. Dalton and Picall witnessed an altercation between four soldiers and a group of ten others, but before they could interfere another band of soldiers appeared around a corner and the citizens fled, those that weren't already prone on the street. At another intersection, three Iandolans were kicking a soldier at the base of a tenement's steps. Dalton shouted, drawing his sword and racing toward them, but the three—two men and a woman—scattered in different directions.

When he and Picall arrived, the soldier was already dead.

They left him. There were bodies everywhere, half a dozen in one street, a singleton here or there, soldier, citizen, mixed. At the base of a fountain at the entrance to a park lay a family of Brovettans. Outside a tavern, two Iandolans, stabbed to death, both reaching for the locked door.

When they finally entered the street with the theater they'd used as a hideout, they found its outer doors blown into the street along with most of its outer walls. The marquee hung across the entrance, attached at only one corner.

Dalton entered through a hole in the front wall. The foyer was mostly intact, but the stairs leading up the balcony where they'd crashed had collapsed on both sides. Inside, the vaulted ceiling above the audience had caved in, the stage piled with debris. The scent of fire and ash hung heavy in the air. Crawling over the remnants of the balcony, Dalton made his way to the center of the theater and turned, taking it all in.

Above, along one wall, the lucent that Devon had repaired flickered, the thin tendrils of the vines dim.

He sank to his knees, sitting on his heels, hands loose in his lap, head bowed. The stone in his chest felt like lead.

Picall worked her way around the room, picking up random pieces of wood, of lucent, and tossing them aside. She ended up beside him.

"What did you come here looking for?" she asked.

"I don't know. A shred of hope? A connection to someone who could help?"

"Like Senn? Or Carbolen?"

He made a sound half growl, half choke. "I won't be seeking Carbolen's *help* ever again." He waited until the hatred faded somewhat. "Perhaps Senn."

Picall shook her head, waved a hand around the room. "Without the theater and the elevators to the sublevel, I don't know how to contact him. Or any of the tullers. Unless you know where they've hidden the Brovettans."

"We didn't want to know. In case any of us were taken." The words caught in his throat, but he swallowed them down. He raised his head, scrubbed at the sweat and grime that coated his face with both hands. "I... don't know what to do. I don't know how to save him. Them."

Picall rested a hand on his shoulder, but said nothing.

* * *

Arrend sat at his desk and tapped his fingers against the wood. A half-empty decanter of wine rested to one side with a glass with some dregs staining the bottom. Dawn's light colored the windows a soft gold, intruding on the glow of the lucents he'd left on all night.

"You know something has happened," he muttered to himself. "Even though all you saw was a stylus and a few drops of blood. You need to tell someone. You need to tell Dalton and the others."

He shifted forward, groaned at the crick in his neck from the awkward position he'd fallen asleep in at the desk and the dull throb of the headache from the wine he'd drunk. Pressing his fingers into his eyes, he rose, then called for his personal acolyte. She appeared at his study's door promptly.

"Arrange a bath and some nondescript clothes. I'll be venturing outside the Lyceum again today. And I'll need a light breakfast as well."

"Of course, proctor."

An hour later, he exited his apartments. More proctors were in the great room than usual, talking animatedly, but he merely frowned, wondering what had started the buzz this time. He swore the proctors were worse than the students when it came to rumors. Nodding at a few of his fellows from afar, he skirted the room and exited the proctors' residence into the bright sunshine outside. He paused on the stairs, taking in the scattered War students on the quad, the amber shard that jutted up out of the grass at its center. Aside from the newness of the grass and the obvious repairs in the surrounding buildings—patches of stone that didn't quite match the original—all signs of the damage caused by the Warding and the battle afterwards had been dealt with. All the physical scars anyway. Not quite all of the emotional ones. There was a clear empty area surrounding the shard of at least twenty feet.

Swift movement caught his eye and he tensed.

Favian approached along the walk, coming from the direction of the mage's dormitory…or perhaps the city beyond.

The Mage proctor caught his eye as he mounted the steps and slowed. "Proctor Arrend."

"Favian."

The mage proctor frowned at the lack of title, eyes taking in Arrend's clothing. "Headed back into the city, I see."

"I have business there again today."

"No doubt. As do I, it seems."

"Then why are you headed into our residence?"

"I need something a little more formal than proctor's robes."

"More formal?" Arrend's chest tightened and he thought of the bustle in the great room. One hand closed into a tight fist. "Why? What's happened?"

"You haven't heard?" Favian's voice came out smooth and smug. "There's to be an official announcement from the Council within the hour, but the rumor is already spreading. There's to be an execution. A public execution."

Arrend's breath caught, but he choked out, "Of who?"

"The rest of those caught during the Warding attack, including their surviving mage—" He drew in a satisfied breath and exhaled slowly. "—and the traitors who aided and abetted the recent Brovettan insurrection…Councilor Varenov and her daughter, Lane."

Chapter Twenty

When Arrend entered the Shandy Quad, the noise quieted noticeably. He recognized some of the students from the Lyceum, saw them casting shocked glances at each other, but he wasn't here for any of them.

As soon as he saw Arch behind the bar, he made his way through the scattered tables, aware of the sudden intense whispering that followed in his wake, the shuffle of chairs.

At the bar, Arch cocked an eyebrow. "What will you have?"

Arrend hesitated—he hadn't come to drink—but caught the blatantly curious look of the Kerpezian History student seated next to him and said, "Whatever Radimansque wine you have."

Arch snorted. "This is a student bar, mostly. They can't afford that."

Arrend waved a hand. "Then whatever Dalton used to drink."

Arch stilled at the name, then reached for something that definitely wasn't wine. He poured a finger's worth into a short glass and plunked it down in front of Arrend, who took it in one hand and sniffed it.

"What is it? Smells…bitter."

"Whiskey."

Arrend took a tentative swallow, gasped, and said hoarsely, "It burns!"

"All the way down," Arch agreed, "but it settles with a nice warmth after a moment."

By the time he'd recovered and taken another sip—smaller this time—Arrend knew what he meant. A strangely pleasant heat filled his chest. And the second swallow hadn't burned quite at much. He also felt a looseness in his arms and shoulders.

He caught Arch's gaze and the bartender said, "Don't."

Arrend leaned forward. "Have you heard? They're going to execute Varenov, Lane, and the Brovettan instigators of the attack at the Lyceum."

Arch glanced toward the Kerpezian student next to him as he said, "What of it?"

Arrend set his glass down, more sharply than he intended. "It's preposterous! Varenov a traitor? *Lane*? Something needs to be done. Some*one* needs to intervene."

Arch shrugged. "I'm just a bartender."

Now the Kerpezian student snorted. She grabbed her drink and wandered away, but not far.

Arrend took her seat. "I need to speak to Nic and Dalton. I have information."

"Not so loud," Arch said, grabbing a cloth and beginning to polish glasses as his eyes scanned the room. "You aren't very good at this, are you?"

"Can you get in touch with them?"

Arch frowned. "It so happens that I can do better than that. Give me ten minutes, then meet me behind the bar."

He wandered away before Arrend could answer. Arrend hesitated, then downed the rest of the whiskey, gasping again, and stood. He wasn't used to such strong drink. His body felt lighter than normal and his fingers tingled pleasantly. That didn't happen with wine, not after such a minor amount.

He made his way toward the door, but before he reached it, the History student stepped in front of him.

"You're going to do something about Lane, aren't you?" she asked. Before Arrend could respond, she added, "Whatever it is, we want in."

A half dozen other students—not just from History, but War and the Sciences as well—fell in behind her.

"I—" he began uncertainly, but one of the others cut him off.

"We didn't like what they did to Devon and Lane after the fight on the quad," a third year from War said.

"They shouldn't have arrested them," Itch from Science said. Arrend knew he'd followed Devon around at the college, even though they'd been a few years apart. "They were the ones who saved us from the Brovettan mages. It wasn't right. And now they're going to kill her and her mother?"

The others nodded and murmured agreement. Arrend glanced over them all, somewhat surprised but also heartened. He'd known Favian's decision had split the proctors along rather solid lines—those that wanted Devon and Lane arrested and those that felt they should be freed—but he hadn't realized it extended to the students as well. It had become mote once the two had "escaped." But perhaps he should have been paying more attention.

"I...I don't know what's going to happen," he hedged. "But involving students wouldn't be ethical. Or in your best interests."

"We don't care," the History student said. "It's wrong. A lot of what's been happening here in Iandolo and at the college is wrong. We did nothing when they took Devon and Lane at the Lyceum and we don't want to make the same mistake again now. There are others that agree with us, other students, even a few other proctors. We've been talking about it, but we haven't been able to do anything about it. But this—this is going too far. We want to help."

Arrend held her gaze, saw the fervor there, the pain and frustration and intent.

He nodded. "Very well. What's your name?"

"Jillian. I'm a History student." The others all mumbled their own names, but he focused on Jillian and Itch.

"Jillian...all of you...as I said, I don't know what's going to happen, but if I can use your help I'll let you know."

They didn't look happy, but they nodded, retreating back toward their table.

Arrend considered for a moment, then left, blinking at the brightness of the sun after the dim interior. He scanned the street, then made his way around to the alley that ran behind the buildings on that block. He found Arch waiting.

"What took so long?"

"Some of the students stopped me to ask a few questions."

Arch grunted. "Probably never seen a proctor in the Shandy Quad before. Follow me."

Arch led him through the back alleys to a wooden staircase, then up to the fourth floor, motioning him inside and stepping in close behind him. The darkened room smelled of sweaty bodies, greasy food, old blood, and a taint of disease.

"You all have a visitor," the bartender announced.

A figure stood as Arrend's eyes adjusted, but he recognized Dalton's voice as he said, "You brought him here?"

"Seemed easier than trying to meet up at the flower shop again. He says he has information."

Arrend stepped forward, catching sight of Nic seated against the far wall, two other women near him, one seated, one standing, and a third woman he hadn't noticed to one side of the door he'd entered. Another older man appeared in the entrance to a separate room and demanded, "Who's this?"

Arrend focused on Dalton. "I know where they're keeping Devon and Lane in the tower. We need to get them out. Now."

Dalton motioned to Arch that it was all right, the bartender departing without comment. "We've heard about the execution."

"It's to happen in two days, at the Pulpit. I went by there before seeking out Arch. They've already started setting the stage up. We need to get into the tower and get them out before then."

"We can't," Dalton said, his voice haggard and weary. Defeated.

"I thought you had someone who could get you in."

"We did," Nic said angrily, standing abruptly and moving to the inner door, the older man stepping aside. "But look at her."

Arrend drifted toward Nic, aware of the tension in the room that lined the weariness and worry.

He sucked in a sharp breath when he saw the woman on the cot inside. "Raven."

He stepped forward, reaching out but not touching the bandages that swathed her practically neck to toe. Blood had soaked through in patches around her chest, her arms, her legs. They stank of infection and the tang of linament. Raven's forehead was beaded with sweat, but she didn't look feverish. In fact, her expression appeared…restful.

"Her fever broke last night," Nic said from behind him.

The older man pushed in front of them with a blanket, draping it over her. "At this point, I'd say she'll survive. *If* we leave her to rest."

Arrend and Nic retreated back into the main room. "Who did this to her?" Arrend demanded.

"Carbolen,"

"But why?"

"Because she left," Nic said. "She seized her opportunity and came with us when we fled. She didn't think she'd return—and she didn't have to—but she came with us and Maupin when the Council went after the Brovettans in order to help. She should have stayed at the tull. She—"

Dalton grabbed his shoulder to cut him off, forced him to look at him in the eyes. "She made her own decision. She knew the risks. And she wouldn't want you ranting about it when there's nothing you can do to change it."

Nic's face hardened, one hand kneading the handle of a sheathed knife at his side. He pulled back from Dalton's grip, but said nothing as he withdrew.

Dalton faced Arrend. "Raven knows a way into the towers, but she's in no condition to take us, and everything Devon told us from the time before indicates we won't be able to find our way in ourselves even with an explanation from her. It's too complicated. For obvious reasons, we're not going to approach Carbolen for help, and now that the Iandolan Army has hit our main bases of operations on multiple levels, we've lost contact with Senn and Maupin. So it's just us." He waved at the six of them in the room. "Plus Arch, although I think we've pushed him as far as he's willing to go."

Arrend glanced at the three women. "I'm sorry. I don't believe I know any of you."

The eldest of the three stepped forward. "Cerelle. Devon and Lane pulled Sadie and I out of one of the Brovettan internment camps. Along with many others. And that young woman at the window watching the alley below is Picall."

"She's from the tull in the Flatlands," Nic added. "Maupin and her people took us in after you helped Devon and Lane escape the Lyceum and Raven helped us escape Carbolen."

Arrend raised an eyebrow. "I see Devon has continued his penchant for stirring up trouble…and finding allies along the way." He considered all of them, then said, "I assume none of you have access to the towers."

"We're Brovettan," Cerelle scoffed.

"And I'd never been into the city until I followed Nic and the others here," Picall said from the window. Her voice was softer than Arrend expected and he adjusted her age downward slightly, closer to Nic's and Devon's.

"So I'm the only one who can enter the tower directly," he said with a nod. "Before anyone asks, no, I can't sneak any of you in. Nor can I pass you off as students and get you in that way. None of the soldiers they have guarding the entrance to the towers now would believe me. I only managed to get in myself by claiming I was trying to find Favian and one of the guards recognized me from the Lyceum."

"But you did get in," Dalton said.

"Yes. I wanted to speak to Varenov, but before I could find her she confronted Councilor Havvelan in the audience hall outside the Council chambers. Havvelan and Prefect Arctus escorted her into the elevators, but they didn't go to either of their quarters in the tower and when the elevator returned there was blood on the floor. The next day, I heard about the executions."

Dalton and Cerelle shared a look. "You said the execution is going to take place at the Pulpit," the former War student said.

"Mid-afternoon. Or so I overheard. I couldn't get Favian to verify it without raising suspicions, but he claims he will be there, along with a few of the other mage proctors. And the Council, of course."

"Any idea how many Iandolan soldiers will be there?"

"Favian didn't say anything about that."

"What are you thinking?" Cerelle asked.

Both Nic and Sadie had perked up, Sadie drifting forward. Picall stayed at the window.

Dalton's gaze drifted over them all. "I'm thinking that if we can't get into the tower to save them, then we'll have to do it at the Pulpit, during the execution."

The others stood in stunned silence, until Cerelle started to say, "How—?"

"I don't know yet," Dalton said tersely. "Maybe we can intercept them before they reach the Pulpit. Maybe we create some kind of diversion and then steal them off the stage before they can be executed. There are only six of us, so there aren't many options. All I know is that we have to try something. Devon would want us to."

They all considered this in silence. Then Arrend stirred. "If we intend to attempt this, we need more information. I'll see what I can gather from Favian and the others at the Lyceum, as well as whatever I can pick up from the citizens. You should know that since the retaliatory attacks on the Brovettans a few days ago, the mood of the populace has shifted. People are becoming more vocal about the Council, the army, and their recent decisions regarding the Brovettans within Iandolo. They're unsettled and unhappy with recent events. It's only a low rumbling right now, but perhaps we can use that."

Dalton nodded, already deep in thought. "We'll see what we can learn about how they'll be transported to the Pulpit. Maybe we can press Arch for more help as well." He glanced up at Arrend. "Once we have Varenov and Lane, we'll figure out how to get Devon out, along with whoever else they've managed to grab."

"And then what?" Nic asked.

Dalton's expression darkened. "And then we're getting out of Iandolo."

* * *

Arrend made his way through the scattered stalls at the market—half the number that would normally be there—moving slowly but with a hint of purpose so that he didn't catch the attention of any of the city guards on patrol. There were more of them on the streets, their number increasing as the execution drew nearer. Iandolan soldiers had been busy securing the Pulpit. Based on conversations overheard at taverns and shops at Mid-level, the route from the city prison to the Pulpit was clear, the prisoners to be transported by barred, enclosed wagons. It was unclear how those being held at the towers were going to brought to the execution. Arrend had been unable to determine if they were to be taken to the city prison first or were being moved secretly by a different method. He'd hoped to learn more from Favian, but the mage proctor had rarely appeared on the Lyceum campus. When he was within the grounds, he and a few of the other mage proctors had secluded themselves within the practice yards. Arrend had been unable to corner him for any direct questions. As his frustration grew, he'd ventured out into the streets, hoping to overhear whatever rumors were spreading about the execution, without much better luck.

"I don't understand it," the merchant two stalls down from Arrend grumbled. "How is this execution supposed to solve anything? We haven't had an execution in the city in decades! Banish them to the Flatlands, that will take care of them. And what did those hits on the escaped Brovettans do? None of it brought my customers back. People are too scared to go out and shop and mingle, except to get whatever's necessary to survive. They aren't lingering. They aren't *buying*."

The man he spoke to—another merchant, Arrend surmised—shook his head. "The Brovettans should never have been put in those camps."

"Who cares about the Brovettans! They weren't bothering me."

"They were some of my best customers."

"And since then the Kerpezians and Bolnians have been leaving, afraid they're next. Where am I supposed to get silk material for these scarves? Or the ingots for my jewelry? Look at this market! Hardly anyone is here!" He waved a hand, his eye catching on Arrend where he'd paused to examine a potter's wares while listening in. The merchant assessed him with one glance, grunted in disappointment, and turned back to his fellow merchant. "The Council needs to take care of these insurgents once and for all. Let the Brovettans leave if they want. And let the rest of Iandolo get back to its usual business."

Arrend listened for a few minutes more, but the discussion devolved into complaints about business contacts and how many of their normal customers had already left Iandolo. But the merchant had raised an interesting point: why an execution? Banishment had been considered the acceptable alternative, the general belief that no one could survive the Flatlands, that they were poisonous. So why an execution now? And how were they to be executed? No one had said. Hanging? Beheading? All of that seemed barbaric compared to banishment.

"They must want to make a point," he muttered to himself, the potter frowning in confusion. He plastered on a smile and waved aside his words, turning to move away—

And almost ran into Jillian, the History student.

He brought himself up short, his heart leaping in his chest. "What are you doing here?"

"Following you."

He glanced up and noticed Itch and two of the other students who'd cornered him at the Shandy Quad the other day—the War student and a mage. He shot an alarmed look around the area, but didn't notice any guardsmen nearby. Nevertheless, he herded the four students back the way they'd come, in the general direction of the Lyceum.

"Why would you follow me?" he asked as they moved.

"Because you're obviously planning something. You've been skulking around the quad, asking after Favian, not following your usual patterns."

He pressed his lips together but said, "We haven't planned anything yet."

"The execution is tomorrow," the War student said.

"We've been gathering information."

"About what?" Itch asked.

Arrend sighed and rubbed his forehead with the fingers of one hand. "How they're transporting the prisoners, what route they're using, what's supposed to happen on the Pulpit. So far, we only know the route they're taking from the city prison, but we don't know whether they're bringing Councilor Varenov or Lane the same way."

"They're not," the War student said succinctly. "Proctor Gallean said they're only bringing some of those that attacked us at the Lyceum with the Warding that way. A spectacle for the public, he called it. The rest are being brought by a different route."

"The others are to be escorted by Favian and a contingent of mages," the mage student added. "I heard some of the sixth-year mages talking about it in the dormitory."

Arrend swore beneath his breath. Of course the students would know more about the event than anyone else. "That's extremely useful information, but you shouldn't be concerning yourself with this. Go back to the Lyceum and stay there. I'll handle it."

He halted, the others taking a few more steps before Itch stopped and turned back, the others following suit.

"Lane was one of us. We can't let them do this to her."

Arrend clenched his jaw. "We won't."

Itch considered, then nodded. All four of them headed back toward the Lyceum.

Arrend waited until they'd rounded the corner ahead, then cut right and made his way toward the apartment where Dalton and the others were watching over Raven. As soon as he entered the alley out back, he felt Picall's eyes on him, even though he couldn't see her. The wooden stairs creaked as he ascended.

Dalton, Cerelle, Sadie, and Picall were waiting when he entered, Picall at the window, the others seated around the table. He remained standing, although he moved closer. He didn't like the table. Its surface was tacky and stained and he couldn't get the image Nic had conjured when explaining they'd used it to care for Raven when they'd first arrived out of his head. He glanced toward the ex-Regular through the open door to the bedroom. She still slept. He didn't see Mindell anywhere.

"Where's Nic?" he asked Dalton.

"I had him fetch Arch." He pulled a paper from a pocket and unfolded it, laying the rough map of Mid-level out on the table. He traced out a route already marked. "This is the route from the city prison to the Pulpit. There's not much of strategic value along the way, which is likely why they chose it."

"And neither Varenov or Lane will be brought that way anyway," Arrend said. He explained what Jillian and the students had told him and about the escort of mages.

"That complicates things. How many mages? Did the students know?"

"I can try to find out."

Dalton rubbed at his eyes and pinched the bridge of his nose. "Picall, how many mages can you take out before they react?"

"Two, maybe three."

"It won't work," Cerelle said. "Not on the street. They'll be guarded by Iandolan soldiers as well as the mages. How will we get through them? That's assuming we figure out what route they're taking from the tower."

"There will be more guards at the Pulpit," Sadie pointed out.

"More people as well," Cerelle countered. "More confusion."

"More confusion where?" Nic asked as he entered the room, Arch trailing behind him. The bar owner flashed an angry look around at all of them, then stepped to the side of the door, arms crossed over his chest.

"The Pulpit," Dalton said wearily. "Cerelle doesn't think a hit on the street will work. Arrend here has learned that Varenov and Lane will be escorted by mages to the execution."

"Then I agree," Nic said, dragging a chair up to the table and plopping himself down. "We can't handle mages and soldiers combined."

"There will be mages and soldiers at the Pulpit as well," Sadie pointed out again, exasperated.

"But with the larger crowd, their attention will be divided," Cerelle said, an edge creeping into her voice.

All of them were tense, Arrend realized, even himself. The entire situation was looking grim.

Dalton glanced at Arch. "Unless you have something to tell us? Something learned from Carbolen?"

Arch fidgeted, then let his arms fall and sighed. "I haven't heard from Carbolen since the Iandolan Army attacked the lair. He's sent no one up to the Quad and any men I send down to contact him are turned away. He's not at the lair. He's gone to ground."

"Then we'll have to get Varenov and Lane back at the Pulpit." Dalton pulled out a second sheet of paper, this one a sketch of the Pulpit and the surrounding streets. "Nic, Picall, and I scouted out the area. The Pulpit is at the intersection of four streets, the main viewing area before the stage a wide, open semi-circle. There are stairs along these arms surrounding the stage. There must be something in behind leading out the back of the stage and the arched roof that covers it, but we couldn't get access to it. As Arrend said earlier, the place is inundated with soldiers preparing for the execution. They've already sealed off the plaza in front."

"That will be opened up tomorrow," Nic said. "They'll want as many people as possible witnessing the execution. And people will come in droves."

"Of course they will," Cerelle said bitterly. "Nothing beats Council-sanctioned slaughter."

"Picall?" Dalton waved the tuller over, Sadie taking her place at the window.

She touched the map near one of the streets. "All of the buildings along the streets are too tall for an effective shot at the stage except for this one. I believe I can gain access to the roof from the side street in the back. I'll take out as many of the mages as I can, then select targets after that until my location is discovered."

"It's up to the rest of us to get Varenov and Lane off stage and out of there," Dalton said. "The best chance we'll have of that is creating as much confusion as possible. Picall taking out mages is a start, but we'll need something more."

They all turned to face Arch.

The bartender stiffened, then glanced through the door toward Raven. His stance eased and he turned back. "I can create some chaos. But neither I nor any of my men will go near the stage. That's up to you."

Dalton nodded. "Fair enough. Picall, wait to fire until after Arch's 'chaos' starts. As for the rest of us—" He glanced around at Arrend, Nic, Cerelle, and Sadie. "—we'll need to get as close to the stage as we can before all hell breaks loose."

Chapter Twenty-One

Dalton hit the edge of the crowd pushing forward to the Pulpit three blocks from the stage itself. He merged with the slow-moving citizens as they shuffled down the street. He glanced behind to see Nic, Arch, Arrend, Picall, and the others doing the same behind him, separating, Picall edging toward the next street over. Cerelle and Sadie were harder to track, with hoods pulled up over their heads to shield their Brovettan skin. Arch vanished into the crowd almost instantly. Dalton's hands itched for the pommel of his sword, but he left it hidden, strapped to his back beneath the cloak he wore. A woman bumped him from behind, jostling it. She shot him a startled look, then stumbled away from him, those she ran into muttering curses until she vanished among the throng.

As he focused forward, the top of the Pulpit's roof visible over the crowd's head, he listened to those around him. He'd expected a thrum of excitement, anxious mutterings about what was going to happen, about the rarity of an execution, and there was a thread of that here and there, but the general atmosphere was one of dark, rumbling tension that only increased the closer he came to the Pulpit. He began to scan the faces more closely.

Most of them were ordinary citizens—Iandolan, mixed with a few Kerpezians and Bolnians and a scattering of the harsher features of those from Lambenesque and Incandesque. But as they neared the Pulpit's plaza, he realized that a smattering of the faces he saw were out-of-place. A man two paces behind him moved stiffly, eyes darting back and forth, mouth set in a grim line. When he noticed Dalton looking at him, he ducked his head and began sliding away. As he did so, Dalton caught sight of a sheath and blade.

A sense of dread slid into Dalton's gut, but he faced the Pulpit. An Iandolan soldier, hidden among the crowd? They'd done such things before, but he doubted the man was a guardsman. He didn't have the stance, the training. But he could be one of the "guards" they'd been using from the recent War colleges, no better than thugs. But then why had the man drifted away? The more likely reaction would have been a confrontation. Or it could have been one of Arch's men, readying for whatever distraction he had organized.

He didn't have any more time to think about it, for the crowd ground to a halt, still half a block from the Pulpit's plaza. Stretching his neck, he could see most of the Pulpit's roof but not the stage itself.

He needed to be much closer.

Many of those around him were grumbling the same thing, a few complaining they couldn't see the stage. He scanned the nearest areas, but the streets were packed in all directions. To his left, some idiot had parked a wagon up against the building. A few industrious people had climbed up onto its top. No one appeared to care. Farther down the street, he saw another wagon, then another, spaced evenly apart. The pattern was repeated on the right side of the street.

The dread deepened.

Sucking in a deep breath, he stiffened his back and threw his shoulders back, taking on the stance of one of the soldiers. Then he said loudly, confidently, "Army business, let me through!"

Those brushing up against him startled at the sudden voice, but backed away as much as they could as he began to plow forward. People grumbled, but they got out of his way, muttering as they closed up behind him.

He angled his way to the side of the street, but stopped calling out as he neared the edge of the plaza. There were real Iandolan soldiers here, spaced out around its edge, eyes scanning the citizens trying to push forward, faces hard. For a brief moment, one of their gazes locked onto his and he felt a sickening moment of panic as he thought they recognized him, but the soldier merely nodded before his eyes moved on.

Perhaps there *were* Iandolan soldiers mixed in with the citizenry.

Moving slowly, using his build and size, he made it through the soldier's line without bringing on any additional attention, then began making his way to the right of the stage. He was close enough now he could see it clearly. A line of Iandolan soldiers guarded the back, couriers and a few prominent merchants and elite already in place, milling around. The front circular portion of the stage that rounded out into the plaza had been left empty. The pale green lucent of the curved roof overhead gleamed in the midmorning sunlight, occasionally dazzling Dalton's eyes with reflected light. Banners depicting the emblems of the seven Crystal Cities lined the edges of the stage, the fabric ruffling in a faint breeze.

"They couldn't have asked for a better day for an execution," Dalton mumbled to himself.

Someone nearby barked out a laugh.

He hesitated, then worked his way to within ten paces of the stage, near the long tier of steps that led up to it.

He had no idea how this was going to work, but it would take Arrend, Nic, and the others longer to get into position without drawing attention to themselves, not to mention Picall getting set up on the roof, so he settled in to wait.

* * *

Picall wound her way through the people headed toward the plaza, thankful that she didn't need to get as close as the others. She'd grown up in the tull where there were few people. This many bodies packed this closely together made her skin crawl. She tried to brush past people without touching them, twisting and contorting in some cases, careful of the pack strapped to her back. Here, a few blocks away, there was enough room, but she could tell that closer in they were going to be shoulder to shoulder.

Cutting into a side street, she moved a block east, crossed that street and into the side street there, and glanced upwards. This was the building she wanted, only four stories, unlike those others, which were higher.

Scanning to either side, she ducked into the alley behind the building, scuffing through collected trash until the alley opened up into a neglected, narrow courtyard with half-dead plants on trellises and a cracked, mossy stone fountain. Water dribbled from the spout on top. Behind it, she mounted the lattice threaded with thick dead vines, scrambling upwards to the balcony it was attached to, then wended up floor by floor until she reached the roofline, using the ridges and niches of the stone and lucent architecture.

She was about to slip up and over the lip of the roof when her eye caught movement.

Settling into a crouch on a narrow ledge, she peered over the edge as a frisson of fear speared through her.

Ten Iandolan soldiers loitered at the roofline overlooking the plaza. Four of them were seated on overturned wooden crates, tossing dice and arguing with each other. Two more were sprawled out with their backs to the edge, asleep. The rest were scanning the crowds below. They held crossbows, with spares already loaded and set to one side.

A trapdoor to the interior of the building lay propped open to Picall's right.

She couldn't take on ten soldiers. She might be able to deal with half of them with the advantage of surprise, but not ten. And getting caught didn't help Nic or Dalton or Lane at all.

Tamping down the burgeoning fear, she considered the trapdoor, then grunted to herself. Too far away; not worth the risk. Glancing downwards the way she'd come, she sighed. "Down is always harder than up," she muttered to no one.

She began retracing her steps, descending balcony to balcony, her grip slipping only once on the rounded, moldy edge of some ornamentation near the bottom. She landed hard, stumbling, palms scraping through the debris and gravel. Brushing the grit aside, hands burning, she shifted to the fountain and splashed some water onto her face. She was sweating now, not only from the exertion. Dalton and the others were counting on her taking out some of the mages, or at least some of the soldiers guarding Varenov and the others.

"How am I going to do that now?" She glanced back up at the roof, then sprinted to the alley entrance, slowing as she reached the side street, then turning the corner. Her heart was beating hard, on the edge of panic. She shoved through the throng, even thicker now than before, working her way down the main thoroughfare along the building's edge. People shouted imprecations after her, but she ignored them. On the next block, she passed a wagon inexplicably set to the side, then another, and then she was at the edge of the plaza.

She searched for Dalton or Arrend or any of the others first. Perhaps she could warn them. But there were too many people, so close together she felt her stomach begin to churn. Nausea fought with the static energy coursing through her arms and legs, making her bounce on her toes. She spat a frustrated curse and forced herself to breathe in deeply, searching again, more slowly, but the plaza was a sea of milling people, most facing forward so all she could see were the backs of their heads.

Hands clenched on the straps of her pack, she began searching the rest of the plaza—the buildings.

"You need height, Picall. Height."

The roof of the Pulpit was worthless, no line of sight on the stage. The building behind her had the soldiers on the roof. The one next to it was far too high; she'd have no accuracy at all, even if the angle wasn't insane. Same for the one to the right. And there was no way to gain access to one of their windows at this point.

She began to mutter a string of curses to herself, getting concerned glances from those around her—

And then her gaze fell on the statues.

At the base of each of the buildings that overlooked the plaza there was a statue—two women and a man, their gazes centered on the Pulpit; all dressed in draped robes. One had her arm raised toward the stage. Picall had no idea who they represented, but she didn't care. They were all about twenty feet high.

Slipping to the side, she reached the edge of the street, the statues on a stone platform about eight feet high. The stone was smooth, but with thin breaks with mortar between each two-foot-high chunk.

She tucked her fingers into one of the spaces. She'd be climbing on fingertips and toes. Mostly fingertips.

"You won't make it," a man beside her said with a thin smile. "A few of us have already tried. It's too slick."

She shot him a defiant glance, then reached upwards, jammed her fingers into one of the cracks, and pulled.

Five second later, she was up over the edge, a startled, "I'll be damned," sounding behind her. Her arm muscles burned, but she shook it off.

The base of the statue stood on gravel, but she kept to the stone edge and shifted behind the statue's feet, back up against the building. She paused long enough to ascertain no one had seen her or was inclined to follow her, then stepped up behind the statue and looked up at the smooth, rippling folds of the man's robes.

Then she began to climb.

* * *

Arrend had only made it halfway through the plaza toward the Pulpit when he saw Cerelle and Sadie break away from him. They'd been following on his heels since Dalton and Nic had told them to scatter and head for the stage. He hadn't minded. Now that they were gone, anxiety set in.

"You're a damned proctor, Arrend, what in hells are you doing here?"

Then he recalled Lane's face at Devon's challenge, when Favian had accused them of blatantly defying the Lyceum's core rules, followed by the betrayal when Devon had revealed Favian and the other mage proctors had actively worked against her passing her own qualifiers. On a fundamental level, the entire Lyceum had betrayed both her and Devon when they'd allowed their arrest after the Brovettan attack with the Warding.

This mockery of justice they were calling an execution went too far. Lane—and Devon—deserved better.

Hands clenched in determination, he pushed forward through the press of bodies, apologizing as he went, but not giving in under the glares and curt words.

Dalton and Nic had said they'd head to the right, so Arrend circled left and stationed himself near the stairs on that side. It took him far longer than he thought it would and, when he arrived, he realized the crowd had grown restless. It was approaching midday and activity on the stage had increased. The number of Iandolan guardsmen had doubled. The merchants and statesmen had begun settling into positions in the background. Three of the councilors had arrived—Secora Arrum, Petrov Orrus, and Gabrella Evitte. Each had four of their own soldiers as escort. Gabrella appeared troubled and Arrend noticed Petrov kept himself close to her, making small conversation as they settled into place. Santigo Allemand of Radimansque arrived shortly after, clearly angry. He avoided the others, taking position as far from them as possible.

Arrend didn't see Havvelan or Iriarte from Lambenesque.

He scanned the crowd again, hand reaching into the folds of his shirt near his waist to touch the sheathed knife he'd hidden there. His fingers tingled as he touched it, a shiver running up his arm. He hadn't wielded a knife since his days as a youth in the lower levels, where it was required to survive. He'd brought it because it felt necessary, although it had taken him most of a morning to find it tucked away in the back of one of his desk drawers. He didn't even know if he remembered how to use it.

New activity on the stage caught his attention, but before he could figure out what was happening, someone snatched at his arm and said, "Proctor Arrend!"

A choked cry escaped him and he spun, hand going to his chest, not his knife. Even as he berated himself, he focused on who clutched his arm. "Jillian? What are you—?" He gasped as he recognized the rest of the students who'd halted him at the Shandy Quad. "Itch, Alan...what are you all doing here?"

"It didn't look like anyone was going to help Lane, so we decided to come and help her ourselves." Jillian's tone was determined and the others nodded their agreement.

"And how were you going to do that?" Arrend demanded.

Jillian's intent gaze faltered.

"That's what I thought," Arrend said, slipping into his proctor's voice. "You shouldn't be here. We have this in hand. You need to head back to the Lyceum. You'll be safe there."

"'We' who?" Jillian asked.

Arrend couldn't answer. The people around them suddenly erupted into a roar of shouts and taunts and jeers and he spun to the stage with a curse. A group of Brovettans were being led onto the platform by Councilor Iriarte and twenty additional soldiers. Ten prisoners were paraded around the curve at the front of the stage, their hands bound behind their backs. Those in the plaza threw garbage at them, some spat, as the soldiers lined them up in a small group near the back, but a good distance from the other councilors and the elite behind them. They were shoved to the floor, a few soldiers kicking their knees out from under them to make them kneel. Most sported bruises old and new. One went sprawling and was jerked back up by the arms, the man moaning in pain as the crowd laughed.

Arrend felt nauseous, but faced the five students from the Lyceum. "It's too late to send you back now. Whatever happens, stay close to me."

A few of them nodded, two with sudden fear in their eyes. Only Jillian, Itch, and Alan—the War student—appeared tensed and focused.

Iriarte passed down the line, grabbed one of the men by the chin and glared at him before thrusting him backwards. Once he was done, he strode to the front of the stage, one hand held high, and shouted, "Behold, the Brovettan traitors who dared to attack Iandolo, tricking us with a false offer of truce and the promise of a treaty, then unleashing the Warding upon us. The slaughter of our soldiers and an untold number of citizens afterwards will be remembered for ages! These are the men we captured after the Warding fell, along with some of those Prefect Arctus rooted out in Luminesque when our army was sent in retribution to clean out the rot in Brovetto. Today, they will face justice!"

The uproar from the plaza was deafening. Iriarte exalted in it a moment, then turned to face the back of the Pulpit.

"Where's Lane?" Itch asked, edging forward.

Arrend straightened, grabbing hold of Itch's shoulder to hold him back. "I think they're going to bring her and Varenov out next."

* * *

When the crowd erupted into catcalls and vitriol as the prisoners were led around the stage, Dalton kept his eyes on those gathered. The longer he'd waited at the base of the stairs, the more he'd noticed certain people in the crowd didn't fit in. Not one or two, but dozens. Men and women scattered among the citizens, faces hard, movements subtle as they shifted closer to the Pulpit. Ten minutes earlier, he'd spied Nic and Arch. He'd signaled a warning to Nic, who'd nodded and gestured to two near his position. When Dalton sent a question, Nic merely shrugged and signed, *Gang?*

Then the noise in the plaza tripled and he spun back toward the stage.

Councilor Varenov, Lane, and another young woman had been led to the front. Thick collars surrounded their necks, linked by short chains. Their wrists and ankles were shackled as well. Even so, Varenov's stance was regal, purposeful, defiant. She glared out at the crowd. Her clothes were dirty and rumpled, as if they'd been worn for days, but she held herself as if she were dressed for a formal event. Beside her, Lane wore the same expression, back rigid. The woman next to them—shoulders slumped, hair unkept and greasy, skin marred with aged bruises—radiated absolute hatred. Her gaze swept the crowds from beneath ragged bangs, her jaw clenched.

Behind them, Councilor Havvelan let everyone vent their fear and frustration as the mages who had escorted the prisoners took up positions around the stage. Seven of them, including Favian. Favian moved to the front, with three to either side, all spaced evenly about the semi-circle that protruded out into the crowd. They were all dressed in mage battle armor, with more formal, ceremonial vestments overlaid on top. Two were carrying staves with the blue and red crystals on top that accompanied nearly every army contingent that went into battle. Dalton remembered rallying around them in the quad at the Lyceum before descending to the waygate during that first intense Brovettan attack.

Prefect Arctus stood with Havvelan.

The mages faced outward at first and the roar of the crowd lessened. Some of those near Dalton drew back and glanced around, clearly uncomfortable. Then the mages turned to face the prisoners.

Councilor Havvelan stepped forward, along with Arctus and a contingent of Iandolan soldiers, who shifted Varenov, Lane, and the other girl back as the councilor stepped up beside Favian.

"Citizens," Havvelan began, and the crowd responded with a rousing cry of support that fell once Havvelan raised an arm in acknowledgment.

Dalton reached to his back and unclipped the straps of his sword, shifting it around and down to his waist. Glancing to the side, he saw Nic position himself near the base of the stairs to the stage. Arch stood farther ahead, closer than Dalton. He didn't see Arrend, Cerelle, or Sadie.

His gaze flashed toward the roofline where Picall was supposed to be and his stomach clenched in horror.

Three—no, five—Iandolan soldiers were visible, scanning the stage and the crowd below.

He jerked his head toward Nic, but the ex-gang member had disappeared.

"Citizens of Iandolo," Havvelan began again, "I bring before you those who would destroy the Council and seize control of the Crystal Cities for their own purposes. Councilor Iriarte has already told you of those we captured after the fall of the Warding, when we regained our own streets and then purged Brovetto of those who'd turned traitor and sanctioned the attack on our city. But I bring before you three even more criminal than that."

He spun and pointed to the enraged young woman slouched beside Lane. "Erilyn Marks, one of the Brovettan mages who attacked us so mercilessly seven months ago. She is the one who set off the Warding at the Lyceum that sealed away your Council and a significant portion of the military that has vowed to protect you!"

The derisive response from the crowd was instant, threats and deprecations hurled toward the young woman, who merely sneered.

Havvelan paced a moment, then waved those gathered to silence as he pointed next at Lane. "I'm certain you've all heard of Lane Illea, the councilor's daughter being trained as a mage at the Lyceum, who saved us all by bringing down the Warding. And yet, since then, she has betrayed us, working with the Brovettan underground here within our own city. When the Council was attempting to protect the Brovettans by secluding them within the quarantine zones, she and her compatriots were stealing them away, concealing them within the city's lower levels with the help of the remnants of the Brovettan rebellion who escaped us. Once we'd established the quarantine zones, she and these same rebels coordinated an attack on the army charged with protecting those inside the quarantine zone. Thousands of our own Iandolan soldiers died during that attack and they destroyed large sections of three different levels. It was during this attack that our own mages managed to capture her."

The reaction this time was uncertain, many as vocal as before, but others murmuring in doubt. As if sensing this, Havvelan swept on to Varenov.

"And lastly, the most blatant betrayal of all, perpetrated by one of our own councilors, Varenov Illea!" He approached Varenov, moving in close, although his voice still projected out to the crowd. "How long have you been working for the Brovettan rebellion, Councilor? How long have you been secretly undermining Iandolo and the Crystal Cities from within the Council itself? Since we arrested your daughter after the fall of the Warding? Was that the moment you turned against us? We know you helped your daughter escape, along with her compatriot, the Science student Devon Alamort."

At this, a low rumble crept through the crowd.

Havvelan smiled. "I don't think that was it, though. I think you've been sympathetic to the Brovettans for far longer. Since their attacks on our city began after the sixteen-year truce? Or has it been even longer?" He circled in behind Varenov, halting slightly behind her right shoulder, so he faced the crowd. "I think you've been a traitor to Iandolo—to the Crystal Cities—since the moment you took your seat on the Council. After all, isn't it true that your lover, your husband for the past eighteen years, is John Senn, the father of your only child...and the leader of the Brovettan rebellion?"

Those gathered gasped, and then protests rolled up and over them all as the shock wore off. The roof of the Pulpit gathered the noise and doubled it, the sound reverberating through the entire plaza, shuddering in Dalton's teeth and bones. He inched toward the stairs, loosened the clasp on his sword. He didn't know what had happened to Picall, but if they were to have any chance of saving Varenov and Lane, it had to happen now. There would be no second chance. Plans for how to deal with all seven mages flashed through his mind, each more desperate than the last. All of them relied on Nic, Arrend, Arch, and the others realizing his intent, one he couldn't communicate to them now.

He tasted bile at the back of his throat.

"That's right," Havvelan shouted, stepping back to the front of the stage. "Councilor Varenov has been consorting with the leader of the rebellion since before she became a member of the Council! That is how she negotiated the treaty with Luminesque seventeen years ago. When she returned from Brovetto with it in hand, she was pregnant with the rebellion leader's child! The Council has found correspondence between Varenov and this John Senn dating back almost two decades. Because of this, because of her complicity in the most recent attacks here in Iandolo, including the attack with the Warding and the assault on those protected within our quarantine zones, the Council has ruled that those involved, including Varenov Illea, shall be executed. Since executions have not been used in the Crystal Cities in over a hundred years, the Council has determined that these deaths shall be carried out…by mage."

The cacophonous roar was deafening, even greater than before. Gritting his teeth, Dalton watched as the seven mages all raised their hands into a familiar position, fingers crooked. The satisfied smirk on Favian's face dug a dagger deep into Dalton's gut. The ten prisoners behind Varenov, Lane, and Erilyn cried out and cowered, some flinging themselves to the lucent floor in protest, others weeping. Both Varenov and Lane appeared stunned, even as the seven mages, in concert, began the base sigil.

Dalton reached the steps, saw Nic begin to climb them to his right, Arch to his left. He hefted himself up, in a crouch, scanning the soldiers closest to them on the stage—

Then, as the roar of the crowd lessened, someone bellowed, "I don't think so."

Everything paused, the noise falling away, the mages halting, though their hands were still raised, poised to start the secondary sigil.

Havvelan moved to the edge of the Pulpit and stared out at a man hovering above the center of the crowd, as if he were standing on their shoulders. Dalton twisted in order to see him better, then spat, "Carbolen."

"Captain Ben Coral," Havvelan said tersely. "Come to save your friends?"

"I don't care about the Brovettans," Carbolen said. "I came for you and the Council. And whoever among the Iandolan Army I can find." His gaze settled on Prefect Arctus, standing behind the prisoners. "You should have left me alone. You should never have attacked my lair."

Motion up high caught Dalton's attention and he glanced toward the roof, where three soldiers were aiming crossbows down at Carbolen. At the same moment, explosions erupted along all of the major streets leading into the Pulpit's plaza.

The shock wave deafened Dalton and flung nearly everyone to the ground. He was shoved hard into the wall on one side of the stairs, managed to catch himself with one hand. A secondary explosion sounded, dampened to a mere thud as his ears began to ring with a high-pitched tone. He shook his head and blinked, blurred vision settling on chaos.

The entire plaza was a shambles, people screaming and scrambling to get away, headed in all directions, panicked.

But not everyone. All of the men and women he'd singled out earlier in the crowd were charging the stage.

"The wagons," he muttered to himself, pushing himself up onto his feet. His words were muffled, but the ringing was fading, his hearing returning. "The damn wagons. And Carbolen."

He didn't see the gang leader anywhere.

Nic appeared at his side and yelled, "Lane!" gesturing to the stage.

All of the mages had been swept to the floor. One of them began to rise, but was caught by a crossbow bolt in the back and was thrown forward, the staff he held clattering to the stage, the red crystal on top snapping off. Two others began to stir and Dalton charged forward. At the back of the stage, Iandolan soldiers were urging the councilors and merchants to the safety of the inner Pulpit, another contingent rushing forward toward the prisoners and mages. Carbolen's men had reached the steps, some leaping up onto them ahead of Dalton, others scrambling up behind. He saw Arch on hands and knees at the edge of the plaza, shaking off the effects of the explosions, and he cursed.

The Iandolan soldiers reached the ten prisoners closest to them and began to slaughter them, stabbing them from behind or swinging at exposed necks or throats. Three fell in the space of a breath, two spun to face the attackers with snarls, cut down in seconds, the rest attempted to flee.

By then, the first of Carbolen's group reached the platform and it became a free-for-all.

Dalton hit the stage behind two gang members, shoving them out of the way as they paused to engage. He and Nic darted to where he'd last seen Lane, breaking free of the main melee and stumbling toward the front.

Varenov crouched protectively over Lane and the Brovettan mage, glaring at where Favian and Havvelan stood, the fight that had broken out in the plaza a backdrop to them all. Two other mages had recovered and stood, both facing the plaza, hands raised. One more had been taken out with another crossbow bolt; the other two hadn't stirred from where they'd fallen.

Havvelan glared at Dalton and Nic. As fire from the mages began to rain down on those in the plaza, the councilor said clearly, "Kill them. Kill them all."

Dalton drew his sword. "Nic, their chains."

The ex-gang member leapt toward Varenov and Lane, while Dalton stepped forward between them and Havvelan and Favian. The proctor had already completed the basic form, had started the secondary.

From behind, Lane screamed, "Dalton, get out the way! That's a cantrip!"

Before Favian completed it, a crossbow bolt slammed into his upper shoulder, spinning him around and flinging him to the floor. Havvelan turned toward the plaza, searching, then pointed toward one of the statues.

"There! The shoulder of that statue!"

One of the other two mages began a form as Dalton caught sight of Picall ducking behind a stone shoulder. He suppressed a grin as he advanced on Havvelan, but Favian lurched to his feet, one arm tucked tight to his side. He grimaced in pain as he straightened, but his hand was already crooked, already moving.

Behind him, the statue where Picall had hidden shattered with an ear-splitting crack, massive chunks of marble rolling down onto the edge of the plaza. People were crushed—both Carbolen's men, Iandolan soldiers, and citizens—but Dalton's gaze was fixed on Favian as he completed his form.

The air crackled as the cantrip sped toward him. He raised his sword, even though he knew it was useless—

And then the cantrip slammed into a shield that shot up from the lucent floor, cutting them off from the front of the stage. Light flared, iridescent and bright, and the entire shield shimmered. On the far side, the concussive wave of impact from the cantrip flung Favian, Havvelan, and the other two mages off of the stage and into the crowd below.

Dalton turned to find Varenov and the other mage, Irelyn, massaging their wrists and necks, the chains lying to one side. Nic and Arch were protecting their flanks, even though the shield encircled them, separating them from the brawl at the back half of the stage.

Arch caught his gaze and shrugged. "So much for my own diversion."

Lane faced Dalton, hand still raised defensively, face etched with tension and hatred. "Where's Devon?"

Dalton's gut clenched as a cold hand squeezed his heart. He lowered his sword. "They still have him."

Lane's face hardened. "Where?"

Chapter Twenty-Two

"We need to get off this stage and away from here," Dalton said, shifting forward.

Lane halted him by grabbing his shirt in one fist. *"Where is he?"*

Dalton stiffened at the intensity of her gaze, at the strength of her grip. "We think you were both held in the towers."

"Then we're going to the towers."

"But—"

"They were torturing him, Dalton. I could hear him screaming."

Dalton sucked in a sharp breath, visions of Raven flashing through his mind. He'd known it was possible, had forced himself not to think about it, but as he stared into Lane's gaze it became a reality. That cold hand squeezing his chest tightened. "Very well. And then what?"

Lane's hand loosened in his shirt. "Then we're getting out of Iandolo." She turned to her mother. "There's nothing left to stay here for, is there?"

Varenov hesitated, glancing around the chaos of the plaza and the Pulpit. "No, nothing."

"Dalton!" someone shouted and he caught sight of Arrend at the edge of the stage, gesturing frantically. Cerelle, Sadie, and what looked like a couple of students surrounded him, fending off the mob in the plaza.

Behind, fire struck Lane's shield, cascading down its side in rivulets. Dalton swore. At least one of the mages had survived the fall from the stage.

He motioned everyone toward Arrend. "Nic, Arch, fall back to the edge of the stage, where Arrend is. Lane, you're going to have to drop the shield, but not until we're ready to move."

They all shifted to the edge of the shield closest to Arrend, the proctor urging them to move faster. Dalton saw Nic snatch up the red crystal from the mage's staff and shove it into a pocket, then he, Arch, and Dalton arranged themselves between Varenov, Lane, Erilyn, and the clashing gang members and soldiers on the stage. A moment before Lane dropped the shield, Dalton saw Havvelan and Favian in the middle of the melee near the stage, surrounded by soldiers holding off Carbolen and his gang.

Then the shield fell and they were rushing the edge of the stage, Arrend reaching for Varenov first, Erilyn rolling over the edge on her own, Lane, Nic, and Arch next. Dalton held ready, although no one approached them, until someone tugged at his ankle. Then he stepped back, knelt, twisted and rolled.

He landed with a jolt of pain in his knees, but ignored it as Arrend steadied him.

"We're heading toward Titchener Street!" Arrend yelled over the clash of swords, grunts, and screams. He held a knife in one hand. Bodies littered the ground in all direction, some dead from the explosion, most from blades. Blood and worse slicked the paving stones as they scrambled across the plaza, avoiding pockets of fighting. A group of seven gang members and five Iandolan guards stumbled into them, breaking their tight formation apart. Dalton dispatched one of Carbolen's men with a quick punch of his sword through his side, shoving the man away as he screamed, flecking his beard with blood and spit, then they were past them, Arch holding a cut along his upper arm, one of the students limping. They broke for the street, the path clear except for the dead or wounded, and then they were beyond the plaza.

They ran for two blocks, slowing only when the limper began to fall behind and Arrend protested.

Tightening up the group, Dalton glanced back and found Nic staring toward the carnage. "Nic!"

The ex-gang member turned toward him, eyes narrowed. "Carbolen is back there." The hand holding his dagger flexed, the blade twisting.

Dalton stepped toward him, placed his hands on his shoulders. "Yes, but now is not the time. We need to focus on Devon."

Nic hesitated, mouth twisting in distaste, but nodded.

When he turned back, he searched out Arrend. "We're headed to the tower, to get Devon and whoever else they have imprisoned there. Then we plan on leaving Iandolo altogether. You and your students should head back to the Lyceum."

"Like hell."

Both Arrend and Dalton glanced at the Kerpezian student. "Jillian, I don't think—"

"I'm not staying here to wait for whatever the Iandolan Council decides to do next." Her jaw set. "I'm coming with you."

"You don't even know where we're going."

She waved a hand. "Doesn't matter. It will be better than here."

Dalton wasn't so certain and drew breath to argue, but Arrend halted him.

"I find I have to agree with Jillian. Iandolo has...changed. I could likely seclude myself in my role as proctor at the Lyceum and survive these changes, but that's not in my nature. I grew up in the lower levels, remember. If you're leaving, I'd like to come with you."

"I as well," Arch said. "Iandolo has become...uncomfortable."

The other students all gathered around Arrend and Jillian.

Varenov cleared her throat, catching their attention. "If we are all going to go, then we're going to need supplies. More than we can simply carry. We'll need a wagon, horses, water, provisions—"

"I'll handle that," Arch cut in. "Someone will have to gather up Raven, it may as well be me."

"And us," Cerelle said, pulling Sadie forward with her. "You can't do it alone."

"There are others at the Lyceum who would likely join us," Arrend said. "Proctors and, I assume, students." Those with him nodded. "We'll head back to the college and gather up who and what we can."

"Get Devon," Arch said, "then meet us at the Shandy Quad."

He and the others scattered, leaving Dalton, Nic, Lane, Varenov, Erilyn, and the War student on the street. When Dalton cocked an eyebrow at the War student, he shrugged. "I figured you could use another fighter in your group." He hefted a short sword. "I stole it from one of the bodies."

Dalton drew in a ragged breath and exhaled harshly. "This is getting out of hand."

Varenov chuckled, the sound lacking any real mirth. "Welcome to the rebellion."

The sound of shattering stone echoed down the street, making all of them jump. The sounds of the fighting were muted, but Lane said, "We should get moving, while they're distracted."

Before anyone moved, someone appeared on the street behind them. Everyone tensed, until Nic said, "Wait, it's Picall."

When the tuller drew near, Dalton could see multiple cuts, abrasions, and bruises on her face and arms. She joined them without comment.

"Let's go," Dalton said.

They angled away from the Pulpit, zigzagging through the streets, heading toward the towers. At first, the city was empty, the only people they saw rushing away from the plaza. A contingent of Iandolan soldiers charged past, the captain shouting for them to get out of the way, to intent on reaching the Pulpit to notice Varenov among them. But the farther they got, the more citizens were on the streets. Many were glancing toward the direction of the fighting, clearly unaware of what was happening, although word was spreading fast. Shopkeepers were shoving customers out and closing up their doors, shuttering windows. Many on the street made sudden decisions to drop what they were about and head home.

They dodged out of the way of another few squads of soldiers as they neared the towers, this one more organized, marching in tight formation. Both Varenov and Lane slid behind an abandoned food cart until they were gone.

Then they reached the courtyard in front of the towers, the wide rounded plaza surrounded by trees. Iandolan soldiers were lined up in front of the entrance to the main tower. Before Dalton could ask how they were going to handle this, Varenov moved forward, stalking across the plaza, the others trailing behind.

Councilor Secora stood at the front of the main contingent of soldiers, along with a captain Dalton didn't recognize. All of the men and women around them tensed as they approached, Varenov halting six feet away from Secora.

"Secora."

"Varenov." She glanced at Dalton and the rest, her gaze lingering on Lane and Erilyn. "I would have thought you would have run, not returned."

"I won't be attempting to stay."

"Then why come at all? It was a mistake."

Varenov stiffened and drew herself upright. "Because Havvelan is holding more of our citizens here, in the towers, in his private little prison. We won't leave them behind."

Secora appeared surprised. "Here? He said—"

"Yes, here. Only a few floors above the Council chambers." She took a step forward. "Did you know he intended to arrest me that day? Did you know he intended to murder my attendant there in the elevators when we left, right before me?"

Secora's eyes widened and she opened her mouth, but couldn't find the words.

Behind her, Gabrella stepped out of the tower and said sharply, "Is this true? Did Havvelan do this under your orders, Secora? With the Council's permission?"

Secora closed her mouth and ground her teeth together.

Gabrella faced Varenov. "The Council agreed to Varenov's arrest, after seeing the papers Havvelan presented as evidence, that was it. Not the death of her attendant. Not a secret prison here in our own tower. Show me this prison."

Secora protested, but Gabrella overrode her. With an escort of soldiers, they entered the tower into the grand foyer, Varenov at the front, behind Gabrella, flanked by two guards. Dalton discreetly motioned Nic and Picall into position around Lane and Erilyn, while he and the War student brought up the rear.

When he glanced back outside, he saw Secora spitting orders at the Iandolan captain.

Inside, Councilor Santigo approached Gabrella. "What is going on?"

"Varenov claims Havvelan kept her prisoner here in the tower, that there are others there now. We're going to verify it." She scanned them all. "We won't all be able to go at once."

"Lane and Dalton will accompany me. Santigo, you can come up with the rest. The ninth floor."

The councilor nodded and Dalton and Lane followed Varenov, Gabrella, and her two guards into the elevator.

When they emerged onto the ninth floor, the halls were quiet. Dalton wanted to rush to each door, fling it open, find Devon, but Varenov forced them to wait for the others.

Gabrella moved to the first door, already opened, and peered inside, her expression darkening. "Cot, table, chair. It certainly appears to be a holding cell." She sniffed and her nose wrinkled. "Recently used."

"That's where I was kept," Lane said.

"I was in the room farther down on the left," Varenov added.

Gabrella tried one of the closed doors. "Locked. With a lucent lock."

"If only Devon were here," Nic said dryly as he emerged from the elevator with Erilyn, Picall, Santigo, Alan, and another few guards.

"How are we going to get them open?" Dalton asked, only a hint of desperation bleeding through.

"Allow me," Lane said, stepping forward, voice hard. She was already beginning the basic form. Everyone in the hall stepped as far away from the door she approached as possible.

Dalton found himself next to Erilyn.

The Brovettan mage sucked in a breath. "Cantrip," she muttered, but frowned. "Only...different."

Dalton tensed. The air before Lane crackled with the same energy Favian had thrown at him at the Pulpit, but smaller, more contained, and then Lane released it.

The door exploded inwards, Lane already surging forward. Dalton lunged to the door. The reek of blood and sweat and rot choked off his breath. Inside, Lane leaned over a nearly unrecognizable, bruised body on the cot.

She glanced up as he blocked off the light from outside and said, "It's Mannert. She's alive."

A shudder ran through Dalton from head to heel as Varenov and Gabrella passed him. Lane stood as Gabrella gasped and Varenov said, "This is what you've allowed Havvelan and Secora to do in the Council's name."

"I never agreed to this," Gabrella protested.

But Lane dragged Dalton out into the hall, moving to the next door. Another cantrip, another door ripped from its hinges, but the man inside was dead. He was missing three toes, two fingers, and his tongue. The woman in the next room was alive, shuddering back from them when they entered, breaking into sobs when she realized they were there to get her out.

The last room with a locked door stood at the end of the hall on the right. Lane gave Dalton's arm a reassuring squeeze, then faced it, her crooked hand already tracing out the sigil.

When the splinters of the door settled, they both stepped into the room, reeling back from the stench. The floor was tacky with dried blood, shit, vomit, and worse. A figure sat tied to a chair in the center of the room, body and head slumped forward, hair dangling in front of the face. Dalton drew in a shuddering, steadying breath, then stepped forward, debris from the doorway crunching under his feet. He knelt down and touched the man's knee.

The figure jerked backwards with a snarl and Dalton unconsciously grabbed him by the shoulders to steady him. The man screamed and Dalton let go, letting the body settle back into its slump. The scream trailed down into a wretched sob, bloody spit dribbling down to the floor.

"Devon?" Lane asked from the door. She hadn't moved into the room. Nic and Picall were hovering out in the hall behind her. "Devon, it's Lane and Dalton. We're here to get you out."

Dalton reached up and drew the figure's hair aside, exhaling in a choked gasp filled with relief and pain. "It's him. Gods, it's him. Help me get him out of this chair!"

Nic pushed forward, Varenov, Gabrella, and the War student now visible. Picall kept them and the other guardsmen back.

When Nic and Dalton eased Devon upright, he screamed again. Lane cut the ropes binding him and his arms dropped to his sides, limp, and the screams doubled.

When they attempted to lift him, he passed out.

They carried him to the door, Dalton shouting at everyone to get out of their way, then laid him out on the floor outside. Dalton touched Devon's bruised face, his hands trembling, his breath ragged, chest filled with fluid. He cursed and swallowed, wiped at the tears already blurring his vision, then began a detailed check of his body. But he kept returning to Devon's face, to the cracked and split lips, the layered bruises, one eye swollen shut, one ear torn, lobe dangling, hair matted and greasy and knotted. He couldn't control his breath, his chest hitching. And his vision kept blurring, no matter how often he swiped at his eyes, until he gave up and cradled Devon's face and hunched over him, as if he could protect him.

Someone touched his shoulder and from a distance he heard Lane say, "He's alive, Dalton. We need to get him out of here. We all need to get out of here."

When someone reached to pick Devon up, he thrust their hands away, then seized control of himself enough to gather Devon gently into his arms, his body so light, so limp, it tore another ragged round of sobs from him. But he was aware enough to know that Nic and the others had gathered up Mannert and the other woman. They descended in the elevator, Santigo, Nic, Alan, Mannert, and a few guardsmen first, Picall, Erilyn, the woman, and the rest of the guards next. Lane, Varenov, and Gabrella remained with Dalton, going down last.

By the time they reached the foyer, rage had begun to seep into Dalton's pain. He emerged from the elevator and moved toward the exit without stopping. Nic and Picall were at the lucent doors, Nic holding Mannert upright, the former Iandolan captain conscious, not as badly beaten as Devon. The other woman they'd rescued appeared to be moving on her own, Alan keeping an eye on her. Outside, the number of Iandolan soldiers had doubled. Councilor Santigo was gesturing and shouting at them, Secora and the captain standing stolidly in his way.

As he approached, Nic said, "He's trying to convince them to let us through."

"We're leaving," Dalton said, his voice still thick with emotion, "whether they're going to allow it or not. Lane?"

Lane and Erilyn shifted in front of him, the others falling in behind. Gabrella ran for the doorway. A few of the guardsmen who'd accompanied them to the ninth floor began to block their path, but Lane crooked her hand and they hustled aside.

The early evening sunlight outside was bright, blinding Dalton momentarily, enough he paused to blink his vision clear. All of the soldiers outside tensed. The argument between Santigo, Gabrella, and Secora ground down to a halt as they took in their group, including Devon's condition and that of Mannert and the woman. Many of those watching fidgeted in unease.

Both Lane and Erilyn raised their hands. Dalton grunted as at least twenty of the nearest soldiers stumbled back. There were no mages on guard here, he noted. They must have been sent to the Pulpit.

"Let us through," Dalton said.

When no one moved, Lane began a sigil.

Santigo shouted, "Wait!" then faced Secora and the Iandolan soldiers. "You have three of the Council here—four if you count Varenov. The majority of us demand that you let these people—these *citizens*—pass."

"That's not a full Council," Secora responded. "Not even close, even if I did still recognize Varenov as a member of the Council."

"That didn't seem to matter when you ordered the attack on the gangs and the Brovettans hiding in the lower levels," Varenov said sharply.

Gabrella turned on the Iandolan captain. "Let them pass. As a member of the Council, I order you to let them pass."

The captain wavered, glancing from Gabrella to Secora and back.

"Go," Dalton said to Lane, voice low.

Lane and Erilyn began moving forward again. The captain stiffened, as if he were going to hold, but then heaved a half-curse and motioned with one hand. "Stand aside!"

Some of the men hesitated, ready to defy the order, but most moved without comment.

Gabrella and Santigo followed them to the far side of the line, but halted in the courtyard.

"You should come with us," Varenov urged. "Word of this will reach Havvelan."

"Let it," Santigo said. "I did not become a Council member to be anyone's proxy." His voice softened. "You should know, I did not vote for your removal from the Council, nor your execution."

"I am ashamed to say that I did," Gabrella said.

"It doesn't matter. If Havvelan hadn't gotten rid of me this way, he would have found another." Shouts came from the far side of the courtyard, a ragged mob beginning to pour from the streets and between the trees. "I'm afraid Iandolo is going to be unsettled tonight."

"It's been unsettled for a while now," Santigo said as the captain of the Iandolan guard behind them began shouting new orders, the soldiers falling into new formations. "You'd better go, while you still can."

Without waiting for a response, Gabrella and Santigo retreated back into the towers, Secora joining them.

Varenov turned back to Dalton and Lane, face hardening. "Let's go."

Their small group fled across the courtyard and the mob and the soldiers clashed behind them. Screams followed them beneath the trees and out into Mid-level. They moved as fast as Dalton with Devon, Nic and Mannert, and the Brovettan woman could manage, Picall scouting ahead, Varenov, Lane, Alan, and Erilyn protecting their flanks. Dusk had fallen, the streets limned with an eerie half-light. As they ran, it bled into the orange-red of sunset, lucent-lined buildings glazed with reflections like fire. In the streets, mobs and bands of regular citizens roamed and fought squads and battalions of soldiers. As they made their way toward the Shandy Quad, the size of the groups and the harshness of their encounters only escalated. At one intersection, they watched a screaming band of at least fifty people race past in the opposite direction, heading toward the towers. On another street, they were forced to reroute around a bloodbath as citizens and soldiers rioted for two blocks.

"Those aren't hardened soldiers," Nic noted as they bypassed them. "Not all of them. They've released those in the War colleges, whether they're ready not. That was a brawl."

"It's like the aftermath of their attack on Carbolen and the Brovettans," Dalton agreed.

"Except that was contained to those levels," Varenov said. "This sounds as if it's going on city-wide."

They reached the Quad as the last of the lurid sunset faded and twilight settled. They approached the bar cautiously, the street quiet. Ten paces from the entrance, the door flew open and Arch barked, "Get in here. Now!"

They hustled inside, the interior surprisingly crowded. Dalton glanced around, noting Arrend at the center of a gaggle of at least ten students and a few proctors, most of them carrying satchels, Cerelle and Sadie huddled at a table in one corner, and a host of rough-looking men and women he assumed were Arch's minions. Mindell shoved his way forward as Nic guided Mannert to a chair and Dalton settled Devon onto a table.

The healer began a detailed once-over, ripping Devon's tattered shirt as he checked the bruising, tested his broken rib, listened to his heart and breathing. Then he moved on to arms and legs, taking an inordinate amount of time with Devon's head.

Dalton stood to one side, his heart thudding hard in his chest, hands clenched to hold in the bitter anger, swallowing back acidic anxiety.

He startled when Cerelle touched his arm, almost lost control again when she said nothing, merely waited beside him as Mindell worked.

The healer suddenly straightened. "He'll be fine. He's been beaten pretty bad, most of the damage done to the head, so he may be addled for a while when he comes out of it, but the rest of his wounds simply require time to heal. They'll be hellish on pain though, especially the cracked rib. It's already started to heal, the bones set incorrectly. It will need to be rebroken. I'll have to give him some painkillers. Strong ones." He turned to give someone instructions on what to do, then turned his attention to Mannert and the Brovettan woman, Nic watching over them both. Supplies were fetched and two people set to work on Devon, including one of the Humanities students.

Dalton didn't feel much relief at Mindell's pronouncement. His anger only seemed to heighten. "This should never have happened." It came out as a low growl.

"And we should never have been placed in those quarantine zones. Scerano shouldn't have had to die to get us out. Lane should never have been set for execution." Cerelle's hand tightened on his arm. "None of it should have happened. But it did. And now we must deal with it. Before that, though, we need to rest, recover—" She glanced toward Devon's ravaged body. "—and the only way we'll be able to do that is if we get out of Iandolo." She jutted her chin out to Dalton's right and he turned.

Arch hovered to one side, but came forward when he saw Dalton look his way.

"I have four wagons out back, already loaded with whatever supplies everyone could find. Raven's already secured in one of the wagons. We'll have to get Devon and Mannert settled in next to them as soon as Mindell finishes, but we need to get the hell out of here as soon as possible."

"The streets have gone mad," Dalton said.

Arch nodded. "And according to reports, it's going to get ten times worse during the night. The citizens—especially those not native to Iandolo—are revolting. The tension has been there since the Brovettans were interned in those damn zones; it only needed a trigger. Carbolen provided that trigger."

Dalton waved at all of those inside the bar. "Who are all of these people?"

"Friends, some family, business associates. That's Mindell's wife over there. His three kids."

"Any of them Carbolen's men?"

"No. Dealers, tradesmen. That's all." When Dalton still hesitated, Arch added, "We're going to need guards for the wagons if we're going to make it out of Iandolo alive."

Dalton didn't like it, but agreed, Arch drifting away. His men were beginning to gather up the supplies the others carried, what they were willing to give up. Some kept certain bundles close.

Dalton turned back to Devon, Mindell's two assistants still working on him, but Cerelle tugged at his arm.

"There's nothing you can do for Devon simply standing here. It will only make it worse for you." She pulled him away.

He circled the bar, checking in on Mannert and the Brovettan woman first. The captain gave him a weary nod, the damage done to her similar to Devon's although not as severe. She visibly pulled herself together when she saw him approaching, sitting straighter in the chair, grimacing, but pressing her cracked lips together and meeting his gaze stolidly.

The Brovettan woman had been one of Terrial's group, captured after the Warding fell. She dealt with Mindell's ministrations without qualm, her eyes glazed with anger, her responses to Dalton's questions curt.

He and Cerelle found Lane next, the mage sitting with her mother, Erilyn, and Sadie in the far corner.

"Mindell says Devon will be fine," he reported.

"We heard," Varenov said. Her gaze wandered over the room. "Quite a motley crew you've assembled here. What are you planning to do next?"

"Me?" Dalton gave a short, bitter laugh. "You're the councilor. You tell me."

Varenov smiled, the sentiment thin and drawn. "My days as a councilor are at an end, I think. This is all you. Even Arch reported to you—for approval and direction. You're their leader now, not me."

"She's right," Lane said. "Look at them all—Arrend, Arch, all of them. Our own group included. We're all waiting for you to tell us what to do."

Dalton tried to splutter a protest, then crossed his arms over his chest when that failed. Lane gave him a tired grin.

He turned on Erilyn, the mage tucked slightly farther back from the others. "And what about you? I'm surprised you didn't abandon us the moment we pulled you off the Pulpit."

The lithe girl—she couldn't have been more than fourteen—slid forward. "I don't know anything about Iandolo. Or anyone here."

"What about her?" He motioned toward the Brovettan woman they'd rescued from the tower.

She looked toward her, but frowned. "She was part of the delegation meant to draw the Council to the treaty signing. The mages didn't interact with them. We had our own goals."

The coldness in her voice made Dalton shift uncomfortably. Cerelle coughed. Varenov stared at the girl, brow creased in thought.

Sadie asked, "So what *is* the plan?"

Dalton let his arms drop. "Arch has wagons out back. We're loading up and then heading for the waygate to Luminesque."

"And then?"

"Brovetto." When Varenov tilted an eyebrow up in silent question, he shrugged. "Let's focus on getting out of Iandolo alive first."

He paused to speak to Arrend, Alan, and the seventeen students and proctors he'd somehow gathered while raiding the storerooms at the Lyceum. Most of them were Science students, like Itch, although there were a smattering from the other colleges, including two mages and four from War.

After that, he hit the back alley, where Arch's men were finishing up throwing supplies into the wagons. Raven lay in the back of the second wagon, surrounded by crates and barrels. Dalton climbed up into the back and settled down on one crate, pulling the blankets that covered her bandaged body up close to his chin.

As he did so, her eyes fluttered open and Dalton stilled as they settled on his face, glazed with whatever drugs Mindell had given her, but aware. Her mouth moved and she croaked out a feeble, "Dal—" before her voice cracked and died.

He leaned forward. "Don't talk. We got you away from Carbolen. I'm sorry we couldn't manage it sooner. We're leaving Iandolo now. You should rest."

At mention of Carbolen, her gaze hardened and focused, but by the time he finished she'd already faded out again, eyes closed.

Arch appeared with Devon, the ex-Science student still unconscious. Dalton stood immediately and gathered him up, settling him next to Raven. With Nic's help, Mannert hauled herself up into the wagon next, resting a hand on Dalton's shoulder.

"I'll watch over them." She sat on the same crate Dalton had used and he noted someone had given her a sword.

Everyone from the Shandy Quad was gathering around the wagons, those with weapons forming a loose perimeter. Mostly Arch's mercenaries, joined by Nic, Picall, Cerelle, Sadie, and Arrend's War students.

Dalton jumped down from the wagon and motioned to Lane. "I want you in the lead wagon, but don't do anything to indicate you're a mage unless absolutely necessary. Erilyn, same thing, but take the back wagon and watch the street behind us."

Both mages separated, heading to their wagons.

Arrend had overheard. "I'll split up the other two mage students between the second and third wagons. They're only fourth year, so they won't be able to contribute much if it comes down to a mage battle though."

Dalton scanned the entire group, noted Varenov sitting with Lane in the front, Arrend climbing up to sit next to Mannert with the Brovettan woman. Then he nodded to Arch, who bellowed an order.

The wagons lurched into motion, those surrounding them shifting to follow, hands falling to swords and knives and crossbows.

The Luminesque waygate was only twenty-four levels away.

Chapter Twenty-Three

"Close ranks!" Dalton yelled as he shoved the press of people that surrounded the wagons back and brought his sword up in warning. Arch's mercenaries all took a step back at the order, weapons raised menacingly. Dalton followed suit as soon as the man he'd shoved backed off. But not without a glare.

In the wagon behind him, Lane muttered, "Only two more levels to go."

Dalton stared at the street ahead and tried not to groan.

They'd traveled the upper levels rather quickly, the streets mostly empty, running into only scattered mobs who were more interested in finding Iandolan soldiers or fixated on other targets like the towers, the city barracks, or the guard stations scattered throughout the city. Dalton felt momentary satisfaction when they passed close to one of the impromptu War colleges and found it burning uncontrollably.

But the lower they traveled, the more citizens were in the streets. Many were rioting like above, but hundreds were simply fleeing as their buildings were raided or torched. Others had grabbed whatever belongings were available and were headed toward the waygates, hoping to escape like Dalton and everyone else in the wagons. Most of these were families, parents clutching children close, faces stoic or fearful, desperate or openly weeping. By the time they reached Level Ten, their group had joined a steady but loose stream of people headed downwards. Fires raged in the city on all sides. Screams echoed harshly from the lurid darkness. People were being beaten and robbed on all sides, the attackers grabbing whatever was available and running, only to be attacked themselves by a larger group two blocks later. Bodies began appearing on the side streets, then on the main thoroughfare they were traveling. Arch ordered the wagons drawn closer together, the mercenaries tightening up. On Level Nine, a small group of twelve gathered up enough courage to attack the rear wagon, attempting to overwhelm the guards. The fight was vicious and brutal, five of the rioters left for dead before the others fled, one of them managing to snatch a satchel from the wagon bed. Only one of the mercenaries had been wounded, a cut along her upper arm. She cursed but shook it off.

By dawn, they'd fought off three additional attacks, lost one of their men, and the wagons had slowed to a crawl as the number of refugees on the streets doubled. They'd reached Level Six by then. Eight hours later, they were on the ramp down from Level Three to Two. The Spoke was crowded, Dalton and the rest enforcing a respectful distance between them and the other refugees, but the random attacks had ended. There were too many people, the wagons barely moving forward, what progress they were making brought on by force as Arch bellowed for those in front to get out of their way and his more frightening men threatening violence if people didn't move fast enough.

"We're never going to make it," he said quietly as they inched downwards.

"We will," Varenov answered. "Be patient. Look around. All of these people have had enough. All of them want out. Most of them aren't even Iandolan, even though they were likely born here, lived their entire lives here. I can see Kerpezians, Bolnians, Turbins. That family over there is Verdun. The Council and its recent decisions have driven them to this. Havvelan and the others can't expect to control them all. Not now."

"They're going to try," Dalton said.

Lane stirred. "I could always force our way through." She crooked her hand.

Varenov covered it with her own, forced it down. "These people aren't the ones who deserve to be punished. They aren't the ones who hurt us."

"It may come to that in the end," Dalton said, "whether we like it or not."

Varenov didn't reply, her lips pressed into a thin line.

The sun was beginning to set off to their right when they finally reached the edge of Level Two and could see down the ramp to the waygate.

Dalton sucked in a sharp breath, shock transforming swiftly into anger. "No wonder we aren't moving at all. The gates are still sealed."

Arch was already headed toward him, brow furrowed. Dalton scanned the layout of the street and waygate below as he waited.

The Spoke ramped down into a massive plaza jammed with thousands of people, all pushing forward toward the waygate. Surrounded by a short wall with stone spires at regular intervals, the plaza contained at its center a faceted amber shard ringed by a pool of water. This and the oval shape of the plaza gave the entire waygate the aspect of an eye.

The area immediately in front of the gate was empty, a line of Iandolan soldiers standing ready behind a shimmering mage shield that kept the refugees at bay. At its edge, citizens were screaming to be let through, the roar from the gathered crowd punctuated by curses and wails and threats.

"They're learning fast," Lane muttered.

"What do you mean?"

She turned to Dalton. "That shield is constructed ten times better than anything I've seen from Iandolan mages up to now. It's nearly as strong as what Terrial erected around Devon and I at the Lyceum, to isolate us from everyone else."

"Can you bring it down?"

Lane returned her gaze to the shield. "I think so. But I'll need to get closer."

Arch arrived, spitting curses under his breath. "How are we going to get through now?"

"Lane can handle it."

"But I need to be closer. I may even need to touch their shield."

Arch spit to one side and looked up at her. "I doubt we can get to the bottom of this ramp, even with me bellowing my head off to get out of the way. There are too many people packed into too tight a space."

Lane considered the crowds before them, on the ramp and in the plaza, then lowered her head.

When she raised it again, her chin lifted. Varenov rested a hand on her arm and said, "Lane. Are you certain?"

"I can't hide in the shadows forever, mother."

Varenov's hand squeezed once, then dropped away. "No, you can't."

Lane drew in a steadying breath, then stood, the wagon rocking slightly beneath her. The driver steadied the horses, but Lane was already completing a sigil.

A blinding orb of white light burst into existence above her. Dalton raised a hand to shadow his eyes, blinking away the black dots that appeared because he'd been looking up at her as it appeared. On all sides, people gasped or cried out, most stumbling away from the wagons. A few fell, caught by those around them, the ever-present low-grade anger and grumbling cut off by shock and fear.

By the time Dalton's vision cleared, he caught Lane finishing off another sigil. And then she spoke.

"You've all heard of me."

She spoke in a normal voice, but Dalton heard the words echoing down the ramp and across the plaza. Those below who hadn't yet seen the blazing orb above her began to turn, their focus shifting from the shield that kept them inside Iandolo to Lane.

"I'm the mage who brought down the Warding. I'm the mage who escaped after they arrested me for freeing them. I'm the mage they've hunted ever since. You've no doubt heard I aided the Brovettans when they were being rounded up and sent to what the Council called quarantine zones. But we all know what they really were—internment camps. Prisons. And you've no doubt heard that I helped in the attack on those camps in order to free those Brovettans. It was during that attack that I was captured and imprisoned yet again. You all know I was to be executed at the Pulpit.

"But I've escaped...yet again. And now the Council seeks to imprison all of us, here in Iandolo, by sealing the waygates."

The crowd around them had fallen silent, but now they began to murmur, their discontent and anger from earlier returning.

"I can free you," Lane said. "Get me to the shield and I can break it, as I broke the Warding, as I broke the walls of the internment camp. Let us through and I will bring the shield and the waygate down."

A roar rippled through the crowd, all the way down to the waygate, a wall of noise that rose as more and more took up the cry. Arch stared at Lane a moment, then snapped out of it and began barking orders to his mercenaries. Ahead, the massive crowd of people began to pull back and the wagon lurched forward, Varenov catching hold of Lane before she could tumble from the wagon's bench. But she remained standing. The orb of light above her didn't waver, flickers of jagged lightning coruscating around it.

As they proceeded down the ramp, people parting before them, then closing in tight behind, the Iandolan soldiers behind the shield burst into a frenzy of activity, their leisurely positions breaking and reforming. Dalton watched them closely and asked from his position off the side of the wagon nearest to Lane, "Can their mages hit us from behind the shield?"

"Not unless they drop the shield first. Or unless they have a mage stationed outside the shield already."

Dalton did a quick scan of the soldiers, the crowd nearest the walls, and the parapet. "I don't see any battalions outside the shield, not even on the top of the wall or the gates, and they wouldn't have a mage without at least a squad of soldiers to protect them." He returned his gaze to the forces behind the shield. "It looks like they have three mages on the gates, based on their formations."

"Then keep an eye on the wall, in case they move one of their mages outside the shield there."

"What if they give up on the shield?"

Lane shook her head. "Everyone in the plaza will rush and overwhelm them in moments."

Which is what would happen as soon as Lane brought the shield down, he realized.

He pushed forward to warn Arch, who had already begun warning his mercenaries. He worked his way down one side of the four wagons, while Arch took the other side. Along the way, he checked in with Mannert. Raven glared at him as the wagon jolted her back and forth. Devon hadn't regained consciousness yet, but Mindell had warned him that the drugs he'd given him would likely keep him under, no matter how rough the ride. He wanted to linger, but dragged himself away to finish with the rest of the wagons.

By the time he reached Nic and Picall at the final wagon, they were rounding the shard at the center of the plaza, the shield stretching into the sky before them. This close, he could see sheets of color cascading down it, like rivulets in a waterfall. A faint thrum filled the air as well, vibrating in his teeth and bones.

"When Lane drops the shield, it's going to be a free-for-all," Nic said as soon as Dalton got close.

"Arch and I are warning all of his men and everyone in the wagons to prepare."

"What happens if we get separated?" Picall asked.

"Head for Brovetto along the wayfare. We'll find each other somewhere on the way."

"And that's it?" Erilyn asked, her voice bitter. "We just flee to Brovetto? Leave Iandolo to them? Leave *everything* to them, after what they've done?"

The harshness of her tone prickled Dalton's nerves. "For now."

Erilyn stared at him a long moment, then faced back toward the three towers at Iandolo's heart and the columns of smoke that drifted up from the city between there and here, her back rigid, shoulders tight.

Before Dalton could come up with something more to say, something more encouraging, the sound of horns filled the plaza, throbbing on the air.

It was answered almost immediately above, from a force no more than two levels away.

"That doesn't sound good," Nic said, following Dalton as he drifted toward the back of the wagon.

"It isn't," Dalton said, listening to the tone and timber. "They're calling for reinforcements, and those reinforcements have answered. They're almost here." He spun toward Nic. "Get everyone back here ready to push forward as soon as the shield drops. We've just run out of time."

Nic had barely nodded before he trotted forward toward Lane's wagon again. On his way, he shouted, "Mannert!" but she cut him off with a curt, "I heard. Securing what we can on the wagons." Behind, Arrend was already taking cues from Nic and the others, rallying his students and fellow proctors at the third wagon. Their sudden frantic activity caught on with the surrounding crowds, the agitation sweeping outwards.

"Lane!" he shouted as he got closer, Arch's men bracing as the people around them began to panic. Lane turned, but at the same time, two new sets of horns blared in answer to either side of the waygate, one of them as close as those above, the other slightly farther away. The noise drowned out his voice and sent the crowd into a frenzy as they realized they were surrounded. People began to flee, moving in whatever direction was available, screams erupting on all sides. Some charged the wagons, regardless of the mercenaries with drawn weapons in their way. Behind, some of them broke through, grasping at the wagon's bed, trying to scramble up inside. Mannert rose and began hacking at their hands and arms with her short sword, cursing as she did so. Behind, Arrend's students were doing the same with whatever makeshift weapons they could find.

Dalton drew his sword and bellowed, "Lane, get that gods-forsaken shield down!" then focused on defending the wagons.

"Arch," Lane commanded, "get me to the shield wall now!"

The wagon at Dalton's back staggered forward as Dalton beat back the panicked crowd, hammering at arms and shoulders and foreheads, trying not to use the blade itself, drawing on all of his training at the Lyceum in breaking up brawls and barfights. Most of those he hit were flailing, frantic, eyes wide, mouths open, hyperventilating. No intent, no malice, simply pure panic. He elbowed a woman in the gut, shoved her upright and aside as she began to fall, her face shocked as she tried to catch her breath and was carried off by the crowd. A man caught him a glancing blow to the cheek that stung and Dalton spat a curse as he punched him in the face, his nose cracking beneath Dalton's knuckles. The man wailed, the sound shrill, but stumbled back and away. A man with two sobbing children clutched to his side careened into the mercenary next to Dalton, unaware of the man's blade; he was calling out a woman's name at the top of his lungs, searching the faces around him. Dalton didn't have time to consider how to help as a grizzled, bearded man suddenly appeared in front of him and spat into his face with a shout of "Blasphemy!" Dalton pounded him in the temple with the pommel of his sword, the bearded man dropping like lead. By the time he turned back, the man with the two children was gone.

And then the cacophony of the crowds was split by the whoosh of flames and the escalation of screams from terror to outright agony.

Above him, Dalton somehow now beside the second wagon, Mannert yelled, "The Iandolan mages are attacking the crowds on the ramp, trying to get them out of the way!"

Dalton cursed and shot a glance over his shoulder. They were almost at the shield.

"Hold the wagons," he shouted to the nearby mercenaries, then scrambled back to the front wagon. Lane and Varenov were watching the attacks on the edges of the plaza and on the ramp in horror, until Dalton reached up and caught Varenov's arm. "Tell Lane to get rid of the orb! They'll use it to target her!"

Realization hit and Varenov snatched at Lane, dragging her down from her perch. Anger flashed across Lane's face, until Varenov leaned in close to speak, hand waving up toward the orb. Lane's eyes widened. Then she began a short, sharp sigil.

The orb began to drift back the way they'd come, toward the amber shard at the center of the plaza.

At the same time, lightning crackled out of the darkening sky, lancing downward, to the orb and below. A sizzling crack sounded as the orb exploded and the hapless people below caught in the bolts writhed where they stood or were thrown clear. The sickening stench of cooked flesh and burnt hair drifted toward them—from the lightning strikes and the fireballs raining down from above.

Lane tried to stand back up, but Varenov yanked her back down.

"I have to try to protect the people," Lane protested.

"You have to focus on the shield," Varenov said, catching Dalton's eye. "It's the only way any of us are getting out of here alive." Then she shoved Lane toward him. "Get her to the shield."

Lane toppled from the wagon, Dalton catching her before she could tumble to the flagstone plaza and get trampled. She righted herself, then turned on Varenov. "Mother!"

Varenov cut her off by pointing. "Look."

Both Dalton and Lane spun. To the left, the Iandolan Army had made significant headway into the plaza.

And then Dalton's gaze focused closer in, to where the chaos of those in the plaza was interrupted by a large group forging their way toward them. He recognized those at the forefront, realized most of them were Brovettan.

"It's Senn...and Maupin," he said. "And the Brovettans we freed."

Within fifteen minutes, Senn and Maupin had broken through to the wagons. The Brovettans and tullers immediately began surrounding them, shoving the crowds even farther back. Maupin nodded at Dalton, while Senn faced his daughter, who'd crossed her arms.

"It's good to see you're alive," Senn said. He reached for her, but Lane stepped back, bumping into the wagon. Senn faltered, but turned his attention on Varenov, whose gaze hardened when he smiled.

"We don't have time for this," she said. "Dalton?"

Dalton stepped between Lane and her father, touching her elbow. "The shield."

Lane nodded.

They headed for the front of the wagon, its progress halted. Dalton motioned to Arch, who immediately gathered up six of the closest mercenaries. They fell into formation around Lane.

Then the small group pushed forward toward the shield, now only six hundred feet away.

Behind, the Brovettans closed up around the wagons, forming their own human shield to protect those inside.

Arch began shoving forwards, his men hacking them a pathway when necessary. The closer they got to the shield, the thinner the panicked crowd became. But more and more trampled bodies littered the flagstones as well. They stumbled over them, slipping in patches of blood or when they inadvertently stepped on an arm or leg.

Twenty paces away from the wall, the crowds vanished and they hesitated. On the far side of the rippling shield they could see Iandolan soldiers, in precise formations. They stood fifty feet back from their side of the wall, but just on the other side, three prefects and two captains watched them. One of them took a step forward, as if in challenge.

Behind, lightning flared and jagged down into the plaza at random and the screams intensified. The sun was setting, the gray of twilight settling in, night close. Bands of lucent began to light up all along the wall, including the dark blue lucent of the gate.

Lane set her shoulders and moved forward, eyes on the prefect. Dalton fell into step behind her, on the right, Arch on the left, the others ranged out behind to keep anyone from approaching. Lane halted within arm's reach of the wall, then, without hesitation, reached out and touched it.

Dalton sucked in a sharp breath, expecting…he didn't know what. A backlash of power. A cascade of energy. A splintering of the shield. But nothing happened, Lane's hands pressed up against the shimmering rivulets of the wall, the light washing down and over her fingers.

She gave the prefect a tiny smirk, then closed her eyes to concentrate.

"Now what?" Arch asked.

Both of them flinched as fireballs took the place of the lightning behind them, exploding into fountains of fire like magma when they hit. Dalton couldn't help but notice the attacks were getting closer. The Iandolan Army had overtaken half of the ramp down from Level Two already, and they were closing in on both flanks.

Those in the plaza were trapped. The only way out now was through one of the four sets of Iandolan forces.

"Care to wager which of the three will get to us first?" Arch asked.

Directly in front of them the crowd began to scatter as stone began to split and crack, the surface of the plaza exploding upwards as if something were gouging its way through the flagstone towards them. Dalton, Arch, and his men all tensed as the invisible force tore through the crowd, ripping its way through the people who were too slow or darted in the wrong direction. The air crackled and snapped and Dalton swore as the magic tore straight towards them. His grip on his sword tightened as he crouched, but there was nothing there to fight.

He drew breath to shout, "Run!" but the vortex of energy suddenly halted, ten paces out, and as the dust and debris settled, Erilyn stepped forward. Behind her, Senn, Varenov, and the rest of their wagons and the Brovettans they'd freed emerged from the panicked crowd.

"I'm tired of running and hiding and being trapped," Erilyn said. "You have until I reach the shard to get out of this plaza. After that, it will be too late."

Then she stalked off to the left, where the fire and lightning was closest, already completing another sigil. Lightning shot from her upraised hand, spreading out in a fan in front of her, slamming into the people in her way and throwing them to the side. Before the jagged bolts faded, the ground began exploding upwards on an angle.

A few of Arch's men muttered small prayers under their breath as she advanced away from them. Arch merely cursed.

Ahead, Nic and Picall shoved their way past Senn and Varenov and raced up to Dalton.

"We couldn't stop her," Nic gasped. "She heard Picall and I talking about what would happen once the shield was down and we'd made our way onto the wayfare, that the Iandolan Army would simply follow us, hound us all the way to Brovetto, cutting us down as we retreated. We didn't even realize she was listening to us. Then suddenly she said, 'I can stop them,' and leaped from the wagon. She blasted her way here to clear a path for us and now she's heading for the shard."

"What's she going to do?" Arch asked skeptically.

Nic waved a hand in exasperation. "It's a shard! A Warding! She's going to do what she did at the Lyceum and set it off, sealing everyone in the plaza and probably a good section of the lower city and waygate inside it!"

Dalton spun. "Lane!"

"I heard." Her jaw clenched. "I'm working as fast as I can. I'm not a lockpick, like Devon."

Pain dug into Dalton's gut, but he resisted turning and checking on Devon in the wagon, instead stepping forward. "Even if Erilyn doesn't make it to the shard, we don't have much time. The soldiers are closing in."

Lane didn't answer. Dalton noticed sweat beading on her forehead and her free hand clenched into a tight fist, knuckles white. He swallowed the words he'd been about to speak, stared instead out at the plaza that had become a killing ground. Erilyn blasted her way to the left, the area around her dancing with flares of lightning and gouts of stone and earth. Jagged shards of ice had joined the fireballs and lightning from the Iandolan mages, the radius tightening with each breath. Those trapped in the plaza had nowhere to run, half of them crushed into the center near the amber shard—the Warding—while the other half flung themselves against the Iandolans in an attempt to escape. He watched in horror as men and women leaped from the sides of the ramp as the soldiers pressed forward, some of them far too high to survive the fall.

"Those on the ramp have reached the plaza," he reported, hand twisting on the handle of his sword. "Arch is pulling the wagons in closer. The soldiers to the left are halfway to our position, those on the right a little farther away."

"You're not helping," Lane said, terse.

Dalton clamped his teeth together. Frustration caused sweat to break out all over his body. He couldn't do anything. He had a sword, he had the training, but in this situation he was worthless.

The wagons and those surrounding them pressed closer. Then everyone flinched as fresh lightning sizzled out of the skies a hundred feet to their left, the thundercrack as it struck deafening. It jagged through the compressed crowd, headed away from the shield wall. The people nearby surged toward them, shoving everyone back. Dalton stumbled into Lane and shouted, "They're almost here!"

But Lane merely said, "Got it," and pulled her hand away from the shield, opening her eyes. She met the gaze of the prefect on the far side and smiled, already beginning a sigil.

The prefect bellowed something, his command muted by the shield, but before he could finish, Lane's hand halted, held, and then dropped.

With a scintillating sound, like ice hissing and cracking, the shimmering rivulets of the shield froze in place, then splintered and began to fall and fade. The background buzz in Dalton's teeth and bones ended.

Voice cracking with force, Dalton roared, "Senn! Maupin! Arch! To the waygate!"

At the same time, fire, lightning, and ice rained down from the night sky as the mages inside the shield let loose on the crowds.

The chaos on the plaza quadrupled as the conflagration hit and those trapped between the other three armies realized the shield had collapsed. Despite the danger and the Iandolan Army waiting, thousands rushed toward the waygate. Within seconds, the portion of the plaza that had been protected behind the shield became a melee.

Dalton snagged Picall's arm and dragged Nic close. "Protect Lane!"

They fell into position around the mage, Lane already focused on the army ahead and the waygate beyond. It loomed above them, arrows already flickering down into the mass of people surging toward it. The dark blue lucent doors, banded with steel, appeared black in the darkness, gleaming with the reflections of the fire and lightning scattered throughout the plaza.

Lane raised her hand and sketched on the air.

The flagstone plaza before them cracked and heaved upwards, the air itself appearing to shatter as the cantrip ripped toward the waiting soldiers. One of the Iandolan mages attempted to erect another shield to protect them, but they were too late. The cantrip shredded it half-formed.

The prefect's shoulders sagged in defeat a moment before the cantrip lifted him from the ground and tore him to shreds. The formation of soldiers behind him broke as it struck them, men and women leaping out of its path. But the cantrip didn't stop. Unlike those Dalton had seen before—small and targeted, like the one Lane had used on the doors in the tower; or large and directed, traveling in a straight path, like the ones Erilyn had used—this one expanded as it moved, growing wider and taller. It drove a bloody course through the Iandolan formations and then slammed into the waygate.

Even over the intense noise of the battle on the plaza, Dalton heard the lucent in the doors crack. He felt the scream of metal as it twisted and bent. But the doors held. Lane was already advancing, had already completed another sigil, a second cantrip headed after the first. Dalton shouted at those behind and raced to catch up to her, Nic and Picall already at her side.

Metal squealed and contorted as the second cantrip hit, lucent cracking and raining down in jagged pieces, a third cantrip already gouging toward the gates. The Iandolan Army was no longer trying to stop them, the formations dispersing, being absorbed by the wave of people from the plaza surging forward.

When the third cantrip hit, the gate shattered and exploded outwards.

Ahead, Lane slowed, then sagged. Dalton grabbed hold of her as Senn and the leading edge of the mixed Brovettan and mercenary guard closed in around them.

Lane looked up at him, her entire body sheathed in sweat, her hair matted and stuck to her face. "It's more exhausting than it looks."

Dalton raised an eyebrow.

The first wagon pulled up beside them. Varenov reached down with both arms from the driver's bench. "Hand her up!"

Dalton sheathed his sword and lifted her, Varenov hauling her limp body into a seated position beside her, arm around her shoulder, all while shouting, "Go!" to the driver.

The wagon trundled forward, not fast enough to outpace the desperate people behind. Senn and Maupin drew their forces tighter around the wagons and the Brovettans as the tide overtook them, a few souls racing out in front, a couple taken out by the Iandolan archers on the walls above the gate. But soon there were too many, the flood surrounding them, shoving them forward. The churned flagstones shuddered beneath their tread. Dalton felt the crunch of lucent shards beneath his boots as they began to pass through the hole Lane had made, the crush of bodies at the narrow opening overwhelming. He pulled himself up onto the edge of the wagon's bench, hanging off the side, and glanced back as the wagon's momentum slowed.

In the darkness of nightfall, flames flared and the white-hot jags of lightning illuminated the plaza and the rise of Level Two behind. Above, portions of Iandolo were lit with the more subdued glow of hundreds of fires amid the radiance of the lucent towers at the higher levels. The play of lights was oddly horrific and beautiful.

And then the wagon was passing through the gate, jagged lucent shards and contorted metal passing overhead. They hit the narrowest point, people screaming at the crush of bodies, a few impaled on the metal and crystal to either side, Dalton swallowing back bile, but on the far side the wagon gained speed. Those who'd escaped were fleeing down along the wayfare, the elevated roadway lit by bands of lucent shooting straight out toward Brovetto ahead of them near the city, lost in darkness beyond. Dalton's wagon began to slow a hundred paces out, to wait for the three wagons behind, but Dalton slapped the man's back and shouted, "Keep going, no matter what! Get as far from the city as possible as fast as you can!"

The man nodded and Dalton jumped free as it sped up again, Lane turning back to watch as he pushed through the surrounding mercenaries and Brovettans guarding them and raced back toward the gate. Nic and Picall broke free and joined him.

The wagon containing Raven, Devon, and Mannert pushed through the gate next, Dalton, Nic, and Picall pulling people through and pointing them down the wayfare, all of them yelling, "Go! Run!" As soon as the wagon cleared, Dalton gave its driver the same directions as the first, then watched it pull away, his heart in his throat. But he faced the gate again, his blood singing in his arms and legs, tingling in his fingers. He couldn't see the plaza any longer, or the amber shard at its center. But he could feel Erilyn getting closer to the Warding. It was only a matter of time.

Arrend's wagon passed through, some of those from the Lyceum on board tending to wounded mercenaries or Brovettans who'd been protecting them. Arrend was hauling one of the mercenaries into the back as the wagon edged by, the man clutching at a vicious wound to his gut, Jillian already applying pressure, his legs dangling from the bed as the wagon gained speed.

The fourth wagon was farther behind, the press of Iandolan citizens slowing it down. Dalton dragged people through the crush—women, children, elderly, even a few Iandolan soldiers—shoving them onto the wayfare. The wagon reached the gate and got stuck, the press of people around it too tight.

Before Dalton could come up with a plan, one of Arch's mercenaries bellowed an order and they all began to attack those nearest, cutting citizens down to clear the way. Dalton roared for them to stop, but they either couldn't hear him over the noise or they chose to ignore them. The screams cut into him, sharper than a blade, and anger swelled.

But then the wagon was free, jolting forward without warning.

At the same time, behind them, through the ragged gate, a beam of amber light shot toward the sky, followed by a thunderous cracking that drowned out all other sounds.

"The Warding."

Dalton turned and began to run, everything else forgotten. Nic and Picall had been behind him and did the same, all three of them bolting down the wayfare. People who'd made it free had staggered to one side to rest or clutch wounds, but he didn't try to warn them. He simply ran.

The light from the Warding brightened, cast his shadow out before him onto the stone of the wayfare, then dimmed and he imagined it rushing toward him, blindingly fast. He pushed harder, although he knew he couldn't outrace it. All he heard was his breath, harsh as it rushed from his lungs. A stitch began in his side, but he ignored it. Pain shot up from his knee, but he merely ground his teeth together and bore it.

Then he stumbled and fell, rolling to a skin-scraping halt, facing back toward Iandolo.

The amber light had halted, less than a hundred feet away on the wayfare, swallowing the plaza, the gates, and a significant portion of the city behind. As Dalton exhaled his pent-up breath in relief, the sizzling crackle of ice that he remembered from the first Warding filled the air, and then the light solidified.

The fourth wagon and those who were guarding it were still inside, frozen in mid-motion, faces filled with terror and determination.

Those who'd escaped its grasp raced past Dalton as he climbed to his feet, hissing as he pushed himself upright with raw, bloody palms. Then he simply stood, heart calming, body shuddering in delayed reaction.

Nic and Picall appeared beside him.

"Are you alright?" Nic asked.

Dalton stared down at his hands, grit ground into some of the scrapes, then back at the Warding and the hundreds, if not thousands, of people trapped inside.

He let his hands drop.

"Let's find the remaining wagons and take stock."

Chapter Twenty-Four

Dalton stood at the edge of where they'd drawn the three wagons up and hunkered down for the remainder of the night. He stood just outside of the perimeter of guards that Senn and Maupin had established, using a combination of the rebels under Senn's command, Maupin's tullers, rescued Brovettans willing to fight, and Arch's mercenaries. Lane had fallen into an exhausted sleep, along with many of the others. Varenov and Arch were taking stock of what supplies had survived and what had been lost in the fourth wagon. Cerelle was taking care of the horses, while Mindell and a few assistants, including the Humanities student, were seeing to the wounded.

They'd fled on pure adrenalin for a few hours, until Iandolo had receded into a scintillant pearl of light behind them. Dalton could still see the lucent-lit towers jutting up from its center, his vision muddled by the lanterns of those on the wayfare. Even so, the stars overhead were multitudinous, the swath of the denser band angling down into the horizon—thousands more than could be seen from within the city, but still not as awe-inspiring as what he'd seen at the tull, where there was no ambient light around at all.

Yet his gaze wasn't focused on the stars, but on the road behind. His arms were crossed over his chest, the fingers of his right hand tapping his upper arm.

He tensed as he caught movement in the shadows, but as the cluster of figures stumbled into view he realized it was merely a family of refugees. They'd passed many of them in the last few hours, expected to see many more in the days to come. This one was composed of five adults and three children. One of the women put out an arm to halt them as soon as she saw Dalton, but he motioned them onward. They hurried past, close to the edge of the wayfare, the Flatlands hidden in the blackness a thousand feet below. He'd let the others deal with them, if they stopped at the wagons. Most moved on, keeping their distance. At least for the moment.

Then two more figures trotted out of the darkness, veering toward him as they drew nearer. Both Nic and Picall looked haggard, Nic hunching forward with his hands on his knees as soon as they drew to a halt, gasping.

"One second," he heaved.

Picall glanced down at him, then said, "No one is following us. I don't think the Iandolans have figured out a way around the Warding yet."

A tension across Dalton's shoulders released and he sighed. "Good. You two should get some rest. We'll likely need you to scout ahead or behind once we begin moving again."

Nic straightened. "You need to rest as well, you know."

He shrugged. "I'm not certain I'd sleep." Although he could feel fatigue creeping up on him, now that he knew they were safe for the moment.

He followed them back to the makeshift camp, passing through at least a hundred people curled up on the bed of the road, whatever they had for warmth drawn up tight around them, must huddled up close to loved ones. He left Nic and Picall at one of the wagons, headed for the one where Devon and Raven were kept, but was drawn off to the side by a handwave from Arch.

The bar owner sat hunched over near one of the wagon wheels. Varenov shifted to the side as Dalton settled to the ground before them. Both looked grim.

"What is it?" he asked.

Arch cleared his throat. "We've gone through the supplies left in the three remaining wagons. Most of it was baggage—stuff those from the Lyceum brought, our own satchels, medical supplies. Not much of it was food. That was mostly thrown into the fourth wagon."

"We would have had enough for those of us who started out from the Shandy Quad for a week, maybe more," Varenov added. "We weren't expecting to run into Maupin and Senn, nor the Brovettans you managed to rescue from the quarantine zones. If we do some extreme rationing and try to feed everyone, we'll only have enough for a few days."

"And more than likely we're going to start picking up some of the other refugees as we travel," Arch said. "Especially once they run out of whatever they managed to escape Iandolo with on their own."

Dalton rested his head in his hands, then scrubbed at his face. "So what do we do?"

Varenov shifted. "There are supply depots along the wayfare, used by the army couriers and other Council envoys moving back and forth between the cities, but the stock there is minimal. The only good news is that there's plenty of water available there. And fodder for the horses. But there won't be enough food for all of us, even then."

"Perhaps I can help."

All three turned at the new voice and Maupin stepped forward, crouching down beside Dalton. He placed a hand on Dalton's shoulder to steady himself.

"You did well," he said. When Dalton scoffed, he added, "You got us out of the city with minimal losses. Everyone here is thankful to be alive. And not trapped in that Warding."

Dalton felt slightly better when the other two nodded agreement. "That doesn't help us with the current situation."

Maupin's hand dropped. "You've been to the tull. You know we have food there."

"We can't take all of these people to the tull—" Dalton began, but Maupin was already shaking his head.

"No, I agree. But we can send a small group of the tullers and some of Senn's rebels for supplies. There are ways down to the Flatlands from the wayfare. Senn and the others have been using them for decades to escape the Iandolan Army. Terrial's splinter group used them to get her own forces and those of the Brovettan Army into the city for their own attacks last year."

"How much can you bring?" Varenov asked.

"Everything I can, without hurting the tullers already there. Some of them may even join us."

"More mouths to feed," Arch said.

Varenov quieted him with a hand on his arm. "More who can carry food back to us." She faced Maupin. "Whatever you can arrange will be appreciated."

Maupin nodded and rose. "I'll see who's willing to go. We'll leave as soon as it's light out." He paused. "Most of us are hunters, know the Flatlands and its dangers. We should be able to hunt along the way as well."

As soon as the tuller left, Senn approached. Varenov tensed, her back straightening, eyes cast downward. Senn appeared to sense it and remained standing.

"Did you know Carbolen had Raven?" Dalton asked, the question bitten off, surprising even himself.

Senn's eyebrows rose. "No, he kept that to himself. Among many, many other things."

Only slightly mollified, Dalton continued, "And what about his attack at the Pulpit? Did you coordinate with him on that?"

Senn was already shaking his head. "We had no contact with Carbolen once the Iandolan Army attacked his lair and some of our base camps and hideouts in the lower levels. We were too focused on saving as many of the Brovettans as we could, moving them to different locations, protecting them, figuring out how to get them out of the city once we realized our access to the sublevels was gone." He drew in a deep breath. "As soon as we realized something had happened in the upper levels, we seized the opportunity and began pulling everyone we could reach down to the waygate."

"And what about my execution?" Varenov asked, drawing his attention back to her. "And Lane's? Did you hear nothing of that?"

Senn's eyes narrowed in confusion. "We didn't. We were deep in the lower levels by then, trying to stay hidden in case the army attacked again. If I'd known..."

Varenov's lips pressed into a thin line.

Dalton fidgeted beneath the awkward silence, then said, "You had something to report?"

It took a moment before Senn said, "My men on guard duty have reported a few of the refugees approaching us for help. So far, we've turned them away—"

"Don't," Varenov interrupted. "Let them in."

"But—"

"This situation was forced upon them, by the Council, by Arctus and the army. We cannot simply leave them to die."

"If we take them all in, we may all die," Senn countered.

They glared at each other, until finally Varenov said, "We haven't reached that point. Yet."

Senn gave a curt nod.

"Was there anything else?"

Senn shook his head and retreated.

Dalton, Arch, and Varenov sat in relative silence, listening to those around them—low, muffled conversation; the occasional cough; a huff and headshake from one of the horses. The prickling tension eased from Varenov's shoulders and eventually she sighed.

"We were in love once," she said. "Now…I'm not as certain. We've been apart for so long. He's changed. I've changed. I sometimes wonder if I made the right decision all those years ago—to abandon him and his cause, to come to Iandolo with his unborn child." She gave a short, choked laugh. "Who would have thought then that I'd be fleeing Iandolo for sanctuary in Brovetto."

She faced Dalton. "You should go check in on Devon. Be with him while you can. And get some rest. We'll want to leave as early as possible in the morning."

"Dawn's only a few hours away," Arch added.

Dalton glanced toward the wagon that held Devon and Raven, realized on some level that he'd been avoiding it since they'd left the Shandy Quad. He'd allowed everything else to distract him, to draw him away.

He stood, brushed off his breeches, hesitated. But he'd have to deal with whatever had happened to Devon eventually. "Find me if anything happens," he said, and left Arch and Varenov behind.

The wagon groaned as he climbed up into the back of the bed. Mannert looked up from where she sat, back up against a crate, Raven and Devon to one side. She beckoned him forward, standing and motioning for him to take her place as she stretched.

"I need to move around," she said in a hushed voice. "Been sitting too long. You can watch over them."

Before he could answer, she hopped down from the wagon and wandered off without a backward glance.

Dalton paused, then settled down in the spot she'd left. It wasn't exactly comfortable, but he found himself drifting off to sleep regardless as soon as he'd settled.

Until someone said in a cracked voice, "Why did you come for me?"

He opened his eyes to find Raven staring at him, face shadowed by the ambient light of a few nearby lanterns and the stars overhead. "Because you would have come if it had been one of us."

"You should have left me." The words were harsh, bitter, but not angry.

"And let Carbolen kill you? For what? Leaving him? Abandoning the gang? If you thought any of us could have done that, you don't know us well at all."

"Nic would have left me."

Dalton chuckled. "Nic was ready to com rescue you all by himself. I think he understood better what Carbolen was capable of. We had to hold him back. He would've gotten himself killed." He caught the look of uncertainty on Raven's face and added more somberly, "We should have come for you sooner. It took us too long to find you. I'm sorry."

Raven's uncertainty shifted into confusion verging on denial, then settled into a blank expression edged with pain.

She held up a hand. "Help me up."

"Mindell said—"

"*Help me up.*"

Dalton grabbed her forearm, her fingers tightening on his own with surprising strength, and then he pulled her up into a sitting position. Her teeth clamped down against a scream and her eyes squeezed shut, tears leaking from the corners. She spent a long moment huffing and wheezing before allowing him to shift her into his and Mannert's old position. Sweat broke out on her forehead at even that small movement. She let her head fall back against the crate behind her as Dalton sat down next to Devon where she'd lain.

"You're leaking."

She glanced down to where Dalton pointed. Blood had soaked through the bandages there, but she waved it off. "I've leaked worse before." She pointed her chin at Devon. "He hasn't woken since the tower, according to Mannert."

Dalton glanced down. A sudden fear lanced up through his gut, unexpectedly sharp and cold. His breath caught, but he held it, controlled it, then let it out in a slow exhale. He reached out and brushed a lock of hair off of Devon's forehead. Someone had cleaned off the worst of the caked-on blood and grit, but the bruising and swelling remained. His breath came in a shallow half-gurgle, half-whistle, as if his airway were constricted, and he smelled of the unguents Mindell had been applying to the wounds.

Dalton eased down beside him, stretching his arm out overhead to use as a pillow, laying on his side facing Devon. He edged up close, careful he wasn't pressing too hard against him. He didn't know the extent of Devon's wounds; he hadn't had time to consult Mindell about the details. He wanted to wrap his other arm around him, pull him tight, protect him, but he didn't dare.

He'd almost drifted off to sleep yet again when Devon stirred. Hands reached for Dalton's face, fingers touching skin as Dalton opened his eyes and found Devon staring back at him.

"Dalton?" he breathed, voice ragged, unbelieving. "Dalton!"

Then Devon's hands were scrambling for Dalton's fingers, drawing his hand up into the light near their faces, counting.

"You have all your fingers," Devon said.

His gaze snapped to Dalton's face, one eye still swollen shut, and then he was prying at Dalton's mouth, feeling inside. His fingers tasted of old blood, sweat, salt, and worse, but Dalton didn't move.

"And your tongue."

He fell back against the crate behind him, stunned.

"You have your tongue," he said again. "It was all a lie."

Dalton shifted up onto an elbow. He wiped tears from his face, fought against the bands tightening around his chest. "Devon, what are you talking about?"

Devon's shoulders began to hitch with uncontrollable, silent sobs, face contorted with horror. "It was all a lie," he heaved between breaths. "It was never you. Havvelan...never...had you!"

"No, Havvelan only caught you and Lane and Mannert. He took Varenov eventually. But he never got me or Nic or any of the others."

Dalton sat up and reached for him, but Devon pushed him away.

"You don't understand," he gasped, curling in upon himself. "You don't understand."

"What don't I understand, Devon? All I know is that we got you out. You and Lane and all of the others."

Dalton reached for him again and this time Devon didn't recoil. He drew Devon's shuddering form up into his lap.

When Devon finally answered, his voice was muffled and choked with phlegm.

"I told them everything. *I told them everything.*"

The Epic Saga Continues
in the third and final novel

CRYSTAL WAR

Find it in ebook and trade paperback
now wherever you buy your books.

Or pick it up at:

www.zombiesneedbrains.com

About the Author

JOSHUA PALMATIER is a fantasy author with a PhD in mathematics. He currently teaches at SUNY Oneonta in upstate New York while writing in his "spare" time, editing anthologies, and running the anthology-producing small press Zombies Need Brains LLC. His most recent fantasy novel, *Crystal War*, concludes the fantasy series begun in *Crystal Lattice* and *Crystal Rebel*, although you can also find his "Throne of Amenkor" series, the "Well of Sorrows" series, and the "Ley" series still on the shelves. He is currently hard at work writing his next fantasy and designing the Kickstarter for the next Zombies Need Brains anthology projects. You can find out more at www.joshuapalmatier.com or at the small press' site www.zombiesneedbrains.com. Or follow him on Blue Sky at joshuapalmatier.bsky.social or on X as @bentateauthor or @ZNBLLC. And check out the Zombies Need Brains Patreon and online magazine ZNB Presents at www.patreon.com/zombiesneedbrains.